At First Dance

Coral Bell Cove, Book Two

USA TODAY BESTSELLING AUTHOR
RENEE HARLESS

ISBN: 978-1-962459-09-9

Cover design by Porcelain Paper Designs

Editor: Nicole McCurdy at Emerald Edits

Editor: Jenny Sims at Editing4Indies

Proofreader: Crystal Burnette at Crystal Clear Author Services

Coral Bell Cove, Book Two

USA TODAY BESTSELLING AUTHOR

RENEE HARLESS

She wasn't looking for a way out. He wasn't looking for anyone at all. Especially not his brother's ex. But sometimes, love finds you right where you land.

After years of living under the weight of her stage name, Ivy Quinn needs a break—from the spotlight, the noise, and the expectations of everyone but herself. A broken-down car on a backroad in Coral Bell Cove, Virginia, wasn't part of the plan. Neither was the gruff, steady-handed cowboy who shows up when her world feels like it's falling apart—the same cowboy who happens to be her ex's older brother.

Rowan Wright is perfectly content with his quiet life on the farm. He's built a routine that works—sunrise chores, family dinners, and keeping his distance from anything that might stir up the past. But when Ivy shows up in town with more baggage than luggage and no idea how to slow down, she disrupts everything... and somehow, it feels like exactly what he needs.

But Ivy's world isn't built for small towns and open fields. And Rowan's not sure his heart can take the spotlight—or the whispers about falling for the woman his brother once claimed.

When the fame threatens to catch up to her again, Ivy has to decide if she's ready to stop running... and Rowan has to believe he's worth being chosen.

A heart-tugging, slow-burn romance about love that grows where you least expect it—and a place that just might feel like home.

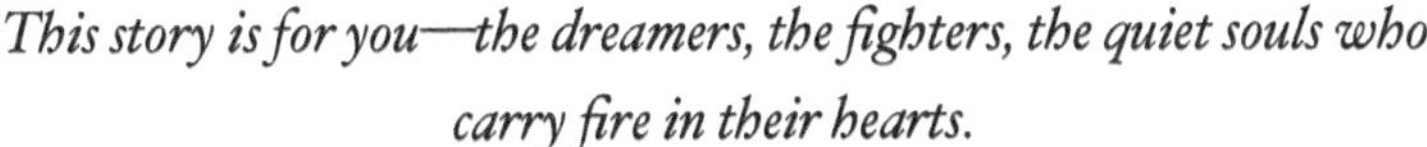

This story is for you—the dreamers, the fighters, the quiet souls who carry fire in their hearts.

May you always remember that your worth isn't measured by what limits you, but by the strength it takes to rise, stand tall, and choose your own way forward.

Chapter One

ROWAN

Of course, she's in the ditch.

I ease the truck onto the shoulder. The gravel *pop-pops* under the tires, and the afternoon heat climbs in through the open window like it belongs here. The road is just a skinny ribbon between scrub pine and marsh, and the electric car nose-dived where the drainage cut dips. It decided to jump the ditch and changed its mind halfway.

She stands beside it, one heel sinking into the soft mud, a long blond ponytail losing the fight with the wind. Oversized sunglasses cover half her face. The rest of her is purpose-built to draw eyes and test common sense: white ribbed tank under a drapey cardigan, shredded light-wash denim, the kind of delicate jewelry that looks like it costs a paycheck, and heels that were never meant for county roads. A phone is lifted in her hand, searching for a bar of service this stretch of county refuses to provide.

I roll to a stop twenty feet back and throw it in Park.

Before I open my door, I take inventory like I always do—damage, surroundings, people. The wheel's pitched wrong because the undercarriage probably kissed a culvert rock. No second car. No filmer tucked in the grass. A cow over the fence chews with judgment.

I climb out slowly, shut the door with the kind of quiet that says I mean no harm, and stay a step or two farther than I usually would. Hands open at my sides, I have nothing in my grip. I know what I look like to a woman alone on a road like this: six-one, broad, boots, and a jaw I never learned to soften.

"Hey," I say, voice steady but not loud. "You alright?"

She startles, then sets her chin like she's bracing for a headline. "Define 'alright,'" she says, cool on the surface but frayed underneath.

I tip my head toward the car. "You're not driving that anywhere today."

"That's a"—she exhales, lips flattening—"shame."

I take two slow steps back—make space, show I'm not between her and any exit—then plant my feet and keep my palms visible. "Not gonna crowd you. Name's Rowan."

She tips her head, like she's scrolling a file in her mind. "Rowan... Wright?" The question mark is there, but faint. "I saw a Christmas picture once—big house, goat on the porch. You were the one in the cowboy hat holding it like it weighed a ton." She doesn't step closer, but her shoulders ease a notch. "Didn't realize I was this close to your place."

She studies me from behind those lenses, if the way she chews on her bottom lip is any indication, and slides her phone into the back pocket of her pants. Wind catches the tail of her hair, and a few strands stick to her peach-glossed lips.

"Ivy," she says finally.

It lands like a dropped glass. Ivy Quinn. My sister, Lila's, playlist staple. The woman my brother, Crew, fake-dated for a year because someone with a spreadsheet said "synergy." Everyone in the family treated it like it was real anyway—Ma set out an extra plate more than once, and Holt asked why Crew never brought her around. I kept my mouth shut and fixed fences. All I ever got from Crew was, "It's work, Ro." He never brought her home, which told me more than the press releases did.

Up close, the details click sharper: the clean line of that tank, the dusting of freckles across a sun-touched collarbone, and tiny hoops in her ears. No glitter. No bodyguard. Just a woman and a bad idea of a road. Through the tinted glass of the spaceship car's back seat, a jacket's slung half-out of a garment bag—navy, slim cut, the brand my brother grabs when cameras bother him. Looks like the one he left at her penthouse during their last PR "touchpoint," if the gossip feeds can be trusted. So she drove out to return it herself or drop it at the carrier in town, clean and private. Less mess than handing it off in Nashville, where ten lenses live on every corner.

"I'm not going to hurt you," I say, because men never have to think to say it, and women are always calculating it. And even though she may recognize me, I'm still a stranger. Ted Bundy could be charming, too. "I'll keep my distance."

Her shoulders drop a fraction. "Thanks."

"Where were you headed?"

She gestures at the car. "Away from here?"

"Good plan. Poor execution."

A hairline crack of a smile appears. Then she rubs her temple. "It made a weird sound, and I overcorrected. I was returning"—she glances at the back seat, then hesitates—"a jacket. To someone who shouldn't have left it where he did. I kind of left on a whim in the middle of the night."

Crew. I don't make her say it.

"Okay." I blow out a breath and keep it practical. "I could tow you out after the wedding if you're not leaking fluids. But that wheel's stuck, and the underside probably isn't pretty. Carl, the mechanic, can get you on a lift tomorrow."

"Tomorrow," she repeats, like the word is a cliff edge.

"Yeah."

Silence creaks between us. She looks like she's balancing ten stories on a spine that forgot how to bend. I do the only smart thing: make it safer.

"You can say no," I add, and hook a thumb toward my truck. "But if you want out of here, I'll get you to town. Or somewhere with air-conditioning."

She eyes the truck. "And if this is the start of a murder documentary?"

My mouth kicks sideways. "Then I'm terrible at it. Give me your phone."

She freezes. I lift my hands again, palms forward. "Selfie. With me. When we get to the property and the service is better, you can send it to whoever would hunt me down if you don't text later."

Her throat works. Then she digs in her back pocket and hands the phone over.

I frame us wide—her sunglasses, my stupidly white shirt I ironed for the first time this year, black jeans, a wedding-appropriate belt Lila bullied me into buying, and clean boots that won't be that way long. I look like a cowboy dragged through an REI. I hate selfies. I take it anyway—one of me stonefaced, one of me trying not to look like I swallowed a nail—then pass the phone back.

"Rowan, Coral Bell Cove," I say while she's tapping out a text. "Otter Creek Farms. If I blink wrong, half this county can find me."

That gets me an actual smile. Not the red-carpet one. Smaller. Real. "Noted."

She slides the phone into her bag. I offer an elbow toward the shoulder. "Let's get you out of the mud."

She hesitates, clocking the distance I've kept, then slips her hand into the crook of my arm like we're strangers on a dance floor that isn't there. Her skin is warm against my sleeve. The vanilla citrus of whatever perfume she uses finds me and stirs up memories I don't want.

At the truck, I pull the passenger door wide and stand back so she can climb in without feeling my eyes on her. She tucks her legs like she's done this in too many borrowed cars and settles the cardigan over her lap, like armor, like decency in a world that tries to devour it.

The cab takes her scent the way cotton takes dye—fast

and indelible. I start the engine and let the low hum do the first round of talking for us. Gravel shifts under the tires. A heron lifts slowly from the ditch, like a curtain going up.

"You really rescue stranded celebrities often?" she asks after a minute, chin tipped toward the window.

"First time."

"Great. I'm a novelty."

"More like an inconvenience."

She huffs out a laugh that sounds like surprise. "Honesty. That's refreshing."

We roll past the hedgerow, and my back acreage opens up on the right—fence lines I mean to fix, shrubs I mean to clear, the kind of work that anchors a man when the rest of life leans too hard. Her knee bounces in a fast, staccato click. I pretend I'm not counting.

I break the quiet with the only thing that makes sense. "Big day ahead," I say, nodding at my shirt. "Sister's wedding."

"Of course," she murmurs. "It's always a wedding in a small town."

"Sometimes a funeral," I say dryly. "Weddings are better."

"That's debatable."

I glance over. "You don't like them?"

She shrugs. "I like the idea of them. The spectacle... not so much."

We pass the hand-painted wooden Otter Creek Farm sign that hangs a little crooked. "You'll be alright," I say before I think about it. "Spectacle or not."

She doesn't answer, but her knee slows. *Progress.*

At my parents' lane, the trees open to white clapboard and a backyard mid-transformation: strings of lights, wildflowers in Mason jars, and chairs in imperfect rows. Music drifts out of the barn—someone doing a sound check on a speaker and a guitar run that sounds like summer. The air hums with the kind of happy chaos you don't get in cities—kids barefoot, aunts already bossing, and men pretending they don't like boutonnieres.

I cut the engine. For a second, neither of us moves.

"You've got two choices," I finally say. "I can stash you in the truck and run interference, or you can walk in with me and allow Lila to squeal in your face."

She pops her sunglasses up to her hair. Her eyes—blue, and not subtle about it—hit me like a bucket of cold well water.

"I'm not hiding," she says, calm as you please. Then a smile that lifts something sharp in my chest. "Also... if this turns into a murder documentary, I want good lighting."

I huff a laugh I shouldn't let her hear. "Come on, then."

I climb out, circle to her side, and offer a palm to steady her hop down. She ignores it on principle, then takes it anyway because the heel sinks, and I'm not letting her face-plant five minutes from a wedding. Her hand fits mine like a problem I could solve if I let myself.

We're halfway around the house when the moment I've been stupidly trying to avoid happens. She reaches up, futilely patting at that wind-battered ponytail again, jaw tight, a little frayed at the edges. Frazzled. Human.

"Hold still," I murmur.

I stop. Turn. And with her chin tipped up, I gently free the snag where her hair caught in the curve of her earring. My fingers slide lower as I smooth the side back, not touching skin, but so close we both feel it. The air thickens. She looks up, lips parted. The world narrows to my breath and a strand of blond pinned behind her ear.

"Rowan." She whispers my name like a secret.

"Yeah," I answer, rougher than I mean to.

"OH MY GOD!"

My older sister Lila's voice detonates like a champagne cork from the backyard. "You brought Ivy Quinn to my wedding?!"

And that—unsurprisingly—ends it.

Lila comes in hot, satin skirts swishing like she's cutting water. I think about stepping between them for a half second. I don't. Ivy straightens on her own, sunglasses slid back into place like she remembered she owns armor.

"You're gorgeous," Lila blurts, then clamps both of Ivy's hands in hers like they've known each other since Girl Scouts. "I mean—hi—welcome—oh my God, I'm Lila, and I'm not usually like this, but today, I am absolutely like this."

"Hi." Ivy laughs, the tension around her eyes easing. "Congratulations."

"Thank you," Lila breathes, and for once, there's no follow-up plan spilling out of her. Just joy. "Eat. Drink. I can't believe Crew invited you and didn't tell me." I don't miss the way Ivy's eyebrows shoot up toward the sky as her eyes dart over to mine.

Thankfully, Lila's swept up by the maid of honor—Ashvi with the flower crown—before I can threaten to revoke speech privileges. The rest of the yard clocks Ivy in a ripple —heads lift, whispers bump, then everything smooths again. Coral Bell Cove is nosy but not cruel.

People go back to shepherding toddlers and topping off tea and arguing about the correct way to hang lights, giving Ivy a chance to breathe. Immediately, I swoop in.

"Okay?" I ask, low.

She tips her chin. "Okay."

"Good." I nod toward the drinks. "You want something?"

"In a minute."

We move through the edges—shady side of the oaks, where the breeze threads cool fingers through shirts. I keep half a step ahead, not to lead, just to clear space—an aunt here, a chair there. She tracks like she's used to slipping past cameras and elbows. She's also barefoot by the time we hit the grass, heels dangling from her fingers. It shouldn't be something I notice, yet I do anyway.

Bailey spots us first—dark hair in a scarf, sundress, brain like a switchboard operator. She's the owner of our town bookstore and someone I look at like an additional sister.

"Ivy Quinn, as I live and breathe," Bailey says, but she says it like the name is a person, not a product. "I'm Bailey. By the look of things, I nominate myself as your handler for the next ten minutes."

Ivy huffs out a real laugh. "I could use one of those."

"Great, because I'm bossy." Bailey tucks herself at Ivy's elbow and aims them toward the dessert table. "We're going to start you with tartlets and end with strawberry cake because I believe in building trust."

"Go," I tell Ivy when she looks at me like she's asking for permission she doesn't need. "Bailey won't let you trip over my family."

"He's right," Bailey says. "I'm a menace, but good at shielding."

They peel off together. Far enough to feel like they're on their own, but close enough that my protective instincts are satisfied. It takes all of thirty seconds for the air to soften around Ivy. Bailey tells a story with her hands, causing Ivy to laugh with her whole mouth. I find myself leaning against the porch post, arms folded, letting the sound run through the tight places I didn't know I'd cinched shut.

Crew, my brother and quarterback for the Tennessee Stallions, finds me like a shadow. He's got sunglasses pushed into his hair and a beer balanced in a way that says he's thinking about nothing and also everything. That smug little brother grin's in place, which means he's bracing for sport.

"You look nice," he says.

"Don't," I warn.

He follows my line of sight. "Huh."

"Don't," I repeat.

"I didn't get word from her agent that she was coming,"

he says, and for once it sounds true. "Thought she was out in California."

"She ran off the road on her way to find you." I keep my voice flat as a pasture .

"Of course she did." He takes a swallow. "You okay? Did she say what she wanted? Never thought I'd see her out this way. Not really her kind of atmosphere."

"You can ask her yourself, Crew. I'm not her messenger. And why wouldn't I be okay?"

Crew shrugs. "Because you rescue damsels like it's muscle memory and then glower at them for needing help."

"I didn't glower."

"You did your version of glowering," he says. "The quiet kind—all jaw, no volume." I drag a hand over my jaw and aim my eyes anywhere but him. Bailey has already crowned Ivy with a flower ring, like she's part of the decor and also the point of it. Ivy tilts her head, and the flowers tilt with her, summer sitting easy on her shoulders for the first time all afternoon.

Crew knocks his knuckles against my arm. "You want me to—"

"No." The word comes out sharper than I intended. I smooth it. "Eat. Be present. It's Lila's day."

He studies me for a beat. Then, surprisingly, he nods. "Yeah. It is." He peels off toward the groomsmen like a man who knows better than to light a match in a dry field.

The backyard swells and settles with the ceremony. The someone's-uncle string band finds its key, the officiant wipes his glasses, and the kids line up like feral ducklings. Ivy ends up three chairs away because Bailey puts her there, and I take an aisle spot because I always do. The vows are honest and a little messy—good ones always are. Lila cries at her own words, Dean kisses her knuckles like he rehearsed, and when the sun drifts under a ribbon of cloud, the whole yard exhales like God dimmed the world for a second to let us see better.

Applause snaps and spills. The band slides into something porch-slow. I'm pinned by handshakes for a minute—neighbors, vendors, and a cousin who thinks I should buy a boat. When I find Ivy again, she's crouched to kid level, listening to a preschooler talk about dinosaurs like it's a TED Talk. She says "no way" with perfect gravity when he reveals a fun fact about T. rex arms, then taps the brim of his tiny paper crown and sends him strutting back across the grass like she knighted him.

I don't want to notice any of that, yet I do.

Bailey steers Ivy back toward me with two champagne flutes. "Hydration," she says, shoving one at Ivy. "Supervision," she adds, handing me the other with a knowing look. "I'm going to track down Aunt Andrea before she redecorates the cake with her opinions."

"Godspeed," I say.

"She's a menace," Ivy murmurs, watching Bailey go with fondness that sounds like it surprises her.

"An effective one." I offer my flute. She clinks without making a ceremony out of it.

We drink. The bubbles are ridiculous and perfect. For a

moment, we stand shoulder to shoulder in a pocket of quiet no one else uses.

"So." Ivy looks over the yard, then at me. "I'm intruding."

"You're here," I correct.

"Uninvited."

"My sister and her now husband claim most of the county. You count by default."

She tips her head. "That sounds like logic you made up just now."

"It is." I let my mouth twitch. "Still true."

Her smile is small and dangerous. "Thank you. For not making this weirder."

I take the opening. "Do you want this to be weirder?"

"No," she says quickly. Then she repeats a softer, "No."

"Good." I nod at the barn. "Avoid the group of older women currently surrounding the dessert table unless you want to be adopted by Ethel Mae."

She mimics my nod like it's a language lesson. "Beware of Ethel Mae."

"Exactly."

We drift to the edge of the porch when the inevitable line dance tries to organize itself without music. She watches, amused and unthreatened, bare toes pressing crescents into the cool painted wood. Close-up, the flower crown is listing like a boat; a strand of blond escapes, tracing the same path I smoothed earlier. I reach to fix it before I think better of it, then my hand closes on the railing instead. I'm not doing that in front of half the county.

"Why Coral Bell Cove?" I ask.

She takes a slow sip, eyes on the yard. "Returning something to Crew. Getting away from something else."

"That jacket."

She doesn't flinch. "Yeah."

"You want me to get him?"

Her gaze flicks to me. "I don't know yet."

I respect that. "Alright."

We watch a while longer—Lila in Dean's arms, his hands bracketed at her waist like he found the exact place she's anchored. The light warms, then leans; the band slips into a waltz that half the town fakes. Ivy's shoulders soften in increments I can track. Her mouth keeps finding the same almost smile, like she's remembering how.

By the time the cake is cut and the kids have weaponized frosting, the margin between noise and night shrinks. The cooler air pulls people toward shawls and porch steps. I find the swing empty and tip my head toward it. "You want quiet."

"Please," she says with relief, and I give her the corner without making a thing of it.

The swing creaks as we set an easy rock. From here, you can see the silhouettes of the oaks against the bruising sky, the barn glow, the slow orbit of lightning bugs like somebody tossed glitter and it learned to breathe.

We sit in the kind of pause that tells on you. If you panic, it's awkward. If you trust it, it's peace.

"You've got a place to stay?" I ask because this is where responsibility lives, and I know for a fact the one inn with a vacancy sign tonight is lying.

She exhales. "No hotel will be thrilled about me showing up. I'm trying not to ruin things for... anyone."

"Alright." I keep my elbows on my knees and my voice simple. "I have a guest cottage. Bed's made. Kitchenette. It's quiet. No one will bother you there."

She turns so fast the swing stutters. "That's—are you sure?"

"Yeah."

Her brows knit. "You don't even know me."

"I know enough."

"What if I'm a terrible houseguest?"

"Then you'll fit right in," I say dryly. "Crew crashes my fridge, Bailey steals my tools, and my sister Hadley leaves floral tape everywhere. I'm adaptable."

Her laugh is a surprised little thing that punches air into my lungs. "What about your parents? Will they be okay with—"

"It's my property. I decide who stays."

"That is an unsettling amount of power."

"Good news is I'm boring."

She watches me for another beat, measuring. Not the calculation of a career girl looking for an angle. Just... a woman deciding whether her rib cage can unclench in a stranger's orbit. "Okay," she says finally. "I'll take you up on it."

"Alright." I rise, the swing scritching under my thigh. "We can slip out the side."

We thread the dark edge of the yard, where the light doesn't press so hard. She puts her hand on the porch post as we go down the steps. I pretend I don't want to take it. The night is cooler, with crickets sawing. Somewhere down by the water, a kid lights a sparkler, and the tiny hiss zips through the grass.

At the truck, I open her door and step back—out of habit, promise—and she climbs in, tucking her feet like she's learned how to take up as little space as possible. I hate that, but I don't say it. I start the engine instead and let the low rumble do what my mouth can't.

The road home is the same one we came in on, but it feels different now that the heat's bled out of it. We pass stretches of ditch that catch star puddles. We pass the bend where the creek throws back moonlight and makes a silver seam.

"You always this... nice?" she asks into the dark, which is funny because the town would describe me two clicks left of nice and four clicks south of social.

"No," I say. "But I'm not stupid."

"That's not an answer."

"It's the one you get."

She huffs, but it's affectionate around the edges. "Fair."

At my drive, I flick the headlights to low and turn under the limbs. The main house sleeps with the porch light on because my mother trained our switches and none of us ever unlearned it. The guest cottage sits under the big oak, butter-yellow paint, new roof, lantern on the stoop already glowing. I turned that light on before I left for the wedding without thinking about why.

I park beside the steps and kill the engine. For a second, we listen to the engine tick as it cools.

I point. "There."

She looks, takes in the square of the soft window, the little railing I sanded myself, the planter box that insists on living no matter how badly I ignore it. "It's sweet," she says, like she didn't expect that word to fit in her mouth.

"It's functional," I counter, because I don't know what to do with sweet.

"Functional works, too."

I hop out, come around, and offer a palm down—not a demand, not a requirement, just a place to put her hand if she needs it. She hesitates one heartbeat, then sets her fingers against mine and hops down onto the crushed shell like she trusts I won't let her ankle roll. I don't.

Inside the cottage, I flick the small lamp by the couch and stand in the doorway to make myself smaller. "Kitchenette's empty. Sorry. Coffee's at the main house. But the shower's hot. Towels are in the basket by the bed. Lock clicks clean; windows take a little tug."

She turns slowly in a circle. The place is simple—white shiplap and old wood and a quilt my mother swore she'd never let leave her house. The salvaged record player in the corner only plays when the moon is in the right mood. It smells like cedar and something lemony. I use it once a week to feel like I'm domesticated.

"It's perfect," she says, and the word lands somewhere behind my ribs and sits there.

I set a key on the counter. "I start chores early. If you want coffee, the main house is unlocked. Or text and I'll bring it by. I'll write my number on the pad by the door. You don't have to see anyone if you don't want to."

Her throat moves. "Thank you."

"Don't make it a habit." I aim for light because anything heavier will crack.

It gets me a ghost of a smirk. She sets her bag by the couch like she's testing the weight of being allowed to put something down.

"Get some sleep," I say. "We'll deal with the car in the morning."

"Okay."

I back toward the door. She doesn't follow. She watches me go with those impossible eyes, and for one wrong second, I want to step back in and find out what vanilla and citrus smell like when the world isn't watching.

I pull the door quietly and let the latch catch. On the stoop, the night hits cooler. I stand there a beat longer than necessary, listening to the cottage settle—floorboards sigh, lamp hums, and the small sounds of a place welcoming a person.

The walk back to the main house feels shorter. The porch bulb throws a circle on the steps, and a moth ping-pongs against the warm glass. Somewhere out in the back field, a horse stamps, and the sound carries.

I tell myself it's just logistics—a roof, four walls, a lock.

The simple math of decency. I let that be the truth I carry into the dark kitchen, where I leave the light above the sink on because that's what you do when somebody new is finding their way by feel.

I shower quickly—cold enough to keep my head straight—then pull on sweats and a T-shirt that still smells faintly like cedar and summer soap. The house is quiet in that old-bones way, boards settling like deep breaths. I check the back lock, flip the porch light off and on out of habit, then stop with my hand on the switch and leave it burning. If she wanders up for coffee or can't sleep, I want the glow to be a promise and not a question.

My phone buzzes on the counter.

> Lila: You disappeared. Rude.
>
> Lila: Also, can't believe you brought Ivy to my wedding after she was stuck in a ditch. I never got the story on why she was here anyway.
>
> Lila: She was lovely. Bailey adopted her. Don't be weird.

I thumb back.

> Me: All set. She's fine. Go be married.

Then I drop the phone face down and lean my hips against the sink, listening to the cicadas rake the night open and stitch it shut again.

It's a funny thing—how quickly a place adjusts around a

new presence. The cottage has hosted cousins and hands and the occasional tourist who wanted more "rustic charm" than they could stomach. But tonight, with a pop star sleeping under my oak, the land feels... steadier. It likes showing off when someone's seeing it for the first time.

I make a circuit—small house rituals I could do blind—to set the coffee, rinse a pan, and leave a dish towel folded clean. When I pass the hallway mirror, I catch my own reflection and snort—clean-shaven jaw I only bother with for weddings and funerals, hair tamed for a total of an hour, and white shirt now rolled to the forearms. Lila's going to frame a picture of me looking civilized if I don't burn the evidence first.

I kill the lamp and head for bed. The ceiling fan turns and turns. Sleep takes me in a blink.

I'm up before my alarm, same as most mornings. My brain snaps to the list before light has time to decide what color it wants to be. Boots. Barn. The horses nicker when I step into the dim area, all soft breath and patient eyes, and the routine slips over me like a shirt I've worn thin: hay tossed, grain scooped, water checked. The chickens complain on schedule. I let them out anyway because nobody likes being penned too long.

By the time I'm back at the porch, dew makes the grass glitter. The kind of damp that clings to your cuffs and your lungs. I pour the smoldering dark liquid and fill two paper cups—one black, one with cream and sugar the way my sisters like it—and add a napkin over the lids because the walk down can slosh if you're not careful.

The path to the cottage runs under the oak's spread, crushed shell crunching just enough to announce me. I slow before the steps and knock my knuckles against the jamb instead of barging in. "Morning."

Nothing for a beat. Then the lock turns and the door swings inward on a soft breath of lemon and cedar and something uniquely Ivy.

She's there—barefoot on the old wood, hair down and mussed from sleep, an oversized T-shirt skimming her thighs like she borrowed it from a life that stayed in bed longer than she did. Sunglasses are nowhere in sight, which means those eyes are. They're not the icy camera blue I'd braced for; they're warmer, stormier. The summer sky decides whether to rain or bless you.

"You weren't kidding about the coffee," she says, voice rough with sleep.

"I'm a man of my word." I hold out the cup with the cream and sugar. "Didn't know how you take it. Guessed right?"

She wraps both hands around the cardboard like it's a heat source. The first sip softens something in her face I didn't know was tight. "Perfect."

I nod at the counter. "I can fetch you a second if you burn through that one."

"You think highly of my caffeine tolerance."

"I think highly of starting the day with more than air." My gaze flicks past her—bed made clean, bag tucked near the couch, and flower crown abandoned on the little table like a surrendered weapon. "You sleep?"

"Shockingly well." A corner smile. "No elevators dinging or footsteps in the hall. Just... quiet." Her eyes lift to mine. "Is that weird to say? That quiet felt loud until it didn't?"

"No." I get it more than I want to explain. "Out here, quiet's not empty. It's just everything else doing its job."

She leans her shoulder to the jamb, the T-shirt slipping off one bare shoulder with a kind of stubborn elegance she couldn't fake if she tried. "Is it always like that? The mornings?"

"Mostly." I jerk my chin toward the back pasture. "Fog settles where the creek bends. The sun burns it off slowly. You should see it when the geese come through—they lift like someone pulled a sheet."

"Say that again," she murmurs.

"What?"

"That thing about the sheet."

I shake my head like I'm not going to repeat myself, then do it anyway. "They lift like someone pulled a sheet."

She closes her eyes for half a second, like the picture lands exactly where she needed it. "Okay," she whispers. "Yeah."

The silence that follows is easy. Birds tune up in the oak. A bee bangs itself stupid against the window screen and remembers the door five seconds later. I take a pull off my cup and try not to watch the way her mouth finds the lip and lingers there like coffee is mercy.

"I'm heading over to help with some chores," I say finally. "You're welcome to come by the farm if you don't want to be alone. There is a walking path, but it's quite a trek. Or sleep. Or whatever."

Her nod is grateful and proud all at once. "I might... I'll figure out a plan."

"You've got time." I look at her, really look, in that quiet minutes-before-the-day way that tells the truth better than night does. This is who she is when nobody's taking: curious and tired, yes, but also something steadier I haven't named yet.

"Okay," she says, like we negotiated a treaty. "Thank you."

"Lock clicks clean," I remind, tapping the knob. "Windows take a tug."

A ghost of a grin creeps across her face. "You said that last night."

"I'm consistent."

She lets me go with a little wave. "See you later, Rowan."

It shouldn't land like it does—my name in her mouth, soft around the edges. I back off the porch and force my feet to find their own rhythm instead of hers.

Halfway up the path, I look back. She's still in the doorway with one hand braced on the frame, coffee lifted, hair bright as old straw where the sun catches it. For a second, I picture that same shape in October, sweater sleeves swallowing her hands, breath ghosting out in pale threads. The oak gone bronze, the pasture cut low, the creek a ribbon.

I turn before I do something I'll regret—like go back and say more—and let the morning take me. There's a fence line to walk, a tractor complaining about a chain I should've replaced last month, and a sister who will absolutely stage a coup if I don't bring her the leftover tartlets she asked for. Routine is mercy if you use it right.

At the house, I set my empty cup in the sink and catch sight of a hoodie slung over the back of a chair—a soft navy with a decade of wash. On reflex, I pluck it up and carry it out. The day will burn hot by noon, but the first hours sit cool and creek-damp. City bones shiver in country mornings. I hang the hoodie on the cottage's porch hook and don't knock or leave a note. She'll find it if she needs it. She'll ignore it if she doesn't.

By the time I hit the barn, the sun has made up its mind. Light comes in at an angle that makes dust look holy. I shoulder into work, gratefully. The rhythm eats thought: measure, cut, mend; lead rope, halter, tie; grease, tighten, test. I'm three bolts into a hinge repair when my phone buzzes again.

Crew: Jacket?

I stare at the screen until the letters blur, then respond.

Me: Ask Ivy yourself.

It's petty and efficient. He'll survive both.

I pocket the phone and step out of the shade. Out across the back field, the line of trees looks like a held breath. Something in my chest mirrors it—and then lets go.

Because here's the inconvenient truth I don't feel like analyzing while holding a power drill: a woman I had no business bringing to my sister's wedding is in my guest cottage sipping coffee, bare feet on my wood floor, and the sky didn't fall. The farm didn't wither. The world didn't tilt except for inside me, and even there, it's not a slide so much as a shift. A click of alignment I didn't ask for and don't quite trust.

I wipe my hands on a rag and get back to work.

I can do this. Be decent without being stupid. Be neighborly without being Crew. Be helpful without making a habit of it. Keep the lines where they need to live.

And if, when the wind changes, a note floats down the lane that smells like citrus and warm sugar, I can pretend I didn't notice.

For now, the list is simple: finish the gate, show up where I'm needed, and—before the sun gets mean—drop off a paper sack on a cottage porch with two breakfast burritos and a Post-it that says

Eat.

Chapter Two

IVY

The porch smells like last night—honeysuckle and wood smoke—and something warmer I can't name until I spot it: a navy hoodie hanging from the hook by the door, shoulders broad, cuffs soft from a hundred wash cycles. My fingers move before my brain does. The fabric is cool in the morning, a little heavy, and when I pull it over my head, it swallows me whole. The hem slides past my hips, sleeves to my knuckles, and neckline brushing my collarbones with the faintest scrape of old cotton.

It smells like him. Cedar. Soap. A note of hay and sun.

The feeling that follows is embarrassingly big for such a simple thing. People give me clothes all the time. Wardrobe racks, stylist pulls, boxes with handwritten notes that don't smell like anyone. This is different. It's a thing that belongs to a person and is offered without ceremony. No cameras. No barter. Just... warm.

A paper bag waits on the little table by the window, a Post-it slapped to the top in block letters.

Eat.

I smile so hard my cheeks hurt. Inside, I find two breakfast burritos wrapped in foil and still pleasantly warm, plus napkins and a plastic fork I definitely won't need. I unwrap one and take a careful bite of the egg, cheese, peppery potatoes, and a little heat that wakes up the back of my throat. I make a noise I'd like to pretend I don't make over food, then lean a hip against the counter and let the cottage be quiet around me.

My phone blinks face down on the counter, the way I left it last night. I turn it over like I'm lifting a heavy stone.

Seventeen texts. Four missed calls. A calendar ping I absolutely ignore.

> Celeste: Where are you? Call me.

> Publicist (Mara): Label wants to confirm your availability for the June slate. Touch base this morning?

> Celeste: You've got a brand meeting at 11a CST. Do not be late.

> Crew: Hey, stranger. Jacket back in your orbit yet?

> Bailey: Want to try a bit of heaven?

The last two make me snort, and I make sure to reply to

them and them alone. I drop the phone and push it away with one finger, like it might bite.

"Not today," I tell the cottage, which does not argue.

When I open the door again, morning air slips inside and tugs at my hair. The yard is dew-damp and gold around the edges, like someone dipped the world in honey and let it drip. I step outside in bare feet and Rowan's hoodie—ridiculous and perfect—and breathe until my ribs feel like they might behave.

By the time I pad down the path toward the bigger house, I've talked myself out of—and back into—texting my mother three times. I land on a compromise. I send Mara a quick note.

> Me: Alive. Safe. Taking a breather. Zoom later?

A text bubbles back instantly.

> Publicist (Mara): Relieved. Take the morning. I'll fend off the dragons.

Bless Mara.

I veer toward the barn, drawn by the rhythm—a steady clank and a low voice of something living. Rowan's inside, and the horses know. They lean heavy necks over stall doors and track him like planets around a sun. He glances up when my shadow spills across the threshold.

"You found it," he says, the corner of his mouth tipping like he knew I would.

"The hoodie?" I tug the sleeve. "It kidnapped me. I'm filing a report."

"Stockholm syndrome sets in quickly." His eyes skate over me—bare legs, big sweatshirt, messy hair—and then do the gentlemanly thing of pretending they didn't. "You eat?"

I lift the other half of the burrito. "Working on it."

"Good." He jerks his chin at a bucket propped by the door. "Walk with me? Just be wary that it will heat quickly once the sun decides to unleash its fury."

I should say no. I have a long list of things to avoid today—gossip sites, my mother, anything with fluorescent lighting—and none of them sound appealing. Following the cowboy in his natural habitat despite the impending heat.

I fall into step beside him, our shoulders brushing once when the aisle narrows. Electricity might be dramatic, but a hum takes up residence under my skin when he's close. We step out into the brightness and past the paddock toward a fence line that looks mostly fine to my untrained eye.

"Two posts loose." He talks like he's narrating for an audience. "One staple popped. Coyotes have been testing it lately."

"Testing?" I echo, eyeing the trees like a wild dog might stroll out with a clipboard.

He gives a slight smile. "They're smart. They watch. They push where you don't think anyone's looking."

"Relatable," I mutter.

He doesn't tease. He just sets the bucket down, then pulls out a hammer, a fist full of U-shaped staples, and a pair of pliers the length of my forearm.

"Want to try?" he asks, mildly.

"Absolutely not," I say, because reflex. My feet betray me and carry me closer anyway. I stop with my hands tucked into the kangaroo pocket of his hoodie like I've handcuffed myself on purpose.

He hears the second answer under the first, but he only nods. "Watch, then."

He braces a boot against the bottom wire, leans the post with a shoulder, and works efficiently and without fanfare. The pliers bite down, the wire sings a clean, bright note, and his forearms rope and release. There's a smear of dust along a vein I have no business staring at. He sets a staple, holds it steady with two fingers, and taps once. Neat. Sure. The metal seats; the line tightens.

"You want tension," he says, eyes on the fence, "but not too much. Yank like hell and you'll snap it. Baby it, and it'll sag, then the first curious nose is through."

"Moderation," I offer.

"Control," he corrects softly. "Let the tool do the work. You guide."

Heat gathers low and ridiculous at the word guide. I lean my shoulder against the next post, pretending it needs supervision. He keeps moving down the run, and the space between us is an elastic thing—stretching, relaxing, humming with everything we're not doing.

He glances over once, quick and unreadable, then sets the last staple and tests the line. It thrums, tight and obedient. My pulse answers like a show-off.

We keep walking. The morning warms by degrees.

Somewhere behind the barn, a rooster finds a reason to be dramatic. When we swing around the north paddock, a sound like a tiny trumpet goes off. I jump because dignity is a luxury, and Rowan laughs.

"Easy," he says, angling me toward the source.

A calf blinks up at me with sticky lashes and a constellation of caramel patches. She gives an indignant snort again and then sneezes directly on my bare thigh. The warmth is unexpected and honestly adorable.

"Oh my God." I press a hand to my chest and start laughing, helpless and bright. "Ma'am. Boundaries."

"She's three weeks old," Rowan says, trying and failing to hide his amusement. "Boundaries are a Q4 goal."

"What's her name?"

"Doesn't have one yet."

"Butterscotch," I say immediately, because of course.

He looks at the calf, then looks at me. "Fitting."

"Welcome to the world, Butterscotch," I tell her solemnly, and she sneezes again for emphasis. I wipe my leg with the inside hem of the hoodie and pretend that's not basically sacrilege.

Back at the barn, he washes his hands at the utility sink and passes me a clean towel without asking. When he turns, his face is easy in a way I'm not used to seeing in men—work done, morning unfolding, company not resented.

"Plans?" he asks, drying his hands.

"Bailey texted," I say. "Said I need to try the cinnamon twists before Coral Bell Cove runs out forever."

"She's not wrong." His mouth tilts. "I'll run you into town if you want."

The offer lands like the hoodie did—simple, unshowy, and kind. I should hesitate, but I don't.

"I want."

After a quick change of my clothes into something less... sleepywear, and tossing Rowan's sweatshirt in the washing machine with plans to confiscate it later, I meet Rowan, who's waiting patiently by his truck, hands tucked casually in his pockets. We take the long way into town, which turns out to be the only way. The road threads between pines, dips past a marsh that flashes silver when the wind skims it, and then climbs just enough that the bay throws a wink through a gap in the trees.

Rowan doesn't talk to fill space. He points, sometimes.

"Old bird sanctuary."

"Don't park by that oak—wasp's nest."

"If you want the best tomatoes, skip Main Street and ask Mrs. Kline at the end of Dock Lane."

I memorize it all like a person who might need these facts more than she needs industry awards.

Bailey's already outside the bakery when we pull up, holding a paper bag like it's a relay baton and this is the handoff. She spots me through the windshield and grins big enough to light the sidewalk.

"There she is," she sings, pulling me inside. The doorbell chirps and the air changes—cold and sweet, butter curling under my tongue just from breathing. "You're in luck. Cinnamon twists are still warm."

"Hi to you, too," I say, laughing.

Rowan trails us, tips the girl at the register like he always has cash exactly where he needs it, and leans a shoulder against the wall while Bailey presses a twist into my hand. Sugar dusts my fingers, which is how I end up licking it off like a scandal in slow motion. The pastry is still soft in the middle, sticky at the edges, and I make that noise again.

Bailey fans herself. "Okay, ma'am."

"Do you sell these in bulk?"

"Only if you promise not to sue us when your nutritionist cries."

"Joke's on you," I say. "She doesn't believe in joy."

Rowan's mouth quirks; his eyes do, too. I've started noticing that his gaze warms when something genuinely amuses him, a sunbeam through branches, here and gone.

We hop down the street to the bookstore, where the air tastes like paper and hope. Bailey's pride and joy. I trail my fingers over spines, whisper hello to the section where my music sits in glossy coffee table collections I pretend not to notice, and end up in front of a shelf of essayists. I pick up a book about living slower and laugh under my breath.

Bailey appears at my elbow like a well-meaning ghost. "That one made me cry on a Tuesday and then bake bread."

"High praise."

"You a paperback or hardcover girl?" she asks, already reaching.

"Paperback," I say, then lower my voice like I'm confessing. "And I dog-ear."

"To jail with you," she says, solemn. "But I'll visit."

I add two books to the stack—one about beekeeping because I'm a chameleon now, apparently, and one about small towns because I want to see if it gets this right—and hand Rowan the bag when it's time to check out. He takes it like he was waiting to have a reason to carry something for me.

We make it three storefronts before Bailey hooks her thumb over her shoulder. "Surprise," she says to me. "No telling."

"I'm right here," Rowan notes, dry as a pasture in August.

"Then stop having ears," she shoots back, and links her arm through mine. "Come on. He can survive twenty minutes without us."

We duck into a shop that is absolutely not for him—linen dresses and sun-faded straw hats and a rack of swimsuits that make me break out in hives just looking at them—but Bailey beelines to the corner where a vintage record player sits atop an antique dresser. She drops the needle on Fleetwood Mac and tilts her chin toward my tote.

"Tell me you have a love of records like me."

I blink. "How did you—"

"Because I am prescient." She pulls a little card from behind the player and holds it up. *Loaner Program.* "Pick a player and five records. Keep them for a week. Trade for another."

"Is that legal?"

She shrugs. "It's Coral Bell legal."

I choose a player, the color of sea glass with an arrangement of blue grass and classic rock records, Bailey scribbles my name on the card, and I walk out with a kind of fizz in my chest that has nothing to do with pastry sugar. Outside, the light is brighter. Or maybe I am because nothing sounds as good as a vinyl record.

We find Rowan on the bench by the planter, one ankle crossed over a knee, paper coffee cup turning in his hands. He looks up as we approach and stands immediately, like he wasn't comfortable without us in his line of sight.

"You rob them blind?" he asks, nodding at the player's case.

"Sanctioned robbery," Bailey says. "We're cultivating taste."

"Coral Bell legal," I add, smug now that I understand the joke.

He shakes his head. "Let's get you back before you start quoting bylaws."

We walk the boardwalk before we leave, because I ask and because he says yes even though I can tell he's not a strolling man. The bay is a sheet of hammered metal in this light, sun biting at the crests. A dog barrels after a tennis ball, then decides the real prize is attention, demanding scratches like payment.

Rowan obliges. Of course, he does.

We lean on the railing. I tilt my head back, breathing this. Bailey snaps a photo of the view and then—because she's not subtle—one of me with a slice of Rowan's jaw in the frame.

"Evidence," she says, not sorry.

"For what?" I ask, even though the answer buzzes under my skin.

"That you looked happy on a Sunday," she says simply. "You can forget, you know? Photographic proof helps."

We leave before the sun gets bossy. Rowan drives, one hand at twelve o'clock, the other on his thigh. My gaze drifts there once. Okay, twice. I tug at the frayed edges of my shorts.

"You good?" he asks quietly, eyes on the road.

"Better than I should be," I admit.

He nods like that's a thing he understands.

Back at the farm, he unloads the record player and my book bag as if he's not cataloging every new thing I've just set inside his life. We're halfway to the cottage when my phone dings.

> Publicist (Mara): Zoom at 3p your time? Quick and painless.
>
> Celeste: Confirmed you for 2p CST. Join the link below.

I type one response.

> Me: 3p works. Thirty minutes, that's all I have.

I don't reply to my mother. The old reflex to obey crackles and snaps, but I step away from it like a live wire.

"Work?" Rowan asks.

"Zoom at three." I grimace. "I'll keep it short."

"You need the big house Wi-Fi?"

"The cottage is fine." I hesitate. "Thank you. For making space for me to... not run."

He tips his chin, eyes searching mine like he wants to check the ground before he nods. "You don't owe me anything."

"Not owing and not being grateful aren't opposites," I say, because maybe he needs to hear it. Maybe I do.

Something in his face shifts—pleased, wary, soft. He pushes the cottage door open and leaves me on the threshold with a brand-new-to-me record player and a new appreciation for small-town life.

"See you later," he says.

I watch him walk away until the oak eats him, then sit cross-legged on the rug and listen to Stevie Nicks tell me not to chain my heart. I make a cup of lemon water. I read five pages without absorbing a single word. At 2:59, I click a link.

Mara's face fills my screen—neat bun, cat-eye liner, smile like a solution.

"You look... peaceful," she says, surprised and delighted. "It's unsettling. In a good way."

"I'm doing a rural immersion program," I deadpan.

"Great. Think we can monetize it?"

We run down the list—deliverables, the three interviews I need to reschedule, and a charity gala I was somehow on the poster for despite not agreeing to attend. Mara promises to deflect, delay, and de-escalate. She uses words like *window* and *reset* and *creative space*. She asks if I'm writing. I don't lie.

"Not yet," I say, tracing a circle in the condensation of my glass. "But there's humming."

"Good enough." She leans closer. "Also, you should know that the internet thinks you're on an enlightenment retreat in Idaho. Shh. Don't correct them."

I laugh. "Bless the internet's geography."

The call ends without stress lodged behind my eyes. That in itself feels like a minor miracle. I sit with it. Then I stand because my body remembers a different kind of ritual I haven't had in months.

I take the record off the player and slide it back into its sleeve. And then I bait fate by walking up to the main house at dusk.

His porch is all long shadows and soft sounds—wind through leaves, insects tuning up, a distant laugh that could be a neighbor or a fox. The screen door is propped with a smooth river rock. I tap my knuckles anyway.

"It's open," he calls from somewhere inside.

The kitchen is small and clean in that unfussy way—no matching canister sets, just a line of jars and a wooden spoon that's earned its keep. Rowan stands at the stove in a gray T-shirt and jeans, bare feet, a dish towel slung over his shoulder like it's a uniform. He turns when I hover in the doorway and does a quick once-over, eyes catching on the clean hoodie I quickly snag off the counter like it pleases him against his will.

"Tomato sandwiches?" he asks. "Got good ones at the market this morning."

"You're speaking a love language I didn't know I had."

He gestures with the knife. "Wash up and slice the other one. Salt's in the pinch bowl."

We move around each other like we've done this a dozen times instead of zero. I wash the tomato, slice it carefully and thinly, then salt it like he said. He toasts the bread and lays down a scandalous amount of mayo without shame. We build something perfect between two palms, then carry plates out to the back steps, where the light turns everything it touches into memory.

I bite. I close my eyes. Rowan makes a small sound that could be a laugh if he were the laughing-out-loud type.

"Okay," I say when I can speak again. "This is... indecent."

"Don't tell the nutritionist."

"She's already crying somewhere," I say through a second bite.

We eat like people who worked for it, knees almost touching, shoulder to shoulder, but not quite. That hum comes back—the one that feels like it starts in the chest and lives in the wrists. His free hand rests on his thigh, fingers splayed, and I have to look away because the very idea of those fingers on me makes my blood do tiny irresponsible fireworks.

After dinner, he rinses the plates. I dry. The domestic choreography would terrify my PR team and thrill my therapist. When the last fork clinks into the drawer, the power blinks—not off, just a hiccup—and the house sighs.

"Storm later," Rowan says, glancing at the window. "You hear it in the way the air sits on the trees."

"You got poetic about geese," I remind him. "Now the trees, too? Dangerous."

"Don't tell anyone," he says, lips tipping.

We step onto the porch just as the first rush of wind rattles the oak. The air is heavier. The world feels like it's inhaled and is waiting to decide what to do with the breath. A strand of my hair whips into my mouth, and I laugh, tugging it free. Rowan reaches out—impulse, instinct—and tucks another behind my ear with a touch so careful that my knees consider giving out on principle.

"Thanks," I say, breath not fully back.

He drops his hand like he remembered himself half a second too late. "You, uh... You need anything tonight? I can leave the truck if you want to run down to town in the morning."

"I'm good," I say. "Bailey said she'll abduct me at ten for something called 'market triage.'"

"Sounds legit."

A flicker of lightning threads the clouds far off, silent for now. We watch it. I think about the woman who couldn't hear herself think in a glass apartment high above the noise, and about this one making lists that include tomatoes and records and learning the weather by the way a tree's leaves turn their bellies up.

"Rowan?" I say, before I decide it's a bad idea.

"Hmm?"

"Thank you. Not just for the big stuff. For... the little ordinary things. The coffee. The Post-it. The hoodie. The fence. The sandwich. Those feel..." I search for a word that isn't *like oxygen,* because that will get me sent to a feelings monastery. "They feel like anchors."

He goes still in that listening way he has. When he looks at me, something unguarded crosses his face and stays. "You're welcome," he says, like he means it from his bones. "You can keep the hoodie, by the way."

My heart does the irresponsible thing again. "Dangerous offer."

"Figured it'd save me a trip to the hook."

We stand there until the first rumble makes itself known, a low roll that feels in my feet before it reaches my ears. He steps back like he doesn't trust himself to stay put if he stays close. I step down because I don't trust myself either.

"Good night, Rowan."

"Good night, Ivy."

The walk to the cottage is short and a little wild—wind playing with the ends of my hair, leaves whispering, and air electric with maybe. I close the door behind me and press my back to it, then grin into the dark like a person who has accidentally stumbled into her own life. I drop the needle on "Landslide" and crawl into bed with a book I don't read.

Outside, the storm thinks about it. Inside, I do, too.

It's only the second day. I am not supposed to feel this... full.

But I do. And for the first time in a long time, I don't apologize to myself for it.

Chapter Three

ROWAN

The storm breaks around midnight and walks all over the roof like it's got a grievance. I lie there and count the space between flash and rumble until the number gets big enough to let my jaw unclench. When it moves off toward the bay, the dark turns plush. Crickets pick up where thunder leaves off.

The first light is clean and silver. The world smells washed and edible.

Coffee, boots, barn. Same order, same pace. Horses blow steam at me like criticism I can live with. The roof still ticks, letting go of the last of the rain. I run a palm down Duke's neck, and he leans his whole soul into it. We all want proof we're real at dawn.

On my way back across the yard, I look at the cottage without meaning to. A curtain moves. It's a small thing, but it lands. The porch light's off—good. She slept. A sliver of navy at the window tells me the hoodie never made it back to the hook. Somewhere between reasonable and reckless. I like that.

I set two mugs on her stoop—hers with cream and sugar, mine black—and knock with my knuckles because it's early and because you don't kick a quiet door when the person behind it is trying to remember how to be a person.

"Morning," she says, voice sleep-rough through the wood. Then the door opens, and I forget about coffee for a second.

Bare legs, damp hair braided over one shoulder, my hoodie hanging off her like a promise I shouldn't make. She's barefoot, toes pink. Her face is clean, no war paint, and there's a softness at her mouth I've only seen when a woman forgets to guard it.

"You brought the good stuff," she says, reaching for the marked cup.

"Bribery works." I hand it over. "Storm treat you okay?"

"Like a lullaby with a bass drop." She tips her chin toward the yard, but I can tell with the way she avoids eye contact that she's holding something back. "Everything still standing?"

"Mostly." I point toward the south pasture. "Corner slipped. I'll fix it after breakfast." I don't add *after I walk you through your morning, so you don't convince yourself you dreamed yesterday,* but it's there, hanging.

She takes a careful sip and makes a sound that registers in places I work hard not to notice. "I have a Zoom at ten," she says, wincing like she hates saying it out loud.

"You need the house Wi-Fi?"

She shakes her head. "I trust your cottage to power my very important call about lipstick and deliverables."

"Bold of you," I say. "Carl texted. He's got your car up on the rack. Says we can swing by after lunch if you want to hear the bad news from a man with hands like motor oil."

Her mouth quirks. "I'll bring him a muffin. Soften the blow."

"Loretta's bakery's got a dozen every morning. She weaponizes carbs," I explain.

"I like her already." She tugs the sleeves over her knuckles and glances toward the north field. "Can I—" She stops, then starts again. "Can I walk with you while you fix the fence? I promise not to touch tools unless supervised."

A laugh sneaks out before I can stop it. "You were a menace with the pliers yesterday."

"I was an apprentice," she counters, chin up.

"Fine." I tip my head toward the barn. "Boots first."

Ten minutes later, she clomps across the yard in a pair of mudroom castoffs two sizes too big and grinning like the sound they make is part of the fun. The sun's up proper now, dripping honey off the grass blades. Everything's brighter than it has any right to be after a night that loud.

We walk the edge of the south pasture in companionable quiet. She keeps pace, eyes everywhere—fence, trees, the way dew beads on spider silk like jewelry. When the bad corner shows itself—stringer warped, staple pulled, my own note in Sharpie on the post from last storm that says FIX ME, IDIOT—she aims an I-told-you-so smile at me without the words.

"I believe *moderation* and *control* were your talking points," she says, parroting me, and I pretend not to like hearing my lecture in her voice.

"Guess I should take my own advice."

I set the bucket down and pass her the pliers like we rehearsed. We fall into the same shape as yesterday without trying—her on the wire, me a breath behind, heat and cedar and the quiet tick of two people deciding not to say the loud thing.

"Here," I murmur, guiding her grip. "Let the tool do the work."

"Control," she echoes, barely audible.

The staple sets clean. The wire hums. So do I.

We're packing the bucket when Butterscotch toddles up and sneezes on Ivy's shin again like it's a sacrament.

"Ma'am," Ivy says, affront softened by delight. "We just did laundry."

"You named her. That's on you." I snag a towel off the fence and pass it over.

"She chose me with bodily fluids. That's basically marriage."

"Depends who you ask," I say, earning a laugh that lands low and warm.

Back at the house, I point her at the kitchen because there's an itch under my ribs that says if I don't let her near the domestic part again, I'll think about it all day. "Tomato sandwiches are a seasonal obligation," I tell her, dropping a fat red one on the counter. "After your Zoom, we'll earn them."

She slides onto a stool and props her chin on a sleeve-swallowed fist. "You say that like there's a test."

"There is." I slice. "You'll pass."

At nine fifty-seven, she hurries back to the cottage with a salute that's half joke, half armor. I head out to check the tractor belts and consciously don't look toward her window while I do it. When the Zoom's over—thirty-eight minutes if my gut's right—she reappears with a victory grimace and a relief exhale big enough to rock a calf to sleep.

"Survived." She blows out a breath.

"Toast," I answer, holding up the bread like a Eucharist.

We eat on the back steps again because the day demands it. She gets mayo on her thumb, licks it off without thinking, remembers I'm there, and then looks anywhere but at me for six long seconds. The air between us goes thick and interesting.

"Carl?" I ask because I'm a coward and a gentleman, and because we both need the change of subject.

"Carl," she confirms, popping to her feet, the sweatshirt long gone after the sun blasts us from above.

The drive into town is slow on purpose. Puddles still glass the low spots where the road dips. Ivy holds her hand out the window and rides the air like a kid in a convertible, hair whipping, laughter quick and surprised when the wind catches under her palm and lifts it. I fight back against the grin but lose miserably.

Carl's bay door is rolled up, radio low, the man himself under her car like a mechanic calendar from 1992. He slides out when he hears us, wipes his hands, and gives me the nod people around here trade instead of handshakes when they've seen each other fix the same stubborn thing three times.

"Morning," he says. "You brought the superstar."

"She brought muffins," Ivy answers, holding out the little brown bag we finagled from Loretta before making our way to the shop.

"Well, that'll soften me," he says, peering into it like it might bite. "Your spaceship's fixable, Ms. Quinn. Needs a control arm and a new tire. Rock in the culvert kissed it where it shouldn't."

"How long?" I ask.

"Two days if the parts's in Norfolk. Three if it's not."

Ivy nods. "I'm not going anywhere," she says, so lightly I almost miss the way it lands.

Carl gives me a look that has nothing to do with cars and everything to do with men who recognize another man skating on thin ice by choice. I ignore him. Mostly.

We leave with grease under my fingernails and a promise from Carl to call when the parts and tire arrive. Ivy insists on paying for the tow even though Carl would have let me run a tab. She signs a receipt with her real name and watches the letters look like a stranger on the paper.

"You okay?" I ask when we're back on the sidewalk.

"Strangely, yes." She tilts her face into the sun and closes her eyes. "Two to three days used to feel like a disaster. Now it feels like... room."

"Room's not a disaster," I say, words coming out rougher than I meant.

"No," she agrees. "It's not." She opens her eyes and pins me with them. Not a crisp, clear blue. Something in between that shifts with the light, the way the bay does when wind runs fingers over it. They are the kind of eyes that make a promise unintentionally and keep it anyway. I need to remember how to breathe.

"Coffee?" I ask.

"Always."

We take it to the boardwalk and lean on the railing the way we do things now—close enough to feel the vibration of the other one's breath yet not touching because that would make the ground tilt too far, too fast. Down the beach, a kid chases his hat and wins. Ivy watches him and smiles with her whole mouth. The wind plays with the loose pieces of her braid until a short curl springs free right above her ear.

"You're going to ignore it, aren't you?" she murmurs without looking at me.

"Absolutely," I lie, and reach anyway, tucking it back with a touch so careful anybody watching would think I was handling glass. Her breath stutters. Mine does too. The moment opens its eyes and stares at us.

We head back to the truck because the chores don't care about my heart having opinions. On the way out of town, a cloud slides across the sun and the temperature drops a notch, the way it does when the day's getting ready to change its mind. Ivy hooks her arm out the window again and rides the wind, hoodie cuff flapping. She is, for the span of a two-lane mile, a woman who forgot to be anyone but herself.

I let her. I drive slowly. The rest can wait.

By the time we crest my lane again, the sun's taken off its morning manners. Heat is honest work—the kind that gets in your shirt and insists you do something with your hands. I give her the easy jobs because I'm not built to watch her bleed. The way she leans into learning is a kind of balm I didn't know I was short on.

We run salt out to the mineral blocks, check the float valve on the north trough, and scare a blue heron off the fence line by accident. She startles, laughs at herself, then points like she just spotted a movie star. "He's huge."

"Thinks he owns the place," I say. "We let him."

A breeze noses across the pasture, warm on my forearms. Ivy tucks stray blond wisps behind her ear and fails since the wind has hands. I pretend not to notice.

"Teach me something harder," she says, chin up like a dare.

"Wire splice," I decide. I grab the little red joiners from the bucket and walk her back to the sagging section by the stand of sweetgums. "If a storm takes the top line out, you can nurse it till I get here."

We kneel in the grass. Her knee brushes my thigh and stays. I don't flinch. I don't move into it. We exist there, a fraction closer than polite, and the world turns anyway.

"Thumb here," I say, guiding her grip on the tool. She's strong—tendons flex under my hand, quick and precise like she's used to choreography that hurts the next day. "Now pull. Slow."

She does, breath feathering my jaw. The joiner bites, clicks, and holds. She grins, proud and all teeth, and it almost knocks me backward.

"Again?" she asks.

"Again."

We work the line until it sings, that hive-deep thrumming a fence makes when it's right. Sweat glows in the hollow of her throat. I look away like I have sense.

I walk Ivy to the far fence where the pasture thins and the creek bends. Old round bales are stacked like tired moons beside a gray barn that's seen too many winters. I tap the door with my knuckles, and it answers with a hollow thud.

"You going to fix this one up, too?" she asks, squinting at the warped boards.

"Eventually." I toe a divot in the dirt. "Be a good spot for kids. Little camp, maybe. Show 'em where food comes from. Feed the goats, plant a row, watch something grow that isn't on a screen."

She stops, and when I finally look over, her gaze is steady on me. "A camp?"

"Just an idea." My voice comes out rougher than I mean. "Been thinking more since Lila married Dean and the boys started tearing around here. Seems like something kids need."

"You'd be really good at it," she says, no hesitation.

That lands in a place I keep boarded up. I shrug like it's

nothing, like I didn't lie awake last night drawing rectangles on an envelope. "I don't know."

"I do." She steps closer, fingers grazing a splintered rail. "You stopped what you were doing to pull a stranger out of a ditch and then made her coffee without asking how she takes it. That tells me everything I need."

I have to look away, out past the hay to where the grass moves like a slow river. Being seen that cleanly feels like standing in full sun. "It's just wood and work," I mumble.

"It's heart," she says softly. "And you've got plenty."

Back at the house, I point her to the spigot, and we wash up side by side, our forearms streaked, droplets making constellations on the boards. She watches the dirt swirl and smiles. "I get the appeal," she says.

"Of soap?"

"Of seeing you did something," she answers, flicking water at me. "There's proof."

Proof. I think about the half-dozen fixes out here no one but me will ever clap for, and the way her saying it out loud lands like recognition in my chest. "Hungry?"

"Always," she says, then winces. "But... Zoom. Part two. At four."

"You'll take it here," I decide, rinsing my hands. "House router's stronger when it gets hot."

Something like relief slips across her face and is gone. She nods, follows me inside, and sets up at the little table with a laptop that probably costs more than my truck. I stack mail, rinse a peach, slice it into perfect crescent moons, and set the plate at her elbow without comment right before the waiting room admits *Celeste Quinn* and *Label Ops – East*.

She looks up at me a beat too long—thank you without words—then pastes on a professional smile I like less than the sleep-rough one and taps *Join*.

I take my peaches and my opinions to the porch.

The call runs forty-two minutes. I know because I learn the shape of their voices through the screen door—Celeste's sweet-knife cadence, a man from the label with a calendar for a spine, and a PR girl who says "just" before every demand. Ivy agrees when she needs to, pushes back twice (soft, smart), and the third time says she's on a break and means it with her whole mouth. When it ends, quiet rushes into the house like wind through a new opening.

She appears in the doorway with her laptop tucked to her ribs, eyes a little too bright. I don't ask if she's okay. I hand her a cold bottle of water and a dish towel for show, because sometimes you need something to hold to remind your hands what they're for.

"They want me in Nashville next week," she says, tone carefully even.

I take a drink so I don't say the wrong thing.

"You want quiet or company?" I ask instead. It costs me.

She opens her eyes and lets me see the truth without the paint. "Company," she says, then glances at the door. "Until you get bored with me not being sparkly."

"Sparkly's a seller's trick," I say. "I'll take you when you're matte."

Her breath catches. Mine, too. We stand in that for

three counts, and then I ruin it by remembering I'm an adult with chores and a huge reason I should say no to everything I'm feeling. "I have to pull the bush hog around and make a pass on the back easement," I tell her. "You can ride if you don't mind being dusted."

"I don't mind at all," she says, grabbing the worn-out baseball cap hanging by the back door. She steals it fair and square. "Let me earn my company."

We rumble the tractor down to the low strip where the property shrugs its shoulders against the creek. She sits sideways on the fender, one hand on the guardrail, the other on my bicep because gravity votes that way when we take the turn. I forget how to shift for two stalls, then blame the soil when it bucks. She laughs against my shoulder and doesn't move her hand.

"You do this every day?" she asks over the clatter.

"Only on days that end in y," I call back.

Dust turns us into something out of a sepia photograph —edges softened, lines honest. The mower coughs once and then settles into a rhythm, knocking back weeds in tidy testimony that someone gave a damn today. We do two passes and call it. We aren't trying to win a ribbon, just keep erosion from eating the land. On the slow drive back, she points at the bend where the creek fattens and then slips narrow under the footbridge.

"You said to sit there when the tide turns," she says. "Why?"

"Because you can feel the river change its mind," I answer, not trying to make poetry and stumbling into it anyway. "Feels like somebody bigger than you just took a breath."

She goes quiet. When we park by the barn, she hops down, dusts her thighs off, and gives me a look I can't file yet. "Show me."

We take the path under the pines, light falling through in fat coins, insects sawing a steady note. The creek's high from last night and moving with purpose, shadowed by overgrown banks. We sit on the flat rock that's been a bench for five Wright kids and half the cousins in three counties. I've carved hearts here I don't admit to. I've thrown stones, insults, and prayers.

"You're not going to narrate?" she teases, fingers skimming the surface.

"You'll hear it," I say.

We do.

When the tide of the bay pushes back up the little artery, there's a stitched moment where the surface goes slick as breath—no ripples, no run—and then the water decides. It shivers, then turns. You can watch the eddies reverse like someone flipped a diagram upside down and dared the world to keep up. Ivy inhales like the relief hurts.

"There it is," she whispers.

"Yeah."

We don't talk for a while. It's good not to. Pines whisper to each other in a language I pretended to understand as a kid and now respect enough to leave alone. A heron reels out a croak that's eighty percent prehistoric. My shoulder brushes hers on purpose or because the rock slopes. She doesn't move.

"Rowan?" she says finally.

"Yeah."

"Do you ever feel like... nothing you say in the city is real? Like words bounce off glass and come back at you wrong?"

"All the time," I say, even though my city is a low building with bad coffee and county paperwork. "That's why I talk to fences."

She laughs, not because it's funny but because I offered a crack for her to climb through. The sound lands on my sternum and makes it easier to stand when we do.

"Come on," I say. "Before the humidity remembers us."

We jog the twenty yards to the house, laughing like kids running to beat the porch. We make it under the eaves and stand there grinning and breathing hard like we just outran something bigger than weather.

"Shower," I command. If she stays right here any longer, I'm going to say a thing I can't unsay. "I'll make dinner."

"You can't always bribe me with food," she says. Then she softens it herself with, "Okay, you can. Thank you."

I slip inside the main house to fry chicken like my mother isn't standing in my head, reminding me not to dry it out. Music through the open windows tells me she's put the record back on and maybe the shower, too. Steam and Stevie drift in tandem across the grass. I stand at the stove and get every timing right that a man can get right when he's not sure what he's doing with his life is right at all.

By the time she appears on the porch in bare legs and damp hair—the tank and shorts swapped for a soft T-shirt that announces a band I haven't heard of—the light is syrup, and the yard smells like hay and my mother's rosemary that refuses to die. I bring the plates out, set them on the little table, and try not to watch her sit down like I set a table for a woman on purpose.

"Looks incredible," she says, lifting her fork.

"Tastes better," I answer, because confidence can be cooked into things even if I can't seem to put it anywhere else today.

We eat. It's quiet in all the right places and talk in the rest. She tells me about a girl in Des Moines who pressed a letter into her hand after a show and said, "You made me feel less alone," and how that ruined her—in a good way— for a while. I tell her about the fourth-grade field trip where I explained photosynthesis to a kid who hated science and watched his face change, and how I keep chasing that same look in kids when I volunteer at the school garden. We are, without either of us naming it, handing each other the little anchors we tie to our ankles so we don't float away.

After, I wash up while she dries, which is a domestic choreography that makes my bones ache in a way swinging a post driver never has. When we finish, she lingers with the towel in her hands, and I point my chin at the porch swing because if we're going to flirt with fire, we might as well sit where I can face the yard and remember I'm responsible for more than my heartbeat.

We swing. Fireflies start up in the low places, a hundred

small yeses. She tucks her feet under her and leans back, head tipping to the board like she trusts the piece of wood and me by extension.

Her phone buzzes on the little table next to us. She flips it, face down, without checking. I raise one eyebrow.

"I'm off the clock," she says.

"Then learn the cricket chorus," I answer, because that's a choice, too. She does, eyes half-closed, mouth going soft in a way that is going to ruin me for years if I let it.

The sky loses its last blue. The swing's chains creak like an older man telling a story he's earned the right to repeat. We're one degree from asleep when a truck crunches up the drive and brakes too quickly.

Crew.

I don't sigh out loud. Ivy sits up, reflexes quick and brittle. "Expecting him?"

"No," I say, which is the problem.

He hops out with a grin and a six-pack, sunglasses in his hair even though the sun bit it an hour ago. "Crashing the party," he calls, too loud for this hour.

I stand. Ivy stands too, a fraction behind me, and it isn't the wrong picture.

Crew clocks it. He's not dumb. His smirk tips to a question mark that I don't have the patience to answer in front of anything with ears.

"Evening, Ivy," he says, easy as a man walking into a room where he expects clapping. "You stuck around after all."

She doesn't flinch. Good girl. "Guess I did."

"Carl says two to three days," I add, like we're sharing a farm report.

He laughs and hands me the six-pack like a peace offering. "You two good?" he asks, finally looking at her with something that isn't entirely show.

"We are," she says, simple as a line drawn right where she wants it.

He takes that in, nods once, and backs down the steps. "See you later," he says. Some party crasher.

When his taillights get swallowed by the trees, the night exhales again. Ivy doesn't look at me, and I don't look at her. We sit back down and swing until the bugs turn from chorus to lullaby, the six-pack resting on the porch earning every drop of condensation.

"I should sleep," she says finally, voice soft as church.

"Yeah," I say, because I don't trust myself to say anything else. I walk with her to the bottom of the cottage steps like I wasn't going to. She climbs two, then turns back —close enough that if I leaned, my mouth would find the place at her temple that feels like a secret.

"Thank you for today," she says. "For... all of it."

"Get some rest," I answer, because I am not a poet, and if I become one on this step, I'm done for.

She nods, opens the door, and the warm square of light swallows her whole. It takes a long time to go off. Long enough to make a man think about the plans he had for staying unbothered and what it means to abandon them.

I sit on my porch with a warming beer from Crew's gift and watch the yard breathe. Crickets trade the line to katydids. An owl stakes its claim at the tree line. Somewhere in the grass, the little calf with the ridiculous name sighs in her sleep. The record in the cottage hits the end of its side and spins against silence, soft, steady, like a heart that refuses to skip.

I sleep like I've been worked, not like I've been worried, which is a trick I learned back when finishing a chore was the only way to tell a day from itself. I'm up before the birds vote on a key. Coffee. Boots. Lists I don't write down because my hands remember them.

By the time I circle back past the oak, a square of light is on in the cottage. She kept the hoodie. I don't see her, but the record player hums low under the morning—needle resting where she forgot to lift it. It's a small, human mess that makes my mouth do something unfamiliar.

"Morning," I say, tapping the frame.

She answers from the kitchenette, hair braided down her back, sleeves pushed to her elbows. "You own any mugs that aren't chipped?"

"Wouldn't trust 'em if they weren't," I say, handing over her coffee—I know the way she likes it enough now that I don't have to guess. She wraps both hands around it like she's claiming something warm on purpose.

"Busy day?" she asks.

I nod once, my answer simple enough. There isn't ever a day that isn't busy on the farm.

She grins, then tips her chin toward the yard. "Put me to work."

I should send her back to the couch with her book and a

command to conserve energy. I don't. I point her at the hose and make a motion of filling the animal troughs. Despite my use of the English language, Ivy seems to understand.

We meet in the middle over the hose when I turn the nozzle wrong and christen her calves by accident. She gasps, laughs, tries to shield herself with her arm, fails, then flicks water at me with the same stubbornness she used on that fence splice yesterday. The drops land cool on my forearms. A ten-second water fight, and then we remember we're adults.

The daily chores pass the time as usual, but it's different with Ivy here. For someone who seems like she lives in such a frazzled state of mind, she brings a calmness over the farm I haven't seen in a long time.

As we wrap up the last chores, we head for the truck and roll back to the house. I promised fajitas, and the way her eyes lit up like I'd handed her fireworks makes it impossible to back out.

We fall into an easy rhythm in the kitchen. Ivy slices peppers from the garden while I sear steak in the cast-iron. She bumps my hip when we trade places at the stove—light, accidental-on-purpose—and I pretend the sizzle in the pan is the only heat in the room.

"Today was... unexpectedly wet," she says, lining the peppers into neat color bars and flicking an imaginary droplet off her wrist.

"Chores, a hose fight, and you declaring war on a water trough," I say. "You're getting the real tour."

"I was merely defending myself," she counters, her smile curving. "You flicked first. For the record, I won," she says, eyes bright.

"You switched the nozzle to jet. That's cheating."

We plate everything and eat at the island like normal people with regular days. She tells me Butterscotch needs her own social media account. I tell her my youngest brother, Holt, swears he can smell rain two hours before it hits, yet he is wrong at least half the time. She laughs and steals the last wedge of lime off my plate without asking.

When the dishes are rinsed and stacked, we take cold tea out to the steps. Dusk folds over the yard, cicadas tuning up. Somewhere down by the creek, a frog starts sounding like a squeaky hinge.

"So Carl should have the part tomorrow or the next day," she says, thumb tracing condensation on her glass. She tries to make it casual but doesn't quite stick the landing. "So... soon."

"Soon," I echo. The word sits between us like a coin no one wants to pick up.

She tilts her head toward me. "You'll help me test-drive my spaceship out of the ditch era?"

"I'll drive behind you with hazards on and a tow strap ready," I say. "Full-service package."

Her smile curves, slow and warm. "Chivalry looks good on you."

"Careful. You'll start rumors."

"About the surly cowboy who makes excellent fajitas?" She nudges my knee with her toe. "Let them."

The porch light throws a soft halo across her bare legs and the hem of her shorts. I should look away. I don't. She catches me and doesn't look away either, and the air gets thick enough to chew for a beat.

She clears her throat first, mercy in the sound. "Thank you. For dinner. For... today."

"Anytime," I say, meaning it more than I should.

She stands, gathering her empty glass. "Walk me back to the cottage?"

"Of course."

We cross the yard shoulder to shoulder, not touching yet close enough to feel it anyway. At her door, she turns, hand on the latch, searching my face like she's memorizing a map she plans to use again.

"Night, Rowan."

"Night, Ivy."

She steps inside, the soft click of the latch louder than it should be, and I'm left on the porch with the taste of lime and the word *soon* humming in my chest.

I watch the square of light take her, then go dark, then flare again when she remembers to blow out the candle, then go dark for good.

I should go to bed. Instead, I do the porch check I always do—gate latched and feed bowl turned upside down because otherwise the opossums leave me thank-you notes. The yard holds the day's heat like a story it plans to tell in pieces. I stand in it and try not to replay every moment where my hand could have been a little braver and wasn't.

Inside, my phone buzzes on the table. *Unknown number*. I let it go dark.

Across the yard, the cottage curtain flashes pale once, twice—the quick pulse of a phone lighting up and going still. A minute later, it happens again. Not frantic, just insistent. The cadence of people who confuse access with care.

I don't have to see the name to guess the sender. Crew's told enough stories about the machine to know how it talks: holds placed, flights booked, "confirm by 9 a.m." disguised as options. The kind of message that treats a woman like a calendar slot.

I stay put. I don't tap on her door. I don't add my worry to her pillow. The frogs take the night back, the creek hums its low note, and the porch boards cool beneath my boots.

I turn my own phone face down and make a promise that sounds a lot like a prayer. I'm going to let her choose. And if choosing needs a picture of what staying looks like, I'll keep it simple—coffee on the porch, a light left on, and a quiet place where nobody wants a piece of her she's not willing to give.

Morning settles easy—the kind of blue that means the heat will take its time. I have feed dust on my forearms, and the horses are talking low when my phone buzzes in my back pocket.

"Wright," I answer, shoulder to the stall door.

"It's Carl," comes the familiar rasp. "Your pop star's spaceship took more than a love tap. Front lower control arm's bent, hub assembly's chewed. Parts are on order—

Thursday if the truck's kind. I can temp-align her if she's desperate, but I wouldn't send my worst enemy past thirty on it."

"Thursday's fine," I say. "Appreciate you."

I hang up as Ivy steps into the barn aisle, hair in a loose braid, and my spare chore gloves tucked in her back pocket like she's been doing this her whole life. She strokes Butterscotch's ridiculous forehead, gets sneezed on for her trouble, and just... laughs.

"News?" she asks, wiping her cheek with the hem of her T-shirt, unbothered.

"Carl says parts by Thursday. He'll call if it's sooner."

"Thursday," she repeats, like she's rolling the word around to see if it fits. "Okay."

Bailey's text pings a second later—three exclamation points and a "kidnap Ivy for town?" like it's a federal order. One that means she's already pulled into my drive. Ivy reads over my shoulder and grins.

"I'll be back by lunch," she says, already backing toward the door. "No, by two. Fine, three. Bailey's persuasive."

"Be careful of her 'just one more stop,'" I warn. "That's how you lose entire afternoons."

"Noted." She tips her chin at me. "Try not to miss me."

I don't answer that. She goes anyway—bare legs, sun, and the flash of that smile thrown over her shoulder like she trusts I'll catch it.

The farm goes quiet once the truck carrying them rattles down the lane. Quiet in the way that makes the windmill creak sound like company. I work the way I always do—fence line, mineral blocks, a new section of drip line in the garden—and catch myself looking for her twice. Three times. I tell myself I'm only checking the time by the angle of the sun.

My ex, Marissa, ghost-walks through my head once—just a shadow, the shape of a lesson: what you think you know about a person can be a story they sold you. I shake it off the way you shake sweat from your brow.

By early afternoon, I'm under the oak with a coil of wire and a stubborn hinge when Dad calls.

"Boy," he starts, which is how you know you're about to get a mix of love and a lecture, "your mama says Hadley saw that singer at the market. She buying honey or buying your silence?"

I grit my teeth, keep my voice flat. "She bought a hat. Honey, too."

He snorts. "You know how this looks, Rowan. Folks talk. I just don't want you in a position where you're cleaning up glitter and a mess at the same time. Again."

"I'm not in a position," I say.

"She's a nice girl, probably," he continues, which is how he softens the edge, "but these visiting types—"

"She won't stay," I snap before I can keep it holstered. The words come out harder than they felt in my head, designed to shut a door and succeeding all the way. "She'll be back on stage soon enough, basking in the cheers and adoration of her rabid fan base."

Silence on the line. Wind through the oak leaves. And—too late—footsteps on gravel behind me.

"Alright, then," Dad says after a beat, as if he didn't hear the way it scraped me raw to say it. "You bring the brush mower up later?"

"Yeah," I say, and hang up.

I turn.

Ivy stands at the bottom of the porch steps, a paper-wrapped bunch of sunflowers in her arms, Bailey's taillights just disappearing at the end of the lane. Her braid's fuzzed from the heat, her cheeks flushed, and there's a carefulness to her face I haven't seen since the ditch.

"Hey," she says, and the word is normal. Everything under it isn't.

"Hey." I nod at the flowers. "Those for Butterscotch? She'll try to eat them."

"For the cottage," she says, voice lighter than her eyes. "It needed color."

I mean to say something that fixes whatever I just cracked. Instead, I hear myself go practical. "Carl called. Thursday's the day."

"Good." She presses the flowers closer, like they could take the weight I just put on her chest. "That's... good."

The rest of the afternoon goes like a day with a limp. We put grain away. I pretend not to notice how she side-steps my hands. She tells me about a bookstore cat that hates everyone but adopted her for ten minutes. I tell her the gate on the east paddock still catches if you don't lift as you swing. Normal words. Not-normal air.

We split leftovers at the porch railing. She eats slowly, smiling when I tell her that at the End-of-Summer Barbecue last year, the kettle corn vendor flirted with me once, and I still bought two bags out of fear. The cicadas tune up; the light leans gold. If I reach six inches, I could tuck the one wild piece of hair back behind her ear. I don't.

"I'm going to finish a thing for work," she says when the plates are clean. Noncommittal. Soft.

"Okay," I say, because I don't push caged animals or people pretending not to be.

She carries the vase of flowers from the porch to the cottage like a bride might carry a bouquet—careful, steady, the act conveys most of the message. Her door clicks. The porch swing carries my weight like it always does, but I can't make it groan the way it usually does. I can't lure it into telling me what to do next.

I sleep, but only because the body insists.

At first light, I make coffee without thinking, two cups, mine black, hers with cream and sugar. The oak dew ices my boots as I cross the yard. I knock lightly and push the cottage door with my knuckles the way I always do.

It opens quietly.

No boots by the mat. No tote dropped carelessly by the couch. The air holds last night's cool and the faintest thread of her perfume like something someone should apologize for.

On the arm of the couch is my navy hoodie, folded clean. On the cushion is a torn page from one of those fancy notepads I don't own.

. . .

Rowan—

Thank you for the roof and the quiet. Thank you for being kind when you didn't have to be.

I don't want to be a problem you have to solve. I'm going to give you your space back and take care of mine.

—Ivy

I READ IT TWICE. THREE TIMES. THE COFFEE GOES COLD in my hand, and I don't notice until the chill hits my skin.

She left the sweatshirt. Left the flowers in a Mason jar vase on the table, bright and defiant and already losing a petal. The bed's made, hospital-corner neat, like a salute.

I stand there like a post somebody never got around to pounding into the ground. Then I do what I always do when the floor moves under me: I move.

Carl picks up on the second ring. "She swing by?" I ask, trying for even but tasting rust anyway.

"Car wasn't ready, but said she'd find a way to handle it. Took an early cab into the city," he says, oblivious to what that sentence does to me. "Bailey dropped her off. She said to tell you thanks. I told her you're as stubborn as a mule and to text you anyway."

"Did she?"

"Don't reckon so," he says gently.

I hang up and brace my hands on the worn counter like it's the only thing that will hold me up.

"She won't stay," I'd said yesterday, all sharp edges and defense.

She heard me.

Of course, she did.

I look at the note again, at the careful way she avoided saying what she didn't want me to hear: that I took something easy and made it hard, that I made myself safer by making her small. The kind of math I swore I didn't do.

The sun pushes through the east window and lands on the folded sweatshirt like a spotlight. I pick it up, press my thumb to the collar where her perfume still clings, and feel something in me shift off its bolt.

I'm not going to chase her yet—not to punish or perform or prove some point to my dad. But I'm not going to let her think that sentence I threw like a shield is the truest thing I have.

I set the sweatshirt on the back of a chair she dragged close to the window because she liked to sit there and watch the field wake up. I rinse the Mason jar and change the water on the sunflowers because that's what you do when you're holding something that wilts without care.

Then I do the only thing I know how to do with my hands when my head is a fight: I go to work. And every task I pick up, every board I straighten, and every bucket I fill turns into a quiet plan for how I'm going to fix the thing I broke without asking for it to be easy.

She won't stay, I'd said.

Not like that, no.

But if she comes back, it won't be because I made the world smaller to keep myself from being hurt. It'll be because I learned how to make room.

Chapter Four

IVY

Bailey's headlights sweep across the cottage wall like a tide I can't hold back. It's not even five—birds haven't decided whose turn it is to sing—and the farm is holding its breath. I slip the note onto the arm of the couch, swallow around the lump that doesn't want to be swallowed, and ease the door shut behind me.

Bailey's idling by the oaks, hair in a messy bun, sweatshirt zipped to her chin. When I climb in, she studies my face and doesn't ask a single question I'm not ready to answer.

"You sure?" she says instead, voice soft enough not to wake the trees.

"No," I admit, buckling in. "But if I wait until I'm sure, I'll never go."

She nods like she understands the language of flight, then pulls onto the lane, keeping the truck lights low until we hit the road.

"Colson's?" she asks.

"Yeah. I want to tell Carl in person."

The town is still blue with almost morning when we roll into the gravel lot. The bay door is half up, light pooling on concrete, and Carl's already there with a thermos and a grease rag tucked in his back pocket. Of course, he is.

"Well, I'll be," he says, eyebrows lifting. "You two beat the sun."

"Didn't sleep much," I say, managing a smile. "I wanted to give you a heads-up. I'm... heading out for a couple of days."

He nods, like people leaving and returning is just another kind of weather. "We got your car up on the lift. The front wheel assembly's bent, and there's some under-carriage rash. Parts are ordered. I'll call when they land."

"Could you—" I press my fingers to the zipper of my Coral Bell Cove windbreaker, steadying. "Could you hang onto it until I get back? I'll handle the bill, I promise. If you need a card on file—"

He waves me off. "We're not the city. You're fine. We'll make her right. You do what you've got to do."

Something eases in my chest. "Thank you."

Carl tips his thermos toward me. "Safe travels, Miss Ivy."

"See you soon," I say, and try to believe the words when they leave my mouth.

Bailey squeezes my forearm, then glances toward the street. "You want me to drive you all the way, or...?"

"I want to walk a bit. Join me?" I ask. Bailey easily falls in step beside me, letting me ruminate in my own thoughts.

We drift through the edges of downtown like ghosts—no destination, no plan, just a gut-deep need to move.

By the time we reach the boardwalk path that leads to the shoreline, my boots have scuffed enough loose grit to fill a bucket. The sky has lightened to a soft blue, but the breeze rolling off the bay chills my face, teasing strands of hair loose from my bun.

I welcome the sting of salt air. It's honest, unlike everything else.

Across the street from the beach access point is a little souvenir shop—one of those narrow storefronts with faded postcards clipped to spinning racks and sunscreen bottles piled beside novelty mugs. A wooden crab above the awning reads *Sandpiper Gifts & Sundries*.

I stand in front of the closed doorway for a second too long, blinking at the cheerful clutter. A small light in the corner blinks on, illuminating the room in a soft, warm glow that feels like a hug.

A wall of hats catches my eye. They're all terrible. Bright colors. Embroidered puns. One says *Shell Yeah* in glitter script.

We walk the path down to the sand, every muscle aching like I've spent the morning climbing a mountain. Maybe I have—emotionally, at least.

The dunes give way to smooth, pale sand peppered with shells and patches of dark grass. A gull cries overhead, diving toward a cluster of seaweed. Farther down the shoreline, a golden retriever chases waves like it's born for it while its sleep-deprived owner sips from a mug.

I find a spot near the weathered lifeguard chair and sit down, tucking my knees up to my chest. The sand is warm beneath me, grounding in a way nothing else has been in days. Bailey silently joins me.

My phone vibrates, and instead of ignoring it, I look.

Celeste: Evangeline Quinn

1 Missed Call. 1 New Voicemail.

I stare at her name. *My* full name, of course. *Evangeline Quinn,* as if *Ivy* is a costume I put on for award shows and press junkets. She rarely uses my stage name.

I don't listen to the voicemail. I don't need to. I can already hear her voice in my head.

"You need to get in front of this. We're hemorrhaging media control.

"Your tour crew is waiting on you.

"There's a makeup campaign pending. You can't ghost them."

What she means is *you can't ghost me.*

I turn the phone off and bury it in my tote bag, the sand curling into the hem of my jeans like it wants to keep me here. For a moment, I let it.

I let the wind rush in my ears. Let the silence grow until it feels less like emptiness and more like space to breathe. And I whisper the thought I haven't dared say aloud yet.

I don't want to go back.

Not to Nashville. Not to my label. Not to the glassed-in apartment with the view of things I don't care about. I don't know what I want yet. But I know what I don't.

The sun starts its slow ascent by the time I brush the sand from my jeans and stand, the hem damp where the tide's crept in.

I don't feel better, exactly. But I feel... quieter. Like all the noise in my head has shifted from screaming to a dull, manageable hum.

Bailey and I start walking past the beach grasses and driftwood piles.

The Needle Palm Resort sits at the far end of Main Street, tucked against a bluff with long porches, shuttered windows, and ivy climbing its siding like it's been painted on by a movie set designer. It's all old-money coastal charm —the kind that wraps itself around you like honey and makes you feel like you belong, even if you don't.

I pause at the end of the drive, heart thudding louder than the rhythm of my steps.

The sign above the front gate reads: *Welcome to the Needle Palm. Stay a While.*

Stay a while.

God, I want to.

I shake my head and turn to Bailey. "I'll call a cab from the corner. Easier that way." Easier not to turn this into a parade of goodbyes I'm not ready for.

We walk the block in silence, the sky lifting from cobalt to lavender. The kind of morning that makes even the cracked sidewalks look soft. At the corner by the café,

Bailey stops with me, thumb hovering over my phone until I give in and unlock it.

"You don't owe me an explanation," she says, gentle but immovable. "But you do owe me a text when you land."

A laugh breaks out of me, fragile but real. "Bossy."

"Efficient." She grins, then pulls me into a quick hug that smells like flour and honey.

I breathe her in, and stupidly, my eyes sting. Bailey isn't an industry person or a hanger-on or someone who's keeping receipts. She doesn't want tickets or a tag or a cut —just proof I'm okay. It's so simple it feels radical. The kind of friendship you don't pay for, the kind that checks in and only asks for a three-word text back. I tuck that feeling somewhere carefully, because it's new and it matters.

"Come back," she murmurs against my hair.

"I will," I whisper into her shoulder, and hope the promise finds its way to the person I'm really saying it to.

Headlights wash the corner. The cab rattles up like it's held together by faith and duct tape. We load my one bag into the trunk. Bailey steps back, gives me a two-finger salute that somehow doesn't make me cry, and I slide into the passenger seat with my phone already open to her contact, thumbs typing.

> Me: Will text when I land. Thank you—for everything.

"Where to, ma'am?" the driver asks, eyes kind in the rearview.

"Tidewater Regional," I say, the words landing like a dare I don't want to take back.

He nods and pulls onto the two-lane, tires hissing over last night's dew. We pass fields stitched with fence lines I recognize too well, the turnoff to Otter Creek Farm receding in the mirror until it's just trees and sky and the ache I swore I wouldn't name.

"You visiting family?" he asks after a mile.

"Something like that." I tug the zipper of the windbreaker higher under my chin. It smells faintly like soap and sun—like a place that isn't mine and somehow feels like it could be.

We don't talk much after that. The road unspools, straight and unforgiving, and I count mailboxes to keep from counting the ways I heard what I wasn't meant to hear. At the edge of town, the water flashes silver, then disappears behind billboards for fireworks and farm equipment. My phone stays face down in my lap. If I flip it over, I'll either be brave or stupid, and I don't trust myself to know the difference right now.

The airport is small enough that the parking lot feels like an afterthought—one terminal, three flags, a flight board with more canceled than on time. He pulls to the curb where the glass doors slide open and shut on other people's arrivals and departures like it's nothing.

"Here we are," he says, easing into park. "You want me to wait?"

I wrap my fingers tighter around the strap of my tote. "No... thank you."

"You sure?"

No. Not even a little. "Yeah," I lie, and manage a smile that doesn't make it to my eyes.

He tips the brim of his cap, which reminds me to tug my own on. "Safe travels."

I hand him cash, more than the meter asks for, because leaving always costs more than you think it will. Then I step out into the thin morning and the automatic doors sigh open like they've been expecting me.

Inside, the air is cold enough to make my teeth click. I stand just past the threshold, heartbeat loud, and tell myself to move. One foot, then the other. Ticket counter. Security. Gate. All the ordinary steps people take every day when they're not running from a sentence said by a man who made them believe in quiet.

Rowan's name lands in my chest again, heavy as a dropped stone, and the ripples push me forward. I keep walking until I can't see the parking lot anymore.

I don't cry. Not yet.

I just sit there, trying to breathe through the knot in my chest. The one that's taken up permanent residence ever since the cameras stopped flashing and the silence got too loud.

My phone buzzes again in my pocket. I don't bother looking. I already know who it is.

Instead, I do something worse. I open Instagram.

The first thing that pops up—of course—is a photo of me leaving Nashville. Sunglasses, hoodie, and an overnight bag slung over my shoulder. My face tilted toward the ground.

Spotted: Ivy Quinn Leaves Nashville in a Rush—What's Going On?

After a string of postponed interviews and whispers of label drama, sources say the pop princess may be making an unannounced exit from her label's summer tour schedule. Quinn, 27, was photographed boarding a regional flight out of Nashville with no entourage in sight. We don't know where she's going—but we'll be watching.

I LOCK THE SCREEN. HARD.

A surge of nausea hits me, sharp and fast. They don't know. Not really. But that doesn't matter. They'll make a story out of anything—out of a glance, a rumor, a single misplaced breath.

And there I am, playing right into it. Running. Again.

I don't even realize I'm crying until a tear hits the fabric of my jeans.

It's all too much. The lies. The pressure. The never-ending game of perception. Pretending I'm fine when everything inside me is screaming that I'm not.

So I do the most ordinary thing I can think of. I make myself small. I skip the lounge, ignore the priority line with my name on it, buy the kind of ticket that doesn't come with a free drink or a curtain to hide behind. I keep my cap low, answer to "ma'am," and let anonymity press over me like a cool cloth. If I can't quiet the noise, I can at least choose where to sit inside it.

Row 17 doesn't make sense for a person whose picture lives in airport kiosks. Which is exactly why I choose it.

Middle seat, wedged between a man who eats almonds one at a time like he's negotiating peace and a woman with a knitting project that could shroud a cathedral. I tuck my knees in, pull my windbreaker tighter, and breathe in the smell of salt and sea that has no business making me feel steady at thirty-two thousand feet.

Celeste would hate this. She prefers first class and visibility, a double-breasted privacy that still exudes opulence. She likes the way people look when they think they might see a star up close. I don't like being looked at, which is a problem when people pay me to be the center of attention.

We skim a foamy seam of cloud. The pilot crackles something about light chop, which translates to hold the armrest and pretend you've got your life in order.

My phone buzzes.

Bailey: How's the sky?

Thank goodness I splurged a bit for Wi-Fi during the flight. I snap a picture of whiteness that could be anything from my neighbor's open window, and reply.

Me: Overachieving.

A second bubble pops up.

> Bailey: Butterscotch tried to eat my braid.
> 10/10, would let her again.

I grin, then swipe to the thread above hers.

We land in the thick, wet heat of Nashville that grabs you under the collar and asks you to explain yourself. I keep the brim of a borrowed cap low, the windbreaker zipped, the pace even. Celeste's assistant is waiting near baggage claim with a sign that says IVY in block letters, like I could be any Ivy and they'd still take me.

"Miss Quinn," he says, snapping to attention. His name is Marlon, and he wears anxiety like cologne.

"Hotel?" I ask.

"Celeste would prefer the office," he says, like we've rehearsed it.

"Celeste prefers a lot of things," I answer, because I'm already exhausted, and I haven't even started performing yeses I don't mean.

He hustles me to a black sedan parked in the loading zone like they own municipal space. The driver flicks his eyes to the rearview and lands on me the way people do when they're trying to calibrate who you are to who you are on their phone. I turn my face to the glass and watch the city crawl by in mirrored pieces.

Billboards shout other faces. Other tours. Other girls whose mothers learned early how to turn talent into leverage and leverage into PR. I tug the cuff of the windbreaker over my knuckles and dig my thumb into the seam until the itch in my throat backs down.

Celeste's office is three floors up in a building that smells like copy paper and ambition. The lobby receptionist smiles with practiced warmth. Marlon swipes us through. Outside Celeste's glass door, a quartet of framed covers stares back at me—magazines that promised I was new, then promised I was inevitable, then promised to tell you what I wore to bed.

Celeste opens the door before I knock because she always knows when she's about to win.

"Darling." She air-kisses both my cheeks, the linen of her dress whispering money. "You look... rested."

Which, for Celeste, means you look like you've been somewhere that doesn't suit our narrative.

"Hi," I say, because I could say other things, and none of them will make this go faster.

Her office is a magazine page with blush chairs no one sits in, a bar cart that holds decanters no one drinks from before five, and a skyline view calibrated for late afternoon self-congratulation. She slides behind her desk and steeples her fingers like church.

"Let's talk plan," she says.

"Let's talk terms," I counter. My voice comes out even.

Her smile doesn't falter, but the edges lose patience. "We have three radio hits warming. The label's asking if the rumors are true. They're hearing you might be exploring a team change. We can manage the narrative, but we need the narrative."

"I'm not changing teams," I say. "I'm changing... proximity."

"To what?"

"To the part where I disappear when the machine isn't hungry," I say. "I need to be a person. You can sell that, can't you? *Girl Finds Her Voice? Girl Chooses Herself?* You taught me how to write the copy."

She leans back. "And Nashville?"

"I'll do the interviews," I say. "I'll do the Zooms. I'll sing when I want to sing, not when you need me to sing to fill a slot on a morning show that will ask about my eyebrows and Crew in the same breath."

At his name, one eyebrow actually lifts, like she rehearsed that trick in a mirror. "Ah, yes. Crew."

"Don't," I say. I'm surprised at the knife in it. "We were content. It's over."

"Content," she echoes. "Darling, everything is content."

For a second, I want to laugh. For a second, I want to ask if she remembers what I looked like the first time she took me to a studio—twelve, shaped like stage fright and stubbornness, singing a verse that wasn't perfect and could have been honest if anyone had let it. For a second, I want to tell her Rowan's hands look like work, and his porch light looks like mercy, and none of that sells ad space.

"Listen," she says, softer—her version of a lullaby. "The label wants to squash the flight rumors. The crew is in town for training. A cordial lunch will calm the waters."

"You mean a photograph someone 'accidentally' leaks?"

She doesn't blink. "If you don't feed the wolves, they eat your calves."

"Butterscotch," I say, because the name slides out before I can stop it. "Her name is Butterscotch."

Celeste misreads. She thinks I'm talking about a hairstyle trend. "Adorable," she says. "Wear the hair down for lunch. People need to believe in softness right now."

"I'll do coffee, not lunch," I say. "Thirty minutes. Public place. No statements."

She tilts her head like she's hearing dissonance and deciding whether to fix it or call it jazz. "Thirty minutes. And a smile."

"I always have one of those," I say, and taste blood.

We let the assistant book it. We let the driver turn circles to waste an hour. We let the city flex its summer shoulders. I ask him to stop three blocks away and walk the rest of the way to the café so I can decide who I am when I get there.

Crew's already at a table near the windows, baseball cap on backward, a T-shirt that says it's a team shirt without saying it's a team shirt. He stands when he sees me, and for a second, I remember what it felt like to be relieved when someone else was the show and I could hide in his light.

"Hey, Vee," he says, like we're still us. He opens his arms like the cameras are already outside and closes them when I don't move into them. "Right," he says, and the word sits between us like a folded napkin we both pretend we didn't drop.

We sit. A server materializes with iced coffee for both of

us because PR plans travel faster than traffic. Crew taps the table with his index finger in a rhythm that's probably a drill I don't know.

"How are you?" he asks.

"I got sleep," I say.

He smiles. It's easy, familiar, the kind of smile that makes men be forgiven for things they shouldn't be.

I know the script he expects. We do the first lines anyway, as if we hadn't just seen each other recently. He asks about the album. I say it's becoming itself. I ask about his shoulder. He says it's gold under a trainer's hands. We both laugh when we hit the timing right. And then we don't pretend.

"I'm not doing this again," I say, wrapping both hands around the wet glass. "Whatever this is. Whatever it was."

His jaw shifts. "We were good at it."

"We were good at behaving," I say, fingers tracing the sweat ring on my cup. "That's not the same thing."

Crew's mouth tips like he's trying not to grin. "You mean you and Rowan."

I roll my eyes. "I mean your brother and me."

"He's careful," Crew says, all teasing gone. "If he's letting you within ten feet of fence pliers, it's not nothing."

"Nothing happened," I answer, but my face betrays me because it wants to smile. "There's the farm. And a man who doesn't talk to fill space."

"That sounds exactly like him." Crew studies me for a beat, the way only someone who grew up reading the same storms can. "You look lighter."

"I think I'm... okay," I say, surprised at how true it feels. "That counts."

"It does." He lifts his coffee. "Look, I'll tell the vultures we caught up over caffeine and moved on. No spice."

"Use your own words," I say. "Make us sound like people."

"Already on it." A flash pops against the window—one, then two, like a reminder. Crew doesn't flinch. He just clinks his cup lightly against mine. "To being people," he says, "and to my brother finally meeting someone who likes quiet, too."

I clink mine against his. "To being people," I echo, and the sound is so small it could be anything.

We part on the sidewalk. He bends for a half hug that lands like gratitude and not a headline because he lets it. I walk away, cap low, windbreaker higher, and nobody gets a shot of my face looking sad or caught or in love with someone I'm not in love with.

Back at the hotel, I lock the door and slide the chain like a ritual. I sit on the edge of the bed and open my notebook. The first line finds me before the pen knows it's writing.

If you knew the weight of quiet, you'd stop calling it empty.

The second line is a fence post. The third is a porch light. By the time I finish the page, sweat lines my upper lip and the weird lightness that comes when a thought finds the sentence it's been chasing. I take a picture of the page and text it to myself because I trust my phone less than paper and more than memory.

Celeste texts at nine.

> Celeste: Tomorrow 10A radio hit. Zoom link. Please use a neutral background. No barns.

I type and delete a dozen responses. I finally land on one.

> Me: Send link.

> Me: I'm flying back after.

Three dots. Then nothing.

> Celeste: We'll talk next week.

I shower. I braid my hair. I lie in the bed and watch the shadow of the curtain move with the AC, the carpet a bland testament to what people do when they don't know where else to go.

At some point, sleep takes me by the ankle and drags me under.

Morning is coffee that tastes like it had to pass through six negotiations to get to my mouth, and a ring light I refuse to use and still turn on. I prop the laptop on a stack of books that the hotel knows they bought for this purpose. The host of the morning radio show has a face for podcasting and a heart like a golden retriever. He asks about the single, about my skincare routine, about my "friend" Crew, because they always ask about my men like they're accessories I borrowed and forgot to return.

"I'm writing," I say. "I'm resting. I'm excited for the tour." All of which are true in the ways they can be.

"You sound... good," he says, which might be the most honest thing anyone's put in a question mark at me in months.

"I think I am," I say, and I mean it enough that it scares me.

I log off. I shut the laptop like it could bite. I throw the ring light a look that could cauterize.

By noon, I'm in a car back to the airport, my cap low, my mouth a straight line I don't let cameras find. The flight is short enough to be a held breath. I keep it that way.

When the pines appear under the wing, something in my chest sits up and looks out the window like a kid. We land, and I walk as fast as I can without looking like a person in a rush. Outside, the humid air wraps me like a body I recognize. Bailey leans against her truck at the pickup curb, arms crossed, sunglasses on, the corner of her mouth etched into a smile.

Bailey pushes off the fender and loops an arm around my shoulders. "Home first to see your cowboy, or swing by Colson's and grab the spaceship?" she asks, like either answer is fine by her.

My heart does a weird, traitorous skip at home. I clear

my throat. "Let's get the car. Then I won't have an excuse to avoid the driveway."

"Colson's it is." She squeezes once. "I'll caravan behind you."

Carl's waiting like he never leaves—rag over one shoulder, grin easy. "All set, Miss Quinn. New control arm, alignment, she's truer than a choir solo." He hands me the keys and a paper with numbers I don't bother pretending to understand. I thank him, promise pastries later, and slide into the driver's seat. The cabin pings awake, and the dash glows a soft, familiar blue. Bailey tucks in behind me, her truck a steady square in the mirror.

Thunderheads stack over the tree line like a crowd gathering. The first fat drops hit the windshield just past the turnoff for the south beach, and by the time I'm on Rowan's road, the sky is a bruise. I keep the speed gentle, hands at ten and two, remembering exactly where the ditch curves mean. The wipers thrum. The air smells like wet hay and electricity. Bailey's headlights sit patiently in my rearview, a lighthouse that moves when I do.

When I turn onto the lane, gravel pops under the tires, and the oaks bow in the wind like they're whispering secrets. Lightning webs the far field. The porch light is on at the main house—gold and steady—and something in my chest loosens like a knot, finally giving way. I park beside the oak, kill the engine, and sit for one breath, palms flat on the wheel, the storm walking in on its own two feet.

Chapter Five

IVY

I'm not even sure he's home.

And if he is...

What if he doesn't want me here?

What if he regrets offering the place?

What if I'm just a complication he didn't ask for and doesn't want to deal with?

What if he has someone home with him?

The thought hits like a cold hand to the back of my neck. My grip tightens on the wheel until the leather bites. I picture boot prints I don't recognize on his porch, a laugh that isn't mine drifting through his kitchen, and a lipstick smudge on a glass by the sink. I hate it—hate how fast the jealousy blooms, hot and shameful. He isn't mine, not like that. I know it. I repeat it. It doesn't stop the small, ugly ache from settling under my ribs.

"Be normal," I mutter, practicing a smile that tastes like rain.

But then a gust of wind slams against the side of the car, and I jump, hands gripping the steering wheel until my knuckles go white. A flash of memory surges—bright lights, muffled voices, that awful helplessness of twitching limbs I can't control. And just like that, I'm moving.

Out of the car. Up the steps. Knocking on the entry door before I can second-guess myself.

Please be home.

Please not tonight.

Please.

The door swings open with a jolt—and there he is. Shirt wrinkled. Jaw tight. The note I left still folded in his hand.

His eyes widen, just for a second, then narrow.

"Ivy?"

I open my mouth, but nothing comes out.

He stares at me. "What are you doing here?"

I swallow hard. "There's a storm." Ignoring how much that phrase is referencing—the weather, my life, my career, Crew—it's a hurricane in motion.

His brows pinch together.

I rush to add, "I didn't know where else to go."

A beat passes.

"I'm not trying to be a problem," I say quickly. "I just... I thought..."

A snap of lightning cracks across the sky. He steps aside without a word.

"Get in."

My relief hits so fast I nearly sag.

I slip past him into the house. It still smells like hay and linen and something warm and earthy beneath it all—Rowan.

"Thanks," I whisper.

He closes the door behind me with a soft click. Final. But not cold.

"I was just putting away the rest of dinner," he says after a moment. "Hungry?"

The answer sits heavy in my chest. Yes. For food. For shelter. For kindness.

But more than anything, for someone who won't walk away when the sky turns against me.

The silence inside the house feels different this time. Not awkward. Not tense. Just... watchful. Like the walls themselves are holding their breath.

Rowan doesn't say anything as I toe off my shoes, my fingers rubbing over my arms like I can smooth away the goose bumps beneath the windbreaker. The air is thick with rain that hasn't fallen yet—and tension that hasn't broken either.

He moves toward the kitchen, his movements efficient and steady. "Sit down," he says without looking back. "You look like you're about to collapse."

I don't argue. I perch on the edge of the worn couch like I'm a guest in someone else's dream.

He pulls a plate from a cabinet and ladles something from a pot on the stove. Cilantro and tomatoes hit me in the chest like a memory. Warm. Familiar. Alive. I didn't even realize how hungry I was until now. I haven't eaten since that granola bar I bought at the airport this afternoon.

Rowan sets the plate in front of me on the coffee table, along with a glass of water. "Chicken and salsa. Nothing fancy."

"It smells amazing," I say, voice softer than I intended . I mean it.

He doesn't respond. Just sits in the chair opposite the couch.

We eat in silence... well, I do. Rowan just stares. The kind that hums with meaning, but doesn't demand it.

Outside, thunder rolls again—closer this time. The silver edges of the storm are pressing in.

When I finally look up from my plate, Rowan is still watching me. Not glaring. Just... observing. Measuring. Like I'm weather and he's trying to decide whether to brace for impact or let it pass through.

"What?" I ask, trying for a smile I don't quite feel.

He reaches for the dimmer to bump the kitchen light a notch—storm static makes the bulb buzz—and the brief flicker skitters across the ceiling. It's nothing, but my whole body goes tight anyway.

"I have epilepsy." I blurt the words out before I can tidy them. "Since I was a kid."

He freezes with his fingers on the switch, then lowers his hand, palms open, like he's showing me he heard me. He doesn't fill the silence or look away.

I swallow. "Last year, I had a seizure on stage. First time it ever happened in public." The memory scrapes. "The strobes, the travel, no sleep—it was a perfect storm. The paps and tabloids ran wild. 'Drugs.' 'Alcohol.' 'Party girl meltdown.'" I huff a humorless laugh. "We even released a statement with my doctor—medical records redacted and everything—to shut it down. It didn't matter. They wrote their own story and stapled it to my face."

His jaw ticks, slow. "I'm sorry that happened to you."

"And then came the... cage," I add, softer. "No flying alone. No hotels alone. No stepping outside without someone 'managing' me. My mom—Celeste—she didn't come to the hospital. She sent an assistant because leaving a label party would cause panic.'" The glass sweats under my fingertips. "So if I get jumpy around flickers or crowds, that's why."

"Are flashing lights a trigger for you?" he asks, voice low, careful.

"Sometimes, but not usually. My big ones are sleep deprivation, stress, and dehydration." I force my shoulders down. "I manage it. I'm good at managing it."

He nods once. "What do you want me to do if it happens?"

Practical. Steady. It unclenches something deep inside me. "Lay me on my side. Don't put anything in my mouth. Time it. If it goes past five minutes, call 911. When I come around, I'm groggy, not broken." I search his face. "You okay knowing that?"

"I'd rather know," he says simply. "And I can kill the overheads—lamps are fine."

I nod, a breath catching on the way out. "And before you ask—yes, I can drive. Laws vary, but it's six months seizure-free here. I'm well past that, cleared by my neurologist." I try a wry smile. "The spaceship is legally back in business."

He huffs, the closest thing he does to a laugh. "Good. Still going to pretend it's a UFO until Carl says otherwise."

Some of the tension slips from my neck. I trace a drop of condensation across the table. "I just... needed you to know it's not what they said. And that if I seem a little off, it's not you."

"It's not you either," he says, meeting my eyes. "It's noise. We don't listen to noise out here."

The storm grumbles somewhere over the fields. He switches the overhead off and leaves the soft heron lamp on, the kitchen sliding into a warmer kind of light. For the first time in months, the truth feels like something I can sit with and eat beside—and not a weapon pointed at me.

The wind picks up again, brushing hard against the windows like a warning.

"You came here because of the storm?" he asks.

I nod. My throat tightens. "They've triggered me before. The thunder. The flashes. I wasn't... I didn't want to be alone."

His posture shifts—barely—but something about him softens. The space between us feels different now. Not smaller, exactly. Just... easier.

"I don't expect anything," I murmur. "I just needed somewhere that didn't feel like a cage."

He leans forward, forearms braced on his knees. "You're not a burden."

I blink. "What?"

"Not here."

Simple words. But they hit me like a safety net I didn't know I'd been falling toward.

"Thanks," I whisper.

Another low rumble shakes the windows.

Rowan stands, collecting the plate.

"I can help—" I start, but he waves me off.

"Sit. You look like you've been walking uphill through molasses all day."

I huff a laugh. "That's disturbingly accurate."

He chuckles under his breath, and something warm stirs in my chest. Something I don't want to name.

I watch him rinse the dishes. He doesn't need to fill the silence. He just... moves through it. Anchored. Intentional. Unbothered by the weight of not having to say everything out loud.

God help me, I don't want to leave.

After a few minutes, Rowan returns with two mugs in hand.

"What's this?" I ask as he passes one to me, the ceramic warm against my palms.

"Chamomile." His tone is gruff. "Don't get used to it. I'm not usually this hospitable."

I smile into the steam. "Noted."

We sit in the low golden light of the old lamp, the only illumination besides the occasional flicker from the stove pilot light behind us. Outside, the wind rattles a branch against the siding, a nervous tap that echoes in my chest.

The air smells like impending rain and something subtler—cedar, maybe. Him.

"Rowan?" I say quietly.

He glances at me over the rim of his mug.

"I'm sorry for showing up like that. I know it was selfish."

"It wasn't."

I pause. "It felt like it."

"You were scared. You came to a place that felt safe. That's not selfish. That's survival."

My throat tightens. I didn't realize how much I needed to hear that—how badly I wanted someone to say it without hesitation, without asking for anything in return.

We sit for a long moment. The mugs grow cooler in our hands, the only sound the low hum of wind pressing against the house.

"You ever think about leaving?" I murmur.

He leans back in the chair, stretching his long legs. "Sometimes."

"What stops you?"

He's quiet for a second, then shrugs. "This place. My family. The land. It's in my blood."

"That must be nice," I say, fingers tracing the edge of my mug. "To belong somewhere."

He turns his head, eyes meeting mine fully. "You don't?"

I try to laugh, but it dies in my throat. "I belong to whoever needs a good headline."

His gaze sharpens. Something flickers there—anger, maybe. Or protectiveness.

"You belong to yourself," he says, low and certain.

My breath catches. He reaches out—slowly—and tucks a loose piece of hair behind my ear. His fingers barely brush my skin, but the contact sparks something deep. Something alive.

We're suddenly too close. Or maybe not close enough. His hand lingers near my cheek, but he doesn't move. Neither do I. My breath hitches. Then the power flickers. The lamp dims and flares, then steadies again.

We both jump as his hand drops. The moment snaps like a taut string pulled too far.

He clears his throat and stands abruptly. "I should check the fuse box."

I nod, heart pounding. "Okay."

He disappears down the hallway, and I sit there on the couch, blanket wrapped around my legs, pulse racing like I've just sprinted a mile. The storm outside howls again. The trees shudder.

The lights settle, a low hum returning to the room just as Rowan reappears, hair slightly mussed, expression unreadable.

"All good," he says.

"Thanks," I murmur.

He hovers in the doorway for a moment like he's not sure whether to sit again. I don't ask him to, but I want him to. He sits anyway.

The house creaks around us. A shutter claps once, then falls still.

"You okay?" he asks, quieter this time.

I nod too quickly. "Yeah. Just... storms."

He waits.

I sigh, running a thumb over the stitching in the blanket. "It's not just the thunder or the lights. It's the way it messes with my head."

He stays still, eyes on me.

"The epilepsy," I say, softer now. "Controlled, mostly. But storms—they do something to me. Sometimes it's not even physical. It's like my body remembers how to panic before my brain does."

"Sensory overload?" he asks gently.

"Exactly."

I stare down at my empty mug. "I'm okay when I'm calm and I feel safe. But today? Between the calls and the hotel and the storm—" I break off, the words sticking.

Rowan leans in just a little. He's not trying to fix it, just carry some of it.

"I've had people treat it like an inconvenience," I say. "Or like it's dangerous. Something to hide. And I hate that I still feel that shame—like it's mine to carry."

"It's not," he says. His voice is firm. "And anyone who makes you feel that way is an asshole."

I huff a soft, surprised laugh. "You always this direct?"

"When it matters."

A slow warmth spreads through me. Not heat. Not arousal. Something gentler. More dangerous.

Trust.

"Thank you," I whisper. "For letting me come here. For not treating me like I'm breakable."

"Stop thanking me. And you're not," he says without hesitation. "You're still standing. That's strong."

The words hit me in the chest.

I glance away, blinking fast. "You make it hard to keep my guard up."

He doesn't smile, not really, but something flickers at the edge of his mouth. "Good. You shouldn't have to carry that alone."

I want to lean into him and say something reckless. To tell him the way his steadiness steadies me, but I don't. Instead, I scoot a little closer on the couch.

And when my head eventually tilts against the back cushion, eyelids too heavy to fight, I don't flinch when he tucks the blanket tighter around me.

And I don't move when he sits on the couch. The couch dips beneath his weight, and for a long, quiet moment, we don't speak. The storm outside hums through the walls, soft now, like it's catching its breath. He settles beside me, his body still and solid, like he's anchoring the whole house in place.

I let mine go.

The blanket he draped over me is warm, but not as warm as the steady pulse of him beside me. We're not touching, not exactly. But I can feel him. In the way the air shifts with his breath. In the way the silence wraps around us like it belongs to both of us.

My eyelids flutter. My body sinks. The kind of exhaustion that isn't just physical—but bone-deep, soul-tired—softens my muscles.

I drift.

And for what feels like forever, I don't wake with a jolt. I don't gasp myself upright or reach for something I can't name. I just... rest.

When I blink awake again, it's dark.

The storm has passed. Or maybe it hasn't. The windows are fogged, and the world outside looks blurred and heavy, like the sky hasn't made up its mind yet.

I shift slightly and realize my head rests on Rowan's shoulder. My breath catches. His arm is along the back of the couch, not quite around me, but not distant either. His head tips just a little toward mine, like he's trying not to move. Like maybe he's afraid I'll wake and bolt if he does.

And I might, but I don't. Because this—whatever this is —it's safe. Gentle. Unspoken.

"I didn't mean to fall asleep," I murmur, voice raspy.

His chest rises. "You needed it."

My cheeks burn. "You didn't have to stay here with me."

"I know."

I glance up. His eyes are already on me. Not intense. Just... aware.

"Rowan—"

"You don't have to say anything."

But I do.

"I don't do this," I whisper. "Show up. Fall apart. Stay in one place too long."

His eyes search mine, steady as a fence post. "I'm not built for leaving," he says quietly. "I set roots, not tents. If you need to go, you go. I'll still be here. And if you stay..."

His mouth tips, almost a vow. "I'm not a man who changes his mind when something matters."

A silence settles between us—dense and humming and full of things we're both too cautious to name. Neither of us budges. His thumb brushes the edge of the blanket where it's slipped off my shoulder, tugging it back into place. It's such a small thing. Barely a touch. But my entire body notices.

I trace the pattern on the blanket with the tip of my finger. "I thought I was just passing through."

He doesn't respond right away.

When he does, his voice is rough. "Are you?"

I want to lie. To say yes. That this is just a detour, a misstep in the carefully controlled choreography of my life. But the truth has already settled in my bones.

"I don't know anymore."

He nods once, accepting it like it's an answer.

The wind picks up outside, rustling the trees again, but I barely hear it. All I hear is my own heartbeat. And his, steady beneath my cheek.

I close my eyes, just for a second, letting myself imagine what it might feel like to stay. To belong to something that doesn't ask me to perform or explain. To be wanted not for headlines or singles or streaming numbers—but for showing up in the rain with shaking hands and asking to be let in.

I'm still not sure what this is, but I know what it's not.

It's not hollow.

It's not fake.

It's not alone.

Chapter Six

IVY

The mornings here start slow.

Not quiet—roosters don't care for poetic timing and the goats across the fence make their opinions known with every passing hour—but slow, like time itself has learned to breathe differently on this land.

I like it.

Like the way the sun creeps over the ridge, brushing golden fingers across the fields like it's waking the world with soft hands. Like how the dew still clings to the wild grasses and even the fence posts look like they have a story to tell.

I like that I can breathe here. Not the shallow, panicked inhale of red carpets and tour buses. Not the rehearsed calm that comes with media training and champagne toasts I never want to give. But a real breath. Deep. Steady.

Alive.

The barn doors creak open as I step inside, hair twisted

in a messy bun, Rowan's oversized hoodie swallowing my frame. I haven't officially asked if I can borrow it again. I just... do.

The scent of hay and wood settles around me. Familiar now. Almost comforting.

"Morning, darlin'."

I turn at the sound of Rowan's voice, a lazy smile pulling at my lips before I can stop it. He stands at the far end of the barn, pitchfork in hand, sleeves pushed up to reveal forearms that have no business being that defined. Not to mention the fading tattoos from spending too much time in the sun.

"Morning," I echo, voice still rough with sleep.

"You sleep okay?"

I shrug. "Storm's gone. That helped."

His eyes linger on mine just a moment too long, then he nods and gets back to work. I linger near the stalls, petting a curious horse who nuzzles my shoulder like we're old friends.

"Hey, Rowan?" I ask.

"Yeah?"

"You said something about a camp once. Give me all the details?"

He glances at me, brow raised.

"For kids," he says, jabbing the pitchfork into the hay with practiced ease. "To learn about farming, animals, and where food comes from. Thought it'd be a good summer thing. Especially for the ones who don't have much else to do."

I blink. "That's... really cool."

He grunts.

"No, I mean it." I step closer. "I would've killed for something like that as a kid."

He pauses. "Yeah?"

I nod, then smile a little. "I was a latchkey kid before I was a headline."

Rowan leans the pitchfork against the wall and crosses his arms, giving me his full attention.

"I grew up in a double-wide trailer behind a gas station. And I say double-wide loosely. Half of it was waterlogged. The entire place should have been condemned. It was nothing more than a shack with vinyl siding," I say. "My mom worked two jobs. My dad was barely a name in my house, let alone a presence. If I wasn't at school or home, I was at the bus stop with a book and a pack of crackers. We didn't have money for summer camps. We barely had money for shoes that fit."

His jaw tightens slightly, but he doesn't interrupt.

"My mom always wanted better for me. But... she doesn't always go about it in the healthiest way. When I won a local talent show at eleven, it was like a switch flipped. Suddenly, she's my manager. My coach. My publicist. There's no more after-school anything, no friends, no weekends." I swallow. "Just rehearsals. Pageants. Auditions."

Rowan's expression doesn't soften. If anything, it sharpens.

"You were a kid."

"Not for long," I say quietly.

Neither of us speaks for a moment.

Rowan pushes away from the wall and crosses to a nearby saddle stand. His voice is low when he speaks. "You ever want to be just... a woman? Out here, mucking stalls, playing with goats?"

I smile at that even though it aches. "Yeah. More than I knew, honestly."

He meets my gaze. "You can be."

Those three words land harder than I expect. Maybe this place really is what I've been looking for all along. Even if I didn't know it.

My phone buzzes in my pocket, and I pull it out to find the screen lighting up with the name I've been avoiding.

Mom – Mobile

The letters glare at me like an accusation.

She called five times yesterday, and I refused to answer. I respond once with a text.

> Me: I'm safe. I need some time.

And that only seems to stoke the fire.

The screen dims, then lights again as the call comes in a second time.

I sigh, thumb hovering. I already know what she'll say. Know the polished cadence of her voice, the veiled threats under every soft word. But letting it go to voicemail again won't help.

I pick up.

"Hi."

A sharp inhale cuts through the line, followed by a clipped, "Evangeline. Finally."

"I've been busy," I say carefully.

"In a town with no name? What are you even doing out there?"

I bite my tongue. "Taking a break."

"You don't get breaks, sweetheart. Not when your fans are still asking questions."

Her voice is too loud, too precise, as if she's already walking through a list of damage-control items in her head.

"The label is panicking. Do you know how many PR people have reached out in the past forty-eight hours since pictures of you and Crew popped up? Spectacular performance, by the way. They want a new single by the end of the month, and your last appearance—whatever that was— has already sparked rumors."

"I need space."

"You don't get to disappear." Her tone dips, almost pitying. "You know that."

"I'm not disappearing," I say quietly. "I'm resting."

"And I need you here," she says sharply. "Which is why I need you to stop playing small-town dress-up and come home. We've worked too hard for this."

I stare out at the field stretching beyond the barn, the hills rolling gently beneath a morning sun that doesn't ask anything of me.

"I'm not coming back again. Not yet."

"Evangeline—"

"I have to go." My voice cracks, but I stand firm. "I'll call you later."

Before she can respond, I end the call. Then I drop the phone into my back pocket and bury my face in my hands.

The ache behind my eyes isn't just a headache. It's years of pushing and pleasing and pretending. Of being Ivy, her perfect little product. For the first time in a decade, I don't want to be her at all.

I was nine when I realized the difference between quiet and alone. Quiet is warm. Peaceful. The stillness right before a song begins. Alone is what I felt most nights—sitting on the back steps of a weather-worn house that barely passes code, listening to the whine of cicadas and the low grumble of the neighbor's truck engine two trailers down.

We didn't have a porch swing or a lawn or even working plumbing some days. What we had was a broken screen door, a collection of empty soda bottles, and my mother's makeup bag permanently open on the kitchen counter, just in case opportunity knocked.

It rarely did.

Mama was beautiful—she still is. Sharp-cheeked and sharp-tongued. She calls herself a dreamer, but mostly she waited tables at The Puddle Duck Diner and left me notes scribbled in eyeliner on fast food napkins.

TV dinner in the freezer. Don't forget to feed Rags.

Rags was the stray cat who refused to leave. I liked him more than most people.

I don't remember when exactly I learned to sing. Maybe

I always had the talent. But I do remember the first time someone noticed. It was the elementary school talent show, a dusty stage in a gym that smelled like chalk and stale orange slices.

I wore a dress too small and a smile too big. My stomach flipped like a butterfly caught in a glass jar.

But when I opened my mouth and sang—really sang— the room went still.

It felt like someone saw me. A lot of someones.

Mama cried that night. Not out of pride, but because a door had opened. A crack in the universe, wide enough to shove a child through.

After that, everything changed.

No more weekends. No more spelling bees or slumber parties. Only voice lessons and auditions and a new name with a star stitched into its bones.

Ivy Quinn. Pop star in the making.

She never asked me what I wanted.

By the time she did, it was already too late.

The rubber boards creak under my boots as I step around the side of the barn, shielding my eyes from the late afternoon sun. I need something—anything—to quiet the noise in my head. And manual labor seems like the best option Otter Creek Farm has to offer.

Rowan has moved near the shed, arms deep in the back of an old four-wheeler. Probably to give me privacy during the call. I hadn't even noticed his leaving.

My eyes are glued to his large body. His shirt clings to

his back, damp with sweat. Grease streaks his forearm as he reaches for a socket wrench.

He glances over his shoulder, face shaded by the brim of his ball cap.

"You lost?"

"No," I say, crossing my arms. "But I could be if it gets me out of my own head."

Rowan studies me, then jerks his chin toward the paddock. "Gate's sagging on the round pen. You ever hang a hinge strap?"

I lift a brow. "You asking if I can handle a drill?"

"Just asking if you're a flight risk around power tools."

"I'll try not to impale myself."

A long, hot minute later, we're at the round pen where the top hinge has slipped, and the gate drags a half-moon in the dust. He hands me a pair of worn leather gloves.

"Here. Hold the gate square while I back the old bolts out."

I slide the gloves on and shoulder the weight; palms braced against sun-warmed metal. It's heavier than it looks. The strain wakes muscles I forgot I owned.

He loosens the hardware, then holds up a fresh hinge strap and a bag of carriage bolts. "You're up. Drill the pilot holes. Level matters."

He passes me the driver. It's warm from his hand. He points at the tiny bubble level fixed to the housing. "Keep that centered. Feather the trigger—don't mash it."

I line it up, but the bit skitters, biting shallow. "It's fighting me."

"You're letting your elbow float." His voice is low at my shoulder, steady as shade. "Here."

He steps in behind me—close but careful—his chest just brushing my back as he wraps one big hand around mine on the grip, the other settling lightly at my forearm to anchor it. Heat rolls off him, slow and sure. The world narrows to cedar, sun, and the weight of his body guiding mine.

"Lock your wrist," he murmurs, breath grazing my cheek. "Let the tool do the work. Straight in."

I adjust, and he stays with me, shaping the angle until the bit bites clean and sings. The vibration travels through my fingers and up my arm, straight to someplace that has nothing to do with carpentry.

"Like that," he says.

My breath stutters. "Got it."

We move as one, hole by hole. He shifts with me, a living bracket—never crowding, never rushing—just there. When it's time to set the bolts, he keeps one palm firm under the gate's weight while I slide the hardware through and spin the nuts on by hand.

"Snug them down," he says, passing me the socket. "Quarter turn past tight."

I work the ratchet while his fingers brush the back of my wrist, steadying, and every nerve I own sits up and pays attention. The final bolt seats with a small, satisfying bite.

"Moment of truth." He eases back, testing the swing. The gate glides clean, no drag, no scrape—just a smooth arc and a clean click when the latch finds home.

A smile breaks over my face before I can stop it. "We're geniuses."

"Hardly." His mouth tilts, eyes on mine. "But you've got good hands."

I pretend that compliment lands anywhere but where it does. "You make a decent teacher."

He tips his chin, approval like sunlight. "Again?"

"Again," I echo even though I'm not sure if I mean gates or this slow, careful way he's touching me without really touching me at all.

He doesn't move, and neither do I. For one brief, pulsing heartbeat, the only sound between us is the soft rustle of grass and the distant call of a mourning dove.

Rowan straightens abruptly. "Barbecue's tonight."

I blink. "What?"

He wipes his hands on a rag, not looking at me. "Town throws one every summer. Burgers, beer, bad dancing."

"Sounds charming."

"Mostly, it's an excuse for people to stare at each other and pretend they don't gossip year-round." He pauses. "You should come."

The words surprise me. I'm not sure if they surprise him too. It doesn't land like a warm-and-fuzzy invite so much as a practical don't-sit-home-and-wallow pass—logistics dressed up as kindness. There's grit in his voice, a careful distance in the way he doesn't quite meet my eyes, like he's still chewing on the fact that I left without a real goodbye. It feels less like a date and more like a lifeline tossed from the shore with a note that says: this doesn't mean anything except you don't have to drown alone. I tell myself I'll take it anyway, even if part of me aches that he didn't ask because he wanted me there, but because it would've felt wrong to leave me behind. "I thought you didn't do town gatherings."

He shrugs. "I don't. Not really."

"So why ask me?"

"Because maybe you need a reminder that not everything out here wants something from you."

That hits harder than I expected.

I nod slowly. "Okay. I'll come."

Rowan meets my gaze then, his eyes dark and unreadable. But something else is there. Something pulling.

He looks away first.

THE BARBECUE HUMS LIKE SUMMER ITSELF—LANTERNS bobbing, a jittery generator keeping the string lights alive, and smoke curling up from three mismatched grills. Kids dart between knees with sparklers. Someone's aunt sets out a pan of cinnamon-dusted funnel cakes like she's starting a holy war. When Rowan parks, the passenger door complains, and I hop down in jeans and a soft T-shirt, hair in a loose braid that's already giving up at the edges.

People look. Of course, they do. But they're not gawking. They're mapping me into the same picture that already holds their kids' school plays and last winter's power outage. Neighbor eyes hit differently.

Rowan falls into step at my side, easy and solid, and the

space around us shifts. His shoulders square, jaw set, a quiet perimeter I can feel even when he's not touching me. Two teens lift their phones halfway—he tips his chin, not unkind, and they lower them. An older couple pauses mid-whisper. He greets them by name, and they pinken, then smile at me like we've been introduced properly.

At the drink table, a knot of kids rubberneck. Rowan angles his body so I'm tucked between him and the coolers, his hand hovering at my lower back—a promise with no pressure. A woman with a messy braid and a toddler on her hip beelines over.

"Rowan? You brought someone?"

"She's a guest," he mutters.

"Could've fooled me." Her grin goes wide. "I'm June. Third plate of cornbread. Zero regrets."

"Ivy," I say, laughing.

"Oh, honey, we know." She winks.

She breezes off, and Rowan leans in, mouth close to my ear. "There's still time to fake a stomachache."

"Please. I've survived award shows. I can survive a grapevine."

He doesn't smile, not really, but the corner of his mouth betrays him. He disappears for a minute and returns with two paper trays and an extra napkin tucked under his forearm like it's a love language.

"Did you bring me brisket?" I ask.

"Don't read into it."

We claim a spot near the edge of the grass—far enough from the speakers but close enough to catch the lantern glow. Our arms brush as we eat, but neither of us moves away. The warmth sits low and steady, like banked coals.

Rowan's arm brushes mine as he sits back. He doesn't move it. And I don't either.

"Watching."

"Me?"

"Not everything's about you."

I give him a look. "It usually is."

He cracks a smirk. Barely.

A few of the townspeople start egging each other toward the makeshift stage—if a plank of wood and two hanging lanterns count. An older man with a banjo starts plucking a tune, and someone yells out, "Give us something, Ivy!"

I freeze.

Rowan stiffens beside me. "You don't have to—"

But I'm already rising. I don't know why. Maybe I need the reminder. Perhaps it's out of duty. Maybe I want to prove that this version of me—barefoot, bourbon-warmed, wearing borrowed denim and a braid—can still sing.

The crowd falls quiet as I step onto the platform, heart thudding.

I ask the banjo man, "Do you know 'Wildflowers in July'?"

He nods, adjusting the tuning keys with a soft smile. "Good choice."

The chords begin, slow and wistful. I wrote this song three years ago in a tour bus parking lot, staring out at a sunrise I never got to touch.

I close my eyes. Then begin.

"I used to run, head full of noise

City lights and plastic poise

But I remember wildflowers in July

Mama's boots and a baby blue sky..."

My voice isn't perfect. It wavers in the middle and cracks just once.

But it's real.

When I open my eyes at the last line, the crowd is hushed. And Rowan is watching me.

The applause is soft. Reverent.

I step down slowly, pulse still racing, but something inside me settles. Like maybe I've stitched a part of myself back together with every note.

Rowan stands as I approach, something unreadable in his eyes.

"Why'd you sing that one?" he asks quietly.

"Because it's the first one I wrote just for me."

He doesn't say anything. Just nods.

"Line dancing starts in ten! Hydrate!" a far-off voice shouts into the crowd.

The band shifts from background to invitation. A fiddle saws out the first bars of a boot-stomper, and a half cheer rises. June reappears and points at the chalk-board: LINE DANCE LESSONS — NO SHAME, JUST FUN.

Rowan looks like a man considering flight. I lace my fingers through his and tug. "Come on, cowboy."

He lets me pull him to the trampled square. Rows form,

loose and laughing. I squint at the feet around me like they're going to reveal state secrets.

"Left, right, kick," I murmur, immediately late.

"Weight on your left," Rowan says, stepping in front of me, palms hovering. "Now step. Toe, heel, shuffle—yeah. Like that."

I try and fail spectacularly. I tip my head back and laugh, bright and uncurated, and feel his gaze like heat on my skin. The line surges forward, I tangle my own ankles, and he's there without thinking, his hand finding my waist, steady and sure. Everything in me leans into that touch like a plant toward the sun.

"Don't let go," I tease.

He doesn't. "Wasn't planning on it."

Two songs in, I almost have it. Three songs in, he starts sandbagging—adding a little heel-click flourish just when I've found a rhythm—smug in a way that makes me elbow him and makes him laugh, startled and boyish. It's ridiculous and perfect, and I can feel parts of me unclench I didn't know were tight.

The fiddle softens, and the rhythm melts. Couples turn toward each other as if the air itself gave the command. Someone kills the floodlights near the grills, and the world narrows to fairy lights, the thrum of summer, and a steel guitar that turns the night to velvet.

Rowan shifts, uncertainty flickering across a face I'm starting to memorize. Then he offers his hand, bashful in a way that kneecaps me.

"Dance with me?" he asks.

I put my palm in his. "Yeah."

He draws me in. One hand finds the small of my back, warm and protective; the other cradles my fingers like they're important. We sway. The generator hum becomes a heartbeat, and the chatter around us goes soft. I rest my cheek against his chest. He breathes in like he's making room for me, and the world tilts into place.

"You're good at this," I say, voice low.

"Lots of weddings," he murmurs. "Lots of waiting."

"For what?"

He considers. "For the right song."

I tip back enough to see his eyes. Lantern light threads gold through green. My thumbs press into the fabric at his shoulders and the small sounds he makes—barely there inhales—go straight to my pulse.

"Your laugh," he adds, almost like he didn't mean to speak. "Sounds like home."

"You don't even know my home," I whisper.

His gaze dips to my mouth and returns, a tide pulling and retreating. "Maybe I don't need to."

The last chord lingers. We don't move. Somewhere behind us, June whoops, a sparkler cracks, and the lights flicker with the generator's hiccup. The spell should break, but it doesn't. It condenses, like rain deciding to fall.

He clears his throat. "Walk?"

"Please," I say, because staying means doing something we can't undo.

We slip along the park's edge, past the hum of grills and the sweet scorch of corn, down the sandy path where the bay lies itself out in ink and silver. Behind us is laughter, a guitar's loose chorus, and kids tracing stars with sparklers that spit and fade. Up by the tree line, a couple drifts into the shadows, and the night politely looks away.

At the truck, he opens my door but doesn't step back. Lantern glow threads gold through the scruff along his jaw and finds the tiny scar at his temple. We stand too close, breath mingling, the kind of nearness that hums in the space where words would go. My fingers skim the door-frame, and his knuckles brush mine. Static jumps. Neither of us moves for a full, suspended second.

A sparkler crackles, and someone whoops. The couple emerges laughing, and the world widens by an inch. He shifts first—just enough to let air through—then reaches past me to steady the handle, forearm warm along my shoulder. I climb in, heart loud, and he closes the door softly like it matters.

On the drive back, windows down, the night pouring cool over our wrists, our hands keep finding each other on the bench seat and retreating. Back of his fingers to the back of mine. A quiet apology. A quiet promise. No talking. Just the road unwinding and the same thought pulsing between us, bright as a sparkler's last flare. Not here, not yet.

Chapter Seven

ROWAN

The road home curves under the moonlight, the truck tires crunching softly over gravel as I keep both hands on the wheel and both eyes decidedly on the windshield.

Not the woman next to me.

Not the goddamn song still ringing in my head.

And definitely not the way my chest squeezes when she sings about wildflowers like she's lived that lyric.

Because Ivy Quinn isn't a song.

She isn't a moment.

She's a headline waiting to happen—and I have no business feeling like I want to hear her voice on my porch every damn night for the rest of my life. My mother always said when I found the one, I would fall fast and hard, just like my father. I didn't believe her then, and I am trying my damnedest not to believe her now.

"You're quiet," she says finally, her voice softer than the leather seat beneath her.

I don't look over. I can't. "Tired."

She hums in response, fingers toying with the hem of her shirt. "You're not a very good liar."

I crack a wry smile, still staring straight ahead. "Never claimed to be."

Silence falls again, but it's not the comfortable kind we've managed a few times before. This one thrums with something I don't want to name—heat, maybe. Possibility. The kind of thing that sneaks in when your defenses are too tired to hold it off.

I clear my throat, reaching to turn the AC knob. "You didn't have to sing tonight."

"I wanted to."

"It showed."

She glances over at me. I can feel it even though I don't return the look.

"You say that like it's a bad thing."

"It's not."

But it could be for me. That's the problem. Everything about her feels like more. More heat. More pull. More mess. And I've built my whole adult life around avoiding mess.

"You were good," I say, finally giving in to the truth. "The whole town will be talking about it for weeks."

"Good." She leans her head against the window. "Then they won't be talking about how I borrowed your hoodie or how Butterscotch blesses me with a sneeze as a greeting."

I huff. "That's your thing now."

A beat passes.

"I saw you talking to that little girl. The one who asked if you were really a singer. You were kind."

She shrugs one shoulder. "Kids don't expect me to be anyone else."

I frown. "You don't either."

She looks at me again. "Don't what?"

"Pretend. Not when it counts."

Her lips part slightly like she's about to argue, but then she closes them again and looks away.

I should leave it there. But the words are already tumbling out. "The camp. That's why I first thought about it. For kids like that."

She straightens a little, twisting in her seat. "You mean... the girl tonight?"

"Yeah."

"I figured. You light up a little around them."

"I don't light up."

"You kind of do. Like an unplugged Christmas tree with one string of working lights."

I bark out a laugh despite myself at the visual, finally letting my gaze flicker to her for a split second. Her smile is small but real.

"I meant it, you know," she says. "What I said before. About helping you with it."

I sober instantly. "You don't know what you're offering."

"I know enough."

"No, you don't."

Her eyebrows draw together. "Then tell me."

"I don't have the money, the time, or the right degree for any of it. It's just an idea I get sentimental about when the house gets too quiet."

"That doesn't make it any less worthy."

I tighten my grip on the wheel. "You don't get it."

"Try me."

"I don't have anything to offer, Ivy." I shake my head. "Not to those kids. Not to you. Unfortunately, anything I can teach them is an art that's falling to the wayside."

The silence that follows is louder than anything she could say. And worse than any lecture.

But still, she replies, gently, "You have more than you realize."

I don't respond. Can't. My throat's too tight with the truth I don't want to admit. When she looks at me like that—like I'm something—every wall I've ever built starts to crack.

We roll to a stop under the wash of starlight, both porch lights casting twin halos—one over the house, one over the cottage. I kill the engine. Neither of us moves. Then she reaches for the handle, and I follow.

We walk side by side until the path splits—gravel veering left toward my front steps, crushed seashells curving right toward hers. The air is warm and quiet, a cricket choir tucked in the fence line. She toes a pebble with her sandal, and it skitters ahead, choosing the cottage for her.

"Thanks for... all of it," she says, voice low. "The food. The... buffer." Her mouth tilts. "The dance."

"Anytime," I answer, which is more honest than I mean it to be.

The porch lights hum. Moths tap and wheel. For a heartbeat, we just stand there inside the overlap of the two pools of gold. Close enough to feel the heat coming off her skin. Far enough that I can't blame the night if I step closer.

"Tomorrow," I say, because I need a safe word, "I'm checking fence lines at first light. Coffee's on at six. If you want to walk the south pasture or head into town later, just knock."

"I want," she says quickly, then tempers it with a breath. "If you're sure."

"I'm sure."

She nods. Her fingers worry the edge of her sleeve. Mine hook into my back pockets to keep from doing anything dumb.

"I liked tonight," she admits, eyes on the seam where gravel meets shell. "More than I expected to."

"Me, too."

That pulls her gaze up. The look we trade is a held match—bright, dangerous, gone if either of us exhales too hard. She shifts a half step, and the light paints her hair in pale honey, her eyes gone dark and thoughtful.

She looks up at me, wide-eyed and unsure, and it feels like we're standing on the edge of something that's been building since the moment she crashed her damn spaceship into a ditch.

I don't mean to step closer. I don't mean to tilt her chin with my fingers.

I definitely don't mean to let my lips brush hers, but I do, and she doesn't pull away. She leans in with just the barest pressure—warmth, promise, chaos. And I break it. Pull back like I've been burned.

Her eyes flutter open. Hurt flickers there, followed by confusion, then anger.

"I should go to bed," she says quickly.

"Ivy—"

"Good night, Rowan," she says, barely above a whisper.

"Night."

She turns down the shell path. I stay where I am, listening to the soft crunch of her steps and the small click of her latch. Her porch light stays on. Mine does too. I don't move until I see her shadow cross the cottage curtain—one sweep, then still.

Only then do I take the left fork, gravel grinding under my boots, the night full of the thing we almost said and didn't.

I run a hand through my hair, fingers digging into my scalp, hoping the sting will knock some damn sense into me. Ivy Quinn is across the way, probably confused as hell. And I don't blame her.

I don't even know what I'm apologizing for in my head—dancing with her or not kissing her fully. Both, maybe. Because either option means I'm a coward.

I stare at the counter, at the empty spot where her cup sat earlier. The space feels bigger without her in it even though she's technically still here. It shouldn't matter. She's only staying another night, maybe two, until she figures out her career situation. Until the press finds a new angle. Until she remembers that men like me aren't part of her world and will never be.

I want to believe I have a grip on this, and I can keep things clean. Distant. She's not a mistake I can forget. And I don't even want to.

I turn off the kitchen light and stalk down the hall, the air heavy with everything I haven't said, every pull I've tried to ignore. The stairs groan under my weight, and I barely resist glancing toward the guesthouse. I don't deserve another look. Not after the way I left her hanging.

In my room, I peel off my shirt, toss it across the back of the chair, and drop into bed. My muscles ache from the long day, but sleep is nowhere in sight. Not with the ghost of her mouth still on mine.

I roll over, then roll again, growling under my breath like that'll make a difference.

I've kissed women before—hell, I've dated. But nothing has ever felt like this. Like kissing someone you don't just want. You *need*. Like everything in your body, soul, and bones recognizes theirs before you even figure out what the hell is happening.

That terrifies me.

I punch the pillow and stare at the ceiling. The fan whirs overhead. A crack in the drywall catches the moonlight.

And I keep thinking about the way she looked tonight —barefoot in the grass, firelight in her hair, and her voice strong and soft all at once. Like a prayer set to music.

And then... that look in her eyes right before I pulled away. As if I've confirmed every doubt she carries.

I swear under my breath, sit up, and pace the room like I can outwalk my own damn guilt.

What the hell am I even doing? She's Crew's ex. Even if it was fake, the lines are still blurry. She's famous. She's been on tour buses and red carpets while I've spent the past decade in dirt and sweat and routine. And she's only here because her car died and fate has a cruel sense of humor.

There's no version of this where I come out clean. And still.... Still, I want to go outside, knock on that door, and ask her what would've happened if I hadn't stepped away.

Would she have kissed me back?

Would she have let me keep going?

Would I have finally stopped pretending I don't feel this thing crackling between us like lightning across a dry field?

I sit on the edge of the bed, elbows on my knees, forehead resting on my fists. "Shit," I mutter.

I'm not good at talking about feelings and never have been. But with Ivy, the feelings come too fast to sort through. It's like stepping into a riptide—sudden, wild, dragging you under whether you fight or not.

And the worst part? I don't want to fight. I want to let go. Just once. Let myself want something—want her.

But then the doubts come roaring back. Crew. The gossip. Her leaving again. Me falling harder than I'll ever admit.

I slam the heel of my hand against my thigh and blow

out a breath, forcing myself to stand. I've screwed up enough for one night.

Yet I cross to the window, peel back the curtain, and look across the property anyway. The cottage light is off. She's gone to bed or wants me to think she has. Either way, I don't blame her.

I let the curtain fall and step back, every inch of me heavy with the weight of what almost was. Tomorrow, maybe, I'll fix it. But tonight, I carry it, just as I always do.

Alone.

The house is quiet. Too much so.

I've walked every inch of this place over the years—tightened hinges, fixed pipes, rewired outlets—but tonight, it feels like a stranger. Like it's not mine anymore, and I'm not supposed to be here. Not with this tight, aching pull in my chest that won't let up.

I try to sleep. God knows I try. But my thoughts won't shut off, and my body is wired, every nerve standing at attention like it expects her to walk back in and call me out for being a damn coward.

I want her to.

So I get up. Again. Bare feet on the hardwood. My boxers and a cotton tee do nothing to block the cool of the air coming through the screen door. I move down the hall like a man chasing a ghost—quiet, aimless, hurting.

When I reach the back window, I stop. The cottage is dark, and I expect that, but then, just as I turn away, a light flickers on inside. Small. Soft. The reading lamp near the window.

And there she is.

Ivy Quinn, sitting on the edge of the bed in that oversized sweatshirt I gave her, hair pulled back, knees drawn up, staring at the same empty night I am.

Something about it hits me so hard I have to brace a hand on the doorframe.

She looks like she doesn't belong anywhere else but here. Wishing she wasn't made of headlines or record deals or glossy magazine shoots. Just a girl who needs rest. Who maybe needs something more than fame and fast lanes and forced smiles. Someone who needs real.

She rubs her hands over her knees, then glances toward the window like she feels me watching her. I don't move; she doesn't either. And for a long, aching minute, we just... look. Two silhouettes in the quiet. Two people carrying more than we ever say out loud.

She tilts her head slightly, like she wants to ask a question. I press my palm flat against the windowpane. She doesn't wave, but she doesn't look away either.

And that says more than either of us can handle tonight.

When she finally reaches up and clicks off the lamp, the space swallows her whole. The window goes dark, but the heat in my chest stays lit.

I stand there for a long time, eyes trained on the dark shape of the cottage, every beat of my heart echoing with a word I don't say.

Stay.

I want it more than my next breath. Or more than the sleep that never comes.

. . .

THE SUN IS JUST STARTING TO RISE WHEN I SLIP MY BOOTS on and head outside.

I haven't slept more than a couple of minutes. Can't. Every time I close my eyes, I see her—those wide, tired eyes in the lamplight. That curve of her lips when I barely kissed her. The way she doesn't pull back.

Hell, I can't even be angry with her for staying in the guesthouse. I offered. I wanted her to say yes. And now that she has, I'm unraveling like barbed wire in a thunderstorm.

The morning air is sharp and dewy, the gravel cool underfoot as I cross the yard. I avoid looking at the cottage. I don't trust myself not to knock on the door.

Instead, I head for the barn. Feed first. Then stalls. Keep moving. Keep my mind out of dangerous places.

I'm tossing hay when I hear footsteps behind me. I don't have to turn around to know it's her. The air changes when Ivy walks into a room. Subtle but real. Like the quiet before lightning cracks.

"You're up early," she says softly.

I keep working, jaw tight. "Farm doesn't care if you sleep like shit."

A pause.

"You're mad at me," she says.

That makes me turn. She stands in the doorway in that damn sweatshirt again, her hair pulled into a messy braid, eyes soft but unreadable.

"I'm not mad," I say.

She lifts a brow.

I sigh. "I'm mad at me. There's a difference."

She takes a few slow steps into the barn. "Rowan, nothing happened really."

"Something happened."

"A peck doesn't count."

I stare at her, tired and exposed and about five seconds from giving in to everything I've sworn I wouldn't.

She looks away first. "Look, I don't regret it. I just... I didn't mean to make things messy."

I toss a forkful of hay into the stall. "Too late."

Silence stretches between us like a rubber band pulled too tight.

Then she clears her throat. "I've been thinking about what you said the other night. About the camp."

I flinch. "It's not happening."

"Why not?"

"I don't have the time. Or the help. Or the funds. Or—"

"Or maybe you're scared it won't be perfect." She crosses her arms.

I turn slowly. "Excuse me?"

"You're afraid it'll flop. Or that the town'll talk. Or that people won't think it's good enough. So instead of trying, you shut it down."

I blink at her. "You don't know me."

"No," she says. "But I recognize fear when I see it. I've lived with it long enough."

I don't answer. I can't.

She steps closer. "What if it works? What if those kids

show up and fall in love with the land the way you did?" I swallow hard. "What if you gave them a place to breathe?" she whispers.

I stare at the pitchfork in my hand like it holds the answers. "I'm not a teacher. I'm not built for that."

"You're built for exactly that," she says. "And if you can't see it, that's your problem. But don't pretend it's mine."

Ivy turns and walks out, boots crunching on gravel as she disappears into the rising sun. And I stand in the barn, heart hammering, walls cracking, because she's not wrong.

I'm terrified. Not of the camp but of hoping. Because hoping means caring. And caring means falling. And falling means losing everything. Again.

The day drags. I mend fences that don't need mending. I clean out the feed bins—twice. I reorganize tools I could find blindfolded. Anything to keep me from pacing the damn yard like a restless fool.

But no matter how hard I work, her voice echoes in my head.

What if it works? What if you gave them a place to breathe?

I hate how much I want to believe her. How easy it is to picture it—kids running through the pasture, barefoot and wide-eyed. Ivy smiling as she watches them dig up carrots or bottle-feed a calf.

I've never told anyone I want to start the camp. Not really. Maybe I mentioned it in passing to Lila once, years ago. Doris, clearly. But that was before I realized how deep my roots had twisted into this solitary, quiet life. Before the weight of responsibility convinced me I didn't have time for dreams.

Now here Ivy is—bright eyes and stubborn hope—trying to shine a light into corners I boarded up a long time ago.

Damn her.

By evening, I'm bone-tired and no closer to peace. I catch sight of her a few times through the kitchen window. She stays near the cottage most of the day, a notebook balanced on her knee, lips moving silently like she's working out lyrics or writing a letter she'll never send.

She never looks toward the house. Never tries to talk to me again. But I feel her there, just the same.

By the time the sun dips behind the trees and the frogs start up their twilight song, I give in and make dinner. Something simple—pan-fried chicken and green beans, cornbread on the side. Enough for two.

Habit, maybe. Or hope.

I sit down at the table, staring at the empty seat across from me, the steam from the plate curling up like it's mocking me. She doesn't come. Of course, she doesn't.

I'm not exactly rolling out the welcome mat.

I scrub the dishes in silence and pour a bourbon, stepping out onto the back deck with nothing but the night and a hundred bad ideas for company.

The sky is streaked with navy and silver, stars just starting to pop. The cottage window stays dark. I lean back in the chair and close my eyes.

She's right. That's the worst part. The thing under my

skin, burning like a goddamn fever. She sees right through me. Not because she's famous or beautiful or used to getting what she wants. But because she knows what it means to carry fear like armor. To live behind glass. To pretend not to want more.

We're not so different. That realization? It hits like a kick to the chest.

I open my eyes again and look toward the dark silhouette of the guest cottage. And I know something has to give. Because she's not going to stay forever. And if I don't figure out what the hell I want soon, I'll lose the one thing I haven't even dared to hope for.

The knock is soft. So soft that I almost think I imagine it. I sit up straighter in my chair, glass still in hand, and wait. It comes again. Three delicate taps against the back door, like a question she's not sure she has the right to ask.

I stand, heart already kicking against my ribs. When I open it, she's there—barefoot in the grass, with her arms wrapped around her middle like she's holding herself together. That sweatshirt swallows her frame, and the porchlight casts her eyes in shadow.

"I didn't know if you were still up," she says quietly.

"I am."

She hesitates, glancing over her shoulder toward the cottage. "I didn't want to sleep yet."

"Can't?"

Her mouth tugs into a half smile. "That's one way to put it."

I step aside, and without a word, she moves past me

into the house. The silence wraps around us immediately. Thick. Charged. Familiar, somehow.

She makes it as far as the kitchen table before she stops. Her hand brushes over the edge like she's grounding herself.

"You made dinner," she says softly.

"Wasn't sure if you'd want any."

"I ate soup," she replies, voice brittle. "Burned it."

Something inside me cracks at that.

She turns to face me, eyes wide but unreadable. "I'm sorry."

"For what?"

"For pushing earlier. About the camp. About... everything."

I step closer. "Don't be."

"I crossed a line."

"So did I."

Her breath catches, and I see it—the memory of the way I leaned in, the moment our lips brushed, the way I backed out like a goddamn coward.

"I didn't mean to make things harder," she says, not quite looking at me.

My reflex is to give her a one-word out, but I make myself do better. "You didn't. I did that all by myself." I rub a palm down my thigh, trying to ground what's sprinting in me. "I have a history with slamming on the brakes when something matters."

Her mouth tilts in a soft admission. "Me, too." She steps closer, tiny grit on the boards squeaking under her bare feet. "I'm scared, Rowan."

"Of?" I ask, even though I can feel the shape of it.

"That I'll never find a place I can be who I am without earning it every day. That if I stop performing, I lose my seat at the table."

Something inside me—that bone-deep part that knows fence lines and first frosts—answers for me. "You don't have to earn anything here," I tell her.

Her eyes lift, sharp and searching. "You don't put on a show either," she says softly. "I like that. I don't know what to do with it, but I like it."

That lands square. I've always treated quiet like a tool and a wall, and somehow, she's managed to read it like a promise. One strand of hair is stuck at the corner of her mouth, fighting every attempt she makes to tuck it away. My hand moves before my head can veto it, knuckles grazing her cheek, tucking it behind her ear. She leans into the touch—barely, but enough that the world narrows to the warmth under my fingertips and the way our breath goes out in the same little rush.

"You almost kissed me last night," she says, not accusing, just placing a marker on a map we're both holding.

"Almost," I admit. "Because I wanted to. And because wanting things has... not always gone great for me."

"Same." Her laugh is breath and nerves. "But I also keep thinking about how it felt to almost have your mouth on mine."

A sound—half groan, half prayer—scrapes my throat. I take a small step closer, because if I don't, I'll spend the rest of the night pacing the boards. "There's something else I have to say before I make that worse," I manage. "You... posed with my brother. The whole world thinks—"

"That I dated Crew," she finishes, gaze steady. "I didn't. We smiled for cameras and did what our contracts told us to do. He was kind. But I never felt like this." Her fingers open and close at her sides, then still. "This is new."

I want to believe her. I do. But there's another knot to untie. "He's a good man. I don't—won't—blindside him."

"You're not." She tips her chin. "We're not sneaking or lying. We're standing in your kitchen in the light. If anything happens, it'll happen that way."

The bulb hums above us like it agrees. The tight band in my chest eases a notch. I exhale, then let more truth out. "I don't always trust myself with good things," I say quietly. "I want them too much, and then I squeeze until they break. With you... I don't want to ruin it by grabbing before we've built anything."

Her eyes go warm around the edges. "Then don't grab," she whispers. "Build anyway. Hold on. Let it take the time it needs."

She says it like it's simple. It isn't. But it sounds possible in her mouth—like cedar and sawdust and early light on the back pasture. I didn't invite this woman into my life; she crashed into it. And now she's the one who made me say out loud the thing I've never given voice to: that I want more than this routine of work-sleep-repeat. A place for kids to learn dirt under nails is holy. A rhythm that belongs to me. She made it feel like lumber I can cut instead of a picture I put away whenever someone walks in the room.

I clear my throat. "I'm not good at leaving," I tell her, and it comes out steadier than I feel. "I'm the guy who stays and fixes boards and shows up with coffee at six. I'll be here tomorrow and the day after. If you go back to lights and noise, I'll still be here. If you come back, I'll still be here. Either way, I'm not changing my mind because it gets hard."

Her breath catches with the smallest sound. She steps the last inch into my space, and I feel the heat of her even before her fingers find the hem of my shirt and hold there, not pulling me in but not letting me go. "Can I be honest?" she asks.

"Please."

"I want you to kiss me," she whispers, voice shaking. "And I'm terrified of what that means."

"Me, too," I say, and then I add the part that matters. "But I want it anyway."

"Okay," she says.

I keep it careful. My palm settles along her jaw, my thumb a slow stroke near the corner of her mouth—asking. Her nod is the smallest permission I've ever felt. I bend, just enough, and our lips meet—soft, patient, the kind of kiss that feels like placing a fragile thing exactly where it belongs. She exhales against my mouth, and her fingers bunch my shirt. Everything in me answers by deepening—barely, a breath—and then I pull back before hunger eats caution.

We rest there, foreheads touching, the kitchen light casting shadows on the boards around our feet.

"I should go back to the cottage," she murmurs, but she doesn't let go.

"You can," I say, smoothing my hand down to her shoulder, tugging the hoodie's edge back into place like it's an excuse to touch her again. "And I'll be here in the morning with coffee. Fence checks at seven. You can come with me or sleep in. Both are allowed."

"If I stay... do we change everything?" she asks, searching my face like she's memorizing a map that only makes sense tonight.

"Things have already changed," I answer. "Back on that shoulder when you stood there behind those oversized sunglasses and asked for help like a person, not a headline."

Her mouth curves, and the ache behind my ribs goes sweet. She loosens her grip on my shirt, then tightens it for one last second, like she's telling herself she can. "I don't want to be another mess you have to clean up."

"You're not a mess," I say, and I don't care if it sounds too big. "You're the reason the house feels less empty. You're the person who made me say out loud the things I only let myself think when nobody's watching. Let me... be the guy who stays. Let me prove it slow."

"I should still go," she whispers, "before I forget how."

I nod, my hand brushing her elbow. "Let me walk you back."

She shakes her head. "Stay here. You've done enough rescuing for one week."

I open the door and watch her step back into the night, moonlight washing over her. Her bare feet barely make a sound on the gravel, the borrowed sweatshirt swaying at her hips.

She turns at the edge of the yard. "You left the porch light off."

"I didn't know if you'd come."

Her smile turns sad—and something else. Something like hope. "Next time, leave it on."

Then she disappears into the shadows, and I stand there like an idiot, heart full and hollow all at once.

There's no going back now.

And for what feels like a long damn while, I don't want to.

Chapter Eight

IVY

The morning air is syrup-thick and golden when I step out onto the porch of the guest cottage. Warm, but not stifling—at least, not yet. Bees buzz lazily around the edge of the flower garden. The only sounds are distant birdsong and the quiet creak of the old wood beneath my feet.

It's the kind of quiet you can breathe.

I wrap my fingers tighter around the chipped mug Rowan left in the cabinet—it says *I Brake for Pie*, and somehow, it's become my favorite. The coffee inside is bitter and too strong, but it grounds me. Anchors me to a place that feels... like it might be something more than temporary.

I haven't seen Rowan since last night.

We haven't talked about the kiss anymore. Or the way his voice went ragged when he said I didn't have to go. But I feel it. All of it. Like an echo I can't shake.

I spent the night replaying every second—the way his

eyes darkened when I touched him and the rasp of his breath when our lips brushed. How he looked like he wanted to run and stay all at once. And how I did too.

I mean to give him space today. Let the tension settle. Let things breathe. But I don't make it past the first sip of coffee.

A sleek black car rolls up the drive like it's been conjured by my worst nightmare.

I blink, heart stuttering in my chest.

No. No, no, no.

The door opens with that same expensive sigh every luxury car seems to have, and out steps a woman in over-sized sunglasses, a linen suit, and four-inch heels that have no business being on gravel.

My mother.

"Evangeline!" she calls, arms wide like this is some twisted family reunion. "There you are."

I don't move. Maybe if I stay very still, like a deer in a field, she'll lose interest. She doesn't.

Instead, she waves off the driver—a new one—and struts up the path like she hasn't just dropped a bomb on my morning. The car stays put... at least that's something in my favor today.

Gravel crunches like a warning before the black sedan even clears the oaks. Perfume hits the porch a beat before she does—sharp, expensive, uninvited. Celeste steps out in linen and sunglasses the size of small satellites. Even blocked, I know her eyes sweep the cottage like she's appraising a fixer-upper.

"Well," she says, taking off the glasses with a practiced sigh. "I had to come all the way out to the middle of nowhere to make sure my daughter wasn't chopped up into tiny pieces and lying in a ditch somewhere. Imagine my surprise to see you hale and hearty—and looking decidedly homeless."

"Mama," I say flatly. "What are you doing here?"

She glides past me into the shade of the porch, gaze catching on my sweatshirt, my bare feet, the mug. "You stopped answering your phone. Your team escalated. The label asked for eyes on you, not 'I need space' texts from a mystery ZIP code."

"I told you I'm fine."

"You're hiding in a borrowed cottage in a town that doesn't have a proper juice bar," she replies, her smile cool and camera-ready. "That's not fine, Evangeline. That's avoidance."

I fold my arms. "Still doesn't explain why you're here."

"It explains it perfectly." She taps a cream-colored envelope against her palm. "We've got fittings, a creative call for the fall rollout, two quick stills for the Lanova contract addendum, and a brand segment the network wants on the calendar before quarter close. All of which you've pushed once. I'm not leaving it to chance—or to your reception out here."

"I'm not going to Nashville," I say, steady.

She blinks, tilting her head. "You don't get to make that call alone. Not when there are signatures, schedules, and seven figures of ad spend with your face attached."

"I'm a person, not a purchase order."

"And I'm your mother, not your concierge," she answers, voice like velvet pulled tight over wire. "Which is why I came to lay eyes on you, confirm you weren't dead in a ditch, and deliver this." She slides the envelope onto the little table by the rocking chair like a summons. "Call sheet. Fitting times. Car service details."

I don't touch it. "You drove all the way out here to drop off paper?"

"I flew," she corrects, crisp. "And I'll be at the Needle Palm on Main Street until tomorrow afternoon. I've told them to hold the suite. A car will be outside this cottage at five. If you're not in it, I'll let the label know you're refusing to meet contractual obligations. They will escalate. You will not like how."

Across the yard, I see movement—Rowan, half in shadow under the oaks, jaw set but not interfering. Every inch of him is a line that reads *I'm here* without making me pick a side. It steadies me and makes my throat ache in the same breath.

Celeste follows my glance and takes him in, filing him away with the same clinical efficiency she applies to budgets. "Is that the cowboy?"

I say nothing.

She slips her glasses back on. "I'll assume it is. Charming. Picturesque. Not permanent." The smile she gives me is TV-warm and ice-cold. "Five o'clock, Evangeline. Don't make me send someone to fetch you like a child."

She turns, her heels finding every rock in the drive and

punishing it, then slides into the back seat. The sedan glides away like the whole visit was a commercial break.

Silence rushes in. The porch smells like coffee and last night's rain. My hands shake.

I pick up the envelope but don't open it.

And for the first time since the sedan appeared, my lungs remember how to do their job. Slipping back into the house, the screen door snapping behind me as if it's just as angry about my mother's arrival as I am, I hover in the kitchen.

I press my palms to the counter, grounding myself. I'm not the girl in the sequined dress anymore. I'm not twelve years old and scared of the electricity bill or the sound of my father's truck door slamming outside the shack. I'm grown. I'm free. And maybe completely freaking lost.

A soft knock comes at the door. I don't answer. It comes again, followed by the gentle creak of hinges and Rowan's voice, low and rough from the field.

"Ivy?"

I turn slowly. He steps inside, filling the doorway with his quiet presence. His hat is gone, hair mussed from the sun. Dirt streaks his forearms, and his boots are caked with red clay, but he looks steady in a way I desperately need.

He takes one quiet step closer, slow enough that I could move if I wanted to. I don't. His hand comes up, rough palm warm against my cheek as his thumb sweeps away the tear I didn't realize had escaped. His eyes are flint around the edges, soft in the middle—angry that someone put salt in my eyes, careful not to add to it.

"You okay?" he asks, voice low and steady, like walking barefoot through warm grass.

I open my mouth, shut it, then try again. "No," I whisper, because lying feels like the wrong kind of hard tonight. "She just... showed up. Said I need to fly back. Meetings. Photos. 'Reset the narrative.' Smile on command." The words scrape my throat on the way out. "It's the machine, Rowan. And I don't know if I can climb back on without breaking something I finally like."

Rowan doesn't speak. I look at him, expecting judgment. Coldness. Distance. What I get is his quiet understanding. Something deeper than pity.

"She says I still owe her. That I signed over my life when I was eighteen and scared and dumb. Back when I was Evangaline Quinn and not this Ivy product I've become."

He steps closer.

"She's not wrong," I add bitterly. "But she's not right either."

"You're not dumb," Rowan says quietly.

I laugh. It cracks around the edges. "You don't know me."

"I know what it looks like when someone's trying to keep you small."

The words hit too close to home. I look down, blinking hard.

He's beside me now, not touching—just close. Present in a way that settles something inside me even as it stirs more up.

"You going?" he asks.

"I don't know," I whisper.

Rowan nods, like he understands the weight of not knowing. Like he's carried that, too.

I reach up to tuck a strand of hair behind my ear, and my fingers shake.

Without a word, Rowan reaches out and gently takes my hand in his. Rough palm against trembling fingers. Ground and air.

It's not romantic, not exactly—no flowers, no speeches—but the look on his face is steady enough to make my throat burn.

"You don't owe anyone your peace," he says, low and certain, like he's telling me which way the tide will turn.

I swallow. "And if I go anyway?"

He nods once, no flinch. "Then go because you chose it. And know this place will be waiting when you're done—same porch light, same coffee, same quiet." His mouth tips, the smallest almost smile.

Something inside me loosens so fast it's almost a dizzy spell.

He lifts a hand, pauses—asking without words—then holds his palm out. "Your phone?"

I pass it over before I can overthink it. He types for all of three seconds, thumb sure and unhurried, then the screen is back in my hand. At the top of my favorites list is a new contact: Rowan. He's already texted himself a single acorn emoji, so he has my number because of course he chose something small and stubborn and alive.

"If you head to Nashville," he says, tapping the contact,

"and the noise gets heavy, you text me one word: home. I'll answer. If you want to come back the same day, you send two words: come get. I won't ask questions."

Heat pricks behind my eyes again—frustrating, embarrassing, and impossible to stop. He sees it and doesn't rush in or back away. He just stands there, big and immovable, like an oak that's learned how to bend for storms.

"I hate that I even have to think about it," I admit, voice small, honest.

"You get to think about it," he corrects gently. "That's the point."

I nod, looking down at his name glowing on my screen, at the word he spoke to anchor it: Home. The letters blur, then sharpen. I breathe.

"I'm not deciding tonight," I say.

"Good," he answers, like that was the right one. "Sleep. Eat. Be a person. The rest can wait."

The late morning sun lays bright rectangles across the yard, dust motes floating in the heat. I slide my phone into my pocket and meet his eyes.

"Thank you," I whisper.

He tips his chin toward the split in the path—one way to the cottage, one to the house. "I'll walk you to the fork," he says, and when our shoulders brush in the shade of the oaks, the touch is as reassuring as anything he just added to my contacts.

At the fork, we pause where both porches throw matching patches of light across the gravel. He nods toward my pocket. "It's not going anywhere."

"Neither are you," I say, and it comes out like a promise.

He huffs a soft laugh, eyes warm. "Nope."

We linger a breath longer in the hum of cicadas, then peel off—me toward the cottage, him toward the house. His screen door snaps softly behind him, and the quiet that settles after isn't empty. It feels held.

Chapter Nine

ROWAN

The bell above the door chimes with a tired little clang, the kind that says it's seen one too many dusty boots and forgotten receipts.

I step into the feed store and scrub a hand over my jaw, trying to shake off the dull ache behind my eyes. The sun's already high, sweat clinging to the back of my neck, and all I want is to grab the damn seed and get out.

"Morning, Rowan," old Ted calls from behind the counter, one hand resting on the register like it's holding him up.

"Hey, Ted. You get that calf formula in?"

"Back wall, third shelf. Just came in this morning."

I nod, eyes scanning the aisles. The place smells like hay dust, motor oil, and rust—same as always. Same as it'll always be.

The TV mounted near the counter drones on with its

usual midmorning entertainment nonsense—background noise. But the moment I hear her name, I stop cold.

"Ivy Quinn and football heartthrob Crew Wright spotted in Nashville the other night..."

I don't turn. I don't have to. The grainy footage flickers in my periphery—her laugh, that signature wave to the cameras, and Crew's hand on her lower back.

Fake, I tell myself. Contract. Optics. All of it for someone else's camera.

But the smile she gives him isn't the stage kind, and when her fingers skim the sleeve of his shirt—like muscle memory, like she still knows where he ends—I feel something hot and unfamiliar lance through me.

Envy.

Of my own damn brother.

I hate it instantly. Hate that Crew's always been the easy one—easy laugh, easy charm—and that for the first time in my life, I want what's in his orbit. My jaw locks so hard it pops. I fix my stare on a stack of seed bags like I can grind them down to dust by will alone. Like if I don't look away, I won't look over and watch her choose him with a touch that should never matter to me.

"No official word on the rekindling of the couple's romance, but sources say the chemistry was undeniable..."

God*dammit*.

I yank the formula off the shelf, grip it tighter than necessary, and stalk back to the register.

Ted glances up at the screen. "Can't believe that gal was at Lila's wedding. Whole town's been talkin'."

I grunt and drop the tub on the counter. "How much?"

"Still, she seemed real sweet. My niece swears she signed her gas station receipt. Said she smelled like heaven."

I don't answer. Ted gives me a look, then mutters the total. I slap down some bills and leave without waiting for change.

The door slaps shut behind me, and the heat smacks me in the face. But it doesn't burn half as bad as the image stuck behind my eyes—*her, with him.*

Crew, grinning like none of it meant anything. Like he hadn't left her behind without a backward glance.

By the time I pull into the drive at Otter Creek Farm, bypassing my house completely, the sun's just past its peak, and sweat clings to the back of my shirt like a second skin. I toss the formula into the barn fridge and grab a shovel without thinking—no real plan, just needing to do *something.*

Keep moving. Keep working. Keep her out of your damn head.

The words loop in my skull like a broken prayer.

I'm elbow-deep in clearing a feed stall when I hear laughter. High-pitched. Familiar.

"Rowan!" Hadley's voice rings out like a bell through the heat and dust. "You're gonna scare the kids with that scowl."

I don't look up. "Didn't know we were hosting a school field trip."

"It's not a school field trip," she fires back. "It's Bailey's weekly reading group. Storytime picnic in the orchard."

That gets my attention.

Bailey. Of course.

Sure enough, Bailey stands at the edge of the orchard in a wide-brimmed hat with a canvas tote bag slung over her shoulder. Her dress is lemon yellow, scattered with tiny blue flowers. She looks like something out of a magazine—sun-drenched and smug.

I wipe my hands on a rag and head over, jaw tight.

"Would've been nice to get a heads-up," I say when I reach her.

Bailey glances up, completely unfazed. "Told Lila last week. Figured she passed it along."

"She didn't."

"Shocking." She arches a brow. "The kids love the goats. Thought it'd be nice to let them see the baby ones."

"And the pecans?"

She gives me a too-sweet smile. "No one's touching anything."

I grunt. Apparently not enough to scare her off. Hadley appears at my side like a damn sprite. "Why don't you go inside and cool off? You look like you're about to sponta-neously combust."

"I'm fine."

Bailey tilts her head. "Are you, though? Because I saw you nearly rip your truck door off earlier."

That needle jabs harder than it should.

I look between the two of them—Hadley's knowing grin, Bailey's calm amusement—and something in me snaps, splitting right down the middle.

"You know what?" I say, louder than I mean to. "Maybe

I don't want people traipsing through the damn orchard every time they feel like it. Perhaps I'd like to have one day where nobody's up in my business."

The silence that follows is instant. Cold. Echoing.

Bailey blinks once. Hadley steps back like I just shoved her. And there it is. The guilt. Immediate. Sharp.

Bailey's voice stays even, but I hear the shift, the careful don't-spook-the-horse cadence she uses when something's already gone sideways. "I'll pack up the kids, and we'll head out."

The words land like a shovel to the ribs. I see the whole scene from outside myself: two little girls no heavier than a feed sack wandering three steps past the rope line, palms itching to touch the first bud on a pecan, and me snapping like a spring-loaded trap. Not at them—at everything else— but they don't know the difference.

How in the hell can I take on a camp full of kids if this is how I fucking react?

Heat climbs my neck, ugly and immediate. The orchard is quiet in that listening way—leaves holding their breath, a wasp ticking against a crate, dust hanging in the sun like evidence. I'm mad at the wrong things: at a photo I didn't want to see, at a brother I didn't want to envy, at wanting a woman I shouldn't be planning a life around. So I barked. And now Bailey's gathering them up like I'm a storm to move around.

"Bailey—" I start, too fast, too late. "That's not what I—"

But she's already moving, steady as a metronome. "Okay,

team," she calls gently to the kids, "let's grab our water bottles and head to the truck." Her smile is warm; her eyes—when they flick to me—are not. The boys pretend not to look at me. One of the girls keeps her hand cupped around her paper baggie of treats.

Self-loathing sits heavy in my gut. I scrub a hand over my jaw and force my voice down where it should've been to start.

"My bad," I say, easing in softer. "I shouldn't have raised my voice—that's on me, not you." I crouch to the littlest. "Wanna know a pecan trick? The best ones are heavy in your hand, and the shuck's split wide open. Next time, I'll show you how to roll 'em out with the side of your boot and use the picker to scoop 'em—no climbing, no tugging on branches." She nods, unsure, eyes flicking to Bailey for confirmation like I'm a dog that sometimes bites. Bailey gives her a small, encouraging nod and keeps ushering them along.

I straighten, shame burning a clean line down my spine. This—this right here—is why the camp feels like a fantasy I don't deserve. It's one thing to build a stage or string lights. It's another to be the kind of man who doesn't let his temper bleed all over a kid's afternoon.

"I'm sorry," I tell Bailey, quieter now. "I'm... not myself today."

"Find him," she says, not unkind, but firm. "He's who they came to see." Then she turns back to the kids, calm wrapped around them like shade.

I stand in the row after they go, hands open, letting the

air move through the leaves and over my skin until the worst of the heat drains off. If I'm going to do this—camp, kids, any of it—my bad moods don't get to steer. Not here. Not around them. Not ever.

Hadley waits until Bailey's out of earshot before she spins on me.

"What the hell was that?"

"I said it's fine," I mutter, jaw tight.

"No. You snapped at her like she drove her minivan through your grove."

I lift my palms. "You're right."

I step back and let them have the row. The urge to fix—the scene, myself—buzzes under my skin, equal parts pride and shame. If a handful of kids in my sister's care can knock me off center, how the hell do I run a camp? I feel that truth settle: something I want doesn't excuse the way I handled five minutes of chaos.

Without a backward glance, I head to my truck, kicking up dust with how fast I leave the farm and dodge across the dirt path that leads to the backside of my property.

I cut across the fence line to my side, oak shade giving way to the open yard. My barn—my mess, my order—waits like an old friend that doesn't ask questions. Inside, the light slants through the boards in dust-thick bands.

A soft head bumps my thigh. Butterscotch. She blinks up at me, lashes full of hay, and huffs like I'm late. "Yeah, I know," I murmur, scratching the warm spot behind her ear. She leans all thirty ungainly pounds into my leg and sneezes for good measure. Ivy's laughter lives in that sound—her grin the day this calf christened her, the way she wiped her hands on my shirt and named the little menace like she had the right.

Guilt loosens a notch. I set a tool in my hands, something I can actually make better—oil the sticky hinge on the south stall, sharpen the loppers, and reset the twine on the baler hook I've been meaning to fix. My brain finds the rhythm of work, and the knot in my chest eases.

Out the wide door, I can see the guest cottage through the trees. Curtains move with the fan. No sign of her, which means she's doing exactly what I told myself I'd let her do: breathe without me hovering. Nashville still hangs like distant thunder, but she's leaning away from it. I can feel that, too. But it's her call to make, not mine.

I pour a Mason jar of sweet tea, walk it up to her porch, and leave it on the rail. No knock. No note. Just proof that I'm here.

Back in the barn, I try to lose myself in work, but my head won't quiet. I over-file a blade edge until it winks thin and useless. Miss a tooth on the chain and nick my knuckle on the next pass. Drop the same bolt twice because my grip's all memory and no attention. The pictures won't quit —old headlines, staged smiles, the way the world thinks it knows her—and every time they flare, my hand slips. One more mistake and I'll be down a finger.

I set the file down, hard. Enough.

I cut across the yard to the house, rinse the grit and blood from my hands at the kitchen sink, and brace my palms on the counter until the sting ebbs. The phone on the table lights up with another alert I don't need. I flip it face down and shove it into the drawer with the takeout menus, like that'll muffle the noise in my head.

The place is too quiet without her humming off-key. I open the fridge, pretend I'm hungry, then close it again. Pacing feels foolish, but I do it anyway—window to door, door to window—until I force myself into a chair and breathe. I think about the way she looked over her shoulder this morning, already deciding to stay and still afraid to say it out loud. I think about those damn photos the world keeps of her—proof to everyone but me that a smile can mean anything you want it to.

I stand, wash my hands again just to do something, and grab a clean Mason jar. Two lemons, a handful of mint, sugar from the blue tin. If my head won't quiet, my hands can at least make something I won't screw up.

When the kettle clicks off, I glance through the window toward the cottage. Curtains still shift in the fan's breeze. I don't text. I don't knock. I let her choose, and I get the house ready in case she decides the choosing is easier with company.

Chapter Ten

IVY

The text from Celeste sits unread at the top of my phone like a bruise I keep poking.

Celeste: Tomorrow. Noon. Nashville.

No heart. No question mark. Just inevitability.

I flip the phone face down and press my forehead to the heron lamp's cool metal shade. The cottage smells like lemon cleaner and the faint, smoky hint of Rowan's laundry soap on the blanket he insisted I keep on the back of the couch. Outside, late summer hums—the whirr of cicadas, a tractor way off beyond the creek, the staccato cluck of indignant hens who have opinions about everything.

"I don't want to go," I tell the empty room.

For the past hour, I've been doing the thing I do when I'm cornered: cleaning what isn't dirty and making lists I'll throw away. My "pros" column has one item:

Rip off the bandage.

The "cons" column takes up half the page and spirals into small, tight handwriting:

spin, misquotes, being handled, feeling twelve, the way my chest caves when Mom says brand like it's my middle name.

Another vibration. I don't check it.

My head's thick in that way that feels like the air is heavier than usual, like I'm breathing through a straw. That happens when I'm stressed—I sleep light, wake heavy, and grow clumsy with my own body. I rub the heel of my hand between my eyes and go for water, telling myself the chalky taste in my mouth is just from not drinking enough and not because anxiety has set up camp in my throat. If I let it get too bad, then the real fear of my epilepsy making an appearance becomes an issue.

Half a glass later, the floor tilts a hair to the left. I brace a palm on the counter until it steadies.

"Okay." I try for light. "That's new."

I pull on shorts and the softest T-shirt in my bag and take the footpath to the main house. The air is warm already, the kind that sticks to the back of your neck. At the top of the path, I pause. Staple sounds: the thunk of a stall door, a low horse snort, Rowan's voice—quiet, steady, a word I can't make out. Something in me unclenches at the sound.

I don't go inside. I turn toward the oak, settle on the cottage steps, and text Bailey.

> Me: Real question: are summer colds a thing here, or is my body staging a coup?

> Bailey: Oh no. Tell me everything.

> Me: Head feels stuffed with wet cotton. sore throat. kind of floaty?

> Bailey: 😬 could be a cold. also could be your nervous system yelling "hey girl take a nap." fever?

> Me: idk. I feel hot then cold.

> Bailey: I'm grabbing OJ and soup. Be there after I drop off an order. Nap now. No arguments.

> Me: Bossy

> Bailey: Useful 😌 lie down. text if you get worse. I mean it.

I set the phone on the step. The shade from the oak shifts, dappled sunlight crawling across my knees. Somewhere close, Butterscotch bleats like she remembers the exact pitch of my voice when I named her. The sound makes me smile, then ache. I want to go pet her soft nose and tell her secrets, but when I stand, my legs feel like they're packed with wet sand.

Nap, then. For once, I don't fight the suggestion. Inside, I pull the blanket down and crawl onto the couch, convincing myself I'm lying here just long enough for the room to stop nudging sideways. I close my eyes, and the list in my head tries to start again. Nashville, flights, outfits that say "adult" and not "doll," what I'll say if Mom uses momentum like it's holy.

Sleep drags me by the wrist anyway.

The dream is loud—the roar of a crowd, the bass of a song I didn't get to finish. I try to sing over it, and my voice won't come. When I wake, my throat hurts like I swallowed sand, and my skin is doing that prickly, too tight thing. I shove the blanket off. Immediately, goose bumps erupt. *Pick a temperature, body.*

Phone. Right. I fumble for it, miss, and nearly fling it into the basket with the extra towels. The screen is a smear of notifications. I squint until Bailey's name comes into focus.

> Bailey: Running 10 behind—line at the bakery was sinful. How are you?

> Me: Fine. just tired.

> Bailey: Liar. temp?

> Me: Don't have a thermometer.

> Bailey: On it. ETA 20.

I put the phone down and try to sit up. A weird wave of vertigo sloshes from my chest to my head. The room doesn't spin, exactly. It ripples. My hands shake, and that little tremor makes my heart beat too fast.

I close my eyes and do the things I've been taught: inhale four, hold four, exhale six. Repeat. Repeat again with my palms flat on my knees. Heat sweeps my face, and a chill sweeps my arms. *This is fine*, I tell myself. I've done stages with bronchitis and label meetings with migraines. This is a nap and a bottle of orange juice. This is not the end of the world. It's not a seizure.

Somewhere in the back of my mind, a quieter voice says, *Or it's your body finally cashing a bill you've been ignoring.*

The knock is soft, two knuckles to the frame. "Ivy?" It's Rowan, not Bailey.

Relief hits so fast I'm embarrassed by it. "Come in," I croak, and wince at my zombie voice.

He steps inside, bringing cooler air with him. He takes one look at me, and a crease cuts between his brows. I've never seen it that deep. "You're pale."

I try for a joke. "That's my new brand."

He doesn't smile. "Bailey said you weren't feeling right. She got called to fix a frosting disaster. I was closer."

I nod, and the simple motion feels like too much. "I'm okay. Just—" I rub my arms, and the shiver that rides up my spine answers for me. "Apparently, summer colds are a thing."

He comes closer and kneels so we're eye level. He smells like sun and hay and the citrus soap he keeps by the kitchen sink. "Can I touch your forehead?"

"Please," I whisper, and the word tastes like surrender.

His palm cups my temple, then my brow. Big hand, careful pressure. The touch finds every frayed wire in my system and smooths it. He frowns. "You're hot."

"Finally, something we agree on," I try, and that gets me a ghost of a smile before it disappears under worry.

He shifts, scanning the room. "You have water?"

I nod toward the counter. "Half a glass."

He gets up and returns with a full Mason jar, the glass beaded cold. When I reach for it, my hand trembles, and I slosh water onto my T-shirt. He takes the jar back and brings it to my lips, steady as a metronome. "Slow."

I sip. It feels like mercy. He tips just enough. When I try to take the jar, he doesn't let me. He sets it on the table within reach and studies me in that quiet way that doesn't feel like being looked at but being looked after.

"Throat?" he asks.

"Scratchy. Feels swollen." My voice scrapes along my vocal cords like they're rusted shut.

"Chest?"

"Fine." I press a hand there, as if to double-check. "Just tired. And cold. And hot. I contain multitudes."

He nods once like he's filing answers. "You have Tylenol? Thermometer?"

"You're very prepared in theory," I mutter. "Less so in this drawer situation." I gesture weakly at the minimal kitchen.

"I have both at the house."

"I can walk." I make the mistake of trying to prove it.

The second my feet hit the floor, the room tips. He's there before I can wobble, hands firm around my forearms.

"Nope," he says, like a man who has decided on the weather. "You're not walking anywhere."

"I'm not made of glass."

"No," he agrees. "You're made of fever and stubborn." He glances at the blanket, then back at me. Something softer moves across his face. "Let me help."

"Okay," I whisper, because arguing takes energy I don't have, and right now, the idea of not being alone with this feels like stepping into shade.

He doesn't go for excuses or dithering. He bends, one arm behind my knees, the other around my back. "Ready?"

"Wait," I say, suddenly. "My bag. The black one. There's a small blue case in there—meds. Just... in case."

His gaze flicks to mine in understanding, not pity. "Got it." He sets me gently back, crosses the room, digs with efficiency, and slides the blue case into his back pocket. "Okay?"

"Okay."

Then he swoops me up with one arm as if I'm nothing more than a rope used to tie things down. I hang on with everything I have.

I want to say something witty, but the truth is, I melt. Not because I'm weak—because every muscle lets go at once. His chest is solid against my shoulder, heartbeat steady enough to sync mine. He smells like safety and the day outside. As he carries me out, he nudges the light off with his elbow, and the cottage settles behind us like a dog told to stay.

The walk across the yard is a pocket of quiet—only the cicadas, the creak of a porch step, and his breath even next to my ear.

He doesn't take me upstairs. He goes straight for the big couch in the living room, the one with the soft, low back I notoriously claimed during a storm. He lowers me carefully, as if he's practiced this a thousand times with things that bruise.

"Pillow," he says to himself, already moving. "Cool cloth." He disappears down the hall and returns with a thermometer, a bottle of Tylenol, a throw blanket and pillow that smell like cedar, and a towel.

"Open," he says gently, and I do. The thermometer rests under my tongue while he wet-wrings the cloth in the kitchen and fills a glass with water from the tap. When it beeps, he reads it and his jaw ticks. He doesn't announce the number. He sets the cloth across my forehead, and it feels like stepping into shade at noon. My eyes sting with the stupid relief of being tended to.

"Small sips," he says, handing me the Tylenol and water. "Then I'm making soup."

"You don't have to—"

"I want to." He says it without flourish, as if he's choosing fence posts. "And I'd like to feed you something not toast."

"This is slander. My toast and I—" The sentence

dissolves in a cough that scrapes my throat raw. He's there with the jar immediately, like he was waiting.

I drink. Blink away the tears pulled to the surface by the cough. He doesn't comment. He tucks the blanket higher and adjusts the cloth like it matters where the corner lies. It does. Everything he touches feels a degree more bearable.

"Tell Bailey I'm here," I manage.

"I will." His eyes flick to the blue case on the coffee table, then back to me. "Anything I need to know? Triggers, red flags?"

Heat that isn't fever rises in my face. "A fever can be… not ideal. But this feels like a plain old virus. I have the nasal spray if it goes sideways. In the blue case. It's labeled."

He nods, absorbing the plan like it's a fence line map. "Okay." He waits a beat. "Do you want me to call—" He cuts himself off. "Never mind."

"Who?" I ask, even though I know.

"Your mom."

A laugh slips out that has no humor in it. "She knows how to find me when there's a camera. She'll be fine."

His mouth tightens, something flint-hard passing through his gaze before it softens again. "Soup," he says, like it's a promise, and strides for the kitchen.

From the couch, I watch him move: the efficient economy of his body, the way he opens cabinets without a creak because he knows exactly how much pressure to use, the quick reach for a pot, the thunk of a drawer as he locates a wooden spoon by sound alone. Water runs. A burner clicks. He hums under his breath, tuneless and low.

It grounds me more than any mindfulness app I've ever been bullied into downloading.

I doze. I come back to the sound of a spoon tapping the rim of a bowl and a soft curse when he tests the heat with his own wrist. He brings the bowl over, steam rising, and sets it on a folded dish towel on the coffee table. The smell—chicken, thyme, and something bright like lemon—makes my throat ache in a good way.

"Can you sit up?"

"Only if the room behaves."

He slides an arm behind my shoulders and slowly lifts me. I try to help and mostly manage not to be dead weight. He settles beside me, thigh to my hip, and fits the bowl into my hands only when he's sure I have it. He keeps his palm near the base anyway, just in case.

I sip. It's hot and perfect, and my eyes burn for the stupidest reason. "You made this?"

"Used to cook after morning chores for Dad if Ma was at the school." He watches my face when I swallow. "Mind the lemon. Lila swears it cuts a sore throat."

"It does." I breathe through my nose, and the sharpness opens something that's been stuck since I woke. "Tell Lila I said thank you."

"She'll take full credit."

We sit like that for a while, me sipping, him quiet, the house settling into evening around us. He keeps adjusting the cloth, swapping it for a fresh, cool one when the first one gets warm. At some point, he texts Bailey again, keeping her updated. She replies with a flurry of heart and nurse emoji and a threat to deliver popsicles at dawn. He turns his phone face down after that, and the room becomes just breath and spoon and the intermittent shift of his weight when he resettles to keep my shoulder supported.

"Do you do this for everyone?" I ask sleepily when the bowl's half gone.

"What—make soup?" His mouth tips at one corner. "Only for the deserving."

"And the undeserving?"

"Toast," he says dryly, and I almost laugh soup into my sinuses.

He takes the empty bowl to the sink and returns with more water, then worries a wrinkle from the blanket with a thumb as if it offends him. I watch his hands and think ridiculous things: that they could hold a life and make a person feel easy in their skin.

The thought scares me, and I must show it, because he goes still. "What is it?"

"Nothing." I shake my head. "Everything." My voice thins. "I was supposed to go to Nashville tomorrow. Meet with Celeste. Be a good little brand."

His jaw ticks. "You don't."

"I know." I breathe once, slow, and the room lists a little less. "This"—I gesture at my fevered body, the way the walls keep doing a soft tide—"is probably just my immune system filing a complaint."

"Or your body saying the quiet part out loud."

I huff a tired laugh. "Since when do you talk like a therapist?"

"Since I figured out fences and people break the same if you overtighten them."

"You calling me a fence?"

"I'm calling you something worth mending right." He says it like the weather , and it lands like weight where I need it.

I look at him, at his steadiness, and the decision clicks into place with a relief that makes my eyes burn. "I'm not going," I say. No apology. No caveat. "I'm staying."

His shoulders ease a fraction. Not triumphant but relieved, like he's been holding a gate against the wind, and it finally latched. "Good," he says simply. "Then the only thing you need to do tonight is sleep."

"I'll text her." I fumble for my phone, thumbs clumsy but sure. *Not coming tomorrow. Health first. Don't schedule anything without my consent.* I hit send before I can massage it into something palatable. The whoosh feels like dropping a stone I've been carrying too long.

I set the phone face down and meet his eyes. "There. Official."

He nods, the approval quiet and warm. "The rest can wait."

"It scares me how much I want this"—I swallow—"to stay simple."

"It's allowed to be," he says. "Here, it is."

I sink back into the pillow. The cool cloth kisses my forehead. His fingers adjust it like it matters where the corner lies. I already have his number memorized—cell and the stupid landline that sounds like it's been ringing since the nineties—but what steadies me is the way he's looking at me now, like he means it when he says he'll be right here.

"Try to sleep," he adds, voice low. "I'm not going anywhere."

"You don't have to sit guard."

"I know." With a half smile, quick and real, he nods toward the blue case on the table. "And if you need more than soup and stubborn, I'll handle it."

The laugh that escapes me is soft and scratchy. I let my eyes close, his palm settling lightly over my wrist like a promise, and for the first time all day, my body believes me when I tell it we're staying.

I close my eyes. The room shifts from bright to dim as the sky moves outside. Time warps the way it does when you're sick and somebody else has their hand on the wheel. I drift. Wake to the scrape of a chair being pulled closer. Drift again to the sound of him talking low on the phone—Bailey, I think—assuring her he's got it, that I've eaten, and my fever's trending down. Once, I wake to a cool hand smoothing hair off my face, and I want to cry with the simple kindness of it.

"Rowan?" My voice is a rumple of blankets. I don't open my eyes.

"I'm here."

"Can you—" The request is ridiculous and small and costs me more than it should. "Will you stay?"

The chair creaks. Warmth moves closer, then his palm

wraps loosely around my wrist, heavy and steady where it rests on the blanket. "I'm not going anywhere, Ivy."

I let that sentence sink into me. It threads through tight places and loosens them. Somewhere in the house, a floorboard pops as the temperature falls. A night bird calls. His thumb drifts absently, barely there, over the inside of my wrist, counting a rhythm my body wants to match.

I sleep.

I surface once in the dark to the sound of rain. I must've asked for the window. The air is wetter, cooler, the scent of petrichor winding into the room. My throat hurts less. My head hurts the same. I turn my face toward the sound and crack my eyes.

He's there on the chair, long legs stretched out, nodding off despite the awkward angle, hand still on my wrist like a promise he forgot to remove. The porch light paints his profile in soft gold—the stubborn line of his nose, the cut of his jaw, and the tired kindness in the set of his mouth even asleep.

Something in my chest expands so fast it's almost pain.

"Rowan?" It's barely air.

His eyes open. He tightens his hand, a reflex. "You okay?"

"Yeah." I find a smile. "You look uncomfortable."

"I've slept on worse." He sits forward, elbows on his knees, close enough that I can feel the heat off him. "More water?"

"In a minute." I swallow. "Thank you."

"For what?"

"For making soup. For not hovering and somehow still not letting me be alone." I wet my lips. "For this."

His gaze drops to where his hand covers mine on the blanket, then comes back to my face like he's landed on a plan. "How do you feel about a bath?" he asks, voice low and sure.

"A what now?"

"The clawfoot in the hall holds heat like a furnace," he says, already rising. "Steam'll help. Epsom salts if you can smell past the fever. I'll make it hot, and you tell me when to stop."

I should say I can manage. I don't. "Okay."

He squeezes my fingers once and disappears down the hall. Pipes groan, water roars into porcelain, cupboard doors thump softly. Lavender drifts back—wild, clean—like a hand smoothing my hair.

He returns, crouches, and slides one arm behind my shoulders, the other beneath my knees. "May I?"

"Yes." Too fast.

He gathers me like I weigh nothing and stands, steady as the house itself. The room wobbles, then my cheek finds his chest—cedar, soap, summer air—and the wobble quits.

Steam curls from the tub as he nudges the door with his shoulder. Bubbles crowd the rim; two towels wait warming on a chair. He thinks of everything.

"Too hot?" he asks, lowering me so my fingers can test the surface.

"Perfect."

He sets me on the closed lid, steadying me until I'm sure

I'll stay. "Clean T-shirt and a robe on the hook," he says, studying the ceiling like it's suddenly fascinating. "I'll be right outside. Knock or say my name if you get lightheaded."

"You're very bossy."

"Only when it's useful." He waits a beat, then murmurs, "Take your time."

The door stays a sliver open—trust and safety in an inch of light. I undress slowly, knot my hair, and ease in. The heat takes me whole. Muscle by muscle, the ache lets go. The lavender settles my pulse like a lullaby.

"You still with me?" he asks after a minute, like he can hear my exhale catch.

"Mmm. Might never leave."

"Good," he says, smiling in the word. "Give me five minutes' warning so I can bring water."

Steam ghosts the mirror. When the fever fog lifts a notch, I call his name.

He knocks once and eases the door wider, eyes on the far wall, a glass of cold water in one hand and a chipped enamel pitcher in the other. "You've got half the tub on your head," he says gently, noticing the crown of bubbles clinging to my hair. "Can I help you rinse? Less work if you don't have to dunk."

I should be embarrassed, but I'm not. "Please."

He rolls his sleeves, keeping his gaze steady and high. A small towel appears from nowhere, and he lays it across my collarbones like a barber's cape—modesty without fanfare— then kneels by the clawfoot. "Lean back for me," he murmurs, sliding one forearm beneath my neck so the curve of his wrist cradles my head. "Tell me if it's too hot. The pressure okay?"

The first warm pour is heaven. He works his fingers through my hair in slow, sure strokes—care, not choreography. Lavender blooms again under his hands, and the ache behind my eyes loosens like a knot finally yielding. He massages the temples with his thumbs, gentle circles that make my lungs remember how to fill. Another pour. Another. He squeezes the ends, rinses until the water runs clear, then pats along my hairline with the towel like he's erasing the last of the day.

"Head up," he says softly, twisting the towel into a loose turban that smells like sun and cotton. "Got you."

He offers the towel without looking, then helps me to my feet, and when the room tilts, his hand is already at my waist to steady me. The warm robe lands over my shoulders like a promise.

He crouches to slip thick socks onto my feet—quiet, matter-of-fact care that undoes me more than any grand gesture. Then he bends, scoops me up again, and carries me back down the hall.

"I'm staying right here tonight," I murmur into his shoulder, meaning more than the room.

"I know." His cheek brushes my hair. "Rest. The world can wait."

He carries me past the living room and turns left instead of right, shoulder nudging a door open. His room is spare and steady—light blue walls, a plain quilt the color of wheat, and a window cracked for rain. It smells like clean cotton and him.

He lowers me onto his bed—fresh sheet, fresh blanket, pillow just so—and tucks the warm towel around my calves. The mattress gives in a way the couch never could, and my whole body sighs without asking permission. He leaves for a moment, then sets a glass of water and a small plate of crackers on the nightstand, like he's thought three steps ahead of me all evening.

"Thank you," I whisper.

"For what?"

"For everything. For... staying."

"That part's easy," he says, eyes steady on mine. "It's what I do. I'll wake you up to give you another dose of medicine later."

He clicks the lamp down to a soft halo, then drags a folded blanket to the floor beside the bed and settles with his back to the frame, one shoulder within reach—close but not crowding. I slide my hand over the edge until my fingers find his. He doesn't startle. His palm turns, warm and broad, thumb skimming the back of my knuckles once, calm and sure.

Rain begins its patient tapping along the eaves. Heat lingers on my skin, lavender in my hair, his presence a counterweight on the rope I've been gripping too tightly. My eyes fall shut. The last thing I feel before sleep takes me is his thumb tracing that slow circle, keeping time with a house—and a man—that hold steady.

Chapter Eleven

ROWAN

I was seventeen. It was the end of summer, hot and humid, and we'd just finished rodeo practice. The sky was streaked with orange. I remember the way she looked under the bleachers—nervous, excited, like the whole world was balanced on the edge of her words.

"I got in," she said. "Early program. Music school in Nashville."

I was stunned. "Why didn't you tell me?"

She smiled, a tight little thing. "Because I want you to come with me."

The air had gone still. My heart jumped into my throat. "Marissa..."

"I'm serious, Rowan. We'll figure it out. I can sing. You can work anywhere. We'll make it. Just say yes."

But I didn't. I couldn't.

"My whole life's here."

"You mean your dad's life. Your siblings'. You don't owe them forever."

I remember how angry she looked. Like I'd betrayed her just by wanting to stay. When I didn't say anything, she nodded like she already knew the answer. And then she walked away, straight into someone else's arms.

Two months later, she was pregnant. And the town whispered *my* name first. Too bad it was the furthest thing from the truth.

I still remember the look in my best friend, Brady's, eyes the first time he saw me after the facts came out. I wanted to deck him. Wanted to burn everything down.

But I didn't. Because, by then, the damage was done. Because the baby wasn't mine—but the shame still was.

People assumed. Small towns do that. Marissa never corrected them, not at first. She said she needed time. That she was confused.

By the time anyone knew the truth, I'd already buried myself in guilt and isolation. I pulled away. From her. From Brady. From everyone.

I stayed here. Fixed fences. Worked cattle. Harvested crops. Shut down any part of me that remembered what it was like to believe in more.

And now Ivy's here, and I'm doing my damnedest not to repeat it. But the past has a crazy way of holding you back when you want nothing more but to move forward.

I sink beside the tree, knees digging into the dirt. I let my head fall back against the bark and close my eyes. Her face flashes behind my eyelids. Ivy in the bath. Voice trembling. Eyes wide.

When I least expect it, flashes of my past with Marissa meld themselves with the photos I've seen of Ivy and Crew. So much so that I spent the entire night lying on my hard floor, unable to tell the two apart. By the time I wake, I'm in a completely different state of mind than the one I had gone to bed with.

And I fucking hate it.

I press the heel of my hand against my chest. This ache—I thought it was anger. I thought I was trying to protect myself. But it's grief, and it's mine.

I'm punishing Ivy for a past she had nothing to do with. And the worst part? I feel more for her than I ever let myself feel for Marissa. More than I want to admit.

Back at the house, I scrub my hands at the kitchen sink. My shirt's damp, stained from hours of walking and chopping wood to burn off the adrenaline.

My phone buzzes on the counter. I snatch it up without thinking, pulse racing like a fool, hoping—Crew.

I almost don't answer. But something in my gut twists, so I pick up.

"You alright?" he asks without preamble.

I lean onto the counter, knowing he's figured I've seen the newest set of images. Jealousy flickers—a mean little match—but I kill it with a breath. "Yeah."

A beat. I can hear film on turf in the background, and somebody laughing too loudly. Then quieter, he asks, "Is she?"

"That's not my place to answer."

Crew doesn't fill the space with noise. He never has. "Okay," he says. "Then I'll ask it this way. Do I need to be worried about her?"

I rub the bridge of my nose and look down the hall where the bedroom lamp glows low. "You don't need to be worried about her safety," I say, careful. "She's... wrung out. I'm handling what I can handle."

He exhales. "Good. The newest photos—" His voice hardens. "They aren't from the other day. They're old. From a charity dinner. PR tossed them back in circulation because someone saw her 'off the grid' and wanted to control the narrative. I told them to pull it."

The tight band around my ribs loosens a notch. I let my jaw unclench. "Copy."

"And before you turn that into me staking a claim—don't." He pauses. "I care about her. Not like that. But I do care. You hearing me?"

"I hear you." The words are gravel and truth. "I didn't love seeing them."

"I know," he says, gentler. "You're not built for that game. She isn't either, not really. She plays it because people like me told her it keeps the wheels on."

I steady my voice. "You calling to clear your name or check on her?"

"Both," he says, honest as a whistle. "And to say—if you're in this, be in it for real. She doesn't need more half-truths. She needs steady."

My throat works. I stare at the condensation ring my jar

left on the counter, at my own hand braced in the circle like I'm swearing to something. "I'm trying."

"Trying is good," he says, "but you've got that Wright talent for holding the door open and standing in the doorway so no one can tell whether they're welcome or not."

That lands.

He goes quiet, then adds, "I can tell you one more thing without crossing a line. She's been fighting to breathe for a long time. If she's breathing easier there, don't make her feel dumb for it."

I look at the hallway again, at the curl of lamplight on the floorboards, at the edge of a blanket I carried from the dryer to the bed. "I won't."

"Good." He clears his throat. "And, Ro?"

"Yeah."

"I'm not your competition. If it ever looked like that, I'm sorry. I won't let my name be used to mess with her head. Or yours."

I let out a breath I didn't realize I'd been rationing. "Appreciate it."

"Always," he says, warmth under the word. "One last thing, then I'll get out of your hair. You don't have to say much but say the part that matters."

"The part that matters," I repeat, tasting the shape of it.

"You know it," he says. "You're just stubborn. Must run in the family."

"Must." I scrub a hand over my jaw. "She's sleeping," I

add before I can talk myself out of giving him anything. "Fever broke. That's all I'm saying."

"That's enough," he says, relief bleeding through. "Thanks."

We sit in the soft crackle of the line like kids on the porch steps after lights-out.

"You going to be around tomorrow?" he asks.

"Here," I say. "Same as always."

"Then be here," he says. "On purpose."

I nod even though he can't see it. "Night, Crew."

"Night, Ro."

I end the call and set the phone face down. The house settles around me.

Say the part that matters.

The sky is fully dark by the time I walk back to the guest cottage. The gravel crunches under my boots, each step heavier than the last.

After an unanswered knock, worry fills me, and I open the door to be met with a snoozing Ivy lying across her bed with a guitar resting beside her that she borrowed from Bailey when she stopped by this morning. Ivy refused to rest in the main house, and before I could argue, she was waddling back to the cottage on her own.

Just the faint scent of peach lotion and the ghost of something that felt like home for a moment. I stand there, chest caving in slow breaths.

I want to carry her back to my bed, but I don't want to press my luck like I did the night before. Instead, I grip the quilt on the back of the couch and lay it across her body.

Gripping the guitar by the neck, I haul it over to the small table, resting it on top with more care than I usually give the musical instrument.

On the bed, Ivy squirms, gripping the blanket in her fist and tugging it closer to her chin. By instinct, I gently rest my palm against her forehead, testing her temperature, which is still warmer than I'd like, but I know sleep is the most important thing I can give her right now.

Gently closing the cottage door behind me, I take a steadying breath. Every part of me wants to be at her side, but she chose to spend it alone today. Something about me taking care of her last night shifted things between us.

The single-seater porch swing creaks in the wind.

I cross to it out of habit, dropping down hard enough that the chain groans. I stare out at the darkening pasture, elbows on my knees, hands laced together like I'm praying to the ghosts of all the mistakes I've made.

And I've made more than I want to count.

I never meant to be this man—the one who lets the best thing to happen to him wonder where they stand to the point they walk away. Unfortunately, that's who I am.

The porch light flickers on beside me. I didn't even realize I flipped the switch.

It illuminates the empty path to the main house.

I press my palms to my face.

Marissa was the first person I ever loved. The first person I trusted with the softer parts of me. And when she left... when she shattered everything we were with one choice, I learned not to offer those parts to anyone again.

Not without cost. Not without hesitation.

I learned that love didn't mean forever. That sometimes people choose their dreams over you. That sometimes they gave up and never looked back.

Ivy wasn't supposed to be anything. Just a beautiful stranger in a ditch. A problem to fix. Yet somehow, she cracked me wide open.

Her laughter. Her bite. Her impossible softness. The way she looked at this broken-down life I built and made it feel like something worth keeping.

She never asked me to change, but God, she made me want to.

And I'm afraid I'm subconsciously punishing her for it.

I swing back and forth once, twice, the old wood moaning beneath the weight of everything I haven't said.

I should have told her she mattered. That she's more than a headline or a PR stunt or whatever the hell Celeste trained her to be.

I should've told her she made me feel again.

Instead, I'm afraid I'll back her into the category I understand: temporary. Because permanent terrifies me. Because building something real takes guts I'm not sure I have.

Because if I build it, and it crumbles? That's on me.

But maybe I've been looking at it wrong. Maybe the real mistake isn't trusting people. Perhaps the mistake is refusing to try.

I push up from the swing, restless energy crawling under my skin. My boots hit the steps hard. I need to move. To do something. To stop sitting in this damn silence that only reminds me of what I lost.

I head toward the barn, my phone's flashlight beam catching on the edges of fence posts and feed buckets, the horses tossing their heads restlessly in the dark. They sense it too. The shift. The unsettled air.

I lean against the stall door, brushing my palm down Maple's nose.

"She's good for us, isn't she, girl?"

The mare huffs softly, nudging my shoulder.

"Yeah. I think so, too."

It's stupid, talking to a horse like this. But it feels safer than admitting it out loud to anyone else. Holt would listen. So would Lila. Hell, even Dad might surprise me.

But Ivy—she deserves to hear it from me. Before she decides I'm not enough.

I leave the barn, the wind sharper now, pulling at the edges of my shirt as I head back toward the main house.

Inside, I dive straight for the living room, dropping onto the couch and yanking the throw blanket over my lap even though I'm not cold.

The lamp near the window glows a soft yellow. I stare at the guesthouse through the glass, my reflection ghosting back at me.

It's too quiet. Too still.

I think about the camp again.

I've been letting the idea die slowly, one unspoken fear at a time. What if it fails? What if I can't give those kids what they need? What if I let them down?

What if I let Ivy down?

Is that it? Maybe I don't want to build it without her. She saw something in me before I saw it in myself. And perhaps that's what real love is—someone who believes in your best parts even when you're terrified they don't exist.

I lean back, one arm flung over my eyes. Marissa wrecked me. Now I'm just a man in the aftermath, trying to find his way back. Because I'm done letting the past decide who I get to love. And I think I've already made my choice.

Chapter Twelve

IVY

The minute I close the cottage door, I tape a hand-lettered note dead center where anyone with eyes can't miss it.

PLEASE DON'T KNOCK. I'M RESTING / WRITING / TRYING NOT TO FALL APART. TEXT ME IF IT'S IMPORTANT.

Bailey helped me pick the wording over text—*kind, clear, a little funny,* she said. I added the last line because honesty has to count for something. The paper looks ridiculous under the sweet brass heron lamp and the whitewashed planks Rowan sanded smooth himself, but I need the boundary more than I need aesthetic harmony.

The cottage breathes around me—quiet, pine soap, and clean cotton, and the faintest echo of hay from my sandals by the door. The bed is made like a promise. The little kitchenette hums. Outside, the cicadas start their sermon, and a dragonfly shoulders the heat like it's paid to. I should be fine. I'm not.

I'm not because three nights ago, a man who doesn't run from anything ran me a bath and washed my hair with the care of someone handling a relic. He carried me to his bed like weight has never meant burden. He slept on the floor with one hand curled around mine and didn't move when I woke and pressed his knuckles to my cheek like a talisman.

No one has taken care of me like that. Not in years. Maybe not ever.

Now I can't tell whether my skin is hot from the fever I finally outran or from the memory of his palm smoothing the towel over my shoulder blades. I only know that every cell in me—tired, wobbly, lavender-scented—keeps turning toward the house like a sunflower toward light.

So I do the only thing I trust to sort the knot. I make tea strong enough to stand a spoon, tuck my hair in a braid, open my notebook, and write until my hand cramps.

The first pages are garbage. Lines that read like notes to myself from a hospital hallway—*you're okay, keep breathing, don't flinch when the world asks you to perform calm.* Then a melody threads through that sounds like rain on a tin roof. Then a chorus that says *stay* without saying his name. I chase it until my eyes blur.

My phone buzzes across the table.

Bailey: Leaving you a basket on the step
in 10 (soup + honey + my last two scones
because I love you). No opening the door
or I'll mace you with elderberry syrup.

I huff a laugh that's really a breath of relief.

Me: You're a saint and a tyrant.

Bailey: Both can be true. Hydrate or I text
Mrs. W.

I could argue, but I don't. I set a timer for water and go back to the page.

Twenty minutes later, the boards on the porch whisper under a careful weight. I stand—because I can't not—and watch from the kitchen window. The basket is there (gingham cloth, of course Bailey), and then there's another shape, broader, framed by the oak's shade. Dark tee, ball cap, forearms clean and nicked. Rowan sets a Mason jar beside the basket like he's leaving a peace offering to a skittish animal. He doesn't try the handle. Doesn't call my name. Just looks at the note for a beat, tips two fingers to the brim of his cap like a promise kept, and walks back down the steps.

The tea in my mug goes cool while I stand suspended in that small, ridiculous grace. I should be the one who knows about cameras and angles and lines you don't cross. He's the one teaching me that quiet can say more than any speech.

I slide the basket inside with a toe and read Bailey's Post-its stuck to everything like leaf tags.

soup: heat low and slow, no boiling (you're not pasta).

scones: eat now, apologize never.

honey: from Wildflower Stan, medicine + dessert.

PS: if you don't text me by 4 pm with ✌ I'm breaking your "do not disturb" and bringing soup sirens.

I text the peace-sign emoji. I add a heart. Bailey responds with fifteen more hearts and a GIF of a woman fanning herself with a church bulletin. My laugh lands in the quiet and stays.

I eat half a scone on the floor with my back against the cabinet, knees up, notebook balanced on my thighs. The song keeps tugging at my sleeve. By midafternoon, there are three verses and a bridge that remembers the shape of his hand on the back of my knuckles and the small circle his thumb traced in the dark like he was keeping time with my breath.

When the sun slants to that late hour where everything turns honey thick, I drive to the market because I need produce and a human face that isn't mine in a mirror.

Coral Bell Cove's farmers' market is the least anonymous place on earth—four dozen people, two dozen folding tables, and one hundred percent certainty that someone will know the way you take your coffee. I keep my sunglasses on for the drive and slip them up when I step under the awning because the kind of attention here isn't the kind that needs a shield. Neighbor eyes. Soft and nosy but hopeful.

I see the jars first—honey like a bottled sunset under a hand-painted sign: **Stan & June's Bees (the bees did the work, we're just proud).** Then tomatoes so red they look like they're daring you. Then Mrs. Wright.

I don't collide with her. Instead, I stop three feet away like a sensible person, and still she reaches for my forearm the way she did when I met her in passing at the wedding, like she's glad I'm tangible.

"Ivy." Her smile sits in the corners of her eyes, where kindness lives. "You look better."

"It's the braid," I say because I still haven't learned how to accept simple care without a joke.

"It's the rest," she corrects gently. "You getting enough?"

"Trying."

"Mm-hmm." She tilts her head toward Stan's jars. "Make sure you take one. Bailey tells me you've acquired a taste."

"I'm being blackmailed with elderberry."

"She's a menace," Mrs. Wright says fondly. "Come here." She pulls me into a hug that smells like flour and line-dried sheets. I stand there stiff for exactly one second, and then I let myself lean into a mother who isn't mine and never will be yet somehow makes me feel like I'm allowed to be tired.

When she steps back, her voice goes conspiratorial. "You might as well know—he's been useless at pretending he's fine."

The he is unnecessary. My heart knows anyway. "I'm the

one with a note on the door that says 'do not disturb,'" I murmur.

"You can be tired and still miss someone," she says, like she's handing me permission on a paper plate. "You can need rest and still choose. Both can be true."

I worry the strap of my tote. "I don't want to make his life harder."

"Do you make his life louder?" Her mouth quirks. "Yes. Harder? No. He knows his own mind, even when he's quiet about it."

I think of his hand around the Mason jar's middle; the thumbprint on the glass when I lifted it later, cool and sweating in my palm. I swallow. "Thank you. For... not treating me like a headline."

She snorts. "I live with men who forget their own birthdays unless someone writes it on the calendar. If you were a headline, I'd still need you to bring a dessert to the potluck."

I buy a jar of wildflower honey and two peaches that smell like July. Mrs. Wright tucks a small bag of pecans into my tote when I'm not looking. "For when you decide to bake something instead of running," she says, and pats my cheek like she's blessing me. "Tell Bailey to stop stealing my scone recipe."

"She would rather perish," I say solemnly.

"Figures."

On my way out, I pass Bailey herself, hair in a messy bun, book in hand. She points two fingers at her eyes, then at me. *"Drink water,"* she mouths. I mime a salute and mouth back, *"I'm okay."* She narrows her eyes, reads my pulse without touching me, and nods once.

Back at the cottage, I set the peaches on the counter and forget about them for an hour because the air is thick and the page is louder. The song turns its head and shows me a new angle—a minor climb that feels like walking toward a door you want opened and aren't sure you should knock on. I play it twice on the guitar I swore I would give back, but now I've grown fond of. The sound fills the small room, and something in my chest loosens like a stuck window.

As if summoned by music, boots thud on the porch boards. The door stays closed. The steps stop.

Silence lengthens. My skin prickles.

"Ivy?" His voice is a low question through wood. Gooseflesh ripples along my arms like I'm the field and wind just remembered my name.

I step closer, palms damp, throat dry. I stare at my own note, at the way the ink bled on the y. I should tell him to come back tomorrow. I should protect the little, fragile edge of peace I carved out. I should—

I open the door.

Rowan stands one step down, as if he made himself shorter before I thought to be afraid. Cap in his hand. T-shirt soft with wear. Eyes steady and sleepless. When his gaze drops to my mouth and returns politely to my eyes, I feel it everywhere I have a pulse.

"Hey," I say, because full sentences have abandoned me.

"Didn't want to ignore your sign," he answers, lifting a

Mason jar sweating with condensation. "Brought you more tea bags."

"I appreciate that." I keep one foot braced against the door because if I don't, I'll invite him into a very small room with a very large amount of unresolved tension.

"I can leave the canister on the rail."

Or I can stop pretending not seeing him is safer. "It's okay," I say. "You can... hand it to me."

He steps up one board. The porch light hasn't clicked on yet. The day's last amber is doing the work, slanting over his jaw, catching on the tiny white scar at his temple I've started measuring my restraint by. He passes me the jar. Our fingers don't touch. It still feels like a spark jumps, a low, clean heat that has nothing to do with summer. "How are you?" he asks, plain. Not a polite formality. A census of the soul.

"Better." It comes out true. "Hungry. Less feverish. Loud in my head."

The corner of his mouth thinks about lifting. "I can handle loud."

I don't know what to do with the ache that sentence wakes up, so I move. "I went to the market and saw your mom. She bribed me with pecans."

He huffs what might be a laugh. "Sounds like her."

"She said you were... being you." I watch his eyes for a flinch or a joke. Neither comes.

"I am," he says. The simplest admission. Then after a beat that feels like it contains three letters I can't bear to spell out, he says, "I heard music."

I glance at the guitar on the chair behind me. "I was just playing around."

He nods, accepting the lie for what it is: protection. "Sounded like you."

I hold the doorframe because my knees have decided to be dramatic. "You heard *me*?"

He studies me the way he studies the sky before a storm —attention sharpened, shoulders loose, ready to move if he needs to. "I heard steady," he says. "Even where it shook."

I can feel the words land under my sternum, warm as a hand. "I was sick," I say, because deflection is a reflex. "You... took care of that."

His jaw works once. He looks past me, over my shoulder, like the cottage might give him an answer. "You scared me," he says, just above a whisper. Not a confession he owes, but one he gives.

My chest goes tight and sweet. "I don't like scaring you."

"I don't like being scared." The honesty sits between us like a Mason jar on a porch rail, catching the light. "But I'll do it, if that's the cost of you being here."

There's a version of me who makes a joke. Another version runs. I do neither. I step onto the top board, closing the inch that has felt like a mile for days. Up close, I can see the gold ring of hazel in his eyes. My hand lifts like I've forgotten I own it. I don't touch him. I let the gravity do the work between our bodies until my throat remembers how to move.

"I'm not going anywhere," I say. "I mean—" I breathe. "I'm trying very hard to mean it."

He nods, once, relief crossing his face so quickly I almost miss it. Then his gaze tips to my mouth and stays there, and all the carefully stacked reasons to be cautious tilt.

The air gets crowded—fireflies starting up in the yard, a car in the distance, and my pulse in my ears. If he steps forward, if I lean, if one of us stops being so damn noble, I don't know where we'll stop.

A screen door slaps somewhere at the main house as a gust of wind picks up. The moment shivers and settles without breaking. Rowan steps back one board like he's saving us both from ourselves.

"Bailey said to tell you she'll drop biscuits in the morning," he says, voice steadying on neutral ground. "I told her you'd bite me if I woke you before nine."

"That's slander."

"That's survival." The corner of his mouth finally, finally lifts. It hits me like a warm front.

I curl my fingers around the basket handle so I don't do something reckless, like hook my hand in his shirt and pull him inside and let the whole question answer itself. "Thank you," I say, and I mean it for more than the delivery service. "For... the bath. The..." I swallow. "For staying."

He nods like I've offered him a job he wants. "It's what I do."

I step backward into the cottage before I say something irretrievable. "Good night, Rowan."

"Night, Ivy." He lifts a hand, palm open to the world, then lowers it to his side and turns toward the path. I stand in the doorway and watch him go until he turns at the fork: left for the house, right for me. He glances once over his shoulder, like a man confirming the stars are where he left them, and then the oaks take him.

Inside, the cottage is the same—and not. The air holds the ghost of his soap, or maybe I'm inventing it. The peaches on the counter glow like they know what they are. I pick up the guitar before the quiet gets ideas.

The chorus arrives whole.

> I don't need the city lights to find me,
> I don't need a headline to believe—
> Call it ordinary holy, call it honey on my
>   tongue,
> You say "stay," and every door in me un-
>   swings...

My throat catches on that last word because it's not real English, yet it's exactly right. By the time the moon ladders up the window frame, I have a song that's too soft for arenas and exactly right for porches. I nod to myself like a person choosing to choose.

I'm washing my mug when the world goes dark for a heartbeat—the bulb over the sink blinks, then comes back. Far off, thunder rolls lazily like a stagehand clearing his throat. The forecast said storms tomorrow. The air says sooner.

I dry the mug and set it upside down, then line it with its match like order will hold what feeling can't. Then I crawl into bed, still damp at the ends of my braid from an earlier shower, and stare at the ceiling fan while the first pinpricks of rain test the roof.

The last thing I think before sleep takes me is not a lyric, not a plan, not a worry I can hold up to the door like a badge.

It's his voice in my ear in the bath, low and sure. *The world can wait.*

Tonight, I let it.

Chapter Thirteen

ROWAN

The heat hangs thick in the air like something waiting to snap. I'm familiar with the feeling.

I've been dancing around Ivy all morning, both of us pretending we don't feel it. She's been in and out of the barn since sunrise, feeding the goats like it's the most natural thing in the world to be back here.

Like she never left.

But I haven't forgotten the pictures. And I haven't forgotten the silence that followed.

Still... when she passed me this morning with that tiny smile, a stray strand of hair caught on her bottom lip, and I had to stop myself from reaching out. From tucking it behind her ear. From dragging my thumb across the soft curve of her mouth.

Instead, I nodded. Silent. Guarded. Like always. It's safer that way. Except it isn't, and we both know it.

Especially not when her top sticks to her skin in this August heat, or when she hums under her breath while brushing one of the horses. She's a walking dare. And I'm not known for backing down from a challenge.

But damn if she doesn't scare the hell out of me. I don't know how to be around her without feeling like I'm going to combust.

And judging by the flush in her cheeks every time our arms brush or her voice catches on my name... she feels it, too.

Hell.

I wipe a hand across my forehead and shove my gloves into the back pocket of my jeans. The sky is too blue. The clouds are too still.

Something's coming. And I'm not just talking about her.

I head to the feed shed, grabbing the bolt cutter I'd meant to fix since May. Ivy perches on the fence across the pasture, legs swinging, that loose braid hanging over her shoulder like it's taunting me.

She waves. I grunt.

Progress.

I turn away before I say something I'll regret.

The radio crackles to life in the work truck, volume cranked low. At first, it's just static, then a voice cuts through—urgent and clipped.

"...dry brush fire reported near the edge of Mrs. Danner's property, off North Ridge Road. Volunteer responders requested. Fire crew is en route from Seabrook, ETA thirty minutes."

Shit.

I bolt for the truck, heart hammering.

Mrs. Danner lives less than two miles from here. Her pasture butts right up against ours in spots, and this time of year, it's bone-dry. All it would take is one spark—one careless flick of a cigarette—to light the place up.

I throw the door open and grab my gear—gloves, rope, shovel, and the old metal water buckets that rattle like hell in the truck bed.

"Let's go, let's go," I mutter, tossing in two spare hoses I keep coiled under the back seat, then I'm tearing down the gravel drive, dust spitting behind me like exhaust.

I hit the turn for Mrs. Danner's pasture doing forty, which is too fast for gravel, but not fast enough for what's ahead.

The smoke's already visible from the rise—a long gray smear climbing into the sky like a signal flare. I can smell it before I even park. That dry, metallic bite of burning brush mixed with scorched earth and panic.

I slam the truck into park and throw open the door.

A handful of familiar trucks are pulled up crooked near the old fence line. Volunteers. Local boys and old-timers who know the drill by now. We've all fought a handful of these over the years. Usually small. Sometimes worse.

Today's riding the edge.

Mrs. Danner stands off to the side, her hands fluttering uselessly as she paces in the tall grass. Her dog barks like it's got something personal against the fire.

"Rowan!" she yells. "It started from the back corner. Might've been the faulty tractor we had out here yesterday."

I nod, already dragging a hose from the back of my truck and uncoiling it toward the fence. "You get the animals out?"

"Goats and chickens are clear. But the wind's shifting."

Which is exactly what I don't want to hear.

"Keep back from the fence line," I call out, waving off her dog and jogging toward the edge where flames lick through dry grass like they're starving. The heat pulses in waves. Nothing too tall yet, but with enough wind, this could jump the ditch and head straight for the hay barn on our side of the ridge.

A few guys I recognize—Ben Carter, Derek from the hardware store—are already beating at the flames with wet feed sacks and shovels. It's half chaos, half coordination.

We've done worse with less.

I anchor one hose to the water tank I keep in the truck bed and pass another to Derek. It's warm. The pressure is weak, but it's something.

"Concentrate on the west end," I bark. "The wind's heading south. We keep it boxed in before it jumps the creek."

I'm soaked in sweat within minutes. Smoke fills my throat, my shirt sticks to my back, and the ground crackles under my boots like dry paper.

Someone yells about more buckets. Another voice calls out for gloves. It's a hell of a dance. And we're barely keeping ahead.

Then, out of the haze and heat, I hear her.

"I have towels!"

I turn, blinking through the smoke.

And there she is.

Ivy.

She's climbing out of her spaceship, balancing a plastic tote in her arms. She's wearing one of my flannel shirts over a white shirt, denim cutoffs, and scuffed boots that definitely aren't designer.

She looks like a goddamn angel.

Or a hallucination.

My jaw clenches. "What the hell are you doing here?"

She pushes past me, dumping the tote near the truck. "Wet towels. First aid. Bottled water. That guy over there is limping and needs ice. Don't argue with me."

I don't.

She disappears into the smoke before I can say another word, like she's been doing this all her life. Just not with me.

By the time the first fire engine rolls up, the worst of it's under control. Blackened patches smolder like dying coals, and the edge closest to the road is soaked through with bucket after bucket of water.

The Seabrook County crew steps in to finish containment and run a perimeter check. Their truck's lights swirl red over the grass, casting an eerie glow that feels more like relief than warning.

I lean against the tailgate of my truck, my shirt sticking to my skin, every muscle aching. But I don't feel it. Because she's standing five feet away.

Ivy.

Hands on her hips, cheeks streaked with soot, lips parted as she catches her breath.

She meets my eyes like she's daring me to say something. Anything.

"You shouldn't have come," I say, voice hoarse.

She walks closer, slowly. "I had to."

"No, you didn't."

"You needed help."

I shake my head. "I needed not to have to worry about you running headfirst into a damn brush fire."

She lifts her chin, unfazed. "I'm not fragile, Rowan."

"I didn't say you were."

"You implied it."

"I—" I scrub a hand over my face, hating how her presence scrambles every part of me. "You just shouldn't be here."

She steps in, close enough I can smell the smoke tangled in her hair. "You mean here at the fire... or here at all?"

I can't answer that.

I look at her. Really look. At the soot on her cheek. The stubborn set of her jaw. The way her hand twitches like she's debating whether to touch me.

And God help me, I want her to. I don't move. Don't breathe. Just... wait. Then her fingers brush my wrist. Just a featherlight touch and the dam nearly breaks. My heart kicks in my chest. My throat tightens.

"Ivy—"

A voice behind us cuts through the moment.

"Danner's fence line is good, but the north corner's still steaming."

We both turn away from each other like we weren't about to fall into something dangerous.

She grabs a bottle of water and tosses it to me. "Try not to collapse before dinner."

I catch it, unscrewing the cap with shaking fingers as she smiles and walks away.

The drive back to the farm is quiet in the way two vehicles can be—her headlights pinned to my tailgate and my eyes flicking to the mirror every few seconds to make sure she's still there. Smoke rides home with us, caught in my shirt and in the crease where her neck met her collarbone when I saw her by the field—ash smeared there, a thin scrape above her knee. I slow for the washboard ruts, throw my blinker on early at the lane so she doesn't miss the turn, and keep the speed steady like a hand on the small of a back.

Gravel chatters under my tires as I pull into the drive and swing wide so she can tuck in by the cottage. We kill our engines within the same breath. Two doors thud open into the quiet, and we meet in the heat-hazed space between our vehicles. She's got that brave face on—chin up, mouth set.

"You okay?" I ask, already scanning.

"Physically? Sure." She huffs a laugh that's more air than humor. "Emotionally? Ask me in an hour."

"Come on." I tip my head toward the porch. "Let's get that cleaned."

We fall into step. She keeps her arms folded, like she's holding something inside in place. I keep my hands loose at my sides so I don't reach for her too soon. The boards complain under our weight. A moth pings the porch light. We don't say anything until the screen door sighs us into the kitchen.

"Sink," I say, dragging a chair out with my boot. "First aid's in the drawer."

She perches, one knee bent, the other leg extended. Up close, the scrape looks worse—angry and embedded with fine grit. I set the kit on the table, wash my hands at the sink, then glance back. "Can I?"

She uncrosses her arms and nods. "Yeah."

I kneel. The kitchen smells like smoke and dish soap and her. "This'll sting."

"When has that ever stopped me?"

I wet a clean cloth and start slow, swiping away ash and dirt in careful arcs. She flinches once, breath catching. My fingers are steady on either side of her knee until the reflex passes. Her skin is warm under the pads of my thumbs. My awareness of that is a problem I pretend I don't have.

"You didn't have to come," I say, keeping my eyes on the scrape.

"I know." Her voice softens. "I did anyway."

"You scared me." The words slip out before I can dress it up.

"Why?" she challenges, not unkind.

Because you're mine to worry about lives right behind my teeth, too loud, too soon. I take the safer road. "Because people panic near fire. You didn't. Still doesn't mean I liked seeing you that close."

After a beat, she murmurs, "I grew up around people who expected me to be strong. Even when I wasn't."

I dab again, gentler. "You were smart out there." I meet her eyes briefly, enough for the truth. "And brave."

Something eases in her shoulders. "You're not used to people showing up for you, are you?"

I look back down and reach for the saline. "Not like that."

The spray makes her hiss. I lean in and blow cool air across the sting without thinking. Her hand curls into the edge of the chair. Mine tightens—briefly—on her calf.

"Sorry," I mutter.

"Don't be." Her voice is just above a whisper.

I pat the skin dry, swipe a thin line of antibiotic ointment, then smooth a large bandage over the worst of it, palm lingering a second longer than medically necessary. The air goes thick and careful. The kitchen clock ticks too loud.

"All patched," I say, voice a notch lower.

She tips her head, studying me like I'm a map she's finally learning to trust. "Thank you."

"Thank *you*, Ivy."

Her mouth pulls into a small, tired smile. "You'll return the favor when I inevitably do something else reckless?"

"Already did." I nod toward the counter. "Water's there. Sit a minute."

She reaches for the glass, our fingers skimming. It's nothing—barely contact—but heat pricks up my arm like I stuck my hand too close to the burner. She feels it too. I see it in the way her breath stalls.

"Ivy," I say, because saying her name buys me a second to pick the right truth, "I'm not good at this part."

"What part?" She holds my gaze.

"The part where I want to wrap you in bubble wrap and also stand back and let you be exactly who you are." I scrub a hand over my jaw. "I'm trying to get it right."

Her lips part. The kitchen gets smaller. "You're doing fine."

I nod once because if I say more, I'll say everything. I ease her foot to the floor, slowly sliding away my fingers. She doesn't move for a beat, then sets the empty glass down, the soft click as loud as a promise.

"I should get cleaned up," she says, glancing toward the cottage through the window's dark pane.

"I'll walk you." My voice comes out rougher than I mean.

We step back onto the porch. The path forks—left to the house, right to the oak and her door. Two pools of light spill onto the gravel, gold halos almost touching. We stop at the seam where they don't.

"Thank you, Rowan." Her eyes shine, not with tears—something steadier. "For the knee. For... earlier."

I tip my chin. "Anytime."

She takes one small step backward into her pool of light. I stay in mine. Our shoulders almost brush where the glow overlaps. Her fingers twitch like she might reach across the gap. Mine do the same.

"Good night," she says, soft as a secret.

"Night, Ivy."

She turns, and I let her go the last few yards alone, the crunch of her steps fading under the hum of cicadas. I stand there until her porch light flips on and her shadow moves across the curtain. Only then do I breathe, slow and careful, like a man who knows the thing he almost touched is still right there, waiting.

My limbs are heavy, like they've absorbed all the heat of the flames we just fought. Or maybe I'm just carrying too much—too much anger, too much regret, too much want.

I toe off my boots and strip off the smoke-stained T-shirt, the collar stiff with ash and sweat. The muscles in my back pull tight when I reach for the hem. Everything aches, but not in a bad way. It's the ache of being alive. The ache of coming close to something I've been too scared to want: Ivy Quinn. That damn woman with fire in her soul and a mouth that tastes like sin. I head straight for the shower, twisting the knob hard until steam pours out in thick curls. The mirror fogs up before I even step inside. The hot water hits my shoulders like a wall, searing and brutal. I close my eyes and let it burn. I need it to. Need to scrub away the scent of smoke. The feel of panic. The adrenaline. But I also need to forget the way her lips parted right before I barely brushed my lips against hers. The breath she caught in her throat. The quiet plea in her voice when she said *kiss me* like it means something. Christ.

I brace both hands against the tile wall, water running down my spine in rivulets. My forehead drops between my arms.

It shouldn't have happened. She was Crew's. Sort of. n ot really. But *once.* The unspoken rule alone should be enough.

Except she came back.

Except she showed up at that fire like she belonged beside me. Like we were something worth fighting for.

And when she leaned in... God. My body knew hers before my brain caught up.

The flash of heat. The *rightness* of it. I twist under the spray, jaw clenched so tight it aches. My chest heaves.

I want her. I haven't let myself admit it—not fully.

But there's no hiding it now. Not when I'm rock-hard under the water, pulsing with need.

It's not just the way she looks—though, damn, I could lose my mind staring at her mouth alone. It's the way she moves. The way she *sees* me.

Like I'm more than a past I don't talk about. Like I'm not broken in ways even I can't name.

I imagine her stepping into this shower. The steam curling around her skin. Her hands sliding up my chest. Her voice low, whispering my name as she presses her curves against me.

I reach down, grip tight around the ache that's been building since that kiss.

A breath escapes my lips.

It's her face I see behind my eyes. Her breathy laugh. The way her lashes flutter when she's nervous. The heat in her eyes when she dares me to close the distance as I wrap my fingers around my throbbing shaft.

I stroke slow and steady. Let the water drown out everything else. She'd be warm against me. Soft and sweet and strong enough to ruin me.

I'd push her against this wall, press my mouth to hers, trace every inch of her with my hands and tongue. I'd whisper all the things I've never said aloud—how I see her. How I *want* her. Not just in the heat of this moment, but in the quiet after.

In the mornings when her hair's a mess and she wears oversized T-shirts and hums songs under her breath like she did in the cottage kitchen that first day.

My hand tightens, pace picking up.

I want to know how she tastes when she's mine. Want to hear her say my name like it's the only word she remembers. I groan, low and rough, the sound echoing off the tile. It doesn't take long. The tension coils. Snaps.

I brace a hand on the wall, eyes squeezed shut, breath ragged as everything inside me shudders loose.

When it's done, I lean against the tile, chest heaving, forehead wet with sweat and steam.

And still, she's there. In my head. In my chest. In *me*.

I rinse off fast, then shut off the water. Wrap a towel around my hips and move through the dark house barefoot and dripping. I don't turn on any lights. Because I know what I'll see if I do.

The empty porch swing. The space beside me where she should be. The ache that lingers long after release.

I fall into bed still damp, towel half loose around my waist, hair wet against the pillow.

Sleep doesn't come.

Not with Ivy etched into every thought, every beat of my heart.

Chapter Fourteen

IVY

The ache in my body is a slow, deliberate thrum—like a warning bell in my muscles, reminding me that I spent the night before hauling wet towels, dragging buckets, and running across a field that had no business being that steep.

I'd expected soreness. What I hadn't expected was the other ache—low, persistent, and entirely Rowan's fault.

Or maybe it's my imagination.

Because I swear, just after I ran back to my car to get my phone that I'd stupidly left in the cup holder, I'd turned to head back to the guest cottage under the cover of night, when I heard him. A groan. Deep. Guttural. One that had no business being that filthy unless someone was doing something filthy.

And I haven't stopped thinking about it since.

Now, as I tiptoe around the small kitchen, trying to

pour tea without spilling it down my tank top, the image won't leave me alone.

Rowan. Naked. In the shower. Water sluicing over every inch of that strong, broad body. His hand wrapped around himself, jaw clenched, breath stuttering out as he thinks about—

"Dammit," I mutter, burning my tongue on the first sip.

It's too early for these thoughts.

Too early to be staring out the window toward the main house, hoping to catch a glimpse of him moving past the kitchen window, shirtless and smug like nothing happened yesterday. Like he didn't nearly kiss me. Like I didn't nearly let him.

I set the mug down harder than necessary, the sound echoing off the small counter. This back-and-forth is giving me whiplash.

It's not just the lust swimming in my bloodstream. It's the confusion. The push and pull. The way he looks at me like he's starving, then closes the door in my face.

The way I came back here thinking maybe—just maybe —he'd be waiting. And all I got was silence.

Fine.

If he wants to act like nothing has happened between us, then I'll confront him like something did. Because I'm tired of pretending. Tired of playing nice and tiptoeing around the burn in my chest every time he walks away without looking back.

I throw on a loose button-down over my tank and head out, not bothering to brush the sleep from my eyes. The morning air is sharp, biting against my legs as I stomp across the gravel toward the barn.

And of course, there he is.

Rowan stands beside the feed bins, sleeves shoved up to his shoulders, sweat already darkening the collar of his T-shirt even though it's barely nine. He's wrestling a wheelbarrow like it insulted his mother, muscles flexing with every motion.

He doesn't see me at first.

Which is probably a good thing, because I need a second to collect the breath he's knocked from my lungs. Even angry—maybe especially angry—he's devastating.

"Rowan," I call, louder than I mean to.

His shoulders stiffen before he turns. Smoke shadows still cling to his jaw, shirt damp at the collar, pitchfork biting the earth. "Morning," he says, clipped.

That's it. *Morning.*

After last night—the way he stood between me and the fire, the way his hand found the small of my back when the wind shifted, the way he cleaned the grit from my knee like it was his own skin—he gives me 'morning'?

I close the distance, not bothering to hide the heat in my voice. "We're just... pretending none of that happened?"

He keeps working a beat too long, like the soil suddenly matters more than oxygen. "Not sure what you mean."

"Oh, I think you do." I fold my arms and plant my feet. "The part where you hovered near enough to catch me if I fell and then acted like you didn't. The part where you watched me like I was a storm you wanted and feared at the same time."

His eyes lift, guarded. "Don't make it into something it's not, Ivy."

"Then what is it?" Softer now, because the bravado is just scaffolding over something far more breakable. "Because you carry me when I'm sick, you show up when things burn, and then you talk to me like we're strangers at the feed store."

The pitchfork teeth thud into the dirt. He drags a hand over his scruff, like the rasp might buy him time. "It's not that simple."

"Try me."

He exhales like he's been holding up the sky all morning. When he speaks, it lands low and unvarnished. "You terrify me."

I blink. "What?"

"You come into this place—into my life—like a spark I didn't ask for. Now everything smells like smoke." His mouth flattens, then loosens. "I think about you when I'm counting fence posts. When I'm supposed to be sleeping. When I'm not supposed to be thinking at all. And I hate it because I know where wanting has taken me before."

"You don't know me," I say, even though part of me aches at how much he already does.

"I know enough." His voice snags on the last word. "I know I'm the guy who stays. And I know you've got a whole world that doesn't look anything like this one."

I take a step closer. The air between us tightens, humming. "Then stop pretending it doesn't matter."

He doesn't answer.

"Tell me you don't want me, Rowan," I whisper. "Say it, and I'll walk away."

Silence.

"Say it," I demand, voice shaking.

But he doesn't. He just *looks* at me. And then he *moves*.

One step forward. One rough hand curling around my wrist, pulling me into him. His mouth hovers over mine, breath ragged.

"I can't," he rasps.

My heart thunders, then his lips crash into mine. It's not tentative. It's not soft. It's hunger. Frustration. Weeks of wanting wrapped into one searing kiss.

His hands grip my waist like he's been waiting forever to touch me. My fingers twist in his shirt, grounding myself in his heat.

He breaks the kiss first, forehead pressed to mine, breath still shaky.

"This is going to ruin me," he whispers.

I smile against his mouth.

"Good."

Rowan doesn't take me back to the barn or the couch or press me up against the wall like I half expect him to. He leads me inside the house—quiet, steady, with his fingers still wrapped around mine like he's afraid if he lets go, I'll disappear again.

I trail him, breath caught somewhere between my ribs and my throat. The door swings shut with a final *click*, the tension between us thick and electric, humming louder with each step.

He doesn't say a word as he leads me through the hallway and into his bedroom. The door closes. The air shifts. And we're alone.

The room smells like cedar, old cotton, and him. There's something unbearably intimate about it—his boots kicked beneath the bed, a flannel tossed across the chair, the sheets rumpled from a restless night.

I barely have time to absorb it before he's on me.

Rowan kisses like he's starved. Like he's been holding back for too damn long. His hands bury in my hair, angling my head just right so he can deepen the kiss, tongue slipping past my lips and dragging a moan straight from my chest.

"You have no idea," he murmurs, voice wrecked, "how long I've wanted to do this."

His hands slide down my sides, lifting the hem of my shirt. I shrug out of it, breath hitching when his palms brush over the thin bra I'm wearing beneath. His thumbs graze my nipples through the fabric, slow and deliberate.

"You're beautiful," he mutters, like it's a confession.

I reach for the bottom of his shirt, tugging it up, and he lets me. His body is exactly like I remembered it—broad and carved from labor, with a thin trail of hair leading down from his chest to where his jeans hang low on his hips.

My mouth waters.

Rowan's hands cup the backs of my thighs, lifting me

like I weigh nothing, and he lays me gently across the bed. His body comes down over mine, heat to heat, pressure against pressure.

I arch into him, moaning when he rolls his hips. There's no denying what's between us. How hard he is. How wet I already am.

"You sure?" he asks, voice thick.

"Rowan," I whisper, wrapping my legs around him, "I've never been more sure."

He groans and kisses me again—slower now, deeper. Like we have time to savor this.

And he takes his time.

He kisses down my throat and nips the sensitive spot just beneath my jaw. His hands explore me like he's memorizing every inch—soft swipes, reverent touches, rough palms, and gentle mouths.

When he finally unhooks my bra, he pauses.

"Goddamn," he mutters, staring at me like I'm priceless art.

He mouths over one nipple, tongue flicking, sucking, until I'm arching beneath him.

"Please," I beg.

He chuckles, low and sinful, dragging his lips down my stomach.

"Patience, songbird."

He kisses lower, hands skimming down my hips, hooking in the band of my shorts and panties. He pulls them off in one smooth motion.

And then he kneels between my thighs, eyes dark and reverent.

"Lie back," he murmurs. "Let me taste you."

My breath catches. He doesn't wait for permission. Just dives in, tongue parting me, slow and steady, licking me like he's starving for it.

I cry out, hips lifting, hands fisting in the sheets.

He groans against me, the sound vibrating through every nerve ending I have. His mouth is skilled—methodical, purposeful, worshipful. He flattens his tongue and laps up everything I give him, sucking my clit until I'm unraveling and shaking beneath him.

"I can't—Rowan—" I gasp.

"Yes, you can," he growls. "Give it to me."

I come hard, body trembling, legs tight around his shoulders as he drinks me down like it's the only thing keeping him alive.

And then—God help me—he climbs up, kisses me, and flips us in one motion so I'm straddling his chest.

"Your turn," I breathe, already reaching for his jeans.

He helps me get them off, and when I finally get his boxers down, I pause.

He's big. Thick. Hard. My mouth waters all over again.

Rowan smirks. "Like what you see?"

I shoot him a wicked grin and slide down, licking a slow stripe from base to tip.

His head drops back. "Jesus."

I slowly take him in my mouth, letting my lips stretch around him. He groans, hand fisting in my hair.

"You're perfect," he rasps.

I swirl my tongue, hollowing my cheeks, moaning around him as I work. I can feel him throb on my tongue and hear the filthy sounds he makes when I suck harder.

"Get up here," he growls, tugging me up his body and twisting me around. "Sit on me like you mean it."

I straddle his face and lean forward, taking him back in my mouth as he goes back to worshipping me from below.

It's filthy. It's perfect.

He licks and sucks while I moan around him, the two of us caught in some messy, glorious rhythm. He groans into me every time I swirl my tongue, and I whimper against him every time his teeth graze my clit.

It's too much. It's not enough. And then I'm coming again, shaking, mouth dropping from his cock as I scream his name.

He lets me ride it out before flipping me again, positioning himself at my entrance.

"Condom?" I ask, barely able to remember my own name.

"Shit. Hold on," he says as he leans back, his abs and chest flexing as he reaches into his nightstand and grabs the familiar aluminum packet.

"Ready?" he pants after sheathing himself.

"Yes," I whisper.

He pushes in slowly, stretching me in the best way. We both moan when he bottoms out.

"Fuck, Ivy," he groans, burying his face in my neck.

He starts to move, slow and deep. Every thrust sends

sparks through me, the tension climbing again, his name a litany on my tongue.

"You feel like heaven," he pants, hooking one of my legs over his shoulder. "Like you were made for me."

I cry out, hips meeting his, the pressure building again. Something about this position hits me in the best way. I can already feel myself shaking beneath him.

"I'm close," I breathe. God, when has anything ever been this powerful?

He reaches between us, circles my clit with his thumb, and I shatter—white-hot, blinding.

He follows with a growl, burying himself deep, coming with a rough cry of my name.

Rowan collapses over me, both of us panting, trembling. After a long moment, he lifts his head and brushes his lips over mine.

"I'm not letting you go again," he whispers.

I don't reply. I kiss him back like I believe it. Like I want to. Because I do.

The silence that follows is anything but empty. It's thick with the scent of sweat and skin and something sweeter— like peace if it had a heartbeat.

Rowan lies beside me, one arm flung across his eyes, the other stretched toward me, palm open like he's not done touching me yet. I turn on my side, pressing my cheek into the pillow, watching the steady rise and fall of his chest. His breath is still ragged. His skin glistens. And there's a crooked smile tugging at the corner of his mouth that makes something low in my stomach flutter all over again.

"Are you smiling because of the orgasms?" I murmur, teasing.

His lips twitch, but he doesn't open his eyes. "All of them. And also because I finally got you in my bed."

My cheeks flush. "So you have been imagining it."

"Since the day you stole my sweatshirt and turned my world inside out."

I let that settle. His world. Inside out. There's a weight to those words I'm not ready to lift.

I stare at the wooden beams above the bed, tracing the lines in the grain with my eyes and grounding myself before I turn the conversation too serious.

"I thought you were going to keep pretending nothing happened," I say, voice quiet now. "After the fire... I heard you. In the shower."

His arm drops from his face. Our eyes meet.

He doesn't flinch or look away. "I thought about you the entire time. You don't want to know how many nights I've done that."

Heat rushes to my cheeks again, this time from something deeper than embarrassment. From want. From ache.

"Then why didn't you say anything?"

He sighs and turns toward me, resting on his side. His hand finds my waist, fingers smoothing over my skin like he needs that anchor.

"Because I was scared," he admits. "I've been living in the past. Letting old scars tell me what I do and don't deserve. But this?" He dips his head, pressing his lips to the spot just below my jaw. "You? I'm not scared anymore."

My throat tightens.

God, he says things like that and makes it feel real. Like we're not going to break under the weight of it all.

I pull the blanket up to my chest and nestle closer, my leg sliding over his. "I wasn't sure you wanted me here."

"I always wanted you here," he says. "Even when I didn't know it."

We lie there for a while, tangled in soft sheets and softer truths. His fingers draw lazy circles on my hip. My hand rests on his chest, feeling the slow, steady beat of his heart.

And in what feels like years, the ache in my chest isn't fear. It's hope. A quiet, steady thing that's still fragile but is finally taking root.

Chapter Fifteen

IVY

The bell over the café door jingles when we step in, and the smell of coffee and buttered toast wraps around us like a quilt. Heat flares under my skin—not from last night, though my body remembers every place he learned by heart—but from the way Rowan's hand finds the small of my back as two ladies at the counter whisper my name like it might bite. He doesn't look at them. He looks at me, checks, the question in his eyes quiet and plain: *you good?*

I am. And I'm not. I feel soft and skinned, fluttery and floaty, like I'm walking around with a secret and everyone can hear it humming.

It's the way he was after. How the edges of him went gentle. How he gathered me closer like I was something breakable and precious, set his mouth to my temple, and murmured, "I've got you," into my hair. How every time the breath hitched in my throat, he stilled and asked—quiet, certain—"This okay?" until the word yes felt like a promise I was making to both of us. When the room finally settled, he slid his palm slowly over my spine, rubbing steady circles until my heartbeat matched his. I fell asleep on his chest with his T-shirt bunched in my fist and woke once to find him tucking the sheet higher, brushing the hair from my cheek, and whispering something I was too drowsy to catch and too greedy to ask him to repeat.

Morning was a softer version of him that I didn't know I was allowed to keep—coffee set on the nightstand the second my eyes blinked open, a clean T-shirt handed over without comment, his thumb skimming the back of my knuckles while he asked if I wanted toast or something real. He kissed my forehead instead of my mouth, like he knew which part of me needed tending first, and stood in the doorway while I tied my shoes, smiling that small, wrecking smile that never makes it to photographs.

On the drive into town, he kept one hand on the wheel and one on my knee—not possessive but present. At the stop sign before the bridge, he traced slow, absentminded circles there, like he was learning a song under his breath. He turned the radio down when a caller shouted, rolled it back up when an old waltz came on, and sang exactly two off-key lines to make me laugh. When we parked, he came around to my side and offered his hand like we were stepping onto a dance floor and not cracked pavement, and I took it, because last night made me brave in a new, quiet way.

He holds the door a beat longer than necessary, palm

out, then weaves us through the morning crowd. First time in public since we... didn't sleep. First time trying on the shape of us outside four walls and a dim lamp and the steady way he breathed after.

He pulls out my chair. Orders me water without asking because he's noticed I forget. When I take off my sweater, he shrugs out of his jacket and drapes it over the back of my chair; protectiveness disguised as practical. The corner of his mouth keeps trying to curve. He won't let it. But it's there. He feels the lightness too.

We take the table near the back—our unspoken preference, offering the most privacy. His knee bumps mine and stays. I could sit here and memorize the new parts of him— the soft after, the way he keeps catching my hand under the table like he's surprised it still fits so well—but I didn't come just to float on last night.

"Gossip mill's working overtime," he says, picking up a menu he knows by heart. "Marge already refilled the sugar like we'll need courage."

"It's either a slow news day," I murmur, "or a pop singer just ruined the reputation of a respectable cowboy."

He shoots me a sideways look. "Respectable?"

"You wear denim-on-denim without irony and say things like rotation schedule in public."

A huff of a laugh. It makes something low and grateful open in my chest. He feels different today—lighter, yes, but careful in a new way too. He keeps checking in without words. When my phone vibrates

Bailey: You alive? Do not forget carbs

His thumb strokes once along the inside of my wrist, and my whole nervous system sighs.

Marge appears with coffee like she's been waiting for this exact moment since 1987. She takes our order with a smile that says she's already decided we belong together. Rowan adds bacon to my avocado toast because last time I stole his. I glare, and he looks smug. It feels ordinary. I didn't realize how much I wanted ordinary until this minute.

The whispers at the counter rise, crest, settle. He watches me, not them. "We can take it to go," he says quietly. "If it's too much."

I shake my head. "I like being seen next to you." Truth, delivered without armor. His eyes flare—barely—but I catch it. A yes that lives in his ribs.

By the time the coffee hits the table, my hands won't stop moving. I fish out a pen and tug a napkin closer.

Rowan leans back, arms crossing, amused and wary in equal measure. "That tone. The one that starts with hear me out and ends with me up a ladder."

I draw anyway. A rough square. Rows inside. A rectangle at the edge. "Camp," I say, because I'm done pretending it's a passing thought. "One field for strawberries, one for corn. A greenhouse for herbs in early spring."

He tilts in despite himself. "That's not how you draw a greenhouse."

"I'm not an architect. I'm a dreamer with caffeine and a

Sharpie." I add little stick figures beside a barn. "This is the petting zoo. This stick kid is petting a goat."

"That goat has antlers."

"*Artistic license.*"

He chuckles, quiet but genuine, and it sends a thrill through me. That laugh is rarer than rain in July.

I keep going, layering the sketch with energy. "Look, I'm not trying to tell you how to run your life. But I've seen the way kids respond to this place. How *you* light up when you talk about teaching them. You're not as much of a hermit as you pretend to be."

He runs a thumb along his jaw, eyes dropping to the napkin. "You think I could do it?"

The raw vulnerability in his voice knocks the wind out of me.

"I think you could change lives," I whisper. "Starting with your own."

Before he can answer, there's a tap at my elbow.

I turn—and see her.

A little girl, maybe seven or eight, with tangled curls and wide brown eyes almost too big for her face. She's wearing a sequined shirt with a unicorn on it and has a pink plastic purse slung across her body.

She's also wearing a medical bracelet.

My heart stutters.

"Are you Ivy Quinn?" she asks, voice small and breathless.

"I am," I say softly.

Her mom catches up to her, cheeks pink with embarrassment. "I'm so sorry. We were walking by and she recognized you from the fireworks video online—"

"You sang on the stage!" the girl chirps, bouncing on her toes. "I have your song on my tablet!"

I blink rapidly. "You do?"

She nods, and for the first time, I notice the tremor in her hands, then I see the bracelet clearly.

Epilepsy.

It's etched in tiny bold letters beneath her name.

And something clicks in my chest—like a light bulb or maybe a match.

"I have epilepsy too," I tell her, scooting to the edge of my seat and leaning down to her level. "And I think that makes us pretty incredible."

Her eyes widen. "You do?"

"Yup. It doesn't stop me from singing. And it doesn't stop you from doing anything you want either."

She beams, and her mom mouths, "*Thank you*," behind her. I stand slowly, heart thudding.

As they leave, Rowan stands beside me, steady as a tree.

"You okay?" he asks, his hand brushing my lower back.

I nod. "That..." I swallow. "That meant more than she knows."

He studies me, then glances down at the napkin I left on the table. "Maybe the camp needs music days."

"And glitter crafts."

He groans. "You're gonna destroy my farm."

I look up at him, lightness blooming in my chest. "Nope. I'm gonna help you build something better."

His gaze drops to my lips. And I think maybe the next move is his.

After breakfast, we don't go straight home.

Rowan drives us toward the edge of Otter Creek, past the vast fields and weathered fences, his hand resting on the gearshift like it belongs there. Like it's sculpted for this life —one of soil and sweat and things that grow slowly but last.

He doesn't say where we're going. Doesn't have to. I let the silence sit between us like an old friend, arms looped around my sketchbook as I watch the trees blur past. The camp flyer napkin is tucked safely between its pages. I don't want it to wrinkle.

We slow at the crest of a hill and turn down a dirt road flanked by tall grass. At the end of it is a massive oak tree, its limbs thick and sprawling like it's been standing here longer than the town itself.

He parks and gets out. I follow.

The air is warm and still. A late summer kind of stillness.

"This was my thinking spot as a kid," he says, running a hand along the tree trunk. "Used to come here to figure things out."

I glance up at him, tilting my head. "You brought me to your brooding tree?"

His mouth twitches. "You're welcome."

We sit in the patchy shade, legs stretched out in front of us, and I lean back on my elbows. The sun filters through the branches, dappled and lazy. A cicada buzzes in the distance. Somewhere far off, a tractor hums.

"So," I say lightly, "are you going to ignore the fact that you almost kissed me again?"

His jaw flexes.

"That obvious, huh?"

"I mean... I practically heard wedding bells in Marge's eyes."

He doesn't smile, not quite, but something softens in his face.

I don't give him time to climb back behind that wall.

"Then why haven't you?" I ask, voice steady even though my pulse does its own stampede.

His answer is a rough exhale. "It's not about Crew. I know what that was." His gaze drags over my mouth like it's costing him. "It's me. It's... everything I haven't figured out how to hold without breaking."

I open my mouth to argue and don't get the chance.

Rowan closes the distance in one sure step, my back finding the warm trunk of the oak. His palm comes to my jaw, the other landing at my hip, and then his mouth is on mine—hungry and reverent, like he's been starving and finally decided to eat. The world narrows to the press of him and the rough bark at my spine and the way he kisses like he plans to remember every second later.

I rise onto my toes. He deepens, a low sound rumbling in his chest that I feel everywhere. Fingers slide into my hair. My hands fist in the front of his T-shirt, hauling him closer like I could stitch us together if I tried hard enough. He breaks only to breathe, then takes my mouth again, slower now, a promise threaded through the heat.

When he finally stops, he stays close—forehead tipped to mine, breath mingling, and his thumb still stroking the corner of my mouth like he can't help himself.

"You deserve more than a man who's still figuring out how to build anything that lasts," he says, voice low and wrecked.

I keep him right there with a hand at the back of his neck. "Maybe you just needed the right person to build it with."

His eyes shutter, then open—clearer, softer, like the choice hurts and heals at the same time. He kisses me once more, quick and certain, then rests his brow to mine again.

"I want to do this right," he says. "Not perfect. Just... true. The kind that holds when storms roll in."

"Okay," I whisper, because it is and I am. "Then we start the way things that last always do—one nail, one board, one breath at a time."

His mouth curves against mine. He laces our fingers—solid, warm, unshowy—and eases us away from the tree like he's learned the exact pressure it takes to keep something precious intact. We don't hurry. We don't explain. We walk back toward the glow of the house, hand in hand, like two people who have finally decided which direction to face.

We sit there like that for a while, our hands locked, the silence between us not heavy anymore, but healing.

When a breeze stirs the leaves above us, he looks down at me and says, "You terrify me, Ivy Quinn."

I smile. "Good."

Back at the farm, Rowan drops me off at the cottage

like he's afraid if he comes too close, he'll lose every last bit of control he's barely holding on to.

"See you tomorrow?" he asks, voice rough.

I nod, already halfway through the door. "You better."

I don't see him again until late afternoon.

I'm weeding the garden behind the cottage—yes, *me*, elbows-deep in dirt with my sunglasses perched on my head and my hair a frizzy halo of sweat. Rowan's voice floats over the fence like it belongs here.

"Hey."

I glance up.

He's leaning on the gate. Sweat-damp shirt, dusty jeans, that eternal I've-been-working-with-livestock look he wears like a second skin.

He holds up a glass jar. "Sun tea."

I blink at him. "You made me tea?"

"Don't make it weird."

I walk over and take it, sipping the warm liquid with a grateful sigh. "It's delicious. You've ruined me for store-bought."

He clears his throat, eyes on my mouth. I step closer. He doesn't move.

A beat. Another. Then his fingers brush mine, and something inside me sparks like a struck match.

And just like that, we're no longer dancing around it.

That night, I sit on the porch of the cottage with the camp flyer napkin in my lap and my guitar beside me. I strum a few soft chords, words blooming from my lips like petals, gentle and easy.

It's not a song yet, but it feels like one, like the beginning of something that matters.

As the stars stretch across the sky and the crickets sing, I close my eyes and let myself believe that this town might have room for a girl like me.

Maybe Rowan does too.

And if I'm lucky…

Maybe he's already letting me in.

Chapter Sixteen

ROWAN

’m up before the sun finishes rubbing the sleep out of its eyes. That’s normal. What isn’t is the knot tucked under my sternum like a pocketed stone. It showed up when Bailey texted at 5:11 a.m.—

Bailey: Story hour at the farm? Ten kids. Maybe twelve. I’ll bring juice. You bring anything that won’t bite. Please. xo

—and it hasn’t budged since.

I feed the horses first. Grain, then hay. Jasper noses my shoulder like he’s owed conversation as well as breakfast. I rub the star on his forehead until his eyelids drop, then run a brush down his neck in long, even strokes that shine the bay back into him. Chickens next. They pour from the coop like somebody cut a ribbon, all bustle and commentary. I check the latches twice even though I’m the one who set them, then I’m headed over to Otter Creek Farms.

The barn breathes with me; it always does. Usually, that's enough to set me right. Today, it gets me halfway there. I keep seeing a line of small faces under the oak, parents close behind, waiting for me to be the kind of man who knows what to do with ten different kinds of worry at once. I can mend a fence in the rain with a headlamp and a pair of pliers. I can read a sky and know when it's thunder or a problem. Kids? Kids are their own weather.

Gravel chatters. Bailey's SUV noses under the oaks and bounces to a stop like it's done this lane its whole life. The back opens, and a flock tumbles out—Velcro, braids, one kid already wearing his sneakers on his hands like puppets. Bailey's got a clipboard, a tote bag, and the look she gets when she's about to herd humanity with a smile.

And then the passenger door opens.

Ivy climbs down in faded jean shorts and a white T-shirt, and the boots that drive my wildest fantasies. Her hair's in a loose braid that the morning has already started to work on. She's got a book tucked under one arm and a light in her eyes I've only seen here—back of the farm light, not stage light. She looks at me first. Not the barn. Not the flock. Me.

"Morning," she says.

"Morning," I answer, and pretend that word doesn't feel bigger in my mouth than usual.

We set the blankets in a half-moon under the oak, the swing nudging at my shoulder in the breeze like an old friend. I haul the water cooler over, stack paper cups, and set a crate for Ivy to sit on. Bailey posts a sheet of construction paper on the trunk with painter's tape: *Walk feet. Farm voices. Ask before touching. Mud happens.* She already has two moms nodding and a dad signing up to bring muffins next time.

"Ready?" Ivy asks, tapping the book cover with her thumb. She means it like *are you okay if I take this?* I nod because of course I am. Because it makes sense here—her voice, kids' knees folded underneath them, sun through leaves.

She starts. "Once, there was a girl who wanted something to grow."

The flock goes quiet in a good way. Not the held-breath way. Shoe-Hands leans forward until he tips and catches himself with his palms. A little girl in polka dots migrates an inch at a time until her knee touches Ivy's shoes like she planned it that way.

"What does a seed need?" Ivy asks, holding her palm out like she's got one in it.

"Water!" three kids chorus.

"Dirt!"

"A song," Shoe-Hands says, deadpan. Ivy tries not to laugh but doesn't quite manage it. "You might be onto something," she tells him.

I don't move from my post near the barn. I don't need to. She has them. She doesn't turn herself into a parade. She makes the room smaller, and every kid feels like the page belongs to them. When the book girl waits, Ivy asks what they'd plant. *A purple bike. A puppy. A thunder that's only sound. A new friend.* That one lands in my ribs like a truth you didn't see coming but recognize anyway. I keep my eyes on the oak's bark and tell myself I'm just checking for beetles like a man who isn't soft.

We finish the book with a soft "The end." Five kids don't move. Ivy hums a simple little refrain—four lines about water and sun and stubborn roots—and by the second pass, the whole blanket hums with her. She doesn't even look at me, and I know exactly what it feels like to breathe easier because she's here.

"Okay," she says, settling the book on the crate. "Want to meet actual chickens?"

We do the rules again. I'm better at rules than songs. "We're going to move as a group," I tell them. "I'll show. Miss Ivy will help. Miss Bailey will make sure nobody rides the chickens."

A hand shoots up. "Can we ride the chickens?"

"Absolutely not," I say, dry enough that two parents laugh. Shoe-Hands looks at me like I just told the best joke anyone's ever thought of.

We start at the coop. I open the latch slowly and walk them through it like my hands are a picture book. "We're quiet in here. We don't chase. We collect like we're surgeons." Ivy crouches beside me with the basket, and we ask who has careful fingers. Seven careful fingers appear. I pick two. Ivy guides them through the straw.

An egg lands in a palm, and the kid whispers, "It's warm," like this is the first true thing he's learned today. It probably is.

We wash up at the foot pump I rigged last winter when

the old handle stuck. "Look at you," Ivy murmurs, not for show, just for me. I shrug like it's nothing and put another cup under a small pair of hands.

In the pasture, I bring Jasper to the fence and put his nose on the rail. He sucks attention like a shop vac and pretends he doesn't. "One at a time," I say. "He likes his forehead rubbed, not his eyeballs." They giggle like I invented comedy. Butterscotch comes up behind me with the swagger of a calf who thinks she's queen. She sneezes directly on Ivy's shin.

"She loves you," Ivy tells the kids.

"She's marking you for later," I mouth back.

I clock a little girl at the edge. Pink medical bracelet, careful posture, the way worry wraps kids' shoulders in a pattern you only learn if you've had to unlearn it yourself. Ivy sees her too because of course she does. She doesn't point. She doesn't coax. She brushes Butterscotch slowly, the big sure strokes you'd use on a skittish horse, and lets the girl come to the brush instead of the other way around. After a minute, Rowan's Rule of Farm Miracles does its thing. The kid steps in, takes the handle, and the calf leans like we put this moment here just for her.

"Brave looks good on you," Ivy says, quiet enough to be just for one set of ears. The kid's shoulders stop trying to tuck under her earlobes. I swallow something that tastes like gratitude and cedar.

We move to the starter table I've set up under the pecans, with trays, a bucket of potting mix, and a bowl of beans. "Pinch," I say, showing thumb and forefinger. "Drop. Cover.

Press." They say it back like a chant. Bailey keeps time with a paper cup. Dirt becomes a possibility a dozen times over. It's messy in the right ways. One kid dumps half his water on his shirt. Shoe-Hands wants to name the worms. "Sir Wiggles," Ivy pronounces, and now I guess we have a worm with a title.

I don't perform for the parents. I don't coo. I show. I wait. I say, "Yeah, that's it," when a kid gets the seed to settle one knuckle deep because work should feel like you did something. I watch Ivy be ten different kinds of patient, and I swear I feel a hinge give way inside my chest. The thought I've been holding under my tongue for weeks—*maybe I could do this, not once, but again*—raises its head like it wants sun.

By the time we circle back under the oak, we've got ten little starters labeled in crooked kid handwriting, two empty water coolers, and a flock of tired happy. Ivy sets the book back on her knee, but the kids steal the moment— one at a time onto the crate, telling me and her what their seed will be. *A bike. A puppy. Thunder that's only sound. A friend who stays.* I could listen to them all afternoon. We don't. We hand out juice. We recycle cups. Bailey schedules two more mornings while I'm standing right there.

Parents drift. One mom with an anxious mouth thanks me with both hands. A dad asks if he can come back and help fix a gate because he misses using a hammer. The polka-dot girl presses the warm egg into Ivy's palm with ceremonial solemnity. "So you don't forget," she says. Ivy's mouth wobbles, and I pretend I don't see it because I know how to give people the dignity of not being watched when they feel.

We wave the last car through the oaks. Dust hangs and falls. Quiet returns in a hurry, the kind the farm carries when the day has done what it came for.

I carry the crate back to the porch. I tip the cooler and watch the last line of water catch sunlight on its way out. When I turn, Ivy's still under the oak, knees up, chin planted. She's looking at the footprints, the smudged blanket outlines, like a general surveying a good kind of battle.

"You were good," I say. It comes out rougher than I meant. I clear my throat. "With them."

She tips me a grin that's more edges than teeth. "They make it easy." She looks past me toward the pasture. "You were... you." She lets it sit like that. "It worked."

I don't know what to do with praise. I keep it anyway. "Nobody rode a chicken."

"They considered it." She angles her chin toward the coop, where Pancake the goat is plotting something she doesn't have the attention span to finish. We both chuckle, and I feel my shoulders drop an inch I didn't realize they'd taken on.

I sit beside her and scrub a hand over my jaw. The egg's still in her palm, warm from one small hand to another. I want to say I'm sorry for dragging my feet. I want to say I'm scared of making something public that I can't control once it lives outside the fences. I want to say *I'm better at mending than starting*, and I don't want that to be true anymore. What I say is simpler.

"They listened," I tell the oak. "Even when I didn't make it... fancy."

"Fancy's overrated," she says. "Showing is enough." She leans her shoulder into mine, light, cautious, like checking the integrity of a new board with your palm. I lean back the same amount. The measure feels right.

"Bailey says she can bring another group next week," she adds, casual if you don't know her tells. I do. She's watching me without moving her eyes.

I open my mouth with a *we should*— and shut it before I get stubborn to prove something no one asked me to. "Let me think," I say instead. "Sleep on it. See how it sits."

"Okay." No push. No pout. Just that steady belief she has that makes me want to build her a porch swing and bolt it into the joists with hardware that could hang an engine on.

A pecan leaf falls and lands in her braid. I pluck it out because I can, and because the world feels simple enough in this second to allow small indulgences. My knuckles graze her temple. She turns her face toward my hand like the cat that lives in the hayloft and tolerates me on Tuesdays.

"Hungry?" I ask, because if I keep touching her, I'm either going to say something too big or do something that asks too much.

"Starving." She tilts her head toward the house. "Is there a rule where I get fed if I do dishes?"

"That's the only rule," I say, and stand. She slips her

hand into mine. I keep it for one extra heartbeat because I haven't learned every smart thing, but I've learned to claim the good quiet when it shows up.

We pack fast—blankets shaken, crate and cooler in the bed, gate latched. I open the passenger door. She climbs onto the seat, arm resting against the center console. My own brushes against hers as I settle in my own seat, neither of us budge. I roll us down the lane, dust lifting behind in a slow ribbon.

The drive is short and easy. Past the pecans, past the bend where the bay flashes silver through the pines, right at the rusted mailbox that still leans like it's thinking about quitting. Wind through the open windows smells like cut grass and sun-warmed salt. She hums the four-line seed song under her breath. I don't say a thing because I like the way it threads the cab.

I turn into my drive and kill the engine under the oaks. We climb out together. Gravel crunches. Somewhere, a gull complains like it's late for something.

We walk the path side by side, and it does what it always does—splits in two: left toward the house, right toward the cottage. Two porch lights that will touch when dusk remembers us. She pauses in that small overlap, like last time. Back then, distance felt like kindness to two people who didn't know what they were doing.

"Left," I say before I can overthink it.

In the kitchen, I slice tomatoes and she salts them like she's baptizing them. I throw bacon in the pan, and the house smells like memory. She perches on the counter and swings her heels, humming the four lines from the wish book. I pretend to study the bread like it's complex machinery. Truth is, I'm smiling into the cutting board like a fool because her plain singing voice does something to the shingles on this house I can't explain.

"You're quiet," she says.

"That's my brand." I flip the bacon and don't look at her. If I do, I'm going to say *I like you here* like a boy, and she deserves an adult.

"Tell me what you were thinking out there," she presses, voice softer. She's not pushing. She's making space. It makes me want to fill it.

I set the knife down. "I kept waiting for something to go wrong. For a kid to slip. For a parent to decide I was doing it wrong and take it personally. For me to say the wrong word and have to watch it ricochet around a dozen heads because that's how I am sometimes, and I hate it." I breathe in. Out. "And then it didn't go wrong. It went... like it was supposed to. Because the work stayed small. Because you held the story together, and I held the edges, and Bailey did the thing where she makes a crowd behave without anyone feeling managed."

I glance up. Ivy's watching me like she does when we're under the oak at dusk, and I pretend I'm staying for the breeze. "I want to be good at the part where you build something people count on," I admit. "Not just the part where you fix what you broke."

"You are," she says. No wobble. No caveats. "You're just used to thinking the only proof is a snapped board and a new nail." She tips her chin toward the window. "Proof looks like ten little names flapping on starter trays."

My throat goes tight on me. I reach for the pepper like it just asked, then set it down again. "You make it sound simple."

"It isn't," she says. "But simple and easy aren't synonyms."

We eat at the counter because tables are for other people. Tomato and bacon sandwiches, juice that tastes faintly of the cooler this morning, two paper plates because dishwater is for the truly committed. Her knee nudges my thigh when she laughs at something I don't remember saying. It occurs to me, with the kind of thud that puts a crack in pride, that I like myself the most in rooms where she is.

"Walk?" I ask when the dishes are done, and she's still on my counter like she plans to live there.

"Always."

We take the long way, skirting the edge of the hay field where the creek thins itself over shale and keeps up a quiet conversation.

Summer sits heavy. A hawk pencils across the high blue. Dragonflies write cursive above the water. We don't talk—boots in gravel, the creek keeping time—until the path splits the way it always does: one track up toward the house, the other tunneling under sycamores to the cottage and the big oak. No porch lights yet, just late gold rinsing everything flat and the first fireflies waking in the reeds.

We stop without planning to. Habit, maybe. She's close

enough that if I leaned an inch, I'd learn things I've been pretending I don't want to memorize by mouth. I turn to her, palms open.

"Thank you," I say.

It isn't for lunch, and she knows it. The corners of her mouth tilt—small, sure—like a woman who can tell the difference between a meal and a day made lighter just by being in it. The choice hangs there a beat, both tracks waiting. Then I tip my chin left, and when she nods—once—we take that turn together, the water at our backs and the fields unrolling ahead.

"For what?"

"For holding the middle today." I find her braid with my eyes again because if I look straight at her, I'm going to overdo it. "I can handle the edges. You're better at the part where people remember what they came for."

She lifts a hand like she might put it on my chest but then thinks better of it. "You did that," she says. "I just sang a four-line song about beans."

"Best one I've heard," I answer, and that makes her laugh in the way that shows the left canine a little more than the right. It's a stupid detail to fall for. I fall anyway.

"Left for me," she says finally, tipping her head toward the cottage. "I'm going to shower and label my moon." She raises the egg. "Then nap like a seven-year-old who survived the petting zoo."

"Right for me." I hook a thumb toward the barn. "I have a strap on the east gate that needs convincing, and the pump by the greenhouse is sulking."

We don't move. Not at first. The thing between us sits there, solid as a fence post, and it isn't asking to be named. Only tended.

She steps in and brushes her shoulder against mine. It's smaller than a kiss, but braver than not doing it. "Later?" she asks.

"Later," I say, and mean it.

She heads left, and I head right, and in the middle of the fork where the porch lights will touch when the day goes soft, I tell the knot in my chest it can let go a little more. I don't have to name anything today. I only have to keep showing up, keep speaking plain, keep letting the mess be part of the lesson. That's a kind of building too.

The farm is the same as it was this morning, and nothing's the same at all. Ten paper labels flap, brave as flags. Sir Wiggles is, predictably, AWOL. The east gate strap forgets itself and holds.

An hour later, I'm back on my own ground, crossing off the dumb little boxes in my head—salt blocks, water lines, mineral tubs—except I'm not really crossing anything off because Ivy's with me, and it turns out, I don't count time right when she is.

We saddle Jasper and the old mare for a slow check along the fence line. She swings up easy, knees braced, fingers light on the reins like she was born knowing how to ask and not demand. We talk about nothing that matters— Bailey's best bee story, and which neighbor's rooster sounds like a smoker's cough. I'd let myself enjoy the way she laughs with her whole face. I like the company. Full stop. So much that I miss the tells I should never miss: wind shouldering out of the south, the metallic edge in the air, the way the calves go still and listen.

I'm watching the way a wisp of hair sticks to her cheekbone. I'm not watching the sky.

The light shifts—drops a note lower—and a white seam splits far off over the pines. The delayed belly-roll hits a few seconds later. Not close. Close enough.

"Damn," I breathe, already turning Jasper. "That's on me."

"What is?" she asks, cheerful, trusting, and I hate that I didn't earn it just now.

"Storm building fast. We should've started back sooner." Another flash, brighter, and my stomach goes cold. I picture the lists Ivy made me promise I'd learn—heat, stress, flashing lights—and I want to kick my own shins for letting the first two pile on while the third announces itself right over our heads.

I edge Jasper alongside her mare and touch her knee, steady. "Hey. Eyes on me, not the sky," I say, calm as I can make it. "We'll cut over to the equipment shed by the north lot. Two minutes."

She nods once. "I'm okay."

"Good. Stay close." I slide my cap off and pull it low on her, then add, "If the flashes bug you, look down at the mane. Tell me if you feel... anything."

"Got it," she says, and I can hear the steel under the soft.

We move out, not a run—steady, smart. The wind lifts

the hay in long shivers. Another flash. I put myself between her and the open, angling her mare to my right so I take the widest slice of sky. By the time we reach the low, tin-roofed shed, the air tastes like rain and pennies.

I get her inside first, swing the door, and drop the bar. It goes dark in that good, even way—no sudden strobe, just the gray of a storm-room. I push a battered canvas coat into her hands and drape it over her shoulders, then crouch to loosen the mare's cinch so she can breathe easier.

"You good?" I ask, close enough that I don't have to raise my voice over the rain starting to drum.

Her palm finds my forearm. "I'm good," she says, and adds, because she knows me now, "Really."

I nod, but the anger at myself has already lit. "I should've been watching the sky. I know better."

"You were talking to me," she says, a little smile in it.

"Not an excuse." I glance at the thin line of light under the door, then back to her. "Next time, I pull us in sooner. If the flashes bother you at all, I'll throw a blanket over the door seam."

She tilts her head. "Next time?"

"Storms happen," I say. "And you're not staying inside just because I forgot my brain."

The rain sharpens until the roof turns into a drumline. She steps in closer, shoulder to mine under the coat, cheek finding my chest like she's choosing the quietest place in the room. I fold her in without thinking—palms open between her shoulder blades, my body a wall against the slit of light at the door.

"I've got you," I tell the crown of her head, steady as I can make it. "You're safe here."

Her fingers bunch in the front of my shirt. "I know."

Thunder rolls, low and long. I feel her breathe with it—inhale when it fades, exhale when the rain rushes back. I match her rhythm on purpose, counting it out like I would for a skittish colt, the way my mama taught me. A minute. Maybe two. Then she tips her head back to look at me, stormlight catching the flecks in her eyes.

"Rowan," she says, my name soft and sure. Not a question. A choice.

Something in my chest shifts into place. I brush a damp strand from her temple and tuck it behind her ear, knuckles grazing skin warm from the dash here. "You cold?"

She shakes her head. "Not even a little."

I mean to kiss her forehead—careful, simple, the way I've been telling myself I know how to be. My mouth finds the corner of hers instead. It's barely a touch and somehow everything at once. She answers with the smallest sound and rises onto her toes, hands sliding up my chest, over my shoulders, hooking behind my neck like she's drawing me down where she wants me.

"Tell me if you want me to stop," I say, already lost.

"I'll say it," she whispers. "I won't."

The kiss is slow—unhurried and deep, all the honesty I'm better at with tools than words. She tastes like rain and something honey-sweet from earlier, and when my thumb skims her jaw, her whole body leans into it like the touch is a door she's been waiting to walk through. The shed hums around us, a small world of our own making—tin roof singing, horses shifting, wind at our backs while we stand still.

I back us toward the stack of folded tarps and drag one down, throw an old canvas blanket over it. We sink together, knees brushing, thighs aligning, the coat falling open and pooling around us like a tent. She pulls me closer by the front of my shirt, mouth opening under mine, and whatever restraint I had gives up politely and steps outside.

"I want to take care of you," I murmur against her cheek, and I mean a hundred things—warmth, water, a hand to hold when lightning trips the dark. She answers by tugging me down until my weight is something we share. Heat sparks everywhere our bodies learn a new map—her palm at the small of my back, my hand splayed over her ribs, both of us moving in the soft, uncoordinated way of people who can't get close enough fast enough.

We don't talk much. There isn't room for it. The words we do manage come out as breath between kisses:

"Here."

"Closer."

"Don't rush."

Thunder answers like it's taking requests. The rain thickens and softens by turns, and I mark time by the way her hands wander—up my spine, over my shoulders, into my hair—and the way she sighs when I learn another place that makes her go quiet and boneless. I keep one eye on the seam of light at the door, an old habit I don't have to think about, the rest of me learning her—how she likes my mouth slower, my hands firmer; how she tips her chin to deepen a kiss like she's been doing it with me for years.

"Rowan," she breathes again, a little wrecked now, and I answer the only way I know—by giving her more, by letting the careful break into something hungry, by meeting every ask with the best of what I have.

When we finally ease back, it's only far enough to breathe. I rest my forehead to hers, both of us laughing that stunned, quiet laugh people do when a storm passes and the world is still standing. My thumb finds the line of her cheekbone; her fingers trace the edge of my jaw like she's memorizing it.

A low, constant rumble settles in my chest as I lay Ivy down on the blanket. Her hair fans out like wildfire against the dark fabric, cheeks flushed, lips kiss-bruised and parted.

She looks like temptation made real. And I'm done pretending I can resist her.

"I don't deserve you," I rasp, fingers dragging over her waist. "But I'm done letting that stop me."

She shakes her head, eyes glassy. "I really wish you'd stop questioning yourself. I don't want perfect. I want *real*. I want *you*."

I crush my mouth to hers again, letting months of restraint finally snap. My hands find the hem of her shirt, pushing it up until she arches to help me pull it over her head. I press kisses down her neck, across the delicate slope of her collarbone, and down the line of her sternum.

She makes this soft sound—half sigh, half gasp—and it undoes me.

"You're shaking," I murmur.

"From *you*," she breathes. "Keep going."

I obey.

I unclasp her bra slowly, reverently, letting it slide from her shoulders before I lower my mouth to one breast. I kiss the soft swell, lick around the nipple until she's arching up into my mouth.

Her hands are in my hair, tugging, needy.

"Rowan," she pants, and the sound of my name on her lips is a fucking prayer.

"Tell me what you want," I demand.

"You. All of you."

I trail kisses down her ribs, over the faint curve of her stomach, dragging her jeans down inch by inch. My hands slide beneath the waistband of her panties, and she lifts her hips, trusting me completely.

God, she's a vision.

I look up at her, lips parted, pupils blown wide.

"This okay?" I ask, voice rough.

She nods, breathless. "Please."

I kiss the inside of her thigh, then again higher, until her legs tremble and her hand fumbles toward me.

I settle between her legs and taste her like I've been dying of thirst.

She gasps, her thighs clenching around me, hips rising in time with my tongue. She's hot, slick, and perfect, and I make it my mission to learn every sound she makes when I bring her closer.

When her cries start to break, I pull back just enough to

slide two fingers inside, curling them just right while my mouth works in tandem. Fucking her with my fingers may be one of my new favorite things.

She comes apart with a sob.

"Oh my *God,* Rowan—"

"Good girl," I whisper, holding her through it. "You're doing so fucking good for me."

She pulls at me then, desperate and impatient, fumbling with my belt.

"I want you," she says. "Now."

My jeans are gone in seconds, my body moving on instinct. I grab a condom from my wallet—never thought I'd need one in a damn shed—but thank God I was wrong.

Ivy wraps her legs around me as I enter her, both of us freezing for a beat at the overwhelming sensation.

"Jesus," I grit. "You feel—God—better than anything."

Her nails drag down my back as I start to move. Slow at first. Deep. Controlled. But she urges me on, gasping my name, hips matching every thrust until we're both trembling.

Her walls clench around my erection, sucking at pulling it farther into the channel. Her ass slaps against my thighs with each thrust, and I can't help but grab one of those glorious globes in my fist.

And when we come—it's not just physical.

It's a release. Of pain. Of fear. Of all the words we haven't said.

I collapse beside her on the blanket, chest heaving.

She turns her head, eyes locked with mine.

"That was—" I kiss her before she can finish.

"Yeah," I whisper. "It was."

We lie tangled in each other's limbs. The blankets are crumpled beneath us, and the storm is tapering off outside the barn. The soft hum of rain hitting the tin roof now sounds more like a lullaby than a warning.

Ivy traces lazy circles on my chest, her breath still uneven, her bare leg draped over mine. I want to say something. Anything. But I don't know what the hell to say.

My throat is dry, my heart too full, and my brain scrambles for the right words that won't ruin this moment. Won't make it too much too fast. Or worse—too little, too late.

I tilt my head toward her, brushing a damp strand of hair from her cheek.

She's not smiling.

Not frowning either.

Just... quiet. Thoughtful. Her expression is unreadable in the pale light that seeps through the warped wooden slats of the barn.

"Are you okay?" I ask, voice hoarse.

She nods slowly. "Yeah. Just... thinking."

I wait. Give her space.

She exhales. "I keep wondering if this changes things."

"What do you want it to change?"

Her lips twist. "That's the thing, Rowan. I don't *know*. I just know I don't want to go back to pretending I don't want this. Last time seemed like a fluke, but now that it's happened twice, I can't brush it aside like you can."

My chest tightens.

She turns on her side, propping her head on her hand. "I don't regret any of it. But if we're gonna wake up tomorrow and pretend it didn't happen—"

"We won't," I cut in. "I *won't*."

I pull her closer, resting my forehead against hers. "You said once that you weren't ready to be sent away. That you wanted to stay. And I never told you the truth."

She doesn't blink. Just watches me like she already knows what's coming.

"I wanted you to stay, too," I admit. "But I was scared. Of this. Of you. Of what you make me feel."

"Why?"

I pause, heart thudding. "Because the last time I let someone in... it almost ruined me."

She swallows, her thumb stroking along my jaw as I reveal the entire story with Marissa. I expect to find a sense of pity in her gaze, but it never shows.

"I'm not her," she says softly.

"I know."

She nods once, then curls into my side, resting her head on my shoulder. We lie like that in silence, letting the storm and our breathing fill the empty spaces between us.

But even as the tension softens, a new one builds.

What happens now? Because sex is one thing. Wanting is another. But feelings? Real ones? Those are where things get messy.

And I'm terrified I'll mess this up before I even have a chance to make it right.

The sunlight spilling through the bedroom window is warm and soft, but it doesn't wake me.

Rowan's arms do.

They're wrapped around me like a fortress, one banded under my ribs, the other draped over my hip. His chest presses against my back, slow breaths fanning over the curve of my neck. It's... still. Quiet. Like the storm never happened. Like last night wasn't a complete unraveling of everything I thought I could hold back.

I don't move.

I don't want to.

His thumb shifts against my stomach, like a reflex, and I feel the softest press of his nose against my hair. My heart lurches.

God, I could get used to this.

To him.

To waking up in his bed, tangled in his sheets, with the scent of cedar and cotton and Rowan wrapped around my skin.

I close my eyes and try to memorize the weight of this moment. His heat. His heartbeat.

And then I remember—I wasn't supposed to stay.

I'd crept over from the cottage after midnight, barefoot and breathless, still aching from the way he'd touched me in the shed. Still reeling from the feel of his body pressed to mine, the low gravel in his voice when he whispered how badly he wanted me.

I'd knocked once. Quiet.

He hadn't said a word. Just opened the door and pulled me in like he'd been waiting all night.

There hadn't been another storm. Not outside, at least. But in his bed, we'd found a different kind of thunder.

This time, it had been slower. Softer. Like he needed to prove something but whether to himself or to me, I didn't know. That I wasn't a regret. That he wasn't a mistake.

That this—whatever this is—could be more.

A groan stirs behind me. Rowan shifts, arm tightening once before his voice comes rough with sleep. "You're still here."

The words hit sideways. Heat crawls up my neck. I start to push the sheet back, mumbling, "Sorry, I fell asleep. I'll just get out of your hair."

His arm bands around my waist and hauls me straight back against him. "Where do you think you're going?" he rumbles into the curve of my shoulder, nose nuzzling the spot that makes my breath stutter. "I'm so fucking happy you're still here. Right where I want you."

The panic drains out like a pulled plug. He tucks me in closer, one big palm splayed over my stomach, thumb sweeping slowly. He presses a lazy kiss behind my ear, then another, softer. "Stay," he says, sleepy and certain.

"I'm staying," I whisper, letting my weight melt into him as the morning settles around us, warm and sure.

"I didn't dream it," he whispers, lips grazing my skin. "You were here."

I twist toward him slowly, facing him now, our noses inches apart on the pillow. "I'm still here."

His hand lifts to cup my cheek, thumb stroking once before it drops again.

For a minute, we just lie there. With a reluctant groan, he rolls onto his back and stares at the ceiling.

"I have to get the horses fed," he mutters. "And the north pasture needs checking."

I prop myself up on my elbow, watching the way his chest rises and falls, his jaw tightening like he's trying to hold something in.

"I can help," I offer quietly.

Rowan turns his head to look at me, eyes narrowing slightly, like he doesn't know what to do with that. With me.

"You don't have to."

"I know."

He studies me for another long second.

Then he nods once. "Okay."

I slide out of bed, feeling the soreness bloom across my thighs and lower back—a delicious reminder of the night before—and pad to the bathroom.

Behind me, I hear Rowan sigh. And I don't know what that sigh means yet, but I want to.

And that's the most terrifying part of all.

We walk in silence toward the barn, our boots pounding over the gravel. The late morning sun climbs higher, warming the world around us, heating the tops of my shoulders through the thin cotton of my shirt. The scent of hay and horses fills the air—familiar, grounding.

Rowan walks a few steps ahead of me, his cowboy hat pulled low, shoulders tense beneath a gray T-shirt that clings to his back with every shift of muscle. He hasn't said much since we left the house.

But as we crossed the yard, his hand brushed against mine. It wasn't much, but it counts for something.

Inside the barn, the horses nicker softly, their hooves shifting on straw as they poke their heads over stall doors. Rowan whistles low under his breath, the sound soothing. He grabs a pitchfork from the wall and starts tossing hay into the feeders with practiced ease.

I lean my elbows on the wooden rail, watching him. The man is made of muscle and grit and quiet competence, and for a long second, I just let myself look at him.

"Hey," I say, nudging his elbow with mine. "You're doing that thing where you take care of everything except what's going on in your own head."

His mouth tips. "Guilty." He threads his fingers through

mine on the tailgate, thumb skating over my knuckles. "It's not nothing. I'm just… pacing myself."

"How's the pacing going?" I tease, softly.

He exhales, eyes finding mine. "Little worried about the weather, little worried about the fence on the north line." He inhales. "Mostly thinking about you."

My chest loosens. "I'm here," I say, squeezing once.

"I know." His shoulders drop like he believes it. "That's why I'm okay."

"Have you thought more about the camp?"

He pauses mid-movement for a second, then continues working.

"Some."

I smile. "Is that Rowan-speak for 'I haven't stopped thinking about it'?"

He huffs out a breath that might be a laugh. "It's Rowan-speak for 'it's a good idea… and it scares the shit out of me.'"

I step off the rail and cross to where he's working. I pick up a stray lead rope from the floor and slowly coil it between my hands.

"You could do it," I say softly.

He glances over at me, brow furrowed beneath the brim of his cap. "You don't know that."

"I do." I step closer. "I saw it yesterday. You care. You're patient. You're stubborn—in a good way. Kids trust you. Their parents trust you."

His throat works as he swallows, and I see it—for a moment—that flicker of hope he's too afraid to admit to.

"Maybe," he murmurs.

I reach for his free hand, wrapping my fingers around it.

"Maybe it's a good start."

And then, from outside, a sharp whistle cuts through the air.

Rowan turns toward the barn door just as someone steps into the sunlight.

Crew.

Baseball cap turned backward, duffel slung over one shoulder, and a familiar grin spreading across his face like he's just landed a punchline.

"Well damn," he says, his voice lazy and amused. "Am I interrupting something?"

Rowan stiffens beside me. "You're early."

"Training got canceled this morning," Crew says, grinning easily. "Figured I'd surprise Mom. Maybe liberate some of her peach cobbler."

Rowan doesn't bristle at first. He tips his chin. "You're late. Lila already requested blackberry for tonight."

Crew laughs, then looks at me. "Hey, superstar."

"Hey." I give him a small smile—automatic, familiar, maybe too familiar—and feel the air shift. Rowan's hay fork pauses mid-lift. Not a slam, not a sulk—just the briefest hitch before he sets the next bale like it weighs more than it did a second ago.

Crew edges closer to the big doors, hands in his pockets, sunlight on his back. "You look good, Ivy."

"Thanks." I feel Rowan move in my periphery, not away but closer, grabbing the water bucket like it needs him right here in earshot. His jaw works once. The muscle eases.

"I saw the press thing," Crew adds, voice softer. "You handled it."

"Working on it," I say, honestly.

Rowan steps between us and the dust motes, passes me a bottled water without looking like it's a gesture. Our fingers graze. A quick static pop that settles the restlessness in my chest.

Crew clocks the exchange, lifts his palms in a peaceable shrug. "Didn't mean to interrupt chores."

"You didn't," Rowan says, finally meeting his eyes. "You here, you help." It's brotherly, not biting. He jerks his head toward the feed room. "Grab the square shovel."

Crew grins and goes, boots thudding. Regaling me with a few of our PR dates and all the ways he consistently screwed them up. My phone buzzes in my pocket. I ignore it for a beat, caught on the way Rowan's gaze skims my face and then centers, like he's reminding himself what's real.

"You okay?" he asks, low.

I nod. "Yeah." A breath. "You?"

His mouth tips. "Pacing myself." Another quick flick of his eyes toward the doorway where his brother disappeared, then back to me. "Stay for lunch?"

"I was hoping you'd ask."

Before he can say anything else, my phone buzzes in my pocket again, relentlessly.

I glance down.

Celeste.

Of course, it's her.

I silence the call without hesitation, but Crew notices.

"You gonna answer that?"

"Nope."

He nods slowly. "Good."

Before I can ask what he means by that, Rowan's voice echoes from behind us.

"Ivy, can you hand me the hose?"

Relieved for the excuse, I move toward him without another word, feeling the weight of both men's gazes follow me.

Something tells me this day is only going to get more complicated.

I slip around the back of the barn, fingers trembling just a little as I pull my phone out of my pocket.

Missed call: *Celeste.*

And a text.

Celeste: Call me back. I don't care where
you are.

My thumb hovers over the screen for a long second. I should ignore it. I should toss the phone into the nearest trough and go back to pretending I don't care.

But I do. Not about what she thinks. But about cutting this off before she finds another way to meddle.

I press **Call** and lift the phone to my ear, my pulse already spiking. She answers on the first ring.

"Well, well. The prodigal daughter returns my call."

Her voice is crisp, coated in sugar and daggers.

"I didn't return your call," I say evenly. "I'm calling to tell you to stop."

A pause. Then a scoff.

"Oh, Evangeline. You've always been dramatic."

The sound of my full name makes something in me snap.

"No. You've always been manipulative."

"Where are you?" she demands. "Still playing house on that farm like some tragic version of Green Acres?"

I clench my jaw. "That's none of your business."

"It *is* my business when your name is still my paycheck. You think you can just run off and pretend this little identity crisis doesn't have consequences?"

"I'm not pretending," I say, voice tight. "I'm living."

"You think anyone gives a damn about *you* without me guiding your career?" she snaps. "I made you. When your father left, you were just a girl in a trailer park with a half-dead cassette player and no idea how to keep the lights on. Who paid for your braces? Your first guitar? That trip to LA when you were fifteen? Me."

I swallow hard. "You helped. But that doesn't mean you own me."

"I built you from the ground up," she hisses. "And now you're going to burn it all down to flirt with a cowboy in a town that doesn't even have a Starbucks?"

I almost laugh. But there's no humor in it.

"I'm done letting you choose who I have to be."

Silence.

Then her voice drops, soft and sharp.

"You're making a mistake, Evangeline. One you won't come back from."

I stare out across the field, where Rowan is still moving between stalls like nothing in the world could shake him. Where his shoulders hold up more than fences and feed bags. Where he hasn't once asked me to be anyone but myself.

"If it's a mistake," I whisper, "at least it's mine."

Then I end the call.

My hands are shaking as I shove the phone back in my pocket, the weight of that conversation pressing down like a summer storm on my chest.

But I don't cry. I just stand there and breathe. One breath. Then another.

Until finally, I turn back toward the barn and start walking—toward the horses, toward Rowan, toward something that feels real.

By the time we get back to Rowan's house, the light is thick and honeyed, the porch casting a long shadow across the yard. My chest still pinches from the call with my mother, but it's Rowan's quiet that tugs at me more. He holds the door, lets me pass, and it swings shut on the breath between us.

Inside smells like wood and lemon oil and him. He goes straight to the kitchen, opens the fridge like it offended him, then shuts it with his forearm. A low sound escapes him—half grunt, half breath.

"Eggs on toast?" I offer, keeping it simple.

He grunts again—then stops himself. Both hands are

planted on the counter. Head drops. He draws a long breath like he's hauling a net out of the water and wants what's caught to come up clean.

"You didn't do anything wrong," he says, voice rough but steady. "I'm... working on not being an ass when I don't have the words yet."

I lean on the island and wait him out.

He lifts his head to meet my eyes. "I got jealous when you and Crew were laughing in the barn." He says it plain, like he refuses to make it ugly. "Not because I think there's anything there. I know what that was—PR, headlines, a job. It's the shorthand you two have. He's known you longer. He knows details I'm still learning. And I wanted"—his jaw flexes—"I wanted to be the one you look at that way."

Something unknots in my ribs. "I was talking about his disastrous attempt at roping. He ate dirt in front of a second-grade field trip."

A reluctant smile tugs his mouth. "Good. He deserved that."

"And," I add, stepping around the island, "you're allowed to say all of this out loud. Preferably before you turn into a storm cloud."

He huffs, nods. "I'm learning. Slowly. But I'm learning."

"Okay," I whisper.

His hand finds the small of my back, tentative. "Let me try again."

"Try."

He takes the pan from me, sets it on the burner. "We're making dinner together," he says, quiet authority back in his voice, but it's softer now. "And then I'm taking you some-where that isn't a kitchen or a café or a barn. I don't want to argue with you. I want to... show you."

"Show me what?"

"That I can be good at this." He swallows. "At you. At us."

Heat stings behind my eyes. I blink it clear and hand him the butter. We move around each other like we've been doing this for years—my hip bumping his gently and his fingers brushing mine when he passes the salt. Nothing dramatic, just the ordinary intimacy I've starved for.

He puts on a playlist from his phone, something low and warm, a steel guitar threading the space. While the eggs set, he catches my hand and tugs me into the open patch of floor. Barefoot on old wood, we sway. No steps to memo-rize, no audience. His chin tips to my hair; my cheek finds his shirt. He breathes out like the tension's finally found a door.

"I don't want to keep messing up," he murmurs. "So I'm going to say the thing instead of making a story about it."

"Rule number one," I say into his chest. "Say the thing."

He pulls back just enough to see my face. "Say the thing: I want you here. With me. And when I get it wrong, I want you to tell me—then let me fix it."

The timer on the stove dings. He kisses my forehead—simple, devastating—and slips away to plate dinner.

We eat at the counter, knees touching, sharing a single fork because the drawer only gave up one and neither of us was willing to wash another. He slides the crispiest corner of toast to my side without comment. I call him noble; he calls me dramatic. It feels like the beginning of something we both recognize and are a little afraid to name.

When the dishes are rinsed, he wipes his hands on a towel and turns to me with that steady, I-built-a-fence look. "Grab your sweater," he says. "And the quilt from the back of the couch."

"Where are we going?"

He tips his head toward the door, eyes gone midnight. "To park my truck in the back pasture and let the sky do the talking."

The back field is a dark bowl edged in trees, the creek murmuring somewhere beyond the grass. Fireflies pulsing like slow applause. He kills the engine and climbs into the bed, then offers a hand and hauls me up like I weigh nothing. The quilt spreads, and we stretch out. He's thought ahead—two Mason jars with sweet tea, a paper bag with peach hand pies tucked inside. Wooing, Wright-style.

"You brought dessert?" I tease.

"Insurance," he says, arranging the jar near my shoulder. "In case my star lecture bores you."

"It won't." Because he could read a tractor manual in that voice and I'd still show up.

He points out familiar shapes—handle, belt, hunter and dog—and the ones I never learned. "That smudge there? The Milky Way. We only get it on the clearest nights." His fingers trace the air, not touching me, and still I feel the line down the center of me go warm.

"Make a wish," I say.

He's quiet for a long moment. "Not a wish," he answers. "A plan."

I turn on my side, pillow my head on his shoulder. "Tell me."

He slides his palm to my waist and rests it there like an anchor. "Plan: I stop shutting down when I'm scared. Plan: I tell you when I'm angry before I weaponize silence. Plan: I take you on actual dates—not just hauling hay and calling it quality time."

"What kind of dates?"

"Picnic at the creek. Sunday sunrise in the flatbed. Dance on the back porch to whatever song you want, even if you make me count." A beat. "Skinny-dip at midnight if you're braver than me."

I laugh against his shoulder. "I am."

"I know." He smiles, small and real, then sobers. "And I learn the ways to look after you that matter. The practical ones—the meds in the truck, the shade when it's too hot. And the other ones—the coffee the way you like it, the quiet when you need it, the noise when you don't."

My throat goes thick. "Rowan…"

"Say the thing," he reminds me softly.

"Okay." I breathe. "I'm scared too. I've been managed more than I've been loved. I don't always trust my own instincts. But when I'm with you, I feel… right-sized. Like I'm allowed to be a person first. I want more of that. With you."

His hand tightens at my waist—just once. "Good," he says, and the word lands like a vow.

The night settles. Crickets. Creek. Our breathing in time. He turns his face, finds my mouth with a kiss that's unhurried and sure. Not a grab. Not a dare. A promise. He kisses me like we have time, like we're going to use it well.

When we finally part, he presses his forehead to mine, voice low. "You deserve more than a man who flinches at his own feelings. I'm not flinching."

"So noted."

We lie there until the quilt dampens with dew, until the jars are empty and the hand pies are crumbs. He points out one last star. I name it ours, to hear him scoff and then relent. On the drive back, his hand finds my knee and rests there. At the fork in the path—left to the house, right to the cottage—we stop where the two pools of porch light almost touch.

"Left?" he asks, not assuming.

"Left," I say, and he smiles like a man who has decided to let himself be happy.

Inside, he flips on the lamp. No storm cloud, no retreat. He hooks a finger in my sweater hem and tugs me into the kitchen for one more slow turn to a song only we can hear. And when he kisses me good night, it's with the same certainty as the stars: steady, simple, bright enough to steer by.

Chapter Eighteen

ROWAN

The morning feels off-balance before I even open my eyes, like the house shifted half an inch in the night and none of the floorboards told me. I reach to the right out of habit and catch an armful of cold sheet. The space she's been warming for a week—gone. Not gone-gone, just... up before me. Which shouldn't rattle me. It does.

Coffee drifts down the hall the same way fog lifts off the creek—slow, patient, inevitable. I pull on sweats and the first T-shirt on the chair, scrub a hand over my jaw, and walk toward the smell.

She's there. Barefoot. My hoodie sleeves shoved to her elbows, hair knotted up like she did it in the dark and didn't care if a halo fell out of it. She knows where the mugs live now. The filter. The drawer that sticks. She moves around my kitchen like she's always had the map.

"Morning," she says, voice smoked with sleep.

"Morning." I try to keep my own voice from showing all the things it wants to carry. It comes out steadier than I feel.

She slides a mug across. Our fingers don't touch, but it feels like they do. She finally looks up and smiles, soft and crooked, but it doesn't quite make the last step to her eyes.

There's a pressure pattern you learn from weather. Heavy air, a hush in the trees, birds that choose not to waste energy—storm logic. The kitchen has that quiet now. It's not the good kind. It's the kind that means something's coming.

"I need to head to Nashville," she says, not sprinting, not hedging—just laying the truth down on the counter between us like a set of keys. "Two, three days. There are meetings I can no longer postpone, fittings, and a film project. I fought for all of it to be in Nashville, not LA or New York. It's... the least loud."

The coffee turns bitter on my tongue. Not her. The idea of the machine that chews up people I love and spits them out shiny and tired.

"How long?" I ask, because practical questions give your hands something to hold.

"Quick," she says, and then, quieter, "I'll come back."

Something under my ribs braces like I'm setting a post. I nod. "I believe you." And I do. That's the terrifying part.

She searches my face. "I don't want you to think I'm running."

"I don't," I say, and I mean it. "I think you're doing your

job. I also think I'd be lying if I said I like the way my stomach dropped when you told me."

Her exhale catches. She comes around the island like she's approaching a skittish horse, then stops when she's close enough that I can see the gold flecks in the brown of her eyes. "Come with me," she blurts, like the thought surprised her too. "Just... for a couple of days. Keep me honest. Remind me where I'm going back to."

The word lands and rings. Come. There's a kid part of me that wants to say yes so fast I forget to pack. There's a man part of me that looks past her shoulder at the chores board: vaccinations tomorrow, feed delivery window, the far north fence that finally sagged like it's tired of pretending it's not weak at the corner.

I picture us on a plane, her hand under mine when it climbs, her head on my shoulder while I pretend I'm not a man who hates leaving the ground. I picture a hotel hallway with a camera flash blooming like summer lightning in a bad place. I picture her squeezed between handlers and stylists and a mother who likes control more than she likes sunrise, and I'm a wall in a room that needs one.

It would be easy to go because I want to. It would be hard to go because I'm a person other people count on. The balance of that is adulthood and I hate it.

I set my mug down, palm flat to the counter to stop the urge to reach for her and say yes to everything. "I want to," I tell her, and the wanting is the truest thing in the room. "Every part of me wants to. But if I go, I won't do it halfway. And right now we've got the feed truck at ten, Jasper's shoe to reset, and

Bailey's third-grade crew coming to read under the sycamores at noon tomorrow. If I bail because I can't stand the idea of you walking into noise without me, that's me making my fear your job. I don't want to do that to you. Or them."

She takes that in. Doesn't flinch. "Okay," she says. "Okay." Then she steps into me like the answer was a place, not a word. Her hands smooth down my ribs under the cotton, around my back, palms warm. "Then let me make this easier."

"How?"

"Rules," she says. "We write them right now."

"Rules," I repeat, because I'm a man who likes fences when they're put in right. "Say them."

"One," she starts, eyes steady, "I call when the plane lands. Not a text. Your voice or mine. Two, if I start to drown in noise, I tell you before I'm fully under, not after. Three, you don't sit here and invent stories about me in a dress on a step-and-repeat I didn't even go to. You call me. You say, 'Tell me where you are and what you can see.' Four, if you want to come later, you come. If you don't, I walk back to you, and we keep the porch light rule."

I huff. "Porch light rule?"

She smiles, and it finally reaches her eyes. "You told me once you can tell whose lights are on because they're up late on purpose and whose because something's wrong. Your house feels like the first one. Keep it on. I'll find it."

I do reach for her then. My hand cups her jaw because that's where I feel her breath when she laughs. "Five," I add.

"We say the thing. Not the version that hides our soft parts."

"Deal," she whispers, and then she kisses me like she trusts me with something irreplaceable. It's not a goodbye kiss. It's a keep-this-in-your-pocket.

She pulls back and frowns at my mouth like she's doing math. "You're thinking."

"I am." I tip my forehead to hers. "About a talisman. Something of mine you take. Something of yours you leave. So neither of us can weasel out and pretend we imagined the last week."

She laughs, soft. "Bossy."

"Prepared."

I tug the leather cord from my neck, the one with the tiny brass acorn my granddad carried as a pocket charm while he rebuilt this place with his hands and stubbornness. "He said it meant patient strength," I tell her, thumb worrying the warm metal. "Also meant 'don't be an idiot about winter.'"

She goes very still, like I just handed her a baby bird. "Rowan..."

"I want you to wear it," I say, and my voice lowers, not on purpose. "For luck. For reminding. For me being with you, even when I'm not wearing my worst button-down in a Nashville conference room."

She slides her hair aside, and I knot the cord at the back of her neck, my fingers clumsy the way they get when I'm doing something that matters. The acorn settles just above her pulse. It looks right. It looks like the room breathed out.

She rushes toward the couch, shuffling through the pages of the notebook she carries with her everywhere, then returns with her eyes darting around nervously. She lifts her hand and settles something in mine in return. A guitar pick, edges worn smooth, a tiny silver star stamped dead center. "First song I wrote for me," she says. "The day I played it without asking if it would trend. I've kept this with me ever since for courage."

"It worked," I say, because I'm not shy about naming bravery when I see it.

"Keep it," she says. "For the days you forget you have enough."

We spend the next hour doing the most domestic things I've ever wanted. Packing without fanfare. Folding the hoodie she steals because it smells like my soap. She writes a list where I'll see it without making a production of it: Butterscotch—AM bottle on the hook (don't forget to warm); Mrs. Carmichael—market eggs; Bailey—text her about rain plan. She adds a dumb little drawing of a chicken and then pretends she didn't.

I want to ask her to stay. I don't, because a relationship, or whatever it is we're doing, without trust is just another fence that bends the wrong direction. Instead, I make her an egg sandwich the way she likes it and wrap it in wax paper for the road and tuck a note inside that says, *Rule #5. Say the thing. You've got me.*

She sees me tuck it. She pretends not to.

She pops the hatch on her car, and I set her bag inside, palms lingering on the edge of the trunk while I ignore the stupid, selfish urge to scoop her up and carry her back into the house like we're the only two people left who know how to be quiet together. Instead, I touch the acorn at her throat and feel the beat under it answer my thumb. "Call me when you land."

She nods. "I will."

"Say the thing," I remind her.

"I love how you stay," she blurts, then laughs, embarrassed and not at all. "I love that you are the same in a storm as you are when the kitchen's clean. I love that you made me a sandwich like it's a spell."

None of this is casual. I lean in and kiss her like the porch light's already on. When I let her go, it's not with fear. It's with a plan.

The car door shuts. Gravel hisses. The taillights blink at the end of the lane like two eyes checking if I'm watching.

I am.

I go back inside and flip the porch light on even though it's full morning and ridiculous.

Rules are rules.

I make the day honest. That's what you do when you want to spiral—you make the list and you do the list so your brain can't draft disaster scenarios in the idle space between fence posts.

Feed. Water. Check the west line. Run Jasper on the hill and not because I'm trying to outrun a feeling. I sharpen the loppers. Oil the chainsaw. Set out the shade tents for

Bailey's readers tomorrow. Measure the blanket space under the sycamores, test the old speaker, and ensure the volume tops out under the threshold the school nurse wrote down for me.

At the market, Mrs. Carmichael asks after Ivy without asking after Ivy. "Saw her with a shine about her," she says, weighing peaches like they tell secrets. "Sun agrees with that girl. So do men with sense."

"I'm working on the sense," I deadpan, and the old woman snorts into her apron.

By the time I get back, the house feels too big, the kitchen too tidy, every surface an absence where Ivy usually is: her mug drying on the rack and her hair tie abandoned on my wrist because I needed it while we fixed the hose. I loop it over the window latch without thinking, and it looks like a flag I don't recognize yet, but I already salute.

I stare at my phone and yank myself away before I can be a man who waits by a window and thinks his wanting makes him noble. She'll call when she lands. I trust that because we said it out loud.

So I go do the thing that scares me in a different direction. I put my number on the school's official volunteer list. It's a small line of text that means big things, and I do it with steady hands.

Then I call my brother.

Crew picks up on the second ring with the breathy background sound of a treadmill. "Say it," he says. "You don't call me before noon unless something is on fire or you have a revelation."

"Ivy's flying to Nashville," I say, and there's a rustle as he slows and then steps off like he's giving the conversation his whole ear and not the part that does laps. "She asked me to go. I said no. Not because I don't want to, but because the work here won't do itself and because if I go every time my fear says jump, I'm not the man I told her I'd be."

"That sounds like growth," Crew says. "Are we proud or alarmed?"

"Both," I admit, and he laughs.

"You okay?"

"I will be," I tell him. "We made rules. Real ones. I gave her Granddad's acorn."

"You did what?"

"Shut up," I say, and he does. Genuinely does. "I want to keep this from turning me into who I was last time—suspicious, defensive, petty, the guy who chooses distance before someone else gets a chance to choose it for him."

"You're not that guy," Crew says, and for once, he doesn't varnish it with a joke. "You're the one who builds. You stayed when it was hard. Do that now too."

The line goes gentle. "Also? If you ever decide you want to surprise her, I'll make sure your dumb flannel and my dumb face don't have to share a doorway with cameras."

I let that sit in the pocket where a yes might live later. "Appreciate it."

After we hang up, I walk the fence line to the creek and let the water sound pull me back into myself. The stones look the way they looked before she came and the way they'll look when we're old. It's hard not to like a truth that steady.

My phone vibrates at exactly the minute the flight tracker I didn't pull up would have promised. Her name takes the whole screen, and the sight of it hits me in the knees like a clean tackle, which I will never admit to Crew.

"Hey," I answer, and the word hurts good.

"Hey," she says, breath a little winded like she ran through the terminal to make the rule true. "I'm on the ground."

"What can you see?" I ask because we said we would.

"People pretending not to stare," she says dryly, and then the smile comes through her voice like sun through leaves. "A sign with my name spelled wrong. A kid in a dinosaur shirt who won't let go of a paper airplane. He's winning."

"Good," I say. "I like him already."

"Me too." There's a shuffle, and I hear the shape of her moving. "Ride's here. I'll call when I get to the hotel."

My throat goes thick for half a breath. "Ivy—"

"Say it," she prompts softly.

"I'm proud of you," I tell her. "Not for the tickets and the headlines. For the way you told me and didn't flinch."

Silence that isn't empty.

"Thank you," she says, small and big at the same time. "Talk soon."

After the call, I walk to the barn, not because there's something to fix but because I like the smell of hay when I'm feeling too human. Butterscotch complains the second she sees me, tail wiggling like she's trying out a dog life by mistake. I feed her, scratch the spot behind her ear that makes her eyes go ridiculous, and swear not to text Ivy a hundred photos of a calf like a man who has lost his mind.

Two hours. Two fence posts set. One lunch I actually taste. At 3:17, my phone chimes with a photo of a hotel window, Nashville skyline beyond, and in the glass a faint reflection of a woman wearing my stupid acorn like it belongs there. The message:

> Ivy: Rule check: I'm safe. Handler tolerable. Room smells like bleach and lavender. Thinking about your porch light.

I don't send words back. I send a photo of my porch with the string lights off because it's daylight and a thumb up over the switch. Her typing bubbles flash, disappear, then flash again.

> Ivy: Turn it on anyway.

I do. Even if I have to pull the shade to see if they're working, even if it's a little crazy. It steadies me like a hand at the small of my back.

That night, I'm supposed to go into town for darts with Holt. I text him a rain check and get back a string of dramatic GIFs, then a simple:

> Holt: Proud of you too, grump.

I stand in the driveway with a cheap pizza box and a stubborn ache in my chest and decide being a grown-up sometimes means letting yourself be a little bit of a teenager again. So I put the pizza in the passenger seat, drive the dirt track to the back field, and park under the quiet sky like a man practicing for her return. The quilt rides shotgun now. So does the jar of tea I didn't drink because I didn't want to finish the last one without her.

I fall asleep there, shoes off, my forearm over my eyes. Even though she took my usual hoodie, I don another one because I'm not above entirely sentimental acts. The owls wake me after midnight, and the first thing I do is look at the porch. The light halos the edges just enough to see the front step. It feels like faith, which is not a thing I would have known how to say a month ago.

The phone buzzes on my chest for a video request.

I swipe without thinking, and the screen fills with her— no makeup, hair down to her shoulders in sleep-tangled waves, my acorn glinting at her throat. "I can't sleep," she whispers into a hotel room that probably costs more than my tractor is worth. "Tell me something true."

I point the phone toward the field so she can hear the crickets. "I fell asleep in the truck," I tell her. "Because it feels like the middle of us."

She smiles like I awarded her a small trophy. "It does. Tell me something else."

"I put my number on the school volunteer list," I admit. "In ink."

She gasps like I told her I bought plane tickets. "Rowan."

"Don't make it a parade," I warn, but I'm smiling too.

"Fine," she whispers. "Stoic fist bump."

We talk until we don't. We fall asleep on video like teenagers but with our bills paid. I wake first, and I watch her breathe for thirty seconds, and then feel like a creep and hang up because I want to keep being the man who does what he says. She texts the second she wakes.

Ivy: I felt you there anyway.

The next two days are a swing between work and small moments of sweetness. She sends a photo of her boots tucked under a chair with duct tape on the sole.

Ivy: Not stage ready. Don't care.

I send a picture of the creek and a single word.

Me: Home.

She replies with three.

Ivy: I know where.

Bailey: Reader headcount up to 22 tomorrow.

I adjust the shade tents again and set up a water station

in a safe location, making a big show of labeling the "quiet corner" so the child who needs it doesn't have to ask. I'm still a guy who grunts sometimes when the words clog. I'm also a guy who can learn.

That night, I stand at the sink shaving. My phone is on the sill so I can hear if it pings. I watch myself in the mirror and don't hate what I see—a man who looks like he works hard, maybe even for the right reasons.

The phone pings with a link from Ivy. It's a clip from some interview from months ago, her face in studio lighting, the host asking about pressure. She answers in the most polished way you could ask for. I remember watching it when it aired and thinking she looked like a deer deciding which way to run.

Ivy: I never want to sound like this again.

Me: Then don't.

I type back.

Me: Sound like you. I'll be the one in the back row not clapping too loud.

She sends a heart. I pretend it doesn't blow a hole in my chest and let light in I didn't know I was still keeping out.

She's due back on Sunday night if the meetings hold. We're both doubtful, though. Nashville doesn't love letting people go on schedule. I decide not to borrow trouble and decide again when the group thread pings—Celeste's name shows up as a calendar color on the screen Ivy shares from the hotel, and my teeth grind on instinct. "She's playing nice," Ivy voice-messages, so gentle it makes me mad at myself for the reflex. "Nice like a cat by a fishbowl, but nice."

"Do you want me there?" I ask. I'm already rolling socks in my head, which is how you know I'm not thinking straight.

"No," she says immediately, then softer, "Yes. Always. But not because I need you to hold me up. I want to prove to myself that I remember how to hold the line. Will you meet me halfway?"

"Pick a halfway," I say.

"FaceTime from the hotel at nine," she answers. "I'll sit on the floor so it doesn't feel fancy. You sit on your porch steps. We'll split the difference."

Nine comes like a ritual I didn't know I needed until it was here—nine at night, porch light on, me on the bottom step, forearms on my thighs, phone face-up like a promise. Some nights she's cross-legged on a hotel carpet that looks soft enough to apologize to. Some nights she sits against a window, city smearing behind her in runway lights and red brake lines. Some nights, the signal hiccups, and all I get is her breath in my ear and the scratch of a zipper as she digs for tea in a minibar that doesn't have any.

We talk about nothing on purpose. A goat that has discovered the single loose board in a mile of fence and is making a life out of it. The weird sock folds people with more money than sense invent. I send her pictures when the service will carry them—Butterscotch in a sunbeam with a blade of hay stuck to her nose; the creek glassed over at first light; an egg on the porch railing that looks like it was laid purely for drama. She sends me ceiling corners and shoes in hallways and the inside of a wardrobe trailer that looks like a spaceship built entirely out of mirrors. Proof of life. Proof of days.

On the third night, she says, "They asked me to add a second brand segment," meaning a man in a suit who says synergy like it buys groceries. "I told them no. My voice shook, but I did it."

I don't bother swallowing the sting in my eyes on my own porch. Let it sit there with the crickets and the gravel and all the words I don't know how to carve. "Good," I say, and it's too small for what I feel. "I'm proud."

"Say it again," she whispers, like it's medicine.

"I'm proud of you," I tell her, slow as a steady cut. "Ivy Quinn, I am proud of you."

Her eyes fall shut on the screen like I just set a warm hand over her heart. "Thank you."

We've been closing the same way, two days running. She lifts her phone and frames the little acorn at her throat. I lift mine to the tin star on the sill. North star and oak. Then she tucks the acorn back under the collar of my hoodie she "forgot" to return, and I stick the star back in its dent, and we hang up before either of us calls the light across the distance what it is.

The fourth night, she doesn't call at nine. The text nails through at 9:17.

Ivy: Running late. Don't wait up.

I don't say I was already waiting. I send a thumbs-up and a picture of the sky cutting itself open in pink over the south field because it costs me nothing to be generous with what the day handed me. At 11:03, she calls from under a hotel duvet, whisper-hoarse, and I sit back down on the step because the porch knows the shape of this better than the couch does.

"Hi," she says, and you can hear the day in it.

"Hi."

"You still up?"

"Now I am."

She tells me about measurements no one needs, a dress that would make more sense as a sculpture, a meeting where everyone used my name as a border around the conversation without knowing they'd drawn one. When she runs out of steam, she asks me for a sound, so I set the phone on the top step and let her listen to rain hit the window. She breathes it in like medicine. I breathe her in like the same.

Day five, Crew texts me first.

Crew: You good?

I look at the screen long enough that the message thinks I died.

Me: Fine. You?

He sends a grainy picture—locker room, laces undone, grin I recognize and remember teaching.

Crew: You hear from her?

I don't have to ask who her is. Nightly, I type, then delete it and write instead.

Me: She's doing her job.

Proud of her, he writes back, and I believe him. The tug that hits under my ribs when I read it, I don't love. I let it sit. Feelings are not facts. Facts are: he looks out for her in rooms I can't enter, and I look out for her in the spaces between.

By the seventh night, I've made a rule of three things I won't do. I won't ask for the return date. I won't double-text. I won't read meaning into delayed replies when half the state's towers fall over if the wind sneezes. I replace those want-to's with three can-do's: pictures of morning; voice memos that sound like the creek; proof that staying isn't a passive act. Some days that look like sharpening the set of loppers I've been ignoring since spring. Some days it feels like driving over two counties to pick up a used bench for the back field, because it seems like something a person who believes in the long version would do.

Bailey catches me throwing the bench into the truck bed.

"You redecorating the outdoors?" she asks, hip hitched

to her car, eyes sharp the way the women who love me run their diagnostics.

"Just making a place to sit," I tell her.

"For you or for her?"

"For anyone who needs it," I say, and she smiles like that's the right answer, even if it isn't exactly true.

On the ninth night, she's cross-legged again on carpet that has never seen a shoe with dirt on it. A different room. A different lamp. Same girl. There's makeup smudged under one eye like proof of life lived and then scrubbed.

"They want to extend," she says, too casual. It slips out on the tail end of a breath like she thought she could trick the sentence into being easier by hiding it in a sigh. "Add two days. Maybe four. They keep saying words like momentum and window."

My stomach drops like an elevator cart pulled along an old rusted chain ready to snap.

"Do you want to?" I ask.

Her mouth does that half-quirk thing that I got good at reading before I admitted I was. "Want isn't the word."

"What's the word?"

"Responsible."

"Then be that," I say, and I mean it. I am not made of the world that's asking for her, but I understand what it is to do the thing you promised when it doesn't feel like your skin anymore. "I'm not a stopwatch."

Something in her face loosens. "I don't want to lose what we've been building."

I look out at the pasture. It doesn't look built when

you're standing in the middle of it. It looks like grass, and some days the grass is defiant. "Then don't," I say. "We're allowed to be steady and far."

"You say that like it's easy."

"It isn't. But it's simple."

She smiles for real then, tired curling up at the edges of it. "Send me a picture of the creek in the morning?"

"Already took it," I admit.

"Of course you did," she says, soft, like it's the best thing she's heard all day.

When we hang up, I sit there long enough for the mosquitoes to locate the parts of me I forgot to spray. Then I go in, pour two fingers of something my dad keeps for happy visitors and funerals, and make a list of tomorrow's chores because doing helps when wanting threatens to take over.

The following morning, the creek throws itself over its own stones like it's performing just for us. I send the picture, and my thumb hovers, but then it doesn't write, *When are you back?*

> Me: The water has that green to it that your dress did at the barbecue. You remember?

She sends back three words that crack me open.

> Ivy: I remember everything.

Days stack. A neighbor loses part of his field line to a storm. I take the truck and four hours of fence in trade for the look a man gives you when he didn't have to ask. The kids come with Bailey for reading on Wednesday, and I pretend I'm not watching Ivy's empty spot on the quilt under the oak while I show six-year-olds how to tell if a tomato wants to be picked or is still thinking about it. Butterscotch has decided gates are more of a mindset than a structure. She licks the back of my hand and bawls like I forgot her birthday. I take her picture and send it with the caption: Your girl misses you.

Ivy answers with a voice memo so tired it sounds like a song: Tell her I'm bringing her a new brush; she likes the purple one.

Crew shows up one afternoon with his shoulder taped like he lost a bet with a refrigerator. He doesn't say he came to check on me, but he eats his mom's cobbler at my table like he's a boy again and not the face on a billboard. "You two okay?" he asks finally, spoon pointed like an accusation he doesn't actually want to make.

"We talk every night," I say, and that's the truest sentence I own right now.

"You gonna go out there?" he asks. "She asked me not to tell you, but…" He stops, that Wright boy line between his brows. "She looks good when she says your name."

I rinse two bowls in water that hasn't decided whether it wants to be hot. "I thought about it," I admit. "Flying into a city that treats me like a guest in my own skin. But this place"—I tap the window frame because there isn't a better word—"it doesn't do really well if you walk away from it when your hands are needed."

He studies me like I'm an event he can't run tape on. "You ever going to admit you're a good man?"

"No," I say, and he barks a laugh. Some part of me that has been clenching since the last airport feed loosens because my brother can stand in my kitchen and laugh at me, and I can laugh back.

On the twelfth night, she video calls from a trailer with a light bulb border and a couch that looks like it was made of credit card points. "Remember when I told you I needed to write by myself?" she says.

"I don't think I do."

She holds up a notebook and flips it open. The page is full of words. She hides the lyrics with her palm like superstition, then reads it anyway, her voice soft and flat the way it sounds when she's not performing. The song isn't about me, and it is, because anything honest is about the people who stood still when you couldn't. When she's finished, she waits without blinking.

"It's good," I say, because it is, and because good is the stone you start with before you start turning it into a house. "It sounds like you."

She bites the inside of her cheek, and my entire torso wants to be a hand pressed between her shoulders. "Say the thing."

"I'm proud of you," I say, and it does the thing it always does—drops into the space and sits there like something heavy that promises it won't slide.

A day becomes two, then becomes four. The calendar does that thing where it pretends it's a neutral party. I don't count. I replace counting with mending a stretch of creek bank the last storm chewed.

On the seventeenth night, she doesn't make nine, and she doesn't make eleven. At 1:24 a.m., the phone goes off on the nightstand like a bird got trapped in the house. I answer before I can think to be dignified.

"I'm okay," she says, breathless.

"I know."

"Do you?"

"I do now."

There's a long exhale, like someone finally opened a window. "We wrapped late. They added a press thing in the morning. I told them I needed two hours blocked out anyway, and when they asked what for, I said 'call the farm.'"

"That what the calendar says?" I ask, and it feels like a kind of sacrament, those three words written next to a slice of corporate pie.

"It does," she says, and laughs. The sound scrapes something tender on its way through me. "I miss the porch."

"It's still here," I tell her. "I left the light on like it could read."

"What if I'm late?" she asks, quiet again, the brave in her voice showing up without armor.

"Then I'll be here when you're not," I say. "And I'll be here when you are."

"You're not... mad?"

"I'm not a timer you set to stun me when you can't get

back by dessert," I say. "I want you home. Want is the honest part. But if the choice is between a want that takes and a want that steadies, I'm going to be the second one every time."

Silence, and then a sound that is not a sob and is not *not* one. "Say it," she asks.

"I am proud of you," I say, and then, because it is true and we are past the point of pretending otherwise, "and I love the way you are being brave for yourself."

The breath she takes is a new kind—sharp on the intake, soft on the out like a hand unclenching. "Rowan."

"I know," I say, because I do, and we aren't going to ruin a good sentence with a hurry.

I'm proud of you, I practice to the frogs and the dark. And: I'll be here.

The night takes both and keeps them safe for later.

The house is too damn quiet.

Not just empty, not just still—but bone-deep quiet. The kind that crawls inside your chest and settles between ribs. The kind that echoes when you walk down the hall and realize no one's humming in the next room. No one's stealing your flannel shirts or leaving coffee mugs in odd corners of the house.

Just me and the silence. And that wouldn't have been so bad... before her. Ivy's been gone a couple of days, and it already feels like the walls are closing in.

I shovel feed into the troughs out back, the chickens kicking dust up around my boots like they haven't missed a beat. The horses nicker in their stalls. The calves stretch and grunt under the morning sun. Life on the farm keeps moving, but I don't. Not really.

Crew's somewhere around here, training in the south pasture. I saw him stretching before sunrise, earbuds in, and that determined look on his face like he's got something to prove. He hasn't said much since she left either, but I've caught him watching me. Waiting. Like he knows something I haven't said out loud yet.

I toss the last bucket of feed into the trough and head back toward my house to rinse off. The kitchen still smells faintly like coffee and citrus, as if the memory of her is clinging to everything. I don't touch her mug. I just stand there, staring at it like it might explain why the hell I feel like I'm missing a limb.

I don't even realize I'm gripping the back of the couch until my fingers brush something soft.

A notebook.

It's small, bound in cracked leather, the edges worn like it's been in and out of too many bags. I lift it slowly, careful like it might break, and flip it open.

Her handwriting is neat, loops and slants that still feel chaotic in a way that's... Ivy.

Some pages are lyrics I remember—songs I've heard her hum under her breath or strum on the porch steps. But one page is different.

New.

I scan the lines, and my throat closes.

> I keep chasing ghosts with dirt under my
>   nails
> Searching for truth behind calloused veils
> He doesn't see it yet—
> The way he's already mine

But I'd wait in silence

If it meant one more time.

My hand tightens around the paper.

It's about me. It's always been about me.

She came back, again and again. She chose this place. Chose me, even when I pushed her away, even when I gave her every reason not to. And now she's gone again—because I couldn't say what I wanted out loud.

I snap the notebook shut and head for the door, heart pounding like I'm about to break into a sprint. Because I remember something. Something old and half-forgotten.

The shed.

It's barely more than a frame and a roof on the far side of Otter Creek Farm, but tucked behind it—buried under dust and canvas tarps—was the start of a stage. My dad built it for one of the county fairs and said it was for the "next Coral Bell Cove talent showcase."

We never finished it. But now? Now I know exactly what I'm building it for.

The door to the old shed sticks, swollen from humidity and years of neglect. I put my shoulder into it, the wood groaning like it remembers me. Dust spills into the light, the smell of old pine and rust curling in the air.

I haven't been in here since before the county fair stopped using volunteers for staging. But it's all still here. Stacks of old boards. Crossbeams leaning in a forgotten corner. Buckets of bent nails and sun-bleached canvas shoved behind a half-broken ladder.

And in the back, under a fraying tarp—what I came looking for. The old stage frame. The bones are solid. Weathered, but strong, like they're waiting for a second chance.

I drop to one knee and tug the tarp free, exposing warped planks and forgotten dreams. My fingers run over the wood, memorizing each knot and splinter like they might tell me what to do next.

I haul the first support beam into the sunlit clearing behind the shed, my boots kicking up dry dirt. The old fairground stage isn't much—just a raised frame and a few crossbars—but it'll be something. It *has* to be something.

If not, she'll have a place to sing when she comes back.

If not… at least I'll know I tried.

By noon, I've cleared the worst of the debris, sweat dripping down my back as I sand the first plank clean. My shoulders burn, but I keep working. Keep moving. Because if I stop, I'll feel the silence again.

I pull my phone from my pocket and stare at the empty thread for a full minute. Then on instinct, I snap a photo of the half-cleared frame. Just enough sunlight. Just enough shadow.

No caption. I don't send it.

Instead, I scroll to her name, thumb hovering over the keyboard.

Me: Hope Nashville's treating you okay.

Simple. Safe. I send it. No typing bubble. No read

receipt. Just silence. I toss the phone onto a toolbox and grab a hammer.

The rhythm of work is the only thing that drowns out her voice in my head. That, and the echo of the song I haven't heard yet—but already know by heart.

The sun is just starting to tilt westward, casting long shadows over the clearing behind the equipment shed. The old fair stage is still mostly bones—rotting planks, half-buried supports, and rusted nails waiting to bite. But the bones are solid enough to stand on. Solid enough to rebuild.

I tug my cap lower and shift the plank into place, sweat clinging to my back and arms. The ache in my shoulders is welcome. It gives me something to do. Something that isn't thinking about the silence Ivy left behind.

I grab the hammer, swing, and drive the nail home. The sound cracks across the clearing like thunder.

"Thought I might find you here."

The voice—low, gravelly with age and too many years shouting over tractors—belongs to my father.

I don't turn. Not right away. My father, Mason Wright, doesn't fill silences unless he has to. He's a man of fences and hay bales, long pauses and looks that say more than most people's words.

"Didn't know I was lost," I say eventually.

He steps up beside me, glancing at the beam in my hands. "You're not."

I finally look over. He's holding two bottles of water, one of them extended my way. His ball cap is sweat-stained at the brim, jeans coated in dust, his button-up rolled at the sleeves. The same uniform he's worn since I was old enough to walk behind him in the fields.

"Thanks," I mutter, taking the bottle.

For a few minutes, we stand there. Me drinking. Him studying the stage like it holds answers. Or maybe like he's trying to remember the last time this thing stood proud.

"You working on somethin'?" he asks eventually.

"Yeah."

"Fair coming back to town?"

I shake my head. "No."

He nods slowly, then looks back at me. "That singer girl. Ivy."

My throat tightens, but I force the cap back on the bottle. "What about her?"

"You building this for her?"

I pause but don't answer.

He doesn't press. Just watches me with that look— steady and unreadable, like the sky before a storm.

"She's good for you," he says after a while.

I blink. "You don't even know her."

"I know you." He kneels beside one of the crossbeams and runs a calloused hand along the grain. "Been a while since I saw you build something for someone."

"I'm not—" I start, then stop.

Because I am.

I'm building this with her in mind. Every board. Every goddamn nail. I'm putting together something better than the mess I made with my words. With my fear.

I'm building something that might show her what I haven't said.

My father looks up at me from where he's crouched. "You want her here when it's done?"

I nod once. "Yeah. I do."

He nods, like that's all he needs to know. Then he pushes to his feet, slow but steady, and picks up the other end of the beam I was about to lift.

"Then let's finish it."

We work in silence for a while. The kind of silence that builds things. That settles over sweat and shared effort and a lifetime of knowing when to speak and when to let your son breathe.

Later, as he loads his tools back into the truck, Dad looks at me over the open tailgate.

"She comes back," he says, "you oughta tell her."

I frown. "Tell her what?"

"That you're not building a stage."

I stare after him as he drives off, the truck kicking up dust along the old gravel path.

Because he's right. This isn't just a stage. It's a promise.

By the time the sun sinks behind the tree line, I'm covered in sweat and sawdust, arms heavy from the work. But it's a good kind of tired—the kind that fills you up instead of emptying you. The kind I only seem to find when my hands are building something that matters.

I drop onto the tailgate of the truck and crack open the water bottle again. The clearing is still. Crickets have started their nightly choir. Somewhere down near the creek bend, a bullfrog croaks.

My phone's still in my pocket, pressed warm against my thigh. I pull it free and swipe the screen.

No new messages.

Just the same old wallpaper—an aerial shot of the ranch fields—and the last text to Ivy, still unopened.

That little gray bubble mocks me.

I don't know what I expect. She said she'd be busy. Said she'd come back. But the longer the silence stretches, the more my chest hollows out.

I tap open the camera and snap a quick shot—nothing posed, just my chest dusted in sawdust, arms crossed, the line of the stage's skeletal frame blurred behind me.

> **Me:** Hard work looks good on me, huh?

I stare at it for too long before I hit send.

Then I type another.

> **Me:** Was thinking about your camp idea today. That napkin sketch keeps rattling around in my head.

Still no response.

I let the phone fall beside me on the truck bed, the metal cold under my thighs. The wind shifts, and I catch the scent of lilac and old wood—faint, but unmistakable. It smells like the cottage. Like her skin when she stood close enough for me to breathe her in.

I lean forward and rest my elbows on my knees, fingers laced together. My head hangs heavy between my shoulders.

I miss her.

Not just the way she filled a room or lit up when she talked about music. Not just the way she curled into my side like she'd always belonged there. I miss her smart-ass remarks. Her stupid socks. The way she looked at my horses like they were mythical creatures.

I miss not being alone in this place.

Eventually, I pick up the phone again and open our thread.

One last message.

> Me: I miss you, Ivy. More than I know how to handle.

I hit send.

Then I toss the phone into the truck cab and slam the door shut before I can regret it.

The moon is rising over the pasture when I finally drive away, gravel crunching under the tires. The unfinished stage fades in the rearview, but the ache in my chest doesn't go anywhere.

She hasn't replied, and I don't know if or when she will. But I do know one thing. If she does come back... that stage will be ready.

The night passes with no sleep, but with determination, I drive the nail deeper, the rough plank shifting slightly beneath my palm. It's coming together now—a little slower than I planned, but the bones are there. The frame of the old stage creaks, stubborn and sun-bleached, but it still holds the promise of something more.

Of her.

I don't look at my phone. Not anymore. It's in the toolbox, screen face down, silent since the last message I sent last night. Just a simple one.

> Me: Miss making your coffee.

And before that? An image of my chest after a long ride, sweat gleaming, saddle strap still hanging low. I don't know what I was hoping for—maybe a little reaction, a smart comment, a "Nice try, cowboy." But there's been nothing.

The silence? It's louder than the hammer.

A car door slams in the distance. Gravel crunches. I glance up just in time to see Hadley's familiar pink aesthetic bounce around the corner of the shed. She's been visiting me incessantly since Ivy left.

Great.

She's got a coffee cup in one hand and a knowing smirk on her face, which means I'm in trouble.

"Still building something or hiding from your feelings?" she chirps, ducking under the open frame of the half wall like she owns the place.

I grunt, wiping my forearm across my brow. "You bring coffee or sass?"

"Both." She hands me the cup. "And maybe a little concern."

"Don't need concern." I sip the coffee and try not to

groan. She went heavy on the vanilla again. "You put syrup in this?"

"Rowan," she drawls. "You've been out here every day for the last few weeks. You're covered in sawdust, and you've sent three shirtless thirst traps to a girl who's probably stuck in more filming than she can count. I think we're past the point of concern."

"Those were not thirst traps," I mutter, turning back to the wood.

"Oh, please. That one yesterday? You even flexed."

I don't answer.

Hadley hops up onto one of the stacked beams and swings her legs, watching me like she's waiting for me to crack.

"So," she says after a beat. "Is this about her?"

I pause, fingers tightening on the tape measure. "I don't know what you mean."

She snorts. "Come on. The entire town's buzzing. Ivy leaves, and suddenly, you're out here playing lumberjack slash mystery man. Mrs. Danner told the post office Ivy 'snuck off like a woman in love with nowhere to go.' And Bailey says you've been acting like a man who either just fell hard or just got dumped."

"Bailey should mind her business."

"Bailey owns half the town's gossip, so good luck with that."

I sigh and lean back against a beam, stretching my arms until my shoulders pop. "It's not like that."

"Oh really?" Hadley folds her arms, cocking her head.

"Because to me, it looks a hell of a lot like a guy who let something good slip through his fingers and is now building a shrine to his feelings."

I blink at her. "It's not a shrine."

"Is it a stage?"

I freeze.

She raises a brow. "Knew it. You always did get sentimental with wood."

I shake my head, jaw tightening. "I'm not doing this for her. Not *just* for her."

Hadley gives me a long look. "Rowan... don't bullshit me."

I take a breath. "I'm doing this because I want her to come back and see something that says... she's worth it. That I'm worth it. That I've finally figured out I don't have to run from things just because I'm afraid I'll mess them up."

She goes quiet, and when I glance her way, her expression has softened.

"That's new," she says gently.

I shrug. "Yeah."

She slides down from the beam and steps beside me, nudging my arm. "You're doing okay, Ro. You're not perfect, and you've been an idiot—but you're trying. And for what it's worth? I think she sees that. Even if she's not answering your... flex pics."

I roll my eyes. "They weren't—never mind."

She grins. "Just... keep going, okay? Whether she comes

back tomorrow or next month, let her find you standing in something you built. Something that matters."

I nod, throat tight.

Hadley turns to leave, then glances back over her shoulder.

"Oh, and if you do send another shirtless picture? Maybe don't do it while holding a hammer. You looked like a horny handyman."

"Go away."

She laughs all the way to her car. And me? I stare down at the stage frame and think about Ivy's notebook, still tucked between the cushions of my couch.

I haven't read past that song. I don't need to. Because the words she already wrote? They said enough. Now it's my turn to do the same—with action. With something she'll see. Even if she never knows why.

The days pass in slow, uneven pieces. Mornings bleed into afternoons marked by sweat, sunburn, and the sharp smell of sawdust. My hands are blistered. My back aches. And still, I work.

Because every bolt I tighten, every board I sand, it's like laying bricks over the gnawing ache in my chest.

Ivy's absence is a hollow thing, though she calls when she can. It's less and less with each passing day. It lingers in places I didn't expect—in the second coffee mug I don't use, in the ghost of her laugh echoing through the barn, in the blanket she folded and left on the porch swing before she left. It's not even *her* blanket, it's mine, but now it smells like her, and I can't bring myself to move it.

By Thursday morning, the stage has started to resemble something more than scrap. The platform is mostly complete, elevated just enough to be visible from the hill. The back beams are upright, and with a little more work, I'll have enough structure for lights or a canvas banner if I get ambitious.

It doesn't take a rocket scientist to figure out who I'm building it for, though, but the reason may be elusive. My dad ambles down from the back porch with two waters and a raised brow.

"You finally giving in to your theater kid era?" Dad asks as he drops onto a hay bale beside me.

I grunt, wiping my neck. "Funny. I'm just fixing it up. Figured we could use it for the summer camp."

It's half a lie.

We *could* use it for the camp. I'd thought about that. But it's not the real reason I've been throwing myself into the project like a man possessed.

My dad watches me for a moment, face lined with the sun and the weight of years lived hard and honest. Then he takes a long swig of water and says, "You know... when your mama was pregnant with Hadley, I built her a porch swing."

I blink. "Yeah?"

"Didn't know a damn thing about woodworking. That swing creaked like hell and leaned to the left, but she sat in it every night for eight months. Because I made it for her."

I nod slowly.

"You never told Ivy how you felt, did you?" he asks quietly.

I stare at the grain of the wood. "No."

"Then maybe it's time to stop waiting for the right moment and just *make* one."

I breathe deep. "I worry she might not come back."

"She might not," he agrees. "But if she does, don't let her walk into a quiet house. Let her walk into something that says, 'You were missed. You mattered. You still do.'"

I don't answer, but I don't need to.

The next day, I'm back at it with fresh screws and a new plan.

It's nearly dusk when Crew finds me crouched behind the stage frame, sketching ideas in the dust with a stick like some desperate caveman architect.

He whistles low. "Damn, Ro. You building a wedding venue or just working out your trauma?"

I roll my eyes. "You're not funny."

Crew tilts his head. "You really are the emotionally constipated one, huh?"

"Don't you have sprints to run?"

"I'm on my break." He studies me for a long second, then sighs. "You could just say it, you know. That you're in love with her."

I pause. The stick in my hand breaks in half.

Crew raises a brow. "That's what I thought."

"I don't know what I am," I admit quietly. "I've never felt anything like this. Not with Marissa. Not with anyone."

"Then maybe it's real."

I look up at the stage, at the way the light hits the edge of the frame. "I think it is."

Crew claps me on the back. "Then finish the damn thing so when she comes back, you've got something better than a text full of horse pictures."

I grunt. "Those were *solid* horse pictures."

He laughs, walks off, and I stare after him. Then I go back to work because this isn't just about Ivy anymore. It's about me being the man I never thought I could be—for her.

For us.

Chapter Twenty

IVY

The fluorescent lights in the PR building hum like angry bees overhead, and I swear, if one more person asks me to "smile for the camera," I might climb onto the conference table and scream.

I don't.

Because that would be bad for brand integrity.

Instead, I sit very still, legs crossed, hands folded in my lap, pretending I don't feel like I've left half of myself behind in a cottage with weathered wood siding and a man who smells like sandalwood and slow Sunday mornings.

"Ivy," my publicist says for the third time, and I blink back into the room.

"Sorry," I murmur. "What was that?"

"The new single. The one you teased last month? We need a firm release date, and we need a track. Something we can build a social campaign around."

I reach for the water bottle and twist the cap, buying myself a breath.

The truth isn't that I'm empty—it's that I'm full in ways I don't want to hand to them yet. I've been writing without my usual notebook: hotel stationery covered in half choruses, the back of a boarding pass with a bridge scribbled across the barcode, voice memos at 2:12 a.m. where I hum the hook into my phone so it doesn't get away. The songs are there. They're just mine right now.

So why am I still here? Because I choose to be—for a minute. I could have dug in and said Zoom only, and most of this could've limped along on video. But fittings for tour pieces need pins in real fabric and hands tugging seams; camera tests for the first video look different in person; choreography tweaks land faster when you're standing on the tape lines; legal wants signatures, not screenshots. If I stack it all now—two days of wardrobe, a half day of camera and lighting tests, one production meeting, one rehearsal block, a quick brand shoot —I can clear weeks later. Fewer "urgent" trips. More uninterrupted days back in Coral Bell Cove to write, breathe, be.

It's not that they couldn't come to me. They could. They'd just bring an entourage and a press leak, and my quiet would be collateral damage. Here, I can herd everyone into three rooms and say no when the schedule grows extra heads. Which I do. I cut the second brand segment. I limit the photo set to one look. I cap the day at six hours. I keep my mornings for writing, even if it's on napkins.

So I sit through "engagement" and "deliverables" and nod like a professional while the parts of me that matter stay tucked in my pocket—ink-stained fingers, a melody that smells like river water, a verse that belongs to a porch and a man who doesn't talk unless he has something to say. When the meeting finally spits me back into the elevator, I press my forehead to the cool metal and let the truth unspool: I'm here because finishing it now buys me freedom later. And because the sooner I do this on my terms, the sooner I get to fly home.

I miss mornings with strong coffee and stronger silences. I miss the rooster I never got to meet. I miss Bailey's little readers and their impossible questions. I miss belonging to something small and beautiful and real.

When I get back to the apartment—my painfully sterile high-rise that smells like someone else's soap—I dig through my bag for my songwriting notebook, then remember I purposely left it shoved into the couch cushions at Rowan's. He hasn't mentioned that he found it, but my nerves bubble to the surface thinking that he has. All my greatest secrets are scribbled on those pages.

I stare at the blank page on my tablet, fingers hovering over the screen like the lyrics might spill out if I stay still long enough. But they don't. They haven't all day.

I've tried everything. Pacing the penthouse suite. Hot tea. My old playlist. A bubble bath that only made me cry.

Nothing.

Not a single verse. Not a line of melody. Not even a

clever metaphor. Because my notebook—the one that holds everything—is with Rowan.

I clutch my mug tighter, ignoring the rising ache in my chest. I don't want to admit it, but that notebook held more than songs.

It held confessions. Memories. The way his voice sounded in the morning. The color of his eyes during storms. The ache in my ribs when I laughed too hard around him. Every single thing I was too scared to say out loud.

And now it's in his hands.

God, I was stupid to leave it, I had that weird hope that maybe he wouldn't find it, but would flip through the pages if he did.

A knock sounds at the door. Before I can answer, it opens, of course. Celeste doesn't wait for permission anymore. Not when she thinks she has the upper hand.

She sweeps in wearing a fitted ivory pantsuit, heels clicking like a warning shot. Her assistant trails her, head down, carrying a folder thick with press clippings.

"You canceled two interviews," she says without preamble, snapping her fingers for the assistant to drop the folder on the coffee table. "The label is panicking. They think you're going soft."

"I needed space," I reply flatly.

"Evangeline, space is for has-beens. Not headliners."

I stare at her, jaw locked.

She begins flipping through the articles, red manicured nails tapping with each turn. "You want to know what the world's saying while you're hiding in your robe and drinking tea like a debutante in mourning?"

"No," I mutter.

She reads anyway. "*Celebrity Page* says 'America's Sweetheart Torn Between Two Cowboys.' *BuzzBeat* ran a poll asking who's more her type—Crew, the golden boy, or Rowan, the rugged recluse."

My stomach twists.

Celeste tosses the papers on the table. "You're trending for all the wrong reasons, Ivy."

"I don't care."

"You should." Her voice turns cold. "You think this is about you and your little farm fling? This is your career. This is everything we built."

"No." I rise from the couch. "This is everything you built. I just kept performing."

Her mouth hardens.

"I don't want to be part of the machine anymore, Mom. I want to live. I want to create on my own terms."

"And what?" she sneers. "Grow tomatoes and braid horsehair? Let some farmhand ruin what we spent a decade building?"

"He's not a farmhand." My voice shakes. "And this—this brand you cling to like a lifeline? It's not living. It's suffocating."

Silence falls, sharp and dangerous.

Celeste's eyes narrow. "You'd throw everything away for a man who hasn't even come after you?"

I flinch.

Because she's right. He hasn't. Except he doesn't have to. We have an understanding.

There is something smarmy in her grin, though. Something I'm afraid to question.

I turn away from her, breath shaky, and open the top drawer of my desk. Pull out another flyer sketch I drew on a napkin—Rowan's summer camp, scribbled in green Sharpie between coffee rings and tears. I hear the door snap shut without a single goodbye.

I smooth the wrinkled edges and grab my laptop. If the songs won't come, I'll build something else.

Rowan's camp. The one he dreams about but won't speak of out loud. I start typing—curriculum, age groups, activities. I create a mock-up. Design a logo. Upload a picture I snapped of the horses when he wasn't looking.

It's easier than writing a love song. The truth is, I already wrote the biggest one, and I left it in his living room.

Glancing at the clock, I know Rowan's out on the field working, but it's been hours since we messaged. Our third rule has already been broken. Instead, I reply to his missed messages with a picture of my own, my bathrobe displaying an indecent amount of cleavage, with his acorn necklace draped between the valley.

But even in my heart, I know that picture isn't enough. Not enough to combat the wild tabloids. If I know my mother at all, I'm sure she and the label concocted this wild tabloid about me, Rowan, and Crew. Anything to keep my name in the headlines. To them, all news is good news.

As I glance around the sterile space, I know my time here is over, even with things unfinished. They've had enough time to get what they needed. Now it's time for me.

I walk to the closet, grab the duffel bag that never quite made it to the shelf, and start stuffing it with clothes. My heart beats faster with every folded T-shirt, every rolled pair of jeans.

This isn't a performance. It's a return. To the place where I started telling the truth. To the man who might still be holding it for me.

Before long, I'm shoving whatever I can find into the bag until I can barely tug the zipper closed. The frustration eats away at me.

It starts with a shimmer.

Not the kind that belongs to stage lights or sequined dresses. This one crawls behind my eyes—slow and electric, like someone lit a sparkler at the edge of my vision.

I blink hard. Once. Twice. Still there. Then let the tears fall until I have nothing left to give but my soul, except it already belongs to a cowboy who roped it up the day we met.

Trying to calm down, I settle on the worn leather. My laptop rests on my thighs, a half-finished mock-up of Rowan's summer camp flyer open in a design program I barely know how to use. Anything to settle my mind and my chest. The screen blurs.

I try to swallow, but my throat feels tight. Too tight.

Breathe, Ivy.

I set the laptop aside, palms bracing against the couch.

My heart pounds, but it's not panic. Not yet. It's recognition. I've felt this before. I know what's coming.

My fingers twitch. The lamp beside me suddenly feels too bright. The sound of the refrigerator hums louder than it should. It's all too much.

I curl forward, breathing slow and deliberate through my nose. This isn't a full seizure—not yet. Just an aura. A warning. Like a distant roll of thunder before the storm arrives.

I should call someone. But who?

My mother would panic—or worse, turn it into a PR narrative about the pressures of fame. Celeste once said, *"Don't let them see you broken. There's no comeback from that."*

I press a trembling hand to my forehead.

I don't want her voice in my head. I want Rowan's. Low and steady. I want the quiet rustle of pasture grass and the gentle creak of the swing on his porch. I want the weight of his gaze, grounding me. Seeing me.

The shimmer swells—bright and buzzy behind my right eye—so I ease down, flat on the couch, and breathe like my neurologist taught me. In for four. Out for six. I thumb my phone and start the timer, a little ritual that keeps the panic from galloping.

My fingers prickle, the world edges glassy, but I'm still here—awake and aware. I can name the room, the day, the person I'd call if I needed to. Ninety seconds. A minute forty. The wave peaks and slides back.

I stop the timer at just under two minutes and let my shoulders sink. No blackout. No second wave chasing the first. I take a sip of water and jot a quick note in my seizure log.

No ambulance. Not this time. My doctor's rule has lived in my bones for years: if it lasts past five minutes or stacks one after another, we go. If it's brief and I stay conscious, I rest, hydrate, and let the edges smooth themselves out.

This one passes. I stay put and let the room come back into focus.

Hours later, my body still feels like it's been wrung out. Muscles shaky. Nausea swirling low in my gut.

But I'm still here, and I'm done pretending this place is enough. That this glass tower and fancy address and bottled water with custom labels can fill the ache that's only ever quieted in Coral Bell Cove.

I push up slowly, legs unsteady, and shuffle to the bathroom to splash cold water on my face. As the water trickles down my cheeks, I glance up. My reflection looks pale. Washed out. But my eyes—they're clear.

And I know without a shadow of a doubt I can't stay here. Not when my body is screaming for peace. Not when my soul is begging to go home. Not when there's a man with rough hands and kind eyes who's probably still wondering why I left in the first place.

I left my notebook at his house, but the truth is, I left more than that. I left myself.

Chapter Twenty-One

ROWAN

The sky is streaked in early morning pink when I step out onto the porch, coffee in hand, and take in the view.

Dew clings to the grass. Stuff that glistens like frost even though it's nearly September. The barn doors are already open, thanks to Holt being an overachiever, and the low rumble of Crew's voice carries on the breeze as he corrals the last of the folding chairs toward the south pasture.

The same pasture where, two weeks ago, I hauled a warped trailer floor and half-rotted lumber out of a shed behind the chicken coop and started to rebuild something I hadn't let myself dream of in years.

A stage.

It's nothing fancy—just a low wooden platform with fresh sealant and new steps, rigged with borrowed fairy lights that twinkle like the start of something. But to me, it looks like hope. Or something I'm not quite brave enough to name yet.

I take a slow sip from the mug and let the silence settle around me. It's the last bit of quiet I'll get before the place fills up with twenty-five screaming kids and a half-dozen volunteer chaperones. My mother and Bailey practically moved heaven and half the PTA to make today happen. I owe her more than I can say.

I'm just thankful Otter Creek Farms already functions as a produce pickup location so we didn't have to worry about parking. Years spent as a strawberry and pecan farm for the town and surrounding counties help.

"Hey!" Crew's voice cuts through the air. He's already sweating through his T-shirt, carrying a stack of laminated signs under one arm. I'm not even sure how he's here since he just played a game in Florida last night. "You planning to supervise or just stand there brooding like a romance novel cover?"

I grunt. "Brooding. Obviously."

He grins. "Figured."

I walk down the porch steps and meet him halfway, taking one of the signs without asking. He eyes me sidelong.

"You sleep at all?"

"Some."

"Liar."

I don't answer. Just drive the stake into the dirt and press down until the "Welcome to Otter Creek Farm

Camp" sign stands straight. The lettering is a little crooked, but the message is clear.

This is happening.

Kids. Laughter. Dirt under their nails. Learning where eggs come from and how to saddle a pony. Maybe even standing on that makeshift stage at the end of the day to sing something into the sky.

And not just because Ivy believed in it. Because I do. Even if she's not here. Even if she's still in Nashville, fighting off the world with a camera in her face and that fake smile she hates.

Crew claps a hand on my shoulder. "It's gonna be good, man. You're good at this."

I nod once. "Hope so."

"I thought she'd come back to see it."

I look out toward the stage.

Every day, but I don't voice that out loud. Part of that is my fault, though. I let my fear keep me from telling her explicitly that we were doing a run-through of the camp this weekend. Though I'm positive Bailey told her.

Instead, I walk toward the barn and call over my shoulder, "We've got gates to tie off."

Because today isn't about her. It's about the kids.

Even if everything in me still wants to believe she'll walk through that field like she did that first day—lost, stubborn, beautiful—and this time, stay.

By 10 a.m., the place is buzzing.

The kind of noise that makes your ears ring, but in a good way. Laughter bounces off the barn rafters. Little boots stomp through puddles I forgot to rake gravel over. One of the goats has already escaped twice.

I haven't sat down once. But my chest? It feels lighter than it has in weeks.

"Rowan!" one of the kids from down the road—Hazel, I think—tugs on my shirt hem. "The chickens won't stop staring at me."

I crouch down to her level. "Did you tell them you're in charge now?"

Her eyes widen. "I can do that?"

"Sure can."

She nods, serious as a preacher, and marches back to the coop with both fists on her hips.

Crew walks past me, balancing three bales of hay on his shoulders like it's nothing. "Did you tell that kid she's the chicken queen?"

"Delegation," I mutter. "It's called leadership."

He laughs and keeps moving. He's been here since sunrise, helping me get this thing off the ground without asking too many questions. That's what Crew does—he fills the space when I can't. Doesn't push when I'm not ready to talk.

Like now. When I'm watching the road with one eye even though I keep telling myself not to.

"You're expecting her," he says eventually, when we're both out behind the shed trying to rig up a tarp for shade.

I don't answer right away.

"She left her notebook," I say finally, voice low. "Wedged in the couch. I found it a few nights ago."

Crew straightens, his hands stilling. "Did you read it?"

"I shouldn't have."

"But you did."

I nod, staring down at the wood grain on the bench in front of me. "There's a song in there. It's... about me. I think. About the farm. About being seen."

He whistles low. "Damn."

"Yeah."

"About Ivy." He waits until I look at him. "When she comes back, it won't be for the journal. It won't be for some cute farm chapter or a photo op. It'll be for you."

Something tight in my chest gives. All those fears and insecurities bubble to the surface. "You sure about that?"

"I'm sure about this." He tips his water bottle at me. "Nothing ever happened with me and Ivy," he says, steady. "Not before, not during, not after. She's like a little sister to me. I look out for her, and that's it. You're my brother. I wasn't competing then, and I'm not competing now."

The barn takes a long breath around us. I take one too. "I was jealous," I say, the word tasting like gravel. "And stupid. You didn't deserve that."

Crew shrugs, easy. "Jealous means you give a damn. Stupid's fixable." He nudges my shoulder with his. "Let it go, Ro. Trust her. And maybe trust me a little while you're at it."

I nod. It's small, but it's real. "Alright."

He grins, quick and crooked. "Good. Because when she walks back up your drive, you don't get to hide behind fences and weather reports. You meet her at the fork in the path."

"Yeah," I say, feeling the truth of it settle. "I will."

I pull out my phone before I can talk myself out of it.

> Me: Stage is up. You'd hate the font on the banner, but the kids love it.

I stare at the screen for a beat. No response.

Just like all the ones I previously sent.

Two hours ago, it was:

> Me: Thought you'd like this.

> <Image attached> Me, dust-covered, on top of the horse paddock fence. Shirtless. Sweaty. Looking like hell but smiling for the first time in a while.

Four hours ago, it was:

> Me: Hope you're drinking real coffee and not that PR-approved caffeine-free crap.

Still nothing.

I lock the screen and shove it back in my pocket, swallowing the ache that keeps rising like bile.

"Maybe she's still working," Crew says gently.

"Maybe I gave her too many reasons to stay gone," I reply.

But even as I say it, I glance out toward the tree line and hope. Hope hard.

By the time lunch rolls around, I've lost count of the

juice boxes, bandaged knees, and goat droppings we've encountered.

The kids are everywhere—climbing hay bales, brushing the horses, and pointing at the cows like they're mythical creatures. I half expect a few of them to start naming the chickens like they're at a Disney petting zoo. And honestly? That's fine by me.

It's chaos. The best kind. The kind that looks like movement. Like growth. The kind that reminds me why I started this thing in the first place.

The small crowd of parents and volunteers who have come to watch sit on hay bales facing the old platform stage we repurposed from the shed. I strung lights across the top this morning. They're not on yet, but they'll glow soft and warm once the sun drops.

It's not perfect, but it's real. It's ours.

Crew walks up behind me and claps a hand on my shoulder. "You should say something."

I shake my head. "Not really my thing."

"Doesn't have to be a speech. Just... a few words. You built this. They should hear from you."

I glance over at the crowd again. A few familiar faces. My parents, of course. Hadley is corralling toddlers with a juice-stained apron. Holt's leaning against the fence with his arms crossed, looking proud and quietly smug. Bailey's sitting next to one of the librarians, jotting things down in a notebook—probably prepping a post about this for the town newsletter while ignoring Crew every time he tries to speak to her.

And me? I'm standing here with my hands too empty and my heart too full.

I walk up to the makeshift stage, brushing my palm over the corner like I'm not sure it's real. The lights are still off, but the midday sun does the job.

The crowd settles when they see me.

I clear my throat. "Uh... thanks for coming out."

A few chuckles. Someone claps. One of the kids yells something about chickens, and I can hold back my grin.

"I, uh... wasn't sure what this was gonna be when we started. Just an idea. Something that felt too big for a guy like me to pull off."

More claps. My mom dabs at her eyes. Dammit.

"But people showed up. They helped. And now here we are. Kids learning where food comes from. Laughing. Getting muddy. Chasing goats."

That gets a louder laugh, and I take a steadying breath.

"And I guess what I'm trying to say is... sometimes the things that scare you the most? The ones you think you're not built for? They turn out to be the things that make you feel the most... alive."

The applause catches me off guard. I step back, giving a small nod, then hop down from the stage.

Crew catches my eye as I walk past. "Nice job, cowboy."

I shake my head, but I'm smiling. I move toward the water station to grab a drink when I hear it.

A car door, then another, and a hush rolls across the field like a summer breeze. I turn, slowly. There, standing just past the gravel loop, hoodie slung over one shoulder, her hair caught up in a loose braid, is Ivy.

She's wearing the denim cutoffs I love so much and boots and that same damn blue tank top that made my brain short-circuit the first time she wore it.

But it's not the clothes. It's her. Her being here and looking like she never left.

My feet start moving before I can think. She meets me halfway. Neither of us speaks right away.

Then her voice, soft and uncertain. "I didn't know if you'd want me here."

I swallow hard, throat thick. "I've been building a stage for when you came back."

Her breath hitches. Then she blinks, and I see it—the thing that's been missing since the night she left.

Hope.

She glances past me toward the kids, the animals, the whole damn setup.

"You really did it," she whispers. "You started the camp."

"You were right. I just needed a nudge."

Her lips curve. "Or a shove."

I chuckle. "Same difference."

We stand there, suspended in that space where everything could still fall apart.

Then she shifts her bag and looks down. "I wrote something on the plane."

My heart thuds once. Loud.

"Yeah?"

She nods.

"I don't know if it's finished. But... I think I'd like to sing it."

I don't speak. I can't. Her words hit me in my chest, calming the ache that grew two weeks ago when she stepped off my porch.

Suddenly, the lights I strung this morning aren't just decorations. The stage isn't just a platform—it's a beginning.

And Ivy?

She's home.

The crowd stirs as Ivy walks toward the stage, the kind of ripple you feel more than hear. People start murmuring—recognition mixing with curiosity. A few of the kids call her name. Parents nudge each other. One of the teens pulls out a phone.

Ivy hesitates near the edge of the platform. She looks back at me, her expression soft and uncertain.

My hand finds hers before I can think.

"You don't have to," I say quietly. "Not if you're not ready."

Her fingers squeeze mine. "I think I am."

I nod once, then let her go.

She climbs the short set of steps and crosses to the center of the stage. Her bag slides from her shoulder with a whisper of fabric as she kneels to unzip it. A notebook—nothing like the beat-up old one I hold in my possession—peeks out, the spine crisp, pages clean and white. She flips it open, her fingers finding a particular page like muscle memory.

The crowd hushes.

She glances out at them, then down at the page. Her voice is quiet, but it carries.

"I wrote this for someone who makes me feel like I'm not lost anymore."

That's all she says.

Then she opens her mouth and sings. No mic. No band. Just her voice and the breeze and the golden light bleeding across the pasture.

Damn, it hits me like a freight train.

The lyrics aren't subtle. They talk about calloused hands and slow mornings. About a porch swing and a denim shirt. About a man who doesn't say much but means everything when he does. A man who holds her steady when everything else feels like it's falling apart.

It's about me. Every word, a thread she's tied from her heart to mine.

I watch the crowd shift as the truth dawns on them—this isn't just a song. It's a confession. And I don't care who hears it.

Her voice catches on the last line. Not from nerves but from emotion.

"...he was the place I didn't know I needed until I finally came home."

Silence clings to the air for a full heartbeat, then the applause erupts.

People stand. Kids cheer. Someone whistles so loud that a horse spooks in the distance.

But Ivy?

She doesn't look at them. She looks at me.

Eyes glassy. Lips trembling with a smile that tells me everything I've been too damn stubborn to say out loud.

I move without consent, my heart guiding me the entire way.

I don't wait for the crowd to calm down. I don't care that half the town is watching. I climb the stage, wrap my hand around her waist, and pull her to me like she's gravity and I've finally stopped resisting.

Her page of lyrics falls at our feet as I press my lips to hers. Soft and certain.

Home.

The applause fades into the background, a dull roar against the sound of her breath and the thump of my heart in my ears.

When I finally pull back, I keep my forehead against hers.

"You wrecked me with that," I murmur.

She smiles, blinking fast. "Good."

I laugh against her mouth. "You think you're clever?"

"I think I'm yours."

That undoes me. Right there.

On the stage I rebuilt from something half forgotten, with fairy lights above us and hay underfoot, Ivy claims me in front of everyone. And I let her. It's about damn time I stopped pretending I don't want to be hers too.

After the song, after the kiss, after the applause dies down and the stage lights flicker to amber with the dipping sun, the world starts moving again.

Ivy and I step off the platform hand in hand.

Crew saunters over, smirking with a red popsicle in his hand as if he's not the reason half the camp is high on sugar. "So...that was one hell of a debut. You're gonna start taking requests, or was that a one-time love ballad just for your grumpy cowboy?"

Ivy grins, cheeks flushed. "No encores."

"Shame," he teases, before clapping me on the shoulder. "Proud of you, man. The camp, the stage, all of it."

"Thanks," I mutter, still overwhelmed.

He leans in and whispers, "You know she's all in now, right? Don't screw it up."

"I don't plan to."

He raises both brows. "Then go do something about it. Because she's got that 'should I have come back?' look again."

He's not wrong. I glance at Ivy, eyes darting at all the kids as they wave in her direction, and something stirs in my chest—protective, possessive, and grateful as hell.

I want her here. Not just now and not just tonight but every day.

"Hey," I murmur when she stands, brushing off grass. "You mind helping me put away a few supplies before dinner?"

"Sure," she says, falling into step beside me, the air between us warm and buzzing with energy we haven't touched yet.

We cut behind the barn while the others light the firepit, laughter and clinking cups fading. Inside, it smells like hay and cedar, with the low shuffle of horses in their stalls.

I walk us toward the tack room, pretending we have something to organize, but really, I just need a second with her without prying eyes and definitely without my mother wiping away another proud tear.

Just Ivy and me.

The moment the door closes, she turns to me, arms crossed loosely over her chest. "So... that was quite a stage you built."

I shrug, trying not to give too much away. "Had the pieces lying around."

"Really?" she asks, stepping closer. "Because it looked a lot like something someone made just for me."

"Maybe I did." I glance down. "Maybe I hoped you'd come back."

Her breath hitches.

I close the distance, my hands settling at her waist, thumbs brushing the hem of her shirt. "Didn't know how else to say I missed you. Especially as your time away extended."

I faintly hear her grumble, "Mother." Then she says clearly, "You built a stage instead."

"Words have never been my thing," I murmur, leaning down, brushing my lips along her jaw. "But I'm trying."

She shivers in my arms, fingers clutching my shirt. "I never wanted to be anywhere else."

"Then stay forever."

"That's the plan."

I crush my mouth to hers again. This time, the kiss isn't for show or stage lights. It's slow. Deep. Familiar in the way only something you've been dreaming about for too long can feel.

I walk her backward until her hips hit the counter beside the tack hooks, and she gasps when my hand slips under her shirt, fingers brushing just across her ribs.

But we stop there. The moment isn't about lust, it's about grounding.

We rest there for minutes—foreheads pressed together, breaths mingling in the quiet of the barn.

Outside, the camp excitement continues to flicker, and kids giggle in the distance. But in here, I finally feel whole.

Chapter Twenty-Two

IVY

He planned this. I can tell the second we reach the top of the ladder and the loft blooms warm with light.

After Bailey packs the last of the picture books and the kids tumble down the lane sticky with lemonade, Rowan murmurs, "Help me shut down the barn?" and palms the ladder like it's nothing. When I climb up behind him, the string lights wink on—soft, low, and gold instead of bright—looped along the rafters like fireflies that decided to stay. There's a quilt spread over the smoothest boards, two pillows, a small battery fan turning lazy circles, and a dented thermos with tin cups. On a crate, he's laid out apples, cheddar, and the last two peach hand pies from the cooler like a man who pretends he doesn't know how to make a moment and then makes one anyway.

"It's not much," he says, that shy edge he gets when he

cares too loudly. "Figured we could... cool down. Hear the creek."

It smells like hay and clean wood. The lights don't flicker—they're the warm kind—and I clock that detail like a love note. No surprises for my brain. He thought about it. He always does.

I settle on the quilt and fold my legs under me while he lingers at the rail, looking out at the dusk settling over the pasture like he needs the horizon to steady himself. His shoulders are loose, but his hands are braced—one of those Rowan tells that says there's a lot inside and he's choosing where to put it.

"Come sit," I say, patting the quilt. He comes halfway, then stops, watching me like I'm the song he can't get out of his head.

"Rowan," I whisper, the crickets taking the rest of the volume. "Talk to me."

He doesn't, not with words. He crosses the space in three strides and drops to his knees in front of me, mouth finding mine like he's been holding his breath since the first kid asked me to sing. The kiss is sure and hungry and a little wrecked. I fall back onto the quilt and pull him with me, fingers fisting in his shirt, the soft halo of those lights turning the world small and golden.

"I missed you," I breathe against his lips.

He groans, low and rough, sliding his mouth to my throat, a hand framing my jaw like I'm something fragile he refuses to fumble. "You don't get to vanish again," he says into my skin. "You don't get to walk in, sing a song like that, and make me feel like—"

"Like what?"

He pulls back just enough to look down at me, his hands braced on either side of my head.

"Like I'm yours."

My chest aches. "You are."

The words break something open between us.

He kisses me again, slower this time, his weight pressing into mine as he slides his hand beneath my tank top. My skin shivers at his touch, and I arch into him, needing more —of him, of this, of the connection I've been starving for since Nashville.

Clothes disappear. His T-shirt. My shorts. The soft cotton of my underwear.

And then we're tangled together, skin to skin, under the soft glow of the lights. Rowan's mouth trails fire down my stomach, his hands rough and reverent as he explores every inch of me like he's memorizing the landscape.

He settles between my thighs, lifting one over his shoulder, and when his mouth finds me—

"Rowan," I gasp, my fingers clenching the quilt.

He doesn't stop. Doesn't even pause. He licks and sucks and groans against me like he's never tasted anything better.

When he slides two fingers inside me, I cry out, the sound echoing off the rafters. He eats me like it's his favorite damn meal, whispering praise between every moan.

"Beautiful... so fucking sweet... been thinking about this every night..."

I fall apart beneath him, shaking, breathless, my thighs trembling against his shoulders. And even then, he doesn't let up. He kisses his way back up my body, mouth finding mine, letting me taste myself on his tongue.

"You're mine," he growls. "You have to know that."

"I do," I whisper, tears stinging the corners of my eyes.

Then I flip him. Straddle him.

I ease him back onto the quilt, and the breath he takes isn't steady—it's the kind you drag in when you're bracing for impact. The string lights honey his skin, turning the hard lines I know by touch into something I want to memorize by sight, slow.

"Hold still," I murmur, already mapping him with my fingers.

Up close, I can see them all. I start with a weather-softened compass on his left shoulder, edges blown a little from sun and years. "Eighteen," he says when I glance up. "Thought it'd keep me from getting lost." His mouth quirks. "Turns out staying put worked better."

Near his inner biceps, a stalk of wheat rendered in fine lines—nearly the color of his skin now. I trace each grain with my nail. "First harvest after Dad named me CEO of the farm," he tells me, voice low. "Didn't think I could do it. We did."

There's a neat line of numbers under his collarbone, almost delicate, that are coordinates. "The bend in the creek," he adds before I ask. "Where I let my mind take a rest."

Over his ribs, a thin, pale scar catches the light—barbed

wire, I know without him saying. I kiss just above it, and he shivers.

"More," I whisper, greedy for the story of him.

And then I see it, tucked just beneath his right pec, where the sweep of muscle meets his ribs: a little songbird perched on a strand of fence wire. New enough that the lines are crisp, the black still a whisper of midnight, the skin around it the faintest pink. My finger hovers, careful. "When?" I ask, breath gone thin.

He swallows. "Week ago," he answers, like a confession. "Couldn't get the sound of your song from the barbecue out of my head. Figured if it was staying, it might as well have a place to land."

Something in me gives, clean and quiet. I press my mouth beside the bird and feel him exhale under me, a rough, helpless sound I want to keep.

"Hi," I say to the songbird, then to him, and keep going, kissing slow paths over old ink and older stories—compass, wheat, creek—letting my hands learn what my eyes are only just catching up to. He's all heat and patient strength and the kind of control that feels like worship. When I circle back to the new lines—the fence wire, the tiny feet—I feel his pulse kick against my lips.

"Careful." His voice is a rasp, not a warning so much as a plea. "She's still tender."

"I know," I whisper, and I do. I treat the little bird like a secret, then follow the trail the ink maps—down the firm plane of his stomach, the dip of muscle where he's strongest. He's already tense beneath me, a question strung tight, and when I look up, hunger and something softer war in his eyes.

"Ivy." My name, wrecked and reverent.

"I'm listening," I tell him, palms sliding to his sides, thumbs stroking where breath becomes body. He catches one of my hands, brings it to his mouth, and kisses the palm like he's thanking it for learning him.

I take my time because I can and because he lets me. Mouth to skin, past ink and the history it carries, tasting salt and summer and the man who puts his body between storms and everyone else.

He's already hard. Already twitching. And when I wrap my lips around him, he lets out a string of curses that echoes through the loft.

He fists the blanket, hips jerking as I suck him slow and deep, swirling my tongue and humming until his legs shake.

"Ivy," he warns, voice wrecked. "If you keep going…"

I crawl up his body again, chest heaving. "Then take me," I say. "Please."

He flips me in an instant, gripping my hips, sliding inside me with one long, slow thrust. We're both so far gone that when he slides to the hilt, I can feel my walls begin to quiver. Rowan's brows furrow as he murmurs about going slow.

But I want nothing to do with that.

Reaching up, I thread my fingers in his hair and yank at the strands as I pull him toward my lips.

"You better fuck me like you own me, Rowan Wright."

"Oh, baby girl, you're about to unleash a wild man," he

says, sliding all the way out and plunging back in my sex. "Too many days I've gone without you."

He persists with the achingly slow thrusts, driving me completely mad. My head whips back and forth on the quilt as his fingers join his cock between my legs, rubbing my clit.

"Am I driving you mad, Ivy? Just like I've been going mad since the day I met you."

"Insane. I need more."

"Beg me for it. Get on your hands and knees and beg me to fuck you hard enough to lose control."

Rowan slips out of me, and I scramble onto my hands and knees, ass facing him, then look over my shoulder with my hair cascading over the opposite.

"Please fuck me. I want to feel you everywhere. I need to."

His calloused palm runs across the globe of my ass before dipping between my legs. I watch in fiery fascination as he lifts the now drenched fingers to his mouth and licks them clean.

God, I'm about to come from just watching him do that.

"Fuck, you taste good," he tells me, aligning his cock with my entrance, gripping my hips with his big hands. "But you feel even better. Your pussy was made for me, Ivy. Now, hold on," he demands, and my hands fist at the quilt before he drives into my sex.

It's a harried pace with no rhythm, but it's exactly what the two of us need. My body rocks back to meet each of his thrusts.

"Give me your wrists," Rowan barks, and without missing a beat, he hauls me back against his chest, gripping my wrists in one of his massive hands while the other reaches around and squeezes one of my breasts.

"You feel so good," I moan as he licks and nips at the side of my neck while his cock sinks farther into my channel. "I'm so close. Don't stop."

"That's it, baby girl, come for me," he rumbles, and we both shatter.

We stay tangled together long after the rush fades, our bodies slick with sweat and breaths gradually slowing. My head rests against his shoulder, and Rowan's arm wraps tight around my waist like he's anchoring us both in place. Like he can't let me go.

I shift slightly, brushing my fingers along the curve of his jaw, feeling the short, scratchy stubble and the slow exhale of his breath against my temple.

"I needed that," I murmur.

His laugh is low, almost shy. "Yeah. Me too."

Silence stretches—warm, humming—until the obvious slides between us and sits down.

"Rowan," I say, barely above a whisper. "We didn't use anything."

He stills. Then his arm tightens around my waist like I might float away. "I know," he says, voice rough. "I got... lost in you. That's not an excuse. I should've—" He breaks off, forehead tipping to mine. "Are you okay?"

"I'm covered," I tell him, steady. "I have an IUD." I feel

him breathe out a small, honest relief. "But I still want us to be smart."

"Yeah," he says immediately. "Tomorrow, I'll go get tested. Not because I don't trust you—but because I want to do this right." He searches my face. "And I haven't... since before all the PR noise. It's been a long time."

"Same," I say, the word easier than I expected.

He nods once, like that answers a question he hasn't let himself ask. His thumb drifts over my hip. "I'll pick up some condoms. Keep them where I can't forget what matters when you look at me like that. It will be your choice, always."

I huff a breath that's almost a laugh. "You mean like you're mine?"

His mouth curves. "Already am."

Something tender lodges under my ribs. I press a kiss to the corner of his mouth—soft and grateful. "Thank you. For not making it weird. For choosing the careful thing with me."

"I want the long thing," he says simply. "If that means patience and errands and doing this like grown-ups, then I'm in."

The string lights hum. The loft holds. I curl closer, palm over his heart, and let the truth stop being scary. "Me too," I whisper into the space between us. "All the way in."

A long pause stretches between us. The kind that usually comes before the part where everything changes. I can feel it hovering, that invisible line we keep toeing. But this time, I don't want to wait for it to crack open on its own.

I lift my head, meeting his gaze. "I need to tell you something."

Rowan tenses beneath me, just barely. "If you're about to say you're leaving again..."

"No," I say quickly, pressing a palm to his chest. "No. I'm not. At least—not unless you tell me to."

His brow furrows. "Why would I do that?"

I look away for a beat. "Because of what I've been hiding."

That gets his attention.

He pulls back slightly, still keeping one hand anchored on my thigh. "Ivy..."

"My mom. The label. They've been on me nonstop since I left Nashville the first time." I swallow. "There were meetings lined up. Press tours. Brand deals. They kept dangling this image of who I'm supposed to be and panicking that I've been 'off-script.'"

Rowan's jaw tightens. "That's what they called it?"

"Yeah." I laugh, but there's no humor in it. "Like being with you—being *here*—was some sort of detour I wasn't allowed to take."

His fingers flex against my leg. "You're not a detour."

"I know that," I say, heart catching. "Now. But I didn't for a long time."

He waits, silent but open, eyes locked on mine.

"I told them I wouldn't do it anymore." I go on. "The

press circuit. The fake romance rumors. The glossed-over version of my life that they keep trying to rewrite."

Rowan raises an eyebrow. "Fake romance rumors?"

I wince. "There's been a... lot. Articles. Speculation. Mostly about Crew and me. Some... implying you're the other man."

Rowan lets out a low curse. "Jesus."

"I didn't write any of it. I didn't agree to it," I say, then the rest just tears loose. "And then the aura hit—this bright edge in my vision—and I was in that stupid cold apartment by myself." My throat works. "The seizure—it wasn't long. Under five minutes. I didn't pass out. I did the breathing, tucked in, then waited for it to crest and go. But afterward I just... shook. I was scared and furious and so, so alone. The kind of alone that makes you feel like a headline instead of a person. I turned my phone off because every call felt like someone trying to own a piece of me." I lift my eyes to his. "That's why I left. Not the press. Not the meetings. I couldn't do another minute of being a body they plan around."

Rowan steps in, palms open. His thumb sweeps one tear I didn't feel fall. "You're not doing that alone again," he says, voice low and certain. "Not while I'm breathing." He tips his forehead to mine. "You don't have to be brave by yourself anymore, Ivy. Not here. Not with me."

I blink back the sting in my eyes. "I want you to know that I didn't choose them. I chose this. *You.*"

He stares at me for a long beat, like he's trying to decide whether he believes me. Then he says, "I know."

I release a breath I didn't realize I was holding. He brushes my hair back behind my ear, fingertips lingering against my cheek.

"You wanna know something else?" he asks quietly.

"Always."

He smiles a little. "I've never seen the kids at the farm light up like they did today."

My heart swells. "Really?"

"Yeah. And it wasn't just the animals or the rides. It was the music. The way you sang. The way you made them feel like they mattered." He pauses. "You're part of this place now, whether you realize it or not."

I curl against his chest, heart thudding.

"I used your sketch," he adds. "The flyer you drew on the napkin at the café. I made copies. Ma's friends handed them out all over town. Bailey helped get the volunteers lined up."

The fact that he took my scribble and made it a plan loosens something in my chest—and with it comes the jolt of what I forgot.

"I left my notebook," I whisper, voice breaking. "That's how I knew I had to come back. Because it holds everything. My songs. My thoughts. *You*."

His expression shifts into something devastatingly tender.

"I know," he says quietly.

I freeze. "You read it?"

He hesitates. "Just one page. The one it fell open to. I'm

sorry. I know it was an invasion of your privacy, but it was like the world left me this little piece of you."

"And?"

"And I've never been the subject of a song before," he says, brushing his knuckles along my jaw. "Didn't know it would feel like that."

"Like what?"

"Like maybe I'm not so bad at being loved after all."

My chest caves.

"You're not," I whisper. "You're... everything."

We stay like that, wrapped in each other beneath the soft string lights, the whole world narrowed to this loft, this moment, this man. I press a kiss to his chest. "So... what happens now?"

He leans down and presses his forehead to mine. "We figure it out."

At some point, the night cools and the lights hum softer. He tugs his jeans back on, wraps the quilt around my shoulders, and kisses my temple. "Ladder's a two-hand job," he murmurs, then scoops me anyway—one arm under my knees, the other at my back—carrying me to the loft ladder like I weigh nothing. We descend slowly, my fingers looped at his nape, the barn dark and sweet with hay. Outside, crickets thicken the air. He keeps me tucked to him as we cross the yard, my bare toes brushing his thigh where the quilt rides up.

"You can't sleep on splinters," he says, mouth curving against my hair.

Inside his house, he sets me on the bathroom counter

and flips the light to low. Warm water, a clean washcloth. He works carefully—wiping hay dust from my shoulders, the smudge on my knee, pulling a straw from my hair with a grin like he's found treasure. "Hold still," he murmurs, dabbing at a tiny scrape. He hands me a soft T-shirt that smells like line-dried cotton and him. I pull it over my head. It hits mid-thigh. His eyes go gentle.

In the bedroom, he turns down the sheets, slides a glass of water and two ibuprofens to my side, and kills the lamp so only the hall glow remains. When he climbs in, it's careful—like he's not sure I'll stay. I turn, fit my back to his chest, and his arm bands across my waist. "Right here," he breathes at the nape of my neck, more vow than words.

"Right here," I echo, and sleep takes us fast.

The morning sunlight filters through the gauzy curtains, laying pale gold across the floor. I stretch, deliciously sore in all the best ways, last night sparking a satisfied ache low in my belly. My limbs are tangled in the sheets—Rowan's sheets—and I don't care that my hair's a wreck or that a stray piece of hay still clings to my calf. I feel... alive.

The bedroom is quiet except for the low hum of a fan and the occasional creak of old wood settling. The scent of cedar and Rowan clings to the room—earthy and warm, with just enough spice to make my thighs squeeze together under the covers. I roll toward the empty space where he should be, my hand brushing over the spot where his body lay just hours ago.

Still warm.

I press my palm flat against it, eyes fluttering shut for a

beat, and then I hear it—muffled clattering from the kitchen, a low grunt, and the clink of silverware.

My heart does something stupid. Something soft.

I slip out of bed and tug on his T-shirt from the floor, the hem brushing high on my thighs. My bare feet hit the cool floor, and I make my way down the hall, pausing just outside the kitchen.

He's standing by the stove, hair damp from the shower, flannel pajama pants slung low on his hips. He holds a spatula in one hand and a mug of coffee in the other. He hasn't seen me yet. He's humming—off-key but earnest— and I want to bottle this moment forever.

I step into the room.

"Smells good," I say, leaning against the doorframe.

Rowan turns, a slow grin spreading across his face when he sees me in his shirt. "Figured you might be hungry. I wore you out last night."

My cheeks flush. "Cocky much?"

He shrugs. "Just observant."

I walk up behind him, looping my arms around his waist and pressing my cheek against the warm skin of his back. "I like this version of you," I murmur. "Domestic cowboy with a spatula."

He chuckles, flipping a pancake. "Don't get used to it. This is a one-time special."

I peek at the counter. There's a stack of pancakes, a bowl of sliced strawberries, and fresh whipped cream.

"I didn't think you cooked anything other than meat and eggs for breakfast."

"I don't usually. Evelyn helped me this morning." He gestures to his phone with the screen still on that reads:

Lila: Use strawbewwies and LOTS of whip. She'll like it. 🩶

I blink, caught off guard by the sweetness of it. "God, I love her."

"She loves you too," he says softly. "They all do."

His voice is so quiet, so full of unspoken meaning, that I freeze.

"Ivy."

I look up.

Rowan's gaze meets mine, searching, serious. "We need to talk."

My stomach dips. "About last night?"

He shakes his head. "About everything."

He sets the spatula down and leans back against the counter, arms crossed over his chest. "I know you've got a life in Nashville. A career. Your mom, your team, all those people pulling you in every direction."

I nod slowly, unsure where this is going.

"But when you're here... when you're with me, it's like I can breathe. Like the chaos shuts up for five seconds."

A lump forms in my throat. "Rowan—"

"I want you to stay and make this place—my house, not the cottage—your home," he says bluntly. "But I'm not gonna ask you to give everything up for me. I just... I needed to say it. I want you here. I want mornings like this.

I want pancakes and Evelyn's texts on Lila's phone and you in my bed."

Something shifts in his expression—something fierce and gentle all at once. "You don't have to say anything."

"I want to," I say, stepping into him. "I love you, Rowan."

His arms are around me in seconds, holding me like the ground might fall out from under us. "I love you too, darlin'. So damn much."

He kisses me, slow and deep, and suddenly, breakfast is forgotten.

He lifts me onto the kitchen counter, his hands under the hem of his shirt—his shirt—pushing it up over my ribs. The granite is cool under my thighs, but his mouth is hot, branding me in all the places that ache for him.

"God, you're everything," he growls, dragging my hips forward.

Rowan drops to his knees in front of me like it's a prayer.

His palms glide up the outsides of my thighs, slow and reverent, before curling around to the backs of my knees. I feel his breath against the apex of my thighs, warm and deliberate, like he's savoring every second before he touches me.

The cool air kisses my skin, but his mouth is warmer. He presses a kiss to the inside of my knee, then higher. Higher.

"Rowan," I whisper, already trembling, toes curling against the edge of the counter.

"You taste better than anything I've ever made in this kitchen," he murmurs with a wicked smile.

And then he buries his face between my thighs.

I gasp, hips rocking forward into his mouth. He groans low, like he's starved for this—starved for me—and God, the way he eats me? It's not fair. One hand spreads me open while the other grips my thigh, grounding me as his tongue strokes and circles, relentless and skillful.

I reach for his hair, threading my fingers through the soft strands, tugging just enough to make him growl. The sound vibrates through me, and I cry out, head falling back as he sucks my clit into his mouth and flicks with a rhythm that makes my knees weak—even though I'm not standing.

And I let him worship me because love looks a lot like this. Like pancakes cooling on the stove. Like laughter and whispered promises. Like flannel and bare feet and the soft groan of wood as the past finally gives way to something new.

"You're gonna make me—" My voice breaks off in a moan.

Rowan doesn't stop. He leans in harder, sliding two fingers inside me with delicious precision, his mouth working me in tandem until I fall apart, breath catching, legs shaking around his shoulders.

I come with his name on my lips, his beard rough against the inside of my thighs, my fingers clenching tight in his hair like it's the only thing tethering me to this world.

He slows his strokes, gentle now, like he's coaxing me back to earth.

When I finally catch my breath and lift my head, he's staring up at me, mouth glistening, eyes dark with heat.

"I'm not done with you yet," he says, voice rough and thick with promise.

My pulse stutters. "Oh?"

He stands, tugging me into his arms effortlessly, and I wrap my legs around his waist.

"Not even close," he murmurs, carrying me through the kitchen like I weigh nothing, past the still warm stove and the forgotten pancakes.

He sets me on the kitchen table with a soft thud, wood creaking under my weight. His mouth crashes into mine as he undoes the tie of his pajama pants, his tongue tangling with mine, desperate and commanding.

When he presses into me, slow and deep, my breath catches again. There's nothing between us—no space, no air, just the raw ache of wanting and finally, finally having.

He moves with measured control, hands braced on either side of my hips, his forehead pressed to mine.

"Look at me," he pants. "I want to see you fall apart this time."

I do. And when I come again, it's with his name on my tongue, his body wrapped around mine, and a love so real it makes my chest hurt.

We collapse together, sweat-slick and tangled, chests heaving, breathless in more ways than one.

Rowan brushes his lips against my temple, still inside me. "You are everything, Ivy Quinn. Everything."

I smile against his neck. "Don't let the pancakes burn."

He laughs, and that deep, gravelly sound makes me want to do it all over again.

"I guess you're hungry now?"

"Oh, I'm starving," I tease, curling my fingers around his biceps. "But not for food."

His eyes darken again, and suddenly, I'm being hauled off the table and spun toward the hallway.

"Bed. Now."

"Yes, sir."

Chapter Twenty-Three

ROWAN

The night smells like grilled meat, honeysuckle, and summer sweat. It's the kind of scent that settles into your skin and stays like a memory. The sun's dipped low behind the pasture, the last of its light glinting off the rusted fence posts and catching the gold threads in Ivy's hair as she laughs beside me.

The breeze is lazy, warm, and constant, rustling the tablecloths we've anchored with old horseshoes and chipped Mason jars filled with sunflowers. String lights arc overhead, glowing soft and amber from the porch rafters to the fence posts, turning the whole backyard into something out of a dream I didn't dare let myself have.

Everyone's here to celebrate the beginning of the pecan harvest and the success of the first camp.

Lila's at the far end of the table, laughing over the potato salad with Bailey, her hair piled high and catching the glow like a halo. Holt's working the grill like he owns it.

Beer in hand, he has his apron on backward, flipping burgers and giving grief to anyone who walks too close. Dad's sitting on the porch steps with Hadley, his arm around her shoulders, both talking quietly like they always do when the world around them gets too loud. And Mom, God love her, buzzes between the kitchen and patio with a dish towel over one shoulder and a glass of sweet tea in the other, stealing bites of cobbler when she thinks no one's watching.

And then there's Ivy, right next to me.

Her hand rests on my thigh—just enough pressure to ground me. Enough to remind me that she's real. That this is happening.

She's wearing a light blue sundress—one that makes my brain short-circuit when she walks. Her hair's up in a loose bun, wisps framing her face in a way that should be illegal. She's been smiling all evening, laughing when Bailey says something ridiculous or Hadley gives Holt hell. And every time she leans into me, my chest tightens. Not in a bad way. In the way that says something's shifted inside me.

Hell, maybe it already did, back on that stage. Perhaps it was the way she looked at me when she sang those lyrics— like I was the song. Like I was the answer.

The table is packed, plates overflowing with hamburgers, grilled corn, and thick slices of bread soaked in butter and love. Glasses clink. Someone breaks into a chorus of "Country Road" for no reason. And for the first time in a long time, I sit back and breathe.

This is what we built.

The camp's no longer a dream scrawled in Ivy's notebook. It's real. It's backed by the town council, funded by local businesses, and well-loved by every damn kid who comes through our gates. We've got dates lined up for the next three months. A rotation of volunteers. Even a local baker who insists on delivering muffins every Tuesday morning.

And Ivy, she's at the center of it. Not because she asked to be, but because she gave it life.

Mom lifts her glass and taps her spoon against it, drawing the attention of the table with the practiced ease of someone used to corralling a rowdy crew.

"I just want to say how proud I am of this family," she says, her voice warm and a little thick with emotion. "What started as a backyard idea became something meaningful. Something kids needed."

Applause echoes down the table. Ivy squeezes my leg, and I glance at her, heart thudding slow and deep in my chest.

Mom's gaze finds mine. "And Rowan... you didn't just build a camp. You built a safe place for kids to be seen. To feel valued."

I swallow hard, nodding once. "Thanks, Mom."

Then her eyes shift to Ivy. "And Ivy, sweetheart, you brought the fire. The spark. You reminded us that dreaming isn't just for kids."

Ivy's cheeks flush pink, and she ducks her head, but I can see the smile tugging at her lips. It lights something inside me, something wild and good.

The whole damn night feels like magic. Which, of course, means it can't last.

Because that's when the sleek black SUV crawls up the gravel drive.

The noise around us quiets as the dust kicks up behind the tires. Holt's fork freezes mid-bite. Lila leans back in her chair, eyebrows raised. Dad stiffens beside Hadley, who blinks twice like she's not sure she's seeing what she's seeing.

Ivy hardens beside me, and my gut churns.

The passenger door swings open before the engine's even off, but I know who it is before she even steps free. Celeste.

Hair perfect. Heels high. Suit crisp. Her phone is still clutched like an accessory she doesn't know how to live without.

The sound of her heels against the gravel makes my shoulders go tight.

"Evangeline," she calls, too bright. Too rehearsed.

Ivy stands before I do.

She doesn't rush. Doesn't hesitate. Just rises like she's been preparing for this moment all her life.

The yard goes still.

My mom sets her sweet tea down harder than necessary. Lila's mouth drops open. Holt mutters, "You've got to be kidding me," under his breath. Hadley looks like she wants to melt into her folding chair.

I move to Ivy's side, close enough for our arms to touch. Celeste barely glances at me.

"I didn't come to make a scene," she says smoothly. "I just want a moment. To talk. Please."

Ivy crosses her arms. "Why now?"

Celeste sighs, like we're inconveniencing her. "Because you stopped answering my calls. Because you're ignoring your team. Because you're throwing away everything we've built—"

"I built," Ivy says, calm and sharp. "You monetized it."

A few murmurs ripple through the family. Mom's expression is stone. Lila stands slowly, moving to Ivy's other side.

Celeste blinks. "I got you record deals. Tours. A platform—"

"A leash," Ivy cuts in. "You gave me a leash."

I see it—the flicker in Celeste's eyes. The crack in the porcelain.

"I'm still your mother," she says.

Ivy's voice drops. "No. You're the manager who used to forge contracts."

A hush falls over the yard. Even the wind stills.

My mom steps forward, slipping beside Lila. She places a gentle hand on Ivy's back, offering support without words. Her gaze, however, is steel when it lands on Celeste.

"You think this town is better than the world I built for you?" Celeste says, her voice rising now, losing its polish. "You think barns and broken fences are enough?"

"I think love is enough," Ivy says.

Celeste blinks like she's been slapped. And what do I do? I move. Not much. Just enough to step in front of Ivy.

"She's not going anywhere she doesn't want to," I say, meeting Celeste's gaze without flinching.

There's silence.

Then Celeste lifts her chin. "I hope you realize how much you're throwing away."

"I do," Ivy says softly. "And I've never felt more free."

Celeste's lips press into a line. She turns without another word, storms to the SUV, and slams the door. Dust kicks up behind her as she drives off.

And just like that, she's gone. I glance at Ivy. She's breathing, shoulders trembling but steady.

"You okay?" I ask.

She nods. "Let's go home."

We leave the celebration without fanfare. No one stops us. No one needs to. The family lets us slip away like they know the moment's ours now.

The drive home is quiet, but not empty. It's the kind of quiet that hums beneath your skin. Charged. Waiting.

I keep one hand on the wheel, the other draped over the console until Ivy reaches out and links her fingers with mine. Her palm is warm. Steady. Her thumb brushes the side of my hand like she's grounding herself in the feel of me.

The porch light is already on when we pull up to the house. A soft amber glow spilling across the steps and the overgrown flower beds. I park the truck, but neither of us moves for a minute.

Then Ivy shifts, her voice breaking the silence.

"She showed up looking like she was about to walk onto a press junket."

"She always like that?" I ask, glancing at her.

She shrugs. "Always. Even when I was fifteen and begging to go to a school dance, she showed up to pick me up in a Chanel suit. Said reputation started young."

"Christ," I mutter.

Ivy huffs a laugh that sounds more like a sigh. "It's always been about the image. Always about the story she could tell other people. Not the one I was actually living."

I squeeze her hand. "You don't have to explain, Ivy."

"I know," she says softly. "But I want to. To you."

That knocks something loose in my chest.

I nod toward the porch. "Come sit with me a while?"

She nods.

We climb the steps together, her bare feet padding against the boards, the hem of her sundress catching the breeze. She settles on the porch swing like she was made for it—knees tucked up, arms around her legs. I drop beside her, the swing groaning softly beneath our combined weight.

We sit like that for a long minute. The stars are just starting to bloom across the sky. Somewhere in the distance, a bullfrog croaks and cicadas buzz in lazy rhythm.

I reach over and tuck a strand of hair behind her ear.

"I never thought she'd actually come here to confront me," Ivy says, her voice quiet.

"Me neither."

"But I'm glad she did."

That surprises me. "Yeah?"

"Because it gave me the chance to say it. Out loud. To her face." She leans her head on my shoulder. "I've spent so long trying not to make waves. Trying to be the version of me she could sell."

"Not anymore."

"No," she says, lifting her head to look at me. "Not anymore."

She's watching me like she sees everything, and I feel the shift. I've seen it building for weeks, since that night on the porch when she climbed into my lap and made me forget how to breathe. Since she sang those lyrics about home and belonging like she meant every damn word.

Now it feels settled. Like we're no longer waiting for the other shoe to drop, and we've both finally chosen the same thing.

She moves then—slow and deliberate—swinging one leg over my lap until she's straddling me again.

"Ivy..." I breathe.

Her fingers thread through my hair. "Shh. Let me say thank you."

"You don't owe me anything."

"I do. I owe you everything."

And then she kisses me.

It's soft at first—like a promise. The kind of thing you say without words. Her lips part, and I taste the sweetness of wine and cobbler, the ache of everything we've held back spilling between us.

My hands slide up her back, under her dress, finding bare skin that's soft and warm and real.

She rocks against me—slow, rhythmic—and I groan into her mouth, gripping the edge of the swing with one hand just to keep from lifting her off the seat and carrying her straight into the house.

"You drive me insane," I whisper against her lips.

"Good," she murmurs. "I want you desperate."

She drags her mouth down my neck, her breath hot against my skin, and I curse under my breath, bucking against her without meaning to. Her hips roll in answer, and the pressure is exquisite—denim rough, cotton damp between us.

"Ivy," I grit, my voice ragged. "You keep doing that, and I'm not gonna last."

"I don't want you to," she says, lips brushing my ear. "I want you ruined. Right here. Just like me."

And she keeps going. Keeps moving.

My grip tightens on her thighs as the pressure builds, sharp and dizzying. Her breath catches. Her eyes flutter closed. Her mouth falls open on a gasp as her nails dig into my shoulders.

Then we're both falling. She trembles against me while I groan her name through clenched teeth as I come hard in my jeans, her hips grinding slowly through the aftershocks.

It's messy. It's primal. It's perfect.

We stay like that—hearts thudding in sync, foreheads pressed together, air thick with heat and honeysuckle.

Eventually, she exhales a breathless laugh.

"Well," she says. "That was..."

"Yeah," I rasp. "That was."

She cups my face in both hands and kisses me again—slow and lingering, like she's sealing something between us.

When she pulls back, there's no hesitation in her eyes. No fear. Just Ivy, choosing me.

I run my hands up her sides, memorizing the feel of her.

The swing sways gently beneath us. The stars shine brighter above. And at this moment, I don't care what the rest of the world thinks Ivy Quinn should be.

We're both breathless and laughing on the swing when reality catches up to my ruined jeans and her wicked little grin. I scoop her up anyway. Inside, I hand her a warm washcloth and grab another for myself. We do a quick triage. I mutter, "Hell of a way to christen a porch," as she kisses the apology off my mouth. In the bathroom, we bump hips at the sink, share the mirror, and brush our teeth like we've done it a hundred times—her in my T-shirt, me in clean boxer briefs. Then we kill the lights and slide under the covers, her back tucked to my chest, my palm spread over her stomach while the house goes quiet around us.

Because I know exactly who she is.

Mine.

The morning creeps in slow, warm light spilling across the hardwood floors of the kitchen. It's the kind of quiet that doesn't weigh on your chest—it settles around you like a favorite blanket. Soft. Familiar. Home.

I pad barefoot through the house, still tasting sleep on my tongue, and there she is—barefoot in the kitchen again, in one of my old hoodies. The same one she wore that first morning after everything changed. Only now, she looks even more like she belongs in it.

The opening hangs off one shoulder, hem brushing her thighs, and her blond hair's still tangled from sleep, but she's moving like she owns the place. Pouring coffee. Humming something soft under her breath.

I lean against the doorframe, arms crossed, just watching her.

This—this is what I never let myself want. The easy mornings. The stolen glances. The girl in the kitchen who knows where everything is and doesn't need to ask.

She glances up and catches me.

"Morning," she says, voice still raspy, one side of her mouth lifting in a sleepy smile.

"Morning," I echo, stepping toward her, one hand dragging through my hair. "You always hum a new song in the morning?"

"Only when I'm not worried someone's gonna sneak up on me."

I slide an arm around her waist, tugging her closer. "You didn't seem all that surprised."

She lifts a brow and presses her free hand to my chest. "You walk like a damn cowboy. All stompy."

I chuckle and duck my head to kiss her forehead. "That so?"

"Mm-hmm." She leans in and rests her cheek against me. "You sleep okay?"

"With you here?" I breathe into her hair. "Better than I have in years."

We stand like that for a beat. Two cups of coffee on the counter. Her body warm against mine. Her scent—vanilla and something wild—twists through my chest.

"Want breakfast?" I murmur.

"Only if you're making it."

I raise a brow. "You're not gonna serenade me with eggs and bacon?"

"Absolutely not. I'm the talent, remember? You're the camp director-slash-handsome cowboy who's good with spatulas."

I shake my head but can't fight the grin. "You're gonna be trouble today, aren't you?"

She slides her hands under the hem of the flannel pajama pants, cold fingers grazing my hips. "Maybe."

I catch her wrists gently. "Careful. I can only take so much before I forget all about that breakfast."

She leans up and presses a kiss to the corner of my mouth. "Save it for later, cowboy. You owe me bacon."

"Damn right I do."

As she hops up to sit on the counter, swinging her legs, I reach for the skillet. The whole room glows with the kind of light that makes memories. I swear I could do this every morning for the rest of my life and never get tired of it.

I slide eggs and bacon onto two plates and set them in front of Ivy. She grins like I just handed her a Grammy.

"Forks, please," I say, easing the last of the soft eggs

onto two plates. "Bacon's crisp, yolks just shy of runny—the way you like them."

She smiles over the rim of her mug. "Smug. But accurate. Even if the bacon flopped, you've got other talents."

I lift a brow. "Name three."

"Rescuing me. Remembering my coffee order. Kissing like you mean it."

"Eat first," I murmur, setting her plate down. "Then we can practice the third."

My body reacts before my brain does, flashing back to last night. To the way she fit against me. To the sound she made when she whispered my name.

I clear my throat and sit down across from her. "You really are trouble."

"Only for you."

We eat in comfortable silence for a few minutes, the kind that makes me forget every doubt I've ever had about letting someone in again. Ivy hums between bites, swaying a little in her seat like the melody in her head is too strong to sit still.

"You've been humming that tune all morning," I say.

She blinks, caught. "Yeah... it's stuck in my head."

"Yours?"

She nods slowly. "A new one. I started it in Nashville, then had the seizure. It's not finished."

I lean my elbows on the table. "Is it about me?"

Her steady gaze meets mine, unflinching. "Recently, they all are."

That hits me somewhere deep. Somewhere old and scarred.

"You know... your notebook," I hedge. "Didn't read the whole thing. Just... a page or two. That song."

She sets her fork down gently. Her lips press together in something like a smile. "Did it scare you?"

I shake my head. "It wrecked me."

Silence stretches between us, heavy and intimate.

"I didn't want to fall for anyone when I came here," she says quietly. "I wanted quiet. Space. Somewhere to remember who I was before everything got so... loud. Hell, I still need to give Crew his jacket."

My chest tightens. "Then what now? The label, your mom... your life. All of it's back in Nashville."

Ivy takes a breath and exhales slowly. "I don't want to go back to that life. Not the way it was. I'm thinking about changing the deal."

"What kind of change?"

"I want to record what I want. Write what matters to me. Maybe start something smaller, on my own terms." She looks down at her plate. "And I want to help with the camp."

I blink. "Seriously?"

"Rowan, I saw those kids' faces. I saw what you built." She tilts her head, her voice soft. "You used my sketch as the flyer."

I nod. "It was better than anything I could come up with."

"It was perfect." She swallows. "I want to be part of this.

Not just as the pop star who showed up once and waved to a crowd. I want to stay. Help. Teach. Sing. Be yours."

My throat gets tight. "That sounds a hell of a lot like a dream I stopped letting myself have."

"Maybe it's time to believe in it again."

I rise slowly and move around the table. She doesn't hesitate—just slides off the stool and into my arms like she was made to be there.

I bury my face in her hair and whisper, "I want all of it. Music. Camp. Mornings like this. You."

She pulls back just enough to look up at me. "Then let's start planning. Together."

Chapter Twenty-Four

ROWAN

The days after the dinner settle into something that doesn't quite feel like reality, but maybe that's the point. Perhaps we've spent so long surviving, dancing around what we are, that now, in the quiet aftermath, we're finally living it.

Ivy's still technically uses the cottage. She insists she needs the space, that she writes better in solitude, but most mornings, I find her curled into my side before the sun comes up, her legs tangled in mine like roots grown into the foundation of this place. Her toothbrush is next to mine. Her hairbrush has claimed a corner of the dresser. And every time she pads barefoot across my kitchen in one of my old T-shirts, I feel it like a shot to the chest—that quiet domestic ache that says this is it. She's it.

The camp is running smoother than I ever imagined. We've got kids from three counties now, some coming back week after week with paint-splattered shoes and stories about the chickens they named.

But Ivy has turned this place into something more than a working farm. She added a music hour. Storytime with Bailey. Little picnic benches shaded by old pecan trees. She strings fairy lights like she's decorating for a backyard wedding, and I let her, because every time I see her humming under her breath with a strand of lights tangled around her shoulders, I fall in love a little harder.

I touch her constantly. I can't help it. A hand on the small of her back when she's walking through a gate. My palm slides across her hip as we pass in the hallway. My fingers brush her neck when I tuck a curl behind her ear. I don't think she even realizes how often she leans into me now. Her body knows mine like second nature.

By midmorning, we fall into the rhythm of the farm like we've been doing it for years. She coaxes Butterscotch out of a sulk with the bottle tucked in her elbow while I haul feed. Later, she pilots the Gator with her hair in a messy knot and her laugh echoing off the trees as I jog beside it, tossing salt blocks like a show-off. We restake tomatoes in the kitchen beds—her glove pressed to the stem while I tie a square knot and show her why it holds—and she hums under her breath, some half-finished melody I don't ask her to name. When the hose kinks, she fixes it and "accidentally" sprays my boots. I retaliate just enough to make her squeal and then pull her in by the waist, water beading on her collarbone, both of us grinning like thieves. We check a creek-side fence, trade sips from a sun-warm canteen, and I realize we've talked all day without once needing the right words.

The sky is painted in streaks of soft copper and blush pink, the kind of sunset that makes you stop and stare, even if you've seen it a hundred times. Ivy's sandal-clad foot nudges my boot as we climb the porch stairs. She doesn't say anything, just laces her fingers through mine and lets the quiet settle between us again.

Inside, the air is cool from the box fan in the hallway. Ivy drops her ball cap on the hook by the door, her sunglasses beside it. She shrugs out of the denim shirt she grabbed from the laundry room, revealing that old concert tee she stole from my drawer and tied at the waist like it was meant for her. She disappears into the bathroom for a minute, and I hear the water run, then silence.

I wait on the porch.

The swing groans softly under my weight as I settle in, leaning back and stretching one arm across the top of the cushion, the other hand around a cold glass of sweet tea. I can still taste the sugar on my tongue and still feel the warm ghost of her hand in mine.

A few minutes later, the screen door creaks again.

I glance up, and the air leaves my lungs.

She's barefoot, her legs bare, wearing nothing but one of my button-down flannels, with the sleeves rolled up. The hem hits just below the tops of her thighs. Her damp hair curls at the ends, falling over her shoulders. She's holding something in her hand.

Her notebook.

My chest tightens.

She walks toward me slowly, like she's not even sure she's doing it on purpose. Like her body just... knows where it belongs now. She eases down beside me, curling one leg under the other, the notebook resting in her lap. She flips it open, pencil tapping against the edge of the page.

For a while, she doesn't speak. She just hums.

It's not the same old tune. It's new. Softer. A little wistful, a little wild.

I don't interrupt. Don't even move a muscle. I watch her—watch the way her lips part slightly as she sings under her breath, the way her eyes skim the page like she's chasing something only she can see. That fire I thought she lost? It's flickering again, low but steady, catching wind.

She pauses.

Glances up at me.

"I think I'm ready to finish it," she murmurs.

I nod, voice low. "Which one?"

"The one I started on the plane," she says, tilting her head toward me. "The one I sang the day I came back."

I smile, and she nods but doesn't look away.

My body tenses under her touch. Not from discomfort—hell no—but from the unbearable sweetness of it. The way she always knows how to unravel me with something so simple.

"I'm not hiding anymore. I chose you over and over again," she says, leaning in.

I turn, meeting her mouth in a kiss that starts soft but

deepens instantly. There's no urgency. No firestorm. Just a slow, steady burn that climbs higher with each pass of her lips.

She shifts, swinging one leg over mine to straddle me.

My hands slide automatically to her hips, steadying her. Her thighs bracket mine, warm and strong, and the swing creaks beneath us as she settles.

"This okay?" she murmurs against my mouth.

I answer by kissing her again—deeper this time. My tongue sweeps slow and deliberate until she whimpers.

Her hands find my shoulders, slipping beneath the collar of my T-shirt, fingers tracing down my back. She rolls her hips once—gentle, teasing—and I grip the swing chain beside me to keep from losing it right then and there.

"Jesus, Ivy..."

"Say my name again," she whispers, breath hot against my jaw.

"Ivy," I growl, pulling her tighter. "You feel like fire."

She grins, teeth grazing my throat. "I feel like yours."

That does it.

I lift her slightly, just enough to push the shirt she's wearing higher. She helps, shrugging out of it without fanfare, leaving her bare to the warm night air and me.

I exhale sharply. "Fuck, baby..."

Her hands are already working at the hem of my shirt, sliding it up, over, gone. She leans in, chest pressing against mine, heat blooming between us like a live wire.

She kisses my jaw. My neck. Down my shoulder.

Her rhythm is slow. Intentional. Not rushed like the last time. This isn't need. This is choice. Worship.

She grinds against me again, the thin cotton of her shorts the only barrier between her heat and my growing hardness. With deft fingers, she unbuttons my jeans and slips my erection free of its confines, pushing the edge of her shorts to the side as she guides me inside her slick core.

My hands slide up her back, down her sides, around her thighs. I kiss her like I'm starving for it because I am.

The porch swing groans with each shift, each roll, and I don't care if the whole damn world hears it. Let them. She's here, and she's mine.

Her breath hitches, and I know she's close. So am I. The pressure is maddening, the friction just right.

Ivy moans against my mouth, and I lose it.

My release crashes through me, teeth clenched, muscles straining as I bury my face in her neck and hold on. She gasps—then follows—hips trembling as her body arches into mine, perfect and powerful.

We stay like that for a long time. Tangled. Breathing hard. Sweating under the stars.

She kisses my jaw and laughs, soft and low as I rip my T-shirt off and use it to clean between her legs.

"I think the swing survived."

I chuckle, chest still tight. "Barely."

She rests her forehead against mine. "Next time, bed?"

"Definitely," I groan.

She climbs off me slowly, body sated, cheeks flushed. She dashes inside, then returns in a blink. She reaches for her notebook and pencil, and curls up beside me again like she never left.

And when she starts humming again—soft and low—I swear, the rest of the world fades to black.

Just us. Just this.

Just Ivy writing her next song under the summer sky.

Chapter Twenty-Five

IVY

oral Bell Cove's public park smells like funnel cake and sunscreen and melted ice cream. Like the perfect end-of-summer night wrapped in sticky sweetness and the hum of cicadas. Music plays softly from the park's speakers, some old country tune that makes you want to sway barefoot in the grass with someone you love. Laughter floats from the kids racing between picnic tables, and the air is thick with heat, joy, and the faint twang of anticipation.

And nerves. God, I'm vibrating with them.

"You good?" Rowan's voice rumbles beside me, warm and calm and so steady it makes my chest ache.

I nod, then immediately shake my head. "I think I'm gonna throw up."

He chuckles, his palm sliding low on my back, grounding me. "You've performed in front of thousands. You'll be fine."

"This is different." I glance up at him. "They know me here. Or... they know you. Us. It's not stage lights and backup dancers. It's your mom handing out lemonade and Lila helping kids on the pony rides."

"And that terrifies you more than a sold-out arena?"

"Terrifies me differently," I mutter.

He tilts his head and brushes a strand of hair off my cheek. "You've already won them over. They've watched you collect eggs and sweep the barn and comfort kids when they scraped their knees. They've seen the real you."

I smile, but it wobbles. "That's the part I want to protect. And share. Which makes zero sense."

Rowan's thumb strokes over my lower back. "You don't have to make sense. You just have to sing."

"Rowan..."

"Ivy." His gaze is steady, voice soft. "Just be you."

And somehow, that makes me breathe easier. Being me doesn't mean being Ivy Quinn tonight. It doesn't mean the label or the pressure or the never-ending PR cycle. It means the girl who fell for a grumpy cowboy and started dreaming of something softer.

The makeshift stage is set up at the far end of the park, strung with lights that twinkle against the deepening dusk. It's not massive, but it's charming—faded wood boards and weathered beams, the kind that feel like home. The town set up benches and chairs, but most people are scattered on picnic blankets or leaning against the fence, waiting.

I spot Rowan's mom refilling lemonade, Bailey organizing crafts for the younger kids, and Holt working the grill like it's a high-stakes operation. Lila waves when she catches sight of me, and Hadley gives me a quick thumbs-up from the other side of the field. It's... overwhelming in the best way.

Even Crew's here, tossing a football with a group of kids, his baseball cap pulled low and a grin on his face. It's a bye week for him. When he looks up and sees me watching, he winks, then subtly tilts his head toward Bailey.

I follow the motion just in time to see Bailey practically bolt behind the craft tent.

I snort. "Poor guy."

Rowan glances at me. "He's been trying to talk to her all summer. She's faster than a jackrabbit."

"Good for her," I murmur, then glance at him. "Not that I don't love Crew, but..."

Rowan's lips twitch. "No need to explain."

The emcee announces a short break before the final performance, and my stomach flutters like I'm sixteen again.

Rowan leans in close. "You've got this."

"I wrote it for you," I whisper.

"I know." He kisses the side of my head. "And I've never been prouder."

I walk toward the stage on legs that feel both too long and too shaky. The crowd quiets as I step into the warm glow of the string lights, and I take a deep breath, letting the guitar strap settle across my shoulder.

This song—this moment—it's not about perfection. It's not about impressing anyone. It's about him.

I scan the crowd until our eyes lock. Rowan stands at the edge of the park with his arms crossed and a steady gaze on me like I'm the only thing in the world worth seeing.

I strum the first chord, part my lips, and sing. The melody floats out of me like it's been waiting for this night, this moment, this man.

The first verse is soft, just voice and guitar—gentle enough to hush the park. The kids are quiet. Conversations fade. Fireflies blink along the hedges, and the town slips into stillness like it knows something important is happening.

I sing about summer nights and porch swings. About laughter that lingers and hands that feel like home. I sing about building something real—slow, steady, sacred.

And I sing about Rowan. About a man with rough hands and a soft heart. About a place where I learned how to breathe again. Where music returned like a tide I thought I'd lost.

The chorus spills out of me, low and aching:

> "I don't need the city skyline,
> Don't need a stage with blinding lights.
> I need the way you say my name,
> Like I'm already enough tonight..."

I spot Rowan near the edge of the crowd, his eyes glossy,

jaw tight. One of his hands is clenched into a fist against his chest, like he's holding himself together with nothing but willpower. His mom slips an arm around his waist without a word. He doesn't look away from me.

The second verse is bolder. Stronger. I let myself feel every lyric. Let myself love him through the music. Not just because he deserves it, but because I do, too.

> "I came here running from something,
> Now I'm standing still for you.
> This small town wrote my ending,
> And my beginning too..."

By the time I hit the final note, the crowd is silent. Not out of disinterest. Out of reverence. Then someone claps. And another. And then the whole damn park erupts into cheers.

I can't help the laugh that bursts from my chest as I step back from the mic, my cheeks flushed, hands trembling. But I don't want to bask in this moment alone. I want him.

Rowan breaks through the crowd as people begin to rise, congratulating, whistling, shouting my name. He doesn't stop to acknowledge them. His eyes are on me like I'm gravity itself.

When he reaches the edge of the stage, I meet him halfway, guitar forgotten behind me. I practically leap down into his arms, and he catches me like he was born to.

"Jesus, Ivy," he mutters, voice hoarse. "That song—"

"It was yours." I bury my face in his neck. "It'll always be yours."

We're standing in front of everyone, but it doesn't matter. I kiss him anyway. Slow, sweet, and unhurried. A promise.

Rowan cups my cheek, and for a second, I think he's going to say something teasing, something to cut through the heat in his eyes. But instead, he leans closer.

"Come with me," he murmurs.

My brows lift. "Where?"

He laces our fingers together, tugging me past the stage lights, past the food stalls, games, and folding chairs. We wind through the trees toward the back edge of the park, toward the walking trail that loops behind the marsh.

When we reach a clearing strung with soft fairy lights—clearly another of his surprises—he stops.

No one else is in sight. Just the sounds of the celebration fading behind us and the faint ripple of water nearby.

Rowan turns toward me, his hands resting lightly on my waist. His eyes search mine with a look so intense it steals my breath.

"I didn't want to do this in front of everyone," he says.

My heart leaps. "Do what?"

He reaches into his pocket and pulls out a small, simple ring. It's not flashy—just a delicate gold band with the sparkle of an antique diamond, warm and real and so perfectly us.

"Evangeline Quinn," he says, voice steady, and it's the first time my real name sounds like a prayer instead of a curse, "you walked into my life like a damn wildfire. And I've been burning for you ever since."

My breath catches.

"I don't care about cameras or headlines or stage lights. I care about porch swings and early mornings and the way your hair smells when it's still wet from the shower. I care about you—here, now, always."

Tears sting my eyes.

"I can live in your world," he says, "if you can live in mine."

I let out a shaky breath. "You don't even have to ask."

But he does anyway.

"Marry me?"

I throw my arms around his neck, laughing and crying all at once. "Yes."

He kisses me with everything he has, and when he finally slides the ring onto my finger, it glints in the fairy light like it's always belonged there.

"Guess I'll have to write another song," I whisper against his mouth.

Rowan grins. "Make it a long one. I'm not going anywhere."

By the time we return to the main park area, the sky has turned the deepest shade of navy—stars blinking to life overhead while the music and laughter carry on. I still feel his kiss on my lips. The weight of the ring on my finger. The hum of everything that just happened was vibrating through my chest like a second heartbeat.

We haven't said anything to anyone yet, and Rowan

keeps glancing down at my hand like he's double-checking it's real.

"Your mom's gonna know the second she sees us," I murmur, elbowing him lightly as we approach the long string of picnic tables again. "You're basically glowing."

"I am not glowing," he grumbles.

"You're totally glowing," I tease, brushing my hand along his back. "I bet Holt makes a joke before dessert."

Rowan lets out a breath of amusement but doesn't deny it.

The tables are lit with paper lanterns now, soft flickers of light bobbing gently from shepherd's hooks staked into the grass. The whole thing feels like a scene out of a movie —rustic and charming and warm enough to thaw the part of me that used to live on defense.

Bailey spots us first. Her brows shoot up, then drop just as fast as she turns and pretends to be wildly interested in folding a napkin.

I notice. "She always this bad at pretending she's not watching?"

"Worse," Rowan says.

Right on cue, Crew's headed toward the table with two sodas in hand. His eyes find Bailey immediately, and before he even opens his mouth, she pivots on her heel and beelines toward the dessert table like she's been summoned by a cherry pie.

Rowan snorts. "That's gotta be the fifth time tonight."

"Seventh, actually," I whisper. "I've been counting."

Crew slows, defeated but not surprised, then drops into the seat beside Lila with a theatrical groan.

"Denied again?" she asks, not even trying to hide her grin.

"She treats me like I'm contagious."

"You are. It's called delusional confidence."

"I call it stubbornness—a common Wright trait."

I catch Rowan's eye, and we both laugh. There's something so easy about being back with his family—no expectations, no filtered conversations. Just this beautiful, chaotic crew of people who've made room for me in ways I never expected.

Hadley waves us over and immediately loops her arm through mine. "Okay, tell me everything. What was that song? You were glowing."

Rowan snickers behind me, but I ignore him.

"I wrote it about the farm," I lie—mostly. "And maybe a little about your brother."

"A little?" Hadley replies, shooting Rowan a look. "He looked like he was about to cry."

"I was not about to cry," he mutters.

"Was too," she and Lila say in unison.

Before he can argue, his mom walks up with a tray of drinks, her eyes falling to my left hand as she hands me a lemonade.

Her gaze sharpens, then softens.

"Oh," she says, gentle and almost reverent.

I smile sheepishly. "We haven't told anyone yet."

She sets the tray down on the table, wipes her palms on

her apron, and wraps me in a hug so tight it knocks the breath out of me.

"You don't have to tell anyone," she murmurs into my hair. "You've already told each other."

When she pulls back, her eyes are glassy, and Rowan's are suspiciously shiny too.

"Mom," he says, voice low.

"I know, baby. I'm just happy." She presses a kiss to his cheek, then mine, and bustles off like nothing happened.

The rest of the night floats by in a blur of laughter and stories. Bailey finally lets Crew hand her a plate of cobbler, but vanishes before he can do more than blink. Holt challenges the kids to a watermelon-eating contest and ends up with juice in his scruffy beard. Someone starts a round of karaoke on the stage, and I hear a warbly version of "Ain't No Mountain High Enough" echoing through the trees.

Rowan doesn't leave my side.

Every time someone pulls me into conversation, he's there—hand brushing my back, fingers lacing through mine, and his mouth at my ear with whispered jokes that make me giggle like a teenager.

"You're touching me a lot tonight," I murmur as we drift away from the crowd again.

"Can't help it," he says, slipping his hand into my back pocket and tugging me close. "You're mine now. Officially."

"I was yours the second you showed me that cottage and gave me sweet tea in a Mason jar."

He hums like that memory is sweeter than anything we're drinking tonight.

"You were always mine," he murmurs. "Even before I had the guts to believe it."

The night stretches long and lazy, stars dancing above the park and the buzz of the party fading into a background hum. I know we'll have to tell more people. Face more headlines. Maybe even deal with more of my past.

But tonight? Tonight, I'm just Ivy. Just his.

Back at the house, we settle on the swing. It's quickly become one of my favorite places.

"I think we should tell people tomorrow," I say eventually, curling my fingers around his. His mom and Bailey know, but everyone else seemed to be too oblivious to notice at the festival. Not that I could blame them, plus twirling the ring around so that the stone pressed against my palm helped.

"Tell them what?"

"That I'm engaged to a cowboy who doesn't write flyers but makes the best damn sun tea I've ever had."

He laughs, low and rough. "And who comes in his jeans on the porch swings?"

I gasp-laugh, swatting at him. "Stop!"

He catches my hand and kisses it.

"No one else gets to see this version of you," he says. "The barefoot goddess who sings in barns and ruins me without trying."

I kiss him again, long and deep. "Only you, Rowan. Always."

The lights twinkle above us, the moon high, and somewhere in the distance, the first crackle of a firework breaks through the stillness—Coral Bell Cove's unofficial end-of-summer tradition.

I lean back in his arms, and for the first time, I don't flinch at the sound. I don't run. I don't brace.

Because I've already found home.

And he's holding me in it.

EPILOGUE - IVY

The road curves gently around the familiar bend, and my heart starts doing that fluttery thing it always does when we're close to Coral Bell Cove. It's been a year—twelve full months of change and growth and late-night laughter in unfamiliar cities. Still, this stretch of rural highway, with its flickering sun through oak branches and the faint scent of hay on the breeze, feels more like home than anywhere I've ever been.

Rowan's hand rests on my thigh, fingers tapping to the rhythm of the country song playing low from the truck speakers. He hums along—off-key, on purpose—and I smile even though he's not looking at me.

His knuckles are still a little rough, calloused from working the farm even after all the changes this past year. Even after we built a new life that looks nothing like what either of us expected.

"Two more miles," he says quietly, glancing toward me. His eyes flick down to my bare legs—propped on the dash like I always do—and the corner of his mouth kicks up.

"You counting?"

He shrugs, thumb stroking slowly against my skin. "Maybe."

We've just wrapped a months-long press tour for my album—an entire loop around the US, from LA to Chicago to New York City, which helped convince my label to push back the world tour to next year.

This is the first time in weeks that the quiet feels real. Like the world's finally catching its breath again. It took some finagling and a few new manager hires, but Rowan was able to leave the farm and animals in good hands. Of course, his father and siblings were also there to help out.

I lean back against the seat, letting my eyes drift shut for a moment, the road humming softly beneath the tires.

"It's going to be weird not waking up in hotel beds," I murmur.

Rowan chuckles. "Better weird than empty."

"You didn't hate it?"

"Waking up next to you in fifty different cities? I'm not that grumpy."

I grin, cracking one eye open. "You sure? You growled at a room service tray in Boston."

"That tray had the nerve to deliver cold bacon."

"You ate it anyway."

"Because you fed it to me," he says, voice dipping lower.

"In bed. Naked. That kind of makes a man forget his standards."

Heat crawls up my neck, but I don't look away. "Good thing I plan to keep doing that everywhere we go."

He makes a low sound of agreement, hand sliding up a little higher on my thigh.

We fall into silence again, the kind that only comes from knowing each other inside out. After a beat, Rowan slows the truck.

My brows knit. "Did we miss the turn?"

"Nope."

He eases onto the gravel shoulder and pulls to a stop in the shade of an old oak tree, right at the edge of a curve where the road narrows. For a second, I don't understand until I look out the windshield and realize exactly where we are.

Right here. This is where it started.

My car had skidded off the road right into that shallow ditch, tires sank, my clothes rumpled, heart pounding, and mascara streaking down my cheeks. It's sitting back in Nashville with a new owner as we speak.

I hadn't even realized I was crying when Rowan pulled up behind me in this same damn truck, arms crossed and jaw tight, looking like a cowboy-shaped wall I couldn't climb. Or maybe like the one I needed to lean against.

He shifts into Park and turns to me, the expression in his eyes softer now, threaded with memories.

"This is it," he murmurs. "Right here. Where you nearly ran your spaceship into a cow sign."

I laugh, hand pressed over my heart. "You were so grumpy."

"You were so lost." He leans back, resting his arm across the back of my seat, eyes sweeping the empty stretch of road and overgrown grass. "You looked like a fairy tale in a car commercial."

"I was a mess."

"You were mine, even then."

The words sit between us, tender and heavy and full of every mile we've traveled since.

Rowan turns toward me slowly. "I don't stop here often. But every time I drive past, I think about what would've happened if I hadn't come around that corner when I did."

I squeeze his hand. "You did. That's all that matters."

He leans in and brushes a kiss over my temple, lips lingering against my skin. "I just wanted to stop. Remind you where we began."

I smile, watery and real. "Like I could ever forget."

We stay there for a moment longer, wrapped in morning light and memory, until the sound of a truck passing behind us reminds us we've got one more stretch to go.

Rowan shifts gears and pulls back onto the road, his hand sliding back to my thigh, grounding me the way he always does. Otter Creek Farm is just ahead, and for the first time in weeks, my shoulders settle. The hum in my chest—that restless, electric pull that always buzzed under my skin when I was away—goes quiet.

Because we're home, not just for a week or two, but for a while, and we made it back together.

We're five minutes from the house when I catch Rowan glancing at me for the fourth time in a mile.

"What?" I ask, raising a brow.

He smirks, the corner of his mouth twitching like he's holding in a secret. Which... he is.

"Nothing," he says, but there's too much warmth in his voice, too much tension in his shoulders.

I narrow my eyes. "Rowan."

"Hmm?"

"You're fidgeting."

"I don't fidget."

"You do when you're sitting on something big."

He shrugs, impossibly nonchalant, but I can see the edge of a smile tugging at his jaw. The way his fingers tap the steering wheel. The way he's fighting the urge to pull me across the seat and spill the thing that's been sitting between us for the past two weeks.

I lean closer, letting my voice drop. "You thinking about telling them?"

"Hadley will freak," he says. "Lila might cry. Crew's gonna pretend he knew the whole time."

"Your mom might throw another dinner party."

"That's the risk."

I bite my lip to keep from smiling too hard. "So... this weekend?"

Rowan glances over at me. Really looks. And then he lifts my hand off my thigh and presses a kiss to the band on my finger—the delicate gold thing we picked up on a whim in a vintage shop just outside of Asheville that matches my engagement ring perfectly. But it's still hidden, still ours.

"This weekend," he confirms, eyes soft, voice steady. "We tell them we're married."

Just like that, my stomach flips in that breathless, delicious way it always does when he says something that feels like a promise.

"I kind of love that we've had it to ourselves this long," I admit. "Just ours."

"Me, too," he says, thumb brushing along the edge of the ring. "But I also kinda want to see your mom's face when she finds out."

I snort. "She'll combust."

He pulls into the long gravel drive, the house coming into view with its wraparound porch and familiar creak of wind chimes. Home. Even better this time. Because it's not just where we began.

It's where we came back to. As *us*.

I reach for the door handle, but Rowan leans over and hooks his finger into my belt loop, tugging me back into his space.

"Hey," he says, voice low. "I know this next year might get loud again. Bigger stages, more flights, interviews, flashing lights... But I meant what I said."

I turn, caught in the quiet storm of his gaze.

"I can exist in your world," he says softly, "if you can still exist in mine."

The emotion catches me by the throat, warm and full and gut-punching.

"I don't want two worlds," I whisper, brushing my nose against his. "I just want *ours.* Whatever it looks like. Wherever we go."

He kisses me then—slow and deep and anchoring.

And just before we break apart, he murmurs against my lips, "Then let's go show them what that looks like."

Newsletter: http://bit.ly/2WokAjS
Author Page: www.facebook.com/authorreneeharless
Reader Group: http://bit.ly/31AGa3B
Instagram: www.instagram.com/renee_harless
Bookbub: www.bookbub.com/authors/renee-harless
Goodreads: http://bit.ly/2TDagOn
Amazon: http://bit.ly/2WsHhPq
Website: www.reneeharless.com

ACKNOWLEDGMENTS

To my family—thank you for being my steady ground and my safe place. Your encouragement, patience, and love carried me through late nights, early mornings, and the moments when I thought the words would never come. You remind me daily why I chase these dreams.

To my incredible editors, Nicole and Jenny—your insight, guidance, and belief in this story made it stronger, sharper, and truer than I could have managed alone. You pushed me to trust my voice and challenged me to grow as a writer in ways I'll always be grateful for.

To my proofreader, Crystal—thank you for your careful eye and dedication. You caught the little things that make the biggest difference, ensuring every page shines.

To my earliest readers, Patricia and Lisa—thank you for taking this journey with me from the very beginning, for falling in love with these characters, and for cheering me on when I needed it most. Your excitement fueled mine.

And to you, dear reader—thank you for choosing to spend your time with this story. For every page you turn and every emotion you carry with you, I'm endlessly thankful. Your support is what makes all of this possible.

ABOUT THE AUTHOR

Renee Harless is a USA TODAY bestselling author with an affinity for wine and a passion for telling a good story.

Renee Harless, her husband, and children live in Blue Ridge Mountains of Virginia. She studied Communication, specifically Public Relations, at Radford University.

Growing up, Renee always found a way to pursue her creativity. It began by watching endless runs of White Christmas - yes even in the summer – and learning every word and dance from the movie. She could still sing "Sister Sister" if requested. In high school she joined the show choir and a community theatre group. After marrying the man of her dreams and moving from her hometown, she sought out a different artistic outlet – writing.

To say that Renee is a romance addict would be an understatement. When she isn't chasing her kids around the house, working her day job, or writing, she jumps head first into a romance novel.

Beauty Beheld

A BEAUTY IS HER NAME NOVEL (BOOK 1)

ZARIAH L. BANKS

Text Copyright © 2023 by Zariah L. Banks

All Rights Reserved.

No part of this book may be reproduced, stored in a retrieval system, or transmitted in any form or by any means, electronic, mechanical, photocopying, recording, or otherwise, without express written permission of the publisher.

Published by eParke Press

hello@lyricalinnovationsllc.com

Cover design by Woodson Creative Studio

Printed in the United States of America

Publisher's Cataloging-in-Publication data

ISBN 979-8-9869693-0-5

Library of Congress Control Number: 2022921107

First Edition

14 13 12 11 10 / 10 9 8 7 6 5 4 3 2 1